KWELENGSEN STORM

Logan's World, Book One

David M. Kelly

Nemesis Press

Kwelengsen Storm: Logan's World, Book One

A Ugan Confluence Novel

Copyright ©2020 by David M. Kelly

All rights reserved. No part of this book may be reproduced in any form by any electronic or mechanical means including photocopying, recording, or information storage and retrieval without permission in writing from the author.

This is a work of fiction. Names, characters, places, and incidents either are the product of the author's imagination or are used fictitiously, and any resemblance to actual persons, living or dead, events, or locales is entirely coincidental.

ISBN-13: 978-1-7771569-2-3

ISBN-10: 1-7771569-2-0

First Published 2020

Nemesis Press
Wahnapitae, Ontario

www.nemesispress.com

Printed in U.S.A.

Dedication

To my readers. Thank you for your continued support.

*"May the stars carry your darkness away.
May the flowers fill your heart
with beauty.
May hope forever wipe away your tears.
And above all, may silence make
you strong."*

– Chief Dan George (Geswanouth Slahoot)

Chapter One

"A marriage, like a house, needs a strong foundation to build from, so buy a good bed."
— Grandfather Twofeathers

Logan Twofeathers looked at the inky, cloudless sky as the pinprick of light crawled toward the eastern horizon. Even through high-powered binoculars, it was nothing more than a bright dot glimmering with reflected sunlight. It wasn't the *Hansen*, the transport ship that had brought them to the planet. At that time of day, the transport's orbit would place it on the other side of Kwelengsen. And the next scheduled supply ship wasn't due for another month.

"Have you got anything?" he said, tracking the dot.

He was standing by the window of the science and communications building of New Hope—the first and so far, only, city on the planet. Behind him, illuminated by the lights from several computer consoles, a shadow moved.

"The ship is broadcasting a transponder ID, but our systems don't recognize it." Logan's wife, Aurore Vergari, sat at one of the computers studying the information on the screen. "And the imaging we can get from down here is inconclusive. It doesn't match anything on the books."

"I thought you were our science expert." Wildan Tejal was the settlement's lead civilian authority, and his dark mustache wriggled over his plump lips like a hairy, oversized caterpillar when he spoke.

"There's no reason for that attitude, Administrator." Logan's jaw tightened. Tejal might be a good politician and competent in a general sense, but he liked to play people. "We're doing what we can, but until our reconsat gets a closer look, our information is bound to be limited."

"We need to know who it is and what they're doing here." Tejal sighed, as if he were talking to a misunderstanding child. "You're supposed to be our technical leads."

Logan gave a humorless smile. "Feel free to issue a request for replacements. I'm sure Earth will be willing to log *another* of your complaints."

A message would take over a day to get to Earth and the same for any response to return. Even with the RoboPony relays invented by Logan's friend Joe, interstellar communication was closer to sending an old-style letter than anything approaching "real-time." Besides, the Combined-Earth Settlement Authority had made its personnel assignments and wasn't likely to change them, short of the community on Kwelengsen failing. Something Tejal was aware of.

"What about Captain Manners?" Tejal said. "Can't the Guard launch a reconnaissance ship?"

"I've apprised her of the situation," Logan said. "They've shown no hostile intentions, and I believe she's happy to wait on the reconsat feedback."

Tejal frowned. "We don't know who they are, or why they're here. The entire settlement might be in danger."

"Then you should raise your concerns with her." Logan stared down at Tejal, holding his frustration in check. "I'm not a soldier."

Tejal took a step back. "Well, no, but you... well, you have influence, shall we say."

Logan glanced across at Aurore, her brown eyes almost black in the subdued lighting. Her nod was meant to reassure him, but they'd discussed how he felt about his past.

"I'm afraid I can't help you," he said brusquely.

Tejal's mouth clamped tighter, making his fleshy jowls look bigger than usual. "I see. I'll be including this lack of cooperation in my CESA report."

"I wouldn't expect anything else, Administrator."

Tejal marched out of the room, his footsteps clicking on the concrete floor.

"He thinks too much of himself," Logan said.

"He's a jumped-up pencil pusher with a stick up his ass," Aurore said. "Why they chose him is beyond me."

"He knows how to smooth ruffled feathers, both here and with CESA."

Aurore sniffed. "Well, he seems to know how to ruffle my feathers, and yours—even though you hide it."

After the discovery of Kwelengsen—the first habitable planet found by humans—Earth's nation-states had scrambled to put together an expedition to explore and settle the new world. Everybody wanted a slice of the new pie, and CESA, the Combined-Earth Settlement Authority, had been created to ensure each political group had equal access. Surprisingly, most historical differences had been put aside, and the first expedition drew its representatives equally from the United States and Provinces, Pan-Asian Confederation, Old Europe, and the United African Democracies—something previously unimaginable for Earth's nation-states.

"If it were a regular Earth ship, they'd make themselves known," Logan said. "That leaves the Atolls and the Corporates. And neither of them like us very much."

"The feeling's mutual." Aurore's expression hardened. "The Atolls are too busy trying to stop their habitats dissolving to worry about us. Besides, they don't like planets."

Since the attacks on the Atolls with the Contravalency Phage, they were preoccupied with looking for a cure for the virus-like substance threatening to destroy them, but Logan knew desperate people often resorted to desperate solutions. "Maybe not. But I don't like it."

Aurore moved closer and gripped Logan's hands. "Remember you're the head of engineering operations, not responsible for the entire settlement. Everyone here came for their own reasons."

She was right, but that did nothing to ease Logan's burden of responsibility. He was the one who'd found Kwelengsen—no one would be here if he hadn't. He'd hoped it would be a new start for Earth people, but increasingly it looked like yet another source of conflict.

She looked up at him and brushed his cheek. "What if I launched ClutterBug early? It wouldn't be hard to do a pass on the ship to check it out, and my surveying mission is open ended."

ClutterBug was the name Aurore had given one of the general-purpose Nomad Transports that had been assigned to science duties. The survey mission worried Logan but not because of the unknown ship's arrival. Aurore would be gone for two weeks surveying the closest planet to Kwelengsen. She'd be alone, and that bothered him despite his confidence in her abilities. Not to mention that whenever she was gone, a hole opened up inside him as big as an asteroid.

"No need for that. You have prep work to finish. We shouldn't let an unexpected ship arrival throw all our plans into a loop."

"You're not concerned about me, are you, Mr. Twofeathers?"

"You have your duties to perform, I understand that."

"Uh-huh." Aurore pulled his head down to meet hers. "I'll miss you too you know."

The communications console behind Aurore beeped several times and she moved over to check it.

"There's a broadcast from the ship." She switched the transmission to the speakers, and a gruff male voice reverberated around the room.

"Kwelengsen, this is Captain Akinyemi in command of Atoll Defense Fleet cruiser *Sarabhai*. We're in orbit around your planet, as I'm sure you're aware, and would like to harvest some of your system's raw materials." Akinyemi hesitated. "We could, of course, simply take what we want, but I thought it courteous to ask."

Logan raised an eyebrow at Aurore. "Surprisingly polite considering what the Atolls are dealing with at the moment."

"I better call Tejal," she said. "This is his decision."

"Include Manners—CEG will consider this a security issue."

Aurore flipped several controls and initiated a three-way connection, excluding the Atoll ship, and played back the transmission.

"Do we know what they want?" Tejal's lips were greasy as

though he'd just started supper.

"They included a list along with the transmission. Water ice, hydrogen, nitrogen, carbon dioxide—all unrefined, and all things they can extract out of asteroids and comets." Aurore ticked the items off. "Basic raw supplies for any deep-space vessel."

"I don't see any harm in it." Tejal nodded. "As they said, they could have taken what they wanted."

"I don't want them on the planet's surface." Manners was as brusque as usual. "They're a security risk."

Logan sighed. "I'm sure they're not interested in coming down. Atollers aren't comfortable on planets."

"That may be so," Manners said. "But right now they're less predictable than a kicked-over hornet's nest."

"A reasonable precaution," Tejal said. "We don't want trouble."

Logan looked from one image pickup to the other. "We might make their lives a little easier."

"How do you mean?" Tejal wiped his mouth with a napkin, as if only then realizing the condition of his lips.

"Everything they need is in the Breadbox." Logan jerked a thumb upward. "More than enough for them to resupply with."

The Breadbox was a large storage vessel in orbit, automatically replenished by several remote mining drones that harvested the system's extensive asteroid fields. The drones weren't fast, but they didn't need to be. Perhaps when the settlement reached double or triple its current size they'd need to look at the capacity, but for now, it wasn't a concern.

"Those supplies are for emergencies," Tejal said. "I can't possibly authorize handing them over to the Atollers."

"That's a tactical asset. I can't permit Tollers to access it either." Manners scowled. "They're the enemy, and we're a long way from home."

Tejal's dark eyes narrowed. "And why should we help them? They have their own equipment. We don't owe them anything."

"Well, I could argue we should do it because it's a friendly thing to do." Logan didn't hold much hope of persuading them. "Or if you want a more pragmatic reason, if we share our resources with them, they might be less of a potential threat. Or look at it from a purely practical point of view—the faster they resupply, the sooner they can be on their way."

"Absolutely not. They can *mine* whatever they want. But that's all." Tejal glanced over his shoulder. "That's my final word. Now, if no one minds, I will finish my supper."

"I will not authorize an Atoll ship to dock with any CESA facility." Manners stared at Logan through the screen, her golden eyes turning a deeper jasper. "End comm."

Both displays darkened, and the room fell quiet. Eventually, Aurore spoke. "Now what?"

"Contact the *Sarabhai*. I'll deliver the message to Akinyemi." Logan's voice had an edge to it.

Aurore frowned and checked the screens. "They'll be out of range in twelve minutes. Do you want to wait until their next orbit?"

Logan shook his head. "This won't take long."

Aurore made the connection, and Akinyemi appeared after a short delay. His face was long, with a slightly pointed chin that was a little at odds with his rounded cheeks, and gave him a gaunt, hungry look.

"Captain Akinyemi." Logan nodded. "I'm Logan Twofeathers. Head of engineering and technical lead for Kwelengsen."

"Good day, Mr. Twofeathers. Thank you for responding to our communication."

"We would have contacted you earlier but we weren't sure who you were. Your ship configuration is an unrecognized type."

Akinyemi rubbed his chin. "It's a new Huanshi design. Procured for this mission."

Huanshi was one of the largest private shipbuilding Corporates. Logan guessed the Atolls had switched to the design to avoid further vulnerability to the Phage that was wreaking havoc on their own technology. "What is your mission, if you don't mind me asking?"

"We're a scout vessel. Searching for habitable planets." Akinyemi smiled, but there was no humor in his eyes. "What else would we be doing at a time like this?"

"Planets?" Logan shifted uneasily.

"I admit it's unusual for us. But desperate times…"

Logan stepped up to the pickup area. "Your request for permission to procure materials is approved. We don't own the entire star system, and are happy to share."

"Well, according to interstellar law, as the first settlers, you do." Akinyemi leaned closer to the pickup, his head getting cut off by the top of the screen. "Is there a charge?"

One does not sell the land, Logan thought. "None. Though if you have any entertainment media we may not be aware of, we'd appreciate the chance to extend our library."

"That's generous of you. I'll have one of my officers arrange an exchange of our entertainment files."

"We could be *more* generous." Logan hesitated. "We have a resource storage facility in orbit, we call it the Breadbox..."

Akinyemi looked puzzled. "We detected it on approach."

Aurore shook her head, but Logan ignored her. "It contains all the materials you're looking for, already refined and separated. You're welcome to use its resources—that would mean less work for you."

Akinyemi said nothing, and the screen went dark.

"What the hell?" Logan looked at Aurore. "Did we lose them?"

"They're in range. Five minutes until they pass over the horizon." She worked the controls. "Looks like they cut the transmission. But Logan, you're not authorized to let—"

The screen lit up again showing Akinyemi, but Logan noticed the background behind the Atoll officer had changed. "Was my offer inappropriate?"

"Apologies, Mr. Twofeathers. I transferred your call to my private office. Your offer is generous, and a little surprising under the circumstances, but I appreciate it. My response, though, is not something I want my crew to hear."

"How so?"

Akinyemi's forehead creased. "The Directorate has issued a complete isolation order, banning all contact between Atollers and Earth personnel or facilities. The Phage is running rampant through our stations and ships. If we don't find a way to block it, our society will be effectively destroyed." A hint of bitterness crept into his voice. "The Directorate is afraid Earth may try to finish what has already started and eliminate us."

"I assure you, our supplies are clean. You can run checks on them to satisfy—"

Akinyemi lifted his hand. "I don't doubt your sincerity, Mr. Twofeathers, but I have to respect the Directorate's orders."

"Are things *that* bad?" Logan's gut twisted—the Atolls might pose a bigger threat than generally thought.

"If we can't stop the Phage, our culture may be all but destroyed within two years."

Aurore gasped.

"I hope it doesn't come to that, Captain." Logan took a deep breath. "There's enough room out here for everyone."

"You would think so, wouldn't you? But potential real-estate is limited." Akinyemi scowled. "If I'm honest, I'm not sure our people are capable of adapting to planetary living."

"It's only been a hundred and fifty years. I doubt there's been much physiological change in that time," Logan said.

"In a biological sense, you're undoubtedly correct. The problem is more psychological. Atollers have mentally adapted to the freedom of space, so being trapped on the surface of a planet seems like a backward step to most."

"You could use some of Earth's recent technology. The Nakaji-Wei habitats would be similar environments."

Akinyemi glanced off to the side. "We're out of time I'm afraid, Mr. Twofeathers. While you're correct, you can understand how reluctant my fellow citizens would be to follow that route."

The screen flickered, filling with static, then the transmission cut off.

Aurore checked the instruments. "They passed over the horizon. Next communications window will be in three hours, unless they change orbit. But Logan, I'm glad he didn't take you up on the offer. You might have lost your position for that."

"I know. I thought we could ease some of..." Logan's voice faltered.

"You tried." Aurore draped herself against his shoulder, turning his chin so he faced her. "You miss being in space, don't you?"

"Not as much as I'd miss you if I'd carried on with it."

"Then what is it?"

Logan didn't answer right away. Despite being overcapacity with engineering projects, he was restless, and couldn't say why.

The settlement was meant to be a fresh opportunity for him as well as everyone else—a chance to build a better world, one where everyone was truly equal for the first time. But sometimes he woke from dark dreams that left him feeling hollow, though he didn't remember the details.

Aurore stared at him for several minutes. "SecOps would take you back in a heartbeat, if you said you were interested."

Logan's skin tingled, and for a moment his adrenaline surged. Then, almost immediately, it was gone. He'd put aside that part of his life, and was determined to stay as far away from the violence and paranoia that always seemed to accompany military ventures. "I'm done with that. Why bring it up again?"

"Because it hurts that you don't trust me enough to talk about these things." The laughter lines on Aurore's face deepened into a frown. "You don't have to hide anything from me."

"I know," Logan said. "And I don't"

"You're not a very good liar."

Logan chuckled. "You should see the estimates I come up with for a job."

Aurore's smile faded. "Have you spoken to Carl recently?"

"Carl... not for a week or so." Logan held up his hands. "I know. But he likes fieldwork—I think that's only because it's a good way of avoiding me."

Carl's father had been Leonard Begay, a family friend of Logan's, and as close to him as a brother. After Begay's death, Logan had pulled strings to get the boy assigned to the expedition. It wasn't what most people would have thought of as a favor considering the settlement's primitive state, but at least Carl would have direction, and an environment with fewer reminders of his father.

"He's been through a lot," Aurore said. "Don't give up on him."

"I thought this"—Logan made a sweeping gesture—"would help him. But perhaps I should have left him where he was."

Aurore put a finger on his lips. "Not everyone wants the same things. And no one can fix the whole world, not even you."

"Worlds." Logan stroked Aurore's hair. "There's more than one now, remember."

"My apologies, oh mighty Lord Twofeathers, conqueror of

worlds." Aurore punched him playfully in the side.

"I haven't conquered anything. Including myself."

"You conquered me." She batted her eyes at him theatrically. "I enjoyed it."

"So I remember."

"Remember?" Aurore drew back. "Has it been *that* long?"

"We've both been busy. Starting a new world isn't easy. Even one as underdeveloped as this."

Aurore pulled him to his feet. "Well, I think it's about time you reminded me how it all works."

Logan stood, letting her think she was pulling his much larger weight. "Remind you? Was it *that* forgettable?"

The following morning dawned clear, with a light haze of cloud, though there were dark patches growing by the distant snow-capped Baraban mountain range to the west, and Logan guessed they might see storms later in the day. The planet's annual cycle was ebbing, and the first cold fingers of winter would soon make themselves felt. He whistled as he strolled over to the engineering offices, feeling as if his feet were dancing over the rough track. Kwelengsen had eighty percent of Earth's gravity, to the delight of everyone who'd settled there.

The office was a prefabricated, gray PlaSteel box like the other first-generation buildings, and sat near the edge of the main city square. A great deal of the early construction wasn't much to look at—grimly functional in a way that would make only a bureaucrat smile. As the city grew, they were making increasing use of local materials such as 3-D printed concrete and wood, and many of the newer designs were more decorative and larger. Despite the office's stark appearance, the work carried on inside by Logan and the other engineers was crucial to the settlement's development—they were literally designing and building the planet's future.

His main focus for several months had been designing and planning the resources for a Space Elevator. The relatively low gravity meant construction was easier than on Earth, and once built, an Elevator would change their future considerably. But, as was so often the case in engineering, it was a question of building the capacity to build something else. They weren't at the point of being able to produce all the raw materials needed, but with the completion of the first nano-fiber plant—scheduled for construction in eight months—they would be close. And once they had an Elevator, it would be cost effective to ship commodities back to Earth, or build orbital habitats.

Logan had left Aurore to finish her breakfast, but not before extracting a promise from her to contact him if there was any further news from the Atollers. She'd be heading for her own office in the science building, to carry on prepping for her mission. So far, they'd only done preliminary scans of the other planets in the star system, and she was excited to be able to do some real core science as she put it, instead of the settlement's day-to-day business.

As he unlocked the office door, Logan spotted two tanglefoxes scratching at some boxes stacked against the wall. It was unusual to see them in the city now, and the ungainly creatures took off when they heard him. They were scavengers by nature, but increasingly avoided contact with humans as the settlement expanded.

Logan lumbered inside and made his way to his desk, distinguished from the others by a row of small shelves stacked with reference data cards. The cards held encyclopedic files on Earth engineering at the time they'd left, as a repository of information to safeguard against a failure of the RoboPony communications relays. Another unspoken benefit was that if anything should happen to Earth, the files would act as a backup of vital information for any survivors. He'd barely sat down when he heard the door open followed by the flat slapping of multiple footsteps on the stairs. He glanced up to see Pasquale and Linnie approaching, two of the engineers working under him.

"Our processing capacity is severely limited." Pasquale Debiasi's words shot out in rapid succession, as if taking the time to breathe was a luxury. "Expanding the Farm has to take second place."

"I swear you bought your degree off some shifty Worldnet company." Linnie Whitker pushed Debiasi out of the way and dropped into the chair behind her desk, flipping the power buttons on her console. "How are you going to increase processing if you can't power it? That's why we need to make the Farm top priority."

"If we don't increase capacity, we can't make the materials for your silly wind farm. You know we could run the processing units with the generators on the Nomads."

"Good luck getting Manners to okay that."

Logan nodded in agreement at Linnie's comment. The settlement had six Nomad Transports available. Two were designated for scouting and research duties and the others assigned for general use under the command of Captain Manners. Manners interpreted that as meaning they were to be held in combat readiness for any military situation that might arise, unless they were on a specific mission. Using them as supplemental power systems was an idea she wouldn't sanction.

"Someone needs to explain to that gung-ho hellcat that this is a civilian settlement, not a military expedition." Debiasi glugged some water and looked at Logan. "Her troops are supposed to be here at the service of the settlement, not the other way around."

"Talk to her directly instead of complaining behind her back." Logan had heard the arguments before. "The captain isn't completely inflexible."

"Maybe with you." Debiasi slumped behind his desk. "She hates me."

"Poor Pasquale." Linnie chuckled. "Tough women scare him. Don't they, baby?"

"Only when they're overly fond of guns and explosives."

Logan smiled. These two were currently working from the office, while the rest of his team were in the field and weren't expected back anytime soon. The two engineers were both young, and close, despite their constant bickering.

This argument over power availability wasn't new. It was a conflict they'd been steadily heading toward as the community grew. They had one general-purpose reactor that covered the basic needs of official settlement business, and a separate solar and wind farm that served the town. The demand for power to support their burgeoning industry was increasing. But every problem was a chicken and egg situation. To complete one project, another needed to be completed first, and *that* required something else before *it*.

"If you're too gutless to face Manners, put in a request for more mini-fusion generators." Linnie was already absorbed by the details on her screen and didn't look up. "If the committee back home approves it, you might have them in a couple of months."

"All we can expect from Earth is people," Logan said quietly. "Both the PAC and United Africa are pushing for higher immigrant volumes, and everyone else will follow suit under the Equal Access rules."

The settlement's development had received full support from all sides, but only after immigration quotas had been agreed. These guaranteed that settler numbers would be controlled by global population percentage. So, while the greater push for moving people came from the PAC and UA, any increase had to be matched by the USP and other nation-states to maintain ratios.

"We don't have the infrastructure. We're already maxed out." Debiasi's words rattled out. "That's why we need access to the Nomad generators. Call Manners, set up a powwow."

Logan frowned. He wasn't deeply traditionalist, but misuse of that word set him on edge. Debiasi was right though—the ships' generators would go a long way toward making up for the shortfall in their capacity until a permanent solution was available. "I'll send a request to CESA for mini-fusion reactors," he said. "You never know—someone might wake up."

"Fat chance," Linnie mumbled, intent on the display in front of her.

"But what about—"

Logan shrugged. "I know. I'll meet with the captain as well. If I explain things to her she might loosen the reins a little."

He stiffened as he spoke. He disliked the political aspect of his position, and especially resented the time it sucked from what he considered to be his real work. He should have been working on the Space Elevator. Once completed, they could assemble a solar station at the top and push power down from orbit at levels far higher than the surface installations could generate.

"I'll head to the CEG compound. Captain Manners might have some time to spare." The unwelcome bite of responsibility nipped at Logan's shoulders.

"You'll be fine," Linnie said. "Just remember, she can smell fear."

Chapter Two

*"Never be afraid to ask for what you need.
But don't expect to get it."*
— Grandfather Twofeathers

The CEG compound was on the other side of New Hope. Both Manners and the civilian leadership agreed it was better to keep some distance between the two in order to reassure settlers they hadn't been dumped at a military compound. Logan hailed one of the field engineers to drive him over. Normally, he wouldn't mind such a walk, but he was impatient to get the meeting over and get back to work. While he waited to be picked up, he called Aurore.

"Hey, Hon." Aurore's face popped up on the small screen on his Scroll. "You playing hooky?"

"I wish. Heading over to talk to Manners about resourcing." Logan stayed out of the building's shadow. Though the sun was high, the cool chill of fall made him hunch inside his light jacket. A couple of birds flapped around in the distance, their triangular wings opening and closing like red and purple semaphore signals. "What's the story on our Atoll friends?"

"They're gone."

"The hairs on Logan's neck prickled. "No further messages?"

"Unfriendly bunch, huh?" Aurore sounded distracted. "I guess they wanted to resupply as fast as possible."

Logan's stomach tightened. "If they were in so much of a rush, wouldn't they have taken advantage of my offer?"

Aurore shrugged. "Who knows what's in the minds of Atollers these days?"

A loud rattling sounded behind him, and Logan looked around to see the bulky shape of a Gator utility vehicle rolling along the gravel-covered street. "Is there any way you can check?"

The large balloon-tired vehicle pulled up next to him. It was electric powered, so there was little noise from the engine, but the chassis and undercarriage groaned as it moved, and every lurch was accompanied by the clanking of metal chains hung from hooks on the side. Logan waved at the person in the wedge-shaped cab, then returned his attention to his Scroll.

"It's difficult to track system traffic from down here." Aurore pursed her lips. "What's wrong?"

"Nothing I know of." Logan shook his head. "Just my gut troubling me."

Aurore frowned. "Your gut is scary—in many ways. I'll see what I can do."

Logan blew her a kiss, then closed the connection. He clambered up a ladder on the side of the Gator and slipped inside the cabin. The driver was Nate Fellows, a burly guy with gray-streaked hair and a dour expression. One of the first-wave settlers, he'd set up a farm on the outskirts of town with his young family. The last time Logan had seen him smile was when his neighbor died unexpectedly, doubling the area of Fellows' farm and giving the man an inflated sense of self-worth—a trait that needed no help.

"Hi Nate, how's the family?" Logan settled into the passenger seat as Fellows engaged the drive, and the Gator shuddered as it rolled forward.

"Doing good, thanks. Becca's doing wonders with the vegetable crops, and Junior and Jeanie are both old enough to help out—at least when they're not wasting time studying. Especially Junior—that boy sure is growing fast."

"I was expecting one of the construction guys to give me a ride." Logan slammed into his seat as the Gator jerked—finesse not one of Fellows' skills.

"Had to do it." Fellows bounced the heavy transport down the street, not paying much attention to anything in front of him. "Don't see why I gotta do community work. Got enough on working my own land."

Everyone above the age of twelve was expected to contribute to the social program—by providing commodities, skills, or labor. "You could donate some of your crops," Logan said. "You grow plenty."

"Ain't nothing but taxation. Came here to get away from all that."

Logan ignored him—the settlers' contract laid out their obligations. "Take it up with your ward representative."

"You think I didn't try that?" Fellows shifted the gears and the Gator lurched again. "She said what they all say. Contribute or else."

Logan knew Fellows had already been fined for not showing up to previous work details. "We have to pull together to build a community. It's the same for everyone."

The Gator splashed through a muddy stream, the black water fountaining up in a V as they passed through, and Logan gripped the nearest handhold to steady himself.

"Not everyone."

"If you mean the CEG people, they *pay* by providing security and transport."

"Sure, *they* protect us. But what about the cops? They sit around all day scratching their asses while the rest of us work. All those bastards are interested in is harassing innocent citizens on trumped-up charges."

"Keep up your civic duties and they'll be happy not to bother you."

The heavy vehicle made a sharp turn around a stand of large trees, then followed a less frequented track through the bush.

"Duties, my ass. I'm here because they promised we'd be free to live how we want."

Logan scowled, his neck muscles tightening. "Move farther out of town. Set yourself up in unorganized territory outside New Hope's boundary and no one will bother you."

"Oh sure... and where would I get my power? And what about getting my produce to the market?"

Fellows was one of those people who wanted everything their way, but didn't want to pay the price. "Have you thought about selling up, Nate? Your place would be worth enough to pay your fare back to Earth. You might be happier."

"Ain't never going back. Besides, Becca and the young 'uns like it here. Damn crazy kids. They'd rather be learning in school than helping with the chores." They turned another curve in the winding trail, and a number of green-sided utility buildings came into view. They were flanked by several H-shaped Nomad transports with the large wedge of the Settlement Lander rising behind them. "But schoolin's important too—man can't get anywhere now without training."

"Same for women, I hear."

"Huh?"

"Never mind." Logan held up a hand as Fellows pulled the Gator in by the main building. "The Social Program is what keeps the school open. Maybe you should consider that."

Fellows looked around. "You have influence here. You could put in a word—"

"Not a chance." Logan clambered from his seat and through the side door. "Thanks for the ride. Wouldn't want to keep you from your work any longer."

The Gator moved off and Logan turned toward the entrance. There was a large sign over the door that read "Combined-Earth Guard Headquarters, Division One." It always made him smile. For one thing, there were only two "divisions"—this one and an area in the mountains several hundred kilometers northwest that played double-duty as a training camp and mining outpost. And besides, everyone knew it was the military base.

Inside was a small waiting area with a desk and a second door that led deeper inside. Again, there wasn't much need for it, but the military had their own practices, many of which were sacrosanct, no matter how crazy they seemed to others. One of the younger CEG soldiers was sitting at the desk and looked up as he entered.

"Mr. Twofeathers? I imagine you're here to see the captain. Do you have an appointment?"

Logan laughed. "You know I haven't, Giorg. Is she in?"

The private glanced toward the door and frowned. "She doesn't want to be disturbed. She's working on performance reports."

"Then she needs a break." Logan sat in the visitors' chair.

"Would you mind checking with her? I'll wait if necessary."

Giorg's forehead scrunched up, his thick bushy eyebrows shading his dark eyes. "Wait here."

"I won't move from this spot."

The private slipped through the inner door and, a few moments later, Logan heard the muffled sounds of voices—Manners didn't sound happy. After a little while, Giorg reappeared.

"The captain will see you, Mr. Twofeathers."

Logan stood. "Thanks. I know my way."

He walked to the end of the short corridor, which had a door on either side. The one on the right opened into the main workshops and storage areas, while Manners' office was to the left. He knocked once and entered. Charlene Manners was standing with her back to him, looking through the window onto the open area to the side of the building. There wasn't anything happening out there as far as Logan could see, but she seemed fixated by the view. He waited, knowing she'd talk when she was ready. Her reputation as a hard-ass was well established, and carefully maintained.

After a few minutes, Manners turned to him. "Do you know how many personnel there are on Kwelengsen?"

It was a rhetorical question—she was referring to those under her command. "Forty-three, including yourself," Logan said.

The light from the window transformed Manners' cropped brown hair into a fuzzy halo around her square skull. "Forty-three. And I have to complete a performance report on forty-two of them. Would you also know how often I have to do that?"

Logan had been recruited to SecOps, the military arm of the USP, while he was employed on construction projects in Low Earth Orbit several years ago. He'd carried on working with them until he'd discovered they'd created the genocidal Contravalency Phage, designed to destroy the Atolls. But even as a civilian contractor, he was aware of how much bureaucracy there was in the system, and the multinational nature of CESA undoubtedly increased that.

"Every two months." Manners sat and clasped her hands on the desk before her. "All because of the profile this damned planet has, I have to report on every single person in my command. And, as if that wasn't enough, I have to provide a complete briefing on any and all security incidents."

Logan frowned. "I don't think we've had any."

"You might think so, but that would be an incorrect assumption." She reached for a control stylus and pointed at the display to her right. "Have you seen the guidance on what *is* categorized as a security incident?"

"I'm sure I don't have the proper clearance," Logan said, silently adding "anymore."

"Everything from a civilian getting fighting drunk to an unexpected meteorological event." The stylus clattered down on her desk. "I'm sorry, Logan. You didn't come here to listen to me rant about red tape. What's the problem?"

Logan remembered the distant clouds he'd seen earlier. Although Kwelengsen was similar to Earth in habitability, it had an axial tilt of around thirty-five degrees, which made the weather patterns less predictable. This, combined with its relatively brief orbital period, meant the seasons were shorter too.

"Better get another report ready, Captain. I think we've got a storm coming in."

"After all this time you're still using my title? Call me *Charlie*. You're not one of my subordinates."

Logan laughed softly. "Old habits, I guess."

"How long until the storm hits? Has meteorology issued a warning?"

"Not that I know of. I'd say tonight, based on what we've seen before." Logan pointed toward the window. "You might want to advise people to close their shutters, in case."

Manners nodded. "We don't want a repeat of last fall."

An unexpected storm a year ago had caught everyone unawares and, although no one was killed, there were several injuries from flying debris, and they'd lost several temporary buildings in the hurricane-level winds. Altogether, the damage and cleanup had cost them months of work.

Manners picked up a comm-set and thumbed the connect button. "Issue a storm warning. I want everything battened down in under two hours." She disconnected and looked back at Logan. "I'm sure you're not here to discuss the weather, either."

"The processing center is running below capacity. We don't make enough power in our grid yet."

Manners smiled, her face drawn tight, making her look like an evil pixie. "Oh yes... I heard something about this. One of your staff was haranguing one of my team about it. No doubt in an attempt to feed information through to me. He needs to learn to fight his own battles."

"I agree. But in this case, I think he's right. The Nomad reactors would go a long way toward making up the shortfall." Logan paused. "In their off-duty time, of course."

"Those ships are never off-duty. They're part of the fast-response disaster unit, and need to be ready to dust off in under ten minutes. The settlement's safety depends on that." Manners pressed a key on her console, and a row of heavy-duty shutters rumbled down the outside of the window behind her. "Anything else?"

"The settlement's future might depend on those reactors being available." Logan leaned back in his chair. "Without them, we're struggling to remain viable."

Before Manners answered, her comm-set buzzed, and she picked it up. "Manners. What? You sure?" She listened for a short while. "Yes, put her through."

She reached out and pressed several controls, then a voice sounded. It was Aurore.

"Logan? Are you there? Captain Manners?"

Logan leaned closer to the console. "What's wrong?"

"I've lost connection with the relays. I'm not detecting a carrier signal," Aurore said.

"High-level atmospherics? I think there's a storm com—"

"Negative. I'd pick up something with the orbital instruments. I can communicate with *them*. The relay is either malfunctioning, or it's not there."

Logan checked the time. They were nowhere near the relay's next scheduled hop, when it Jumped to the nearest star system to transmit its stored messages and pick up any waiting ones before returning. The relays allowed them to stay in contact with Earth at interstellar distances. They might be a relatively slow form of communication, but they were a quantum leap from sending signals crawling at the speed of light.

"Have my people confirmed this?" Manners said.

"Yes, I checked with them first..."

Logan sensed Aurore's hesitation. "What else?"

The silence was so long and deep he thought they'd lost the connection, but then her voice came back on. "I can't find any trace of the *Sarabhai* either. She's gone."

"The Atoll ship?" Manners spat the words out. "So, they mined what they wanted and Jumped."

"Not unless they did it within an unsafe distance." Aurore paused. "They didn't have time to move one A.U. away, let alone collect any materials."

"That's strange," Logan murmured.

"They must have changed their minds." Manners glanced at her console. "The reconsat shows nothing either?"

"Only empty space."

Manners drummed her fingers on the metal table. "What the Atolls choose to do is none of our business. But the relay *is*. We need that repaired ASAP. That's our lifeline to Earth."

Logan gathered his thoughts. The relays were built around technology that wasn't readily available to them. "That's a tricky job. And, even if it's a simple failure, it's a long way from here. You'll need someone with piloting skills and a technical background to pull that off."

Manners nodded. "Thanks for volunteering."

"Wait a sec—"

Manners disconnected the call, cutting off Aurore's objections. She stared at Logan, the challenge clear in her eyes. "Are you in?"

Logan let out a soft laugh, remembering the number of times his friend Joe had been in the same position. He didn't want the job, but there wasn't anyone better qualified. "The Nomads are useless for such a trip. I'll need to take the *Hansen*. But it's not a job for a single person. Aurore is qualified."

Manners shook her head. "You'll take someone from my team. There are security implications here."

"I understand that, but my wife *has* security clearance. Plus she's got exp—"

"This isn't up for debate." Manners' jaw set in a hard line. "Those are my orders."

The sky visible behind Manners was darkening, and the muscles in Logan's arms and legs trembled. He wasn't under her command, but that didn't change the fact that they needed to restore communications, and he was the best one for the job. "I need to launch now. Before the storm grounds us."

Manners reached for her comm-set. "Head for the Nomad compound. Someone will meet you."

Logan called Aurore as soon as he was outside. The storm was approaching faster than he'd anticipated.

She answered immediately. "You're not going up there alone."

"Manners is assigning someone to go with me." Logan marched toward the compound holding the boxy Nomads, his long legs making short work of the distance. "We'll dock with the *Hansen*, and use it to check out the relay."

There was an awkward moment of silence. "I can fly both of those."

"I know. I told Manners I wanted you along, but she insisted on sending one of her people."

Aurore's breathing was audible through the comm-link. "I can meet you there. She can't stop me."

Logan hesitated. There was nothing he'd rather do than agree with her. He looked beyond the trees that lined the edge of the compound. Black clouds obscured the mountains now and billowed toward the capital from the west, their dark underbellies ample evidence of the amount of rain—or worse—they held. "No time—the storm is coming. Make sure you seal everything tight. I need to know you're safe. And see if you can get hold of Carl."

Logan heard a scraping noise, then Aurore's voice returned.

"That storm is a big one. Meteorology has issued a severe thunderstorm warning with possible heavy snow squalls. You have around thirty minutes before it hits."

Logan smiled. One of the things he loved about Aurore was her calm, logical manner in a crisis—the exact opposite of her passionate nature in private. He reached the first Nomad and triggered the door hatch, scrambling into the cluttered interior and making his way to the cockpit. "I need to go."

"I know." Aurore's voice cracked almost imperceptibly. "Don't make me come looking for you, you big dope."

Logan flicked the switches for the engine start-up sequence, as a military buggy pulled up outside and a soldier sprinted toward the ship.

"I'll be back. Count on it," Logan said. The ship vibrated as the rear engines fired up. A few seconds later, the indicator for the main door turned green to show it was locked. He pressed the starter for the front engines and they burst into life too. "Now, make sure you're safe."

The soldier dropped into the co-pilot seat and strapped in as Logan tested the controls, checking the rotating thruster units were working. A wave of slushy rain splashed against the cockpit like a semi-frozen blanket, temporarily blotting out the view. He trundled the ship into the launch clearing.

"Don't wait for me, Chief," the soldier shouted.

Logan clenched his jaw. It may have been meant as a casual remark, but he had no time to worry about it as a flash of lightning arced across the sky and another torrent of sleet plastered the windows. The engines increased in pitch as Logan operated the throttles, then the Nomad shuddered as he tilted the engines to lift them into the sky. The ship skipped upward as the winds caught them from beneath.

"Watch it, you damn crazy Indian."

The thrust increased, and the ship rose as black clouds gathered around them. Logan grunted at the g-forces pressing them against the seats and heard a gurgle from the co-pilot chair. It would have brought a smile to his lips, if he hadn't been disabled by the acceleration and buffeting. He pulled back on the side-stick and the vibration eased as the Nomad started to fly aerodynamically rather than relying on the pure thrust of the engines. The ship punched through the turbulent clouds into sunlight, and Logan looked across at the other man.

"My name is Logan. Use it."

"Huh? What's got you so strung out?" The soldier glanced at the bewildering array of instruments in the cockpit. "I'm Tepfer, I guess you can call me Lee… or sergeant." He tapped the stripes on his shoulder.

The sky darkened into a deep violet as they climbed. At the altitude limit for the air-breathing engines, Logan switched the ship to the stored oxygen supplies, and the atmospheric intakes whirred as they closed, sealing the ship.

"You must love it here," Tepfer called over the engine noise. "All the wilderness. Living wild, in touch with the spirits and all that."

"I wouldn't call New Hope wild." Logan fought to hold his temper in check.

"Sure, but you get the chance to put on the warpaint again, now and then, eh? Living with nature. Isn't that what you people are all about?"

Outside, the stars were showing as their altitude increased. Logan rolled the ship, to put them in a better orientation for orbital insertion.

"You mean engineers?" Logan growled. "Quiet. I need to concentrate on the trajectory—unless you want us stuck up here."

"Sure, go ahead, Chief."

Manners couldn't have known about Tepfer's attitude, surely. The idea of being trapped with him for two weeks didn't bear thinking about. At top speed, the RoboPony relay was five days each way. Luckily, the *Hansen* was big enough that they wouldn't have to spend much time in proximity. He smiled. Perhaps he could lock the soldier up for the duration.

Opening up the navigation controls, Logan scanned for the *Hansen* to plot an approach vector, but before he found it, the proximity display flashed up a signal too near to be their ship. "Something not right here."

Tepfer's gaze bounced around the instrument panel. "What is it?"

"The sensors are picking up another ship." Logan tried to lock down the readings but they kept shifting. "Larger than the *Hansen*."

"Ours?"

"Sensor data is crazy. Might be Corporate. But it's bigger than anything I've ever seen."

The energy requirements of the Jump limited the physical size of the ships that could be built. The biggest one in use by CESA and the USP was the Zenith class, at three hundred meters in length, but if the sensors were right, this ship was at least twice that.

"Where?" Tepfer looked through the windows, jerking his head in every direction. "I don't see anything."

"Trying to get an image." Logan tapped on the controls, transferring the optical feed to the main screen.

A gray, cylindrical ship dominated the view, silhouetted by the sun, like a giant, metallic version of Moby Dick. Barely visible flickers danced between it and the optical pickup, like dark snow or interference on the transmission.

"Damn!" Logan activated the comm system and punched in the frequency for the open comm channel for the settlement. "New Hope. This is Logan Twofeathers. Flight designation 1172-FL in low orbit. I have detected a large vessel and several smaller ones in orbit. I believe they are hostile. Take approp—"

"What are you talking about?" Tepfer swallowed. "Stop bullshitting, man. Is this because I—"

"Repeat. Kwelengsen is under attack. Take defensive action." Logan switched to the science team's comm channel. "Aurore. If you're monitoring, pick up."

"Stop with the chatter, you stupid bastard." Tepfer tore at his harness buckles. "Take evasive action or something."

"That's not an option. We're in orbit," Logan yelled.

"Logan?" Aurore's voice came over the comms. "What's going on?"

"We're under attack. The planet I mean. Warn everybody. Call Manners..."

The link went dead. Logan checked the instruments. They were transmitting but something was blocking their signal.

"Tighten those belts. I'm taking us down." Logan set up a de-orbit burn and triggered it.

A flash lit up the cockpit, and the ship lurched. Someone was firing at them. Logan checked the sensor screen. Two, or possibly three, smaller craft were vectoring in on them. They could have been manned fighters or remote drones—it didn't matter; the Nomad was relatively helpless in orbit. They had some weapons but he ignored them. It was more of a utility ship than a combat vehicle. Their best chance was to drop back into the atmosphere.

A cacophony of popping noises rattled through the ship, and several warning lights flickered.

"They're shooting at us?" Tepfer said.

"We're venting O2 and fuel." Logan fought to stay calm. "I'm jettisoning the fuel reserves."

"Don't be stupid. You can't land without fuel."

"If I don't, we'll blow up on reentry."

He hit the button to release the fuel and the ship slammed to one side. Tepfer shouted incoherently and grabbed the sides of his chair, while Logan struggled with the controls. Something had ignited the dumped fuel. The ship rolled and bucked as it plunged through the upper atmosphere. The hull temperature indicators rose. They were coming in too steep and he strained to lift the nose and slow them. The maneuvering thrusters hissed and popped several times, but the ship's response was sluggish.

As they dropped, the sky brightened, and after several minutes, the ship responded to the airflow around them. Without fuel, they were a falling brick, but Logan managed to get some directional control using the short wings connected to each engine. He glanced down to check their location. From the craggy rock and snow-covered terrain below, they had to be somewhere over the Baraban mountain range. Logan banked the ship into as tight a turn as possible, attempting to point them toward New Hope without bleeding off too much airspeed.

The city came into sight through the cockpit window and Logan gasped. They were too far away to see details and New Hope was half obscured in the storm, but despite that, a pall of black smoke was visible over the city. Several small dots circled the cloud, taking turns to swoop in attack like a swarm of angry midges.

An alarm sounded, and Logan tore his eyes away to check the controls. Two of their attackers had followed them and were closing from behind.

"Hang on." Logan jerked the control stick to bank the Nomad hard-left. The ship responded, but far too slowly. The shrill scream of heavy QuenchGun fire reached them a fraction after they heard the trip-hammer explosions as the needles tore through the aircraft's tail. He pushed the stick the other way, pulling back in an effort to break the lock on them. The ship pitched clumsily, and another volley of the high-velocity projectiles ripped through the fuselage. The control panel lit up in a blinking frenzy as almost every system reported damage or failures.

Logan pushed on the stick, forcing the protesting ship into a dive. He glanced at the targeting system for the onboard missiles, but it was dead. Even it hadn't been, he doubted he'd have gotten a successful lock on their attackers.

"I thought you could fly this thing!" Tepfer yelled. "Pull up, you cra—"

Logan pulled back hard on the flight controls, but the Nomad had other plans. Plans that included diving nose-first into the rocks below. He opened a general distress channel. "Mayday, Mayday, Mayday. New Hope Traffic Control, this is Nomad 1172-FL, Logan Twofeathers and Sergeant Lee Tepfer on board. We are under attack and our ship is critically damaged. We are approximately ninety kilometers due west of the city."

He didn't expect any assistance. If there were any settlement aircraft still flying, they'd have their hands full. He was broadcasting in the hope there would be a record for Aurore of what had happened to them. Logan realized Tepfer hadn't spoken for a while and glanced across, while fighting to pull the nose up. The sergeant's head lolled on his chest, a dark red river of blood pumping from a tear in his upper torso.

Logan cursed and turned his attention back to the controls. The ship was responding, but nowhere near fast enough, and rolled clockwise. He struggled to correct the movement but the spiral continued. A blur of rock, snow, and trees hurtled toward them, then a brutal impact slammed him against the restraining belts.

Chapter Three

*"When we show respect for other living things,
they respond with respect for us."*
— Crazy Horse (Tȟašúŋke Witkó)

Logan was hanging upside down, unable to see anything but the roof of the Nomad. It was covered in debris and snow that had blown in through the shattered cockpit. Intermittent white flashes lit up the darkness starkly as one of the electronic circuits popped and sparked. The acrid smell of burning plastic irritated his nose, and he coughed as foul smoke filled his lungs.

"Tepfer?" he mumbled. There was no answer, and he tried to twist to look at the soldier, but spasms of pain shot through his left arm, as if he'd plunged it up to the elbow into a steel furnace.

He scrabbled at the straps holding him into the seat. They had a quick-release buckle, but his hands seemed to have a life of their own, and he struggled to find it. When he did, he crashed face-first into the debris below. He lay there for several minutes, the icy snow ironically easing the pain of impact.

The shattered remnants of the cockpit were spread around Logan. The Nomad's nose had been smashed in and the roof flattened, narrowing the view. Jagged rocks interspersed with fir-like trees poked despairingly through the drifting snow, as if unwilling to surrender to the carpet of white. The snow swirled around him, as though he was caught inside the wintry whirlwind of a child's toy.

A flickering orange hue reflected off the snow, and for a while, Logan couldn't understand why. Then it came to him—fire. Groaning, he forced himself upright. His left arm was useless, and he grunted in pain when he tried to use it, but his other compensated enough to allow him to drag himself to his feet. Tepfer was locked in his chair, his wound dripping thick red drops onto the snow. Logan checked for a pulse. It took a while, but he found one—weak, but steady.

With his good arm, Logan tried to stop Tepfer from falling while scrabbling for the release buckle, but his injured arm wouldn't cooperate. Finally, he wedged his left shoulder under Tepfer's chest to brace the soldier and used his right hand to jerk the buckle open. The full weight of Tepfer's body hit him, and they both dropped to the floor like discarded machine parts.

"Neck off." Tepfer barely seemed conscious and blurted out the words like an automatic response.

Logan pulled himself back upright and looked toward the rear of the ship. The large cargo door was missing, leaving a torn, gaping hole. The tail had broken away.

"No time for rubbernecking," Logan muttered, his breath freezing as he spoke. "It's too damn cold in these parts."

Scrambling through the twisted access corridor, Logan edged around the fractured metal hull and peered upwards. He wasn't sure how long it had been since they'd crashed. Their attackers might still be around. He took a moment to listen, but heard nothing other than the howl of the icy wind through the trees. Their impact had apparently been convincing enough that the enemy had moved on.

Several fires were dotted around the wreckage but they were all dying out, and Logan sighed in relief. They didn't appear to be in immediate danger from an explosion. The wind sliced through his clothes and he shivered. He needed to find shelter, otherwise they'd both freeze in short order.

Memories of boyhood camping flooded back, and he considered what around them might help. There was an outcrop of rocks a few meters farther up the mountain. If there was a cave there, they might be in luck. He stumbled through the snow to reach it, but the outcrop was smaller than it had appeared from a distance, and there was no cave to help them. He shook uncontrollably, each tremor sending agonizing stabs through his injured arm.

"Come on, Logan. Think, you dumb bastard."

On one side of the outcrop was a wide crevice and a ledge. It wasn't deep enough, or large enough, to shelter one man, let alone two, but if he pulled together some material, it might make a good base for a lean-to, and if he blocked up the ends it might offer better—and safer—shelter than the smashed aircraft.

Logan staggered over to the wreckage, the wind tearing at his thin clothing. Even one-handed, it didn't take much effort to pull off a larger panel from the outer skin of the trashed Nomad. The composite material was light and strong enough to take anything the weather threw at them. At least for a while. Then came the harder task of dragging Tepfer out of the cockpit.

The soldier was unconscious, making it doubly hard to move him. "Dammit, Logan," he muttered. "Move it, or we'll both die out here."

Soon, he had Tepfer laid out on the panel and dragged both uphill like a ramshackle sled. After laying the other man on the rock, Logan leaned the panel against the outcrop, forming a sheltered alcove. Then he stripped the foliage from trees around them, using the branches to block up the remaining openings as well as possible. It was crude but the best he could manage in short order.

He checked Tepfer again. There was no sign of any foreign material in the wound. Logan guessed that the needle had drilled straight through the soldier's torso. They were high-velocity and capable of piercing medium armor. An unprotected human body wouldn't slow one down.

Leaning back against the rock, Logan almost drifted off. He scraped his palm against the jagged slab, the sharp surface cutting deep scratches in his hand and triggering a burst of adrenaline to wake him up. The shelter was one part of their life equation—they also needed a source of heat. Moving the branches to one side, he slipped back outside. The snow was heavier, and he struggled to see the ship through it. There should be an emergency kit in the cockpit, though what condition it might be in was anyone's guess.

Logan staggered toward the downed ship, the moisture around

his eyes prickling as it froze. He wasn't sure how much more of the low temperature he could take. As he approached, a shadowy figure loomed out of the blizzard and stopped, facing him. He heard a low staccato ululation, recognizing it as the noise a tanglefox made instead of growling.

"Go on," he yelled through chattering teeth and waved his good arm. "Get out of here."

The creature eyed him for several seconds, then turned abruptly and vanished into the desolate landscape. Logan hurried forward and clambered inside the smashed ship. At least it was sheltered from the wind. As he scrambled through the rear compartment, his eyes darted around looking for anything useful, but other than debris it was empty.

In the cockpit, he strained to reach up and check under the pilot's chair. Sure enough, there was an emergency pack, the white plastic box designated with a red diamond. Wrestling it out, he winced as the intense cold bit deeper and the strength in his good hand faded. He wondered what the temperature was. Winter should have been a couple of months away, but at this altitude temperatures rarely rose above freezing. He started back to the makeshift shelter, stumbling blindly through the squalls. The box seemed far heavier than it should for its size, and he dropped it several times.

By the time he squeezed back inside the lean-to, Logan's feet were blocks of ice inside his hiking shoes, and he was shaking so hard he had to fight to coordinate his movements. He struggled to open the emergency box. The contents were packed tight, but not for long. Scrabbling through the pack he found a flattened bundle of survival blankets and tore them open. He draped one over Tepfer, then wrapped a second one around his shoulders. It wasn't much but should help.

Digging deeper, he found what he'd hoped would be there—an emergency catalytic heat block. He pushed one end of it under his knee and pulled the other with his good hand, feeling the snap as its internal wall broke, allowing the contents to mix. After a few seconds, the heat from the block penetrated his jeans. He lifted the mylar blanket covering Tepfer and pressed the block against the soldier. Tepfer moaned slightly but didn't wake. The chemical reaction in the pack would provide heat for around twenty hours, hopefully enough to allow them to ride out the storm.

There was a spray can of MediSkin and some patches, but they wouldn't help with Tepfer's wound—it was too big and deep. The box also held an assortment of gauzes and dressings, again nothing large enough, but they might help staunch the bleeding. Logan opened several of the packs, rolled the soldier onto his back, and pressed the gauze against the wound, taping it clumsily. There were also two NanoBiotic-filled Biojet injectors, which he grimly hoped he wouldn't have to use. While they were good at combating infection, they had a number of side effects that could prove lethal in their current situation. The last thing he found was a box of painkillers—ordinary household items rather than prescription medicine, but if they helped even a little, it would be an improvement, and he swallowed two of the bitter pills.

"I'm no MedTech, dammit," Logan mumbled.

Logan lifted the blanket covering the soldier and slipped under it, then pulled the other blanket over the pair of them. Their combined body heat should help, especially with the heat from the pack. Something hard and metallic pressed into him—Tepfer was armed. He pulled the service pistol out of its holster and placed it on the rock next to them.

After lying there for a while, Logan warmed up. The thin sheets reflected the heat back and kept it inside the blankets. Up until that point, he'd been focused on pure survival, but now he wondered about Aurore and what had happened in the city. *Was she alive? Or Carl? Was anybody alive, in fact?* The invaders were well prepared, and the settlement had scant defenses. Everyone was welcome on Kwelengsen, so why attack it? *And what about that ship? How could something so large make a Jump?*

He shivered, even though the warmth was starting to thaw him out. He had to get back to Aurore, no matter what it took.

Several hours later, Logan woke from a barrage of fitful nightmares where his mind conjured up apparitions of Aurore being imprisoned, tortured, and worse. Sitting upright, he looked around. Snow had piled up on the outside the shelter, but the gray light of dawn penetrated the snow-packed fronds crudely blocking the ends. He examined Tepfer once again. The soldier was cold to the touch, and for a minute Logan was sure he was dead. Then he felt the gentle rise and fall of his chest, and Tepfer let out a low, rasping breath.

Slipping out from under the covers, Logan made sure they covered Tepfer. He moved the branches aside by the makeshift entrance and blinked in the weak sunlight. The sun was low in the sky, and his breath frosted, but the air was warmer than when they'd crashed. To have any chance, they needed more supplies. The emergency box might keep them going for a day or so, but after that, they'd freeze.

Logan remembered the tanglefox and grabbed Tepfer's pistol. He'd never heard of them attacking a human, but they were pack animals. If there were enough of them, they might be a threat. He checked the gun over. It was a standard military issue MalCheck 12MP, loaded with a sixteen round magazine. The polymer frame was cold and he tucked it inside his jacket. At least he was familiar with the weapon.

He didn't want to leave the relative warmth of the shelter but had no choice, and crawled out before he changed his mind. His arm hurt, but he decided it wasn't broken. If it had been, their odds of survival would have dropped to near zero. He knew he should check it thoroughly, but it would have to wait until he came back. At least he was mobile enough that they had a chance—no matter how slim.

The Nomad was covered in a thick layer of snow and almost impossible to pick out from the broken rocks around him, which in some ways was good. Anyone double-checking the crash site would have a hard time finding it. Although with the right detection gear it was possible. He clambered in through the gaping rent at the rear. The ship was a dual-purpose civilian and military craft, so it could have any number of items inside it, if they hadn't been scattered all over the mountainside.

Seeing the transmitter, Logan wondered if there was any power. He switched it on, and the front panel lit up but dimmed again almost at once. After the attack, there'd be little chance anyone would be listening. All it would do was potentially alert the enemy, and he stabbed the off button.

Logan checked under the co-pilots chair. The Nomads were used by the settlers as well as the soldiers, and were equipped with basic survival gear. He pulled out a heavy, triangular fabric case and unzipped it. Inside was a collapsible carbine, and a spare magpack. He slung it over his head and checked the case again, finding a broad-bladed folding knife that he clipped to his belt.

He carried on searching, hastily gathering a pile of everything he thought might be useful. In one of the intact compartments, he found a three-pack of duct tape and smiled. It was said you could do anything with the silvery wrap, and it seemed he was about to find out.

Gathering everything up, he waded back to the shelter, his teeth chattering again. The catalytic heat pack was still working and, though it wasn't a roaring fire, it raised the temperature to a level more bearable than outside. Tepfer was still unconscious, but the dressings needed changing, and it would be easier if the soldier was awake enough to sit up. But Logan didn't want to wake him unnecessarily.

Logan took stock of what he'd recovered. There was the rifle and knife, three rolls of duct tape, three short pencils, around twenty pieces of paper, some loose, and some in the form of a safety booklet related to the Nomad, a tiny high-efficiency flashlight that doubled as a lamp, and a partly eaten roll of Neetomints.

"If I was Joe Ballen, or the Rocket Ranger, I'm sure I'd be able to make a spaceship out of that lot. Too bad I'm not," he murmured, then checked the weapon he'd found.

The carbine was an ASC3, also by MalCheck, and a variation on the basic QuenchGun format. The two magpacks held twenty-five needles, and provided the power to operate the coils that propelled them. It was rugged and simple, with a single power setting. Logan examined the knife: a blade with a partial saw edge, a signal whistle, and a magnesium fire starter. The latter looked like a godsend, given there was only one more heat pack in the emergency kit, and he didn't relish lighting a fire the traditional way.

"Pull up..." Tepfer murmured.

Logan moved the silvery blankets away from the soldier's face. Tepfer's eyes danced around, unfocused. "Sergeant? Do you hear me?" Logan half-whispered.

Tepfer rolled over partially, then yelled as his wounded shoulder hit the rock. "Oh crap. You still here, Chief?"

Logan's jaw clenched. "Still here."

"Was hoping you were part of the nightmare."

"The nightmare is that Kwelengsen has been attacked." Logan put his good arm under Tepfer and helped him upright. "And we're stuck on top of a mountain."

"Christ, that hurts." Tepfer coughed. "What the hell did you do to me?"

"You took a round when we were attacked. I tried to cover it, but it needs looking at."

Tepfer grimaced as Logan moved the shiny material away and pulled back his uniform to see the wound. It was a mixture of dark red and purple, the skin around it bloated and inflamed.

"I need to dress it better." Logan reached for the emergency supplies and other items he'd recovered. "It's getting infected. And you're losing blood."

"Don't tell me you're a goddamn medicine man as well?"

Logan's temper flared. "I'm the man trying to help you. So, how about dropping the insults?"

"Jeez, touchy, aren't we?" Tepfer moved again and groaned. "Do what you have to."

Logan shook his head and teased back the dressings, which were clotted with thick, congealed blood. Using some alcohol swabs from the supplies he cleaned up the front and back. "Looks like a large caliber needle drilled all the way through."

"Well, ain't I the lucky one." Tepfer's breath was ragged, and a thick stream of blood oozed from the wound. "Knew I shoulda got that mega-buck insurance package."

"We need to stop the bleeding."

"I get it," Tepfer said, the lines on his face deepening to canyons. "Build a fire, cauterize the wound and all that."

"You've seen too many Solidos." Logan pressed the bandages back, hoping to disturb the wound as little as possible. "If I did that, you'd be dead from infection in a few days."

"Sure thing, Chief. You're the doc—uhhhhh…" Tepfer's voice cracked as Logan eased him up against the rock.

"Try not to move. I need to take your coat and shirt off for a few minutes, okay?"

Tepfer screwed his eyes tight, but nodded.

After pulling the clothes away, Logan applied more of the absorbent dressings, then sprayed a film of MediSkin over the whole mess. The spray foamed and set in a rubbery layer. The stuff wasn't made to be used on large wounds, but he hoped it might create a decent seal to keep further infection from getting in. Then he grabbed one of the rolls of duct tape and taped up the front and back of Tepfer's chest, looping it several times around the soldier's torso and shoulder.

"You into bondage, Chief?"

Logan ignored him, and helped him back into his shirt and fatigue jacket. "Try not to move too much."

"I was thinking of going for a fifteen-klick run. Wanna race?"

"Sure. As soon as you've rested."

"I'm cold." Tepfer pulled the survival blankets back over him.

"You've lost a lot of blood, and you're probably hungry."

Logan dug into the emergency box again. There were half a dozen ration packs, which would keep them going a few days. He unwrapped one and broke off a piece of the thick bar. It reminded him more of fiberboard than food, but he pushed it under Tepfer's nose.

"E-rations?" Tepfer sneered. "That all we got?"

"If you eat your greens, you can have a Neetomint for dessert."

"I thought you people knew how to live off the land," Tepfer muttered after finishing the last of his ration. "Get out there and hunt down some real food. I could do a nice, juicy steak, right now—you know what I mean? Still bleeding."

Logan wondered how anyone living on Kwelengsen could be so ignorant. The native life on the planet was different from Earth organisms, and although it was based on the same twenty amino acids and general protein structures, little of it was compatible with the human digestive system.

"I'll get on it. As soon as we hit the first Steak Factory."

"Now you're talking. Always figured I'd get a franchise for one of those places when I retired." Tepfer laughed, but it turned into a wet cough, making Logan regret his joke.

"Try to get some sleep."

"Any more blankets?"

"A couple, but I was saving them. They don't have much bulk, so they reflect rather than insulate—limited effectiveness."

"My balls are dropping off here." Tepfer's voice weakened, as though he was fading again. "'Chutes on the No…"

Logan checked, but Tepfer had passed out. Which was no bad thing under the circumstances.

So, where are we?

Physically, he knew they were in the Baraban range. He'd seen New Hope as they came down, so they must be on the east side of the peaks. The nearest of the foothills was over seventy kilometers away from the city, which meant they were at least eighty or eighty-five in total. A person could walk at about five kilometers per hour on flat ground, making them roughly seventeen hours away, but the mountains complicated that. Even if they were both one hundred percent fit, Logan would have been surprised if they were able to maintain half that speed.

That put them at least two days away, but with Tepfer's condition, it would take longer—if the sergeant could make it at all. Tepfer's size suggested he'd made full use of his military Geneering credits and, in normal circumstances, would have out-paced Logan, but given his wound, the soldier would be lucky to get out of the mountains alive.

If winter was setting in early, they needed to get to lower altitudes before their heat sources ran out. Logan was capable of starting a fire, especially now he had the knife and fire starter, but the local wood didn't burn without a lot of drying. And to make it worse, they didn't have the right clothing for traveling any distance in such conditions. Tepfer was better off in his fatigues than Logan, but neither was dressed for low temperatures. Without more to insulate them, they were pretty much stuck where they were. But if they didn't leave soon, they wouldn't make it.

"Maybe I could train the tanglefoxes to pull us out," Logan muttered, before remembering what Tepfer had gasped before passing out. "'Chutes. On the Nomad. Why didn't I think of that?"

Logan dragged himself back outside. The sky was ugly and overcast. More bad weather was coming in. The pilot seats had ejection capabilities, with parachute packs built into the chairs. If he retrieved the material, it could make the difference between life and death.

He rushed across to the wreckage and examined the chairs. The ejection mechanism was zero-zero rated, which meant once activated, powerful rockets would shoot the seat and occupant up through an escape hatch in the roof. With the ship on its roof, if Logan triggered them, the rockets would have nowhere to go and almost certainly burn the 'chutes.

The activation mechanism was a simple electromechanical trigger. Logan disconnected the power to the rocket motors on both chairs. The cold made his fingers shake, to the point where he could barely control them. But after ten frozen minutes, both seats were neutralized. The 'chutes formed the back of the chairs, and he cut the straps and other sundry connectors away. They'd be easier to transport while wrapped up.

The second 'chute came out the same and he gathered them both, ready to return to the shelter. As he was leaving, a thought struck him and he turned back to the seats. They were covered in a tough, rubberized material and he sliced off sections, adding them to the pile, along with the nylon bag the rifle had been stored in. To survive, he needed everything he could lay his hands on.

Chapter Four

*"When climbing a mountain
it's easier to go downhill."*
— Grandfather Twofeathers

When Logan returned to the shelter, he checked his arm. It was throbbing, and when he pulled up his sleeve, he found a long slice down his forearm. It wasn't deep, but his shirt was a blood-soaked, congealed mess. After cleaning the wound, he sprayed it with a thin layer of MediSkin. There wasn't much of it left, and he wanted to make sure to leave enough for Tepfer's dressing changes, though how he was going to manage that he wasn't sure. The MediSkin was designed to fall off once healing was complete. Pulling it off partway might do more harm than good, but it was the only way he had of sealing such a large wound.

The parachutes came apart easily enough, but the amount of material made them awkward to handle. He piled the first one over Tepfer to give the soldier greater insulation, then turned his attention to the second. At the moment, Logan was wearing regular clothing, suited for fall in the lowland regions. To move anywhere, he needed better protection from the elements. He sliced up the voluminous, silken material, sticking it together with duct tape to fashion an extra layer. Hopefully, it would be enough to allow him to get clear of the mountains.

There was a small geological station at the bottom of the foothills. He'd helped Aurore set it up to monitor for dangerous seismic activity in the early days after they landed. That was his immediate goal. As well as the seismic equipment, it should contain a few supplies and a radio—which might well be their only lifeline.

Logan warmed up now he was better covered, and he took the time to think about the rest of his gear. His hiking shoes were sturdy enough, but only ankle high. After lining them with the duct tape, he added makeshift socks from the 'chute material, rushing the job as his feet were freezing.

He cut up the thick parachute cover to form mittens, using scraps from the thinner canopy material as additional insulating layers. Then he taped the heavy fabric around his ankles and lower leg, to act as crude gaiters that would help insulate and keep snow from getting inside his shoes. Finally, he cut several square pieces of the silky cloth and taped them around his head, creating a crude hood.

After these preparations, Logan was ready to set off, but before moving Tepfer he checked on his condition. The wound looked no worse than earlier, but no better either. And the soldier's skin was hot to the touch. There was no choice—he had to use the NanoBiotics. He grabbed a Biojet injector, stripped off the sterile wrap, then pressed it a few centimeters above Tepfer's wound. The short silver tube hissed as it delivered its healing payload.

"What the hell…?" Tepfer roused, though barely. "You gonna steal my organs?"

"What makes you think they're worth anything?" Logan said, but Tepfer didn't answer. He'd slipped back unconscious.

Wrapped in his newly created clothing Logan went back outside. This time the temperature didn't bite as much, and he scouted around the area. He located two straight branches in the nearby trees, cut them down and trimmed the needle-like foliage from them, then carried them back.

A thick blanket of snow covered the panel leaning against the outcrop, and Logan brushed it off with one of the branches before pulling the composite sheeting from the rocks and tipping it over. The smooth outer surface would make a sturdy sled to carry Tepfer, and would continue to work as a lean-to as needed. He tied the branches onto the edges using cord from the 'chutes and tested the weight to make sure he was strong enough. He managed to hold it, though his left arm twinged.

Tepfer groaned as Logan dragged him onto the panel but didn't appear to wake up. Logan piled on the rest of their scant supplies, then covered the lot with the thermal blankets and parachute material. He grabbed the branches and heaved. The improvised sled moved, but he almost dropped the left branch. His arm felt like the flesh was being stripped from the bone. He gripped it again and gritted his teeth.

Once he found the rhythm, it wasn't too hard to keep the panel sliding. And that lowered the strain on his arm, reducing the pain to a point where it was merely excruciating. His route was circuitous, made slower by the rocks buried under the snow. Every other step was a scrabble or lurch, and always held the risk of twisting an ankle or worse.

"Just keep heading downhill," Logan muttered, his breath freezing against the makeshift hood.

It wasn't easy to do that. Often he was forced to detour around larger outcrops and steeper areas where he couldn't be sure of holding onto the sled. In thirty minutes, he was sweating, and they'd only traveled seven or eight hundred meters. If there'd been a clear run, Logan might have been tempted to toboggan down the mountainside, but the saw-edged rocks would have sliced the panel, and them, to pieces.

Snow buffeted him in white waves, scouring his exposed skin like a hail of frozen razor blades. He focused on counting his steps, but kept losing track as he slid and staggered over the rocky ground. His hand slipped on the left pole, and the sled dug in, twisting him off his feet. He collapsed face-first. The snow was wet and heavy, and melted against his face and lips but, even with the discomfort, he was unable to move and lay there trembling.

His left arm was a raw stump of pain so intense that Logan checked it was still there. After reassuring himself it was, he crawled over to the sled and scrabbled under the parachute to find the emergency supplies. It seemed to take far longer than it should, but eventually, he found the box and pulled out the painkillers.

He swallowed a handful without counting them. It didn't

matter if the dose was safe. He needed relief, no matter what the cost. As he pushed the box back under the cover, he heard the same low, warbling tanglefox sound he'd heard earlier. But this time, it was coming from several animals.

Easing himself up, Logan looked over the pile on the sled covering Tepfer. He spotted at least six of the creatures spread around his position in an arc. Their fluffy, satellite antennae-like ears pricked upright, and the nearest one opened its pointed mouth to emit a high-pitched trilling whistle. Almost immediately, another sounded from behind Logan. He twisted around to see another four or five of them staring at him, snouts wrinkling as they showed their all-too-sharp teeth plates.

"Easy now." Logan spoke in low, even tones, not wanting to startle them. Although not usually threatening, a pack that size could do a lot of damage and might even overwhelm him if they attacked together. He'd put the pistol back in Tepfer's holster, assuming the soldier would be unhappy if he found it missing, but he had the rifle slung over his back.

"If you fellows want to run along, I'd be happy to see you go," he said, keeping his words soothing.

The closest tanglefox cocked its head, making a sound a little like the short mewl of a goat. Logan lifted himself to his knees. Perhaps if they saw his size they might become less interested in challenging him. He didn't know if they were intimidated by eye contact or not. Some animals shied away from it, while some saw it as threatening, but how these alien creatures might react was unpredictable, and no one had established such details yet.

Logan raised himself higher and the closest animal edged back, crouching and emitting a shrill hiss. Realizing he'd frightened them, Logan lowered himself again.

"Okay," he said, hoping he sounded friendly. "Let's try something else."

The tanglefox relaxed momentarily, then hissed louder, its teeth plates snapping into their extended position. Then it vanished in an explosion of skin, scales, and bones, as a thunderous crack and searing blast hit Logan from behind. The other animals scampered away, disappearing into the trees and rocks. He looked around.

There was a small gap in the mound of material, and he spotted Tepfer's grinning face above the squared-off pistol barrel.

"Looked like you needed some help, Chief. Maybe you need to bone up on those fox whispering skills…"

Despite the cold, Logan's anger blazed. "They might not have attacked."

"Didn't wanna take the chance." Tepfer's grin faded. "I'm chewed up bad enough as it is."

All Logan wanted to do was punch Tepfer, but he saw a trickle of sweat on the man's forehead and instead checked his temperature. "You're running a fever. We need to find shelter so I can have another look at you."

"Go for it, Chief." Tepfer closed his eyes, and the gap in the pile vanished.

Now they were lower, the clumps of trees were thicker, making it harder to find rocky patches. Logan took up the branches of the makeshift sled and pulled again. All he could do was continue down and hope he'd find a resting place soon.

He counted another five hundred steps, then checked the time. They'd been going another thirty minutes and it was getting close to noon. Progress was painfully slow, but there wasn't any alternative. If he stopped, the cold would undoubtedly kill both of them in short order. He started again, dazed from the numbness and exhaustion invading his body. Pain was biting its way through his arm, despite the drugs.

He hesitated at the lip of a steeper incline and looked down. The increased slope would make it harder, and he wasn't certain he'd manage the extra strain. Logan examined the terrain to the left and right, but the ridge disappeared into the trees in both directions, and he couldn't tell how far a detour would take them.

Pulling on the sled, Logan edged over onto the steeper ground. He'd have to risk it and hope for the best. It was at least four hundred meters down to where the land became flatter, but the ridgeline extended at least half that distance in both directions. "I hope someone appreciates this," he mumbled.

He was about fifty meters down the incline when his foot caught a rock under the snow. Logan swore and pushed against it, meaning to clamber over the obstacle. The rock slid under the blanket of white, and he tumbled. He jabbed his hands into the snow to stabilize himself, but the angle was too steep, and he pitched over again, tumbling like a snowball rolling down the steep wash of snow.

He tried to keep his eyes on the sled, but was enveloped in a spray of white powder kicked up by his flailing plunge. He'd almost struggled right-side-up when a fallen tree trunk snagged him, and he catapulted into the air like a rubber ball. The snow engulfed him and broke his fall somewhat. Then his head smacked into something much harder, and the whiteness turned dark.

Letting out a groan, Logan forced his eyelids apart. He was sure they were open but couldn't see anything. After a while, he realized he was lying face-down in the snow, and colder than he'd ever felt in his life. Pushing down, he lifted himself and looked around. He had no idea how long he'd been out, but the sky seemed a deeper blue than he last remembered, which meant it was later in the afternoon. He checked his watch, but it stared back at him with a lifeless black screen.

He'd also lost one of his makeshift mittens and, when he clambered out of the snow, he realized several other pieces of his improvised clothing had been stripped away in his fall. He looked back at the slope. There were two clear trails gouged erratically in the snowfield—one leading to him and a larger one leading farther off to the north. They'd made it down the incline, or at least *he* had.

"Nice going, Logan. Quickest way down..."

He trudged toward the other track, supporting his aching ribs with his good arm. Logan suspected he'd hit something else solid on the way down, or the carbine slung over his back might have punched him in the ribs as he tumbled.

The lower ground formed a natural shallow bowl that provided some shelter from the biting winds as he wove between the trees, searching for signs of the sled. Then he saw it—a wide, sliding path that cut through the snow into a thicker stand of vegetation. Logan struggled through the icy drifts and, after a few minutes, spotted the panel wedged awkwardly into the scrub.

It didn't seem to have tipped, and when he reached it, the pile of parachute material was safely on top. He grabbed the material and lifted it. Tepfer was breathing, but each inhalation was rough and wheezy. When Logan reached down to check him, the soldier's eyes flickered open.

"I demand another pilot." Tepfer gave a labored wink. "This one's trying to fly with no wings."

Logan placed his hand on the soldier's forehead, feeling the burn of fever in his clammy skin. "Wait here, I'll take a look around."

"Wasn't goin' anywhere," Tepfer whispered, then closed his eyes.

Logan stumbled farther along to where the ground started to rise. That might be a sign there was shelter in that direction. His hand and feet were getting increasingly numb where he'd lost his glove and gaiters, but he forced himself to keep moving. There was something dark and gray visible up ahead through the trees, and he moved toward it. A small rock outcrop came into view, and he waded closer. There was a deeper darkness in the middle of the outcrop—a fissure that might lead inside.

Bending low, he squeezed through the narrow cleft. It was too dark to see much, and he pulled out the flashlight. The passage appeared to open wider deeper in, and it was a better option than anything else at that moment. Logan backed out and headed over to Tepfer. The cave might be home to some creature, but he was willing to risk that for the sake of having some shelter.

As he waded through the snow, Logan heard a distant scream, like the cry of a large animal. But it was too constant to be natural and grew in volume until it was deafening. The speed of its approach meant it had to be some type of air vehicle. Presumably, their attackers had got around to checking the area where the Nomad had gone down.

A rumble of artificial thunder shot overhead, and Logan caught the blur of an aircraft above him. He doubted they'd seen him, but with the sensors on their ships, it wouldn't take them long.

Grabbing the sled, Logan pulled with all his strength, grunting at the pain in his arm and ribs. Stabbing his legs into the snow, he dragged it through the trees toward the cave. If he could get them inside, the rock might hide them from detection. Though if it didn't, it might be their grave.

They were close to the cave when the noise grew louder once more. Using the last of his strength, Logan tugged his burden to the lip of outcrop and pulled the cloth off Tepfer. Now the soldier was visible, Logan saw fresh blood. Whether from the fall, or because the wound wasn't dressed properly, he didn't know, but he had no time to worry about it. The aircraft was closing.

Rolling Tepfer off the panel, Logan put his arms under the sergeant's armpits, dragging him back through the jagged split in the rock. Tepfer must have weighed around one hundred and fifty kilos, and Logan laboriously pulled him inside. Jamming his feet against the edges of the fissure, he used his leg muscles to bodily heave the soldier inside. Once through the entrance into the wider area, he collapsed, gasping heavily. Logan feared the worst for Tepfer after manhandling him that way, but he would have to wait. The supplies were outside, and with the right equipment, the enemy might detect them.

Logan wanted to lie there in a heap but forced himself to move. Crawling back through the cave entrance, he scrambled to his feet and swept everything up in the parachute. The roar of the aircraft passed overhead as he dragged the bundle inside the cave, and he hoped he'd been in time.

Logan switched the flashlight back on. It was a risk, but he needed to check on Tepfer. The light flickered on, filling the cave with a dim, but stark, white illumination. They were in a chamber, about three by four meters, with the narrow entrance behind him and a smaller hole running deeper into the rock. Logan didn't miss the telltale signs of thick, gray hair coating the ground around them.

It might be from an animal not frequently seen by the settlers called arktomys. Many people considered them similar to bears, though the creatures were anatomically closer to large rodents, and about the size of a pig. Based on the few human encounters, they were known to live in the mountains and possess heavy coats to protect them from cold temperatures, but beyond that, information was scarce. The limited studies that *had* been done suggested they were omnivorous, so definitely a potential threat. The cave might be an existing lair, or one that had been abandoned.

Logan examined Tepfer. He was sweating profusely, though his skin was cold and clammy. Despite being sheltered in the cave, Logan's breath froze with every exhalation. He laid one of the thermal blankets on the floor to isolate Tepfer from the icy rock and rolled the soldier onto it. Digging back into the supplies, Logan grabbed the remaining NanoBiotic dose. The Biojet hissed when he pressed it against the soldier's upper chest, the sound echoing in the small cave. Finally, he wrapped a second of the silvery blankets over Tepfer, before piling on the rest of the material.

Logan would have been happy to use one of the remaining heat packs, but that would have sent a signal as bright as a flare to the enemy above them. He clamped his jaw tight to stop his teeth chattering, wrapped the last blanket around himself as best he could, then crawled under the pile of material alongside Tepfer.

He couldn't hear the airship anymore and was slipping into an exhausted doze when he woke with a start. The floor of the cave trembled, and a barrage of explosions tore through the air from outside. After a lengthy bombardment, they stopped, leaving him wondering what was happening. Logan wanted to look outside, but his strength failed and he collapsed against the rock.

There was another rattle of explosions, like a stream of high-pitched thunder. They're going to bury us, Logan thought, waiting for another round. After several minutes of silence, he decided they must have had enough and moved on.

Logan clutched the short rifle, ready for anything, but eventually he dozed, then jolted awake. He forced himself to concentrate on Aurore, hoping she was okay wherever she was, but the idea that she might not be tightened his chest and made his breath come out in harsh rasps. He listened again but heard nothing, and decided to check outside for any signs of the enemy. For all Logan knew, they might have landed and were now searching for them on the ground. Poking the carbine before him, he scraped his way back through the narrow opening.

Staying carefully hidden inside the rock, Logan looked out. What had been almost pristine snow a short while ago now looked like a wintry plunge into hell. Giant scorched pockmarks were scattered around the area, and dozens of trees had been reduced to splintered stumps. The panel he'd used as a stretcher had vanished. If the aircraft's sensors had detected it, that might have prompted the enemy to fire, either as a precaution, or to justify being there. It was unlikely they'd consider the panel a threat, so presumably, they'd used it as an excuse to let off steam.

He heard a distant roar, like a train approaching on its tracks, yet he knew there were none on the planet. It might have been the aircraft coming back, but the sound was deeper and more intense, as though an immense thunderstorm was approaching. A vibration tingled in his hands from the rock, and he looked up. The snow seemed to shimmer, then he realized the haze was closing, and what it was.

He couldn't turn in the narrow passage and instead was forced to shuffle back from the entrance. He'd barely moved a meter before the view through the opening was obliterated by a flood of falling snow. It piled up outside and started encroaching into the cave as the weight built up above. Logan scrabbled back, the rock tearing at his hands and knees, until he was in the cavern and could roll onto the floor. He lay there gasping, a slick warmth of blood coating his hands.

"Out of the pan, into the flames," he said, laughing softly. "I think somebody doesn't like me."

Logan squatted on the floor and tried to stretch out his back, but his large frame wasn't meant for small spaces like the entrance. He was only partly successful, and the freezing temperatures didn't help untangle the knots in his muscles. They had one heat pack left, but he wasn't sure how safe it would be in the confined space. The catalytic heaters didn't consume oxygen in the same way a fire did, but would still use some. He glanced around at the smaller hole leading into the rock. That might open to air somewhere, but he couldn't be certain.

"Great choice—freeze to death, or asphyxiate."

He rolled over and looked at the narrow entrance. The snow had come in about half a meter, but that wasn't what worried him. *How deep are we buried?*

Chapter Five

*"We will be known forever
by the tracks we leave."*
— Crazy Horse (Tȟašúŋke Witkó)

Logan dozed fitfully, woken several times by skittering noises. Whether they were real or only in his imagination, he never found out, as when he checked he saw nothing. After the fourth or fifth disturbance, he fell into a deep, exhausted sleep. When he finally roused, he checked Tepfer again. The soldier was tough for sure, and alive despite his high temperature and ragged breathing. Logan chewed joylessly through half of an e-ration, saving the rest for later. He left Tepfer sleeping—there seemed little point bothering him until Logan had a way out.

While he ate, Logan fashioned replacements for his lost clothing from the scraps of material that remained. Then he crawled back through the fissure to where the avalanche had penetrated. He wasn't sure if he saw light through the snow or not, even when he switched off the flashlight. Maybe it was dark outside, or they were buried too deep to make digging out practical.

The snow had compressed almost to the point of being a solid block of ice, and he hacked at it with the knife—all he had that would break up the concrete-like mass. After working at it for half an hour, he'd only cleared about ten centimeters. The rock seemed to press in on him from all sides, the rough edges digging into his skin as he hacked at the icy plug. His breath was coming more sharply, and he fought to keep it steady. He'd spent countless hours inside his spacesuit surrounded by deadly vacuum. It was ridiculous to let something as trivial as a tight rock fissure affect him.

Logan tried to focus on digging, but that didn't help. He forced himself to think about Aurore instead, imagining her smiling and reassuring him that everything would be okay. He dozed, his head dropping a little. Then he roused and snapped back upright, gasping as his neck and skull slammed into the flinty roof.

He pulled back, but found he was snagged on the roughened passage. He struggled harder, his stomach tightening as the rock seemed to grab at him, refusing to let him go. He pushed again, unable to breathe in anything but gasps. *I'm going to die, trapped in the rock and buried under the snow for eternity.* He tried to swallow, but his throat was painfully dry.

Something tugged at his leg, and Logan kicked out, not knowing what it was. Some creature from inside the cave? He felt it again. Several pieces of his clothing ripped as he scraped against the rock and was dragged backward. Then he was inside the wider chamber once more.

Logan rolled onto his back, breathing heavily, and closed his eyes. When he reopened them, Tepfer was alongside him. Somehow the soldier had used his Geneered strength to pull Logan out of the hole, but the cost to Tepfer was clear as blood oozed around his taped-up wounds.

Tepfer grinned. "You people always need our help to pull your asses out of the fire. Or ice."

Logan's hands clenched. "Who's dragging you off this damn mountain?"

"Can't you take a joke?" Tepfer tried to laugh, but it came out as a wheeze. "You okay?"

Logan's breathing slowly returned to normal, and he nodded. "Sure. Had a moment there."

"We stuck?"

Logan thought about it. There was no other way out. If he couldn't dig them out, they'd be dead within hours of the heat pack going cold. His muscles tightened as a grim determination filled him. "Needed a breather. We'll be out soon, don't worry."

Tepfer didn't answer, and Logan realized the soldier had passed out again. After wrapping his patient back in the blankets and parachute, he looked back at the crevice-like entrance.

"Think small, Logan." He turned onto his stomach and shuffled into the hole. The knife was waiting, and he attacked the icy block once more.

This time he worked for about fifteen minutes, then edged back inside the cave. He sat cross-legged on the floor, taking long steady breaths, forcing his thoughts to focus on being reunited with Aurore and walking hand-in-hand through fields of yellow canola in the heat of summer. It helped to keep the panic at bay. After a short break, he was digging again.

He was deliberately not counting how many cycles of this pattern he repeated. But he'd cleared the packed snow beyond the rock opening, enough to get his full chest past the entrance while lying down. Logan twisted onto his back and hacked at the crust above him. The cold tingled his upper body painfully and, after a short while, he wormed inside the relative warmth of the cave. When he stopped shivering, he grabbed his silver blanket and edged back through to the outside, wrapping it around him to preserve his body heat.

By now, Logan sensed the light clearly above him, but it took another three attempts before he finally punched his hand through. A patch of deep-blue sky peered jauntily through the small hole he'd made, but the adrenaline rush made him feverishly smash his way out, and he stood. They were free.

The avalanche wasn't as deep as he'd feared. He stood waist-deep in the small hole he'd made and sucked in breaths of fresh air, looking around at the wash of snow that had tumbled down the mountain. It could have been a lot worse.

When the chill started to bite, he crawled inside the cave. Tepfer hadn't moved, and Logan lifted the covers. "Tepfer? Sergeant?"

Tepfer didn't answer, and Logan checked for a pulse, his cold touch rousing the soldier.

"Huh? Wha?"

"I've dug through the avalanche. We can get out."

"Dug? What avalanche?"

Logan checked. Tepfer's temperature was still high. Maybe he didn't remember what had happened. "I'm going to see what I can find to carry you. I'll be back in ten minutes at the most." He moved toward the entrance.

"Leave me," Tepfer croaked.

Logan turned back. "No way. Not after everything we've been through." He added a silent *and after what you've said to me.* "You're not thinking straight."

"Listen, you dumb-headed Indian. I ain't got a chance in hell of getting off this rock alive, and we both know it. If you try carry me down, we'll both die."

"Self-sacrifice isn't your style. Stick to racism—you're better at it."

"Listen. When you get down, you can send help to get me. You can move quicker on your own. Leave me bundled up. I'm too mean to die out here. But that's the only way either of us has a chance of surviving."

"That heat-pack won't last more than another two or three hours. After that, you're dead. I can't get down in that time. And you're in no shape to make fires."

"I got extreme temperature survival enhancements. Gather up some wood before you leave. I can put together a fire and keep it going, if the stuff is within reach."

What Tepfer said was true—it would be slower with the two of them, but Logan doubted that the sergeant had used up valuable Geneering credits on something like cold survivability.

"You're a bad liar, Sergeant."

Logan ducked down again and crawled outside. He was better protected now, and the cold didn't seem as bad. He waded through the drift of snow over to the trees and sawed at several of the thicker branches. It was hard going with the all-too-short knife, but after a while, he had two fairly long and straight—albeit rough—poles that would do as a basis for a litter.

The sergeant was asleep again and the shock of the cold didn't wake him when Logan pulled him through the tiny passage. Logan had taped several pieces of the remaining parachute material to the branches and piled Tepfer and the rest on top, making sure the heat pack was pressed against the soldier.

The contraption was even harder to pull than the panel had been, but Logan gritted his teeth and dragged it forward. Once they reached the trees, the snowpack thinned, making it easier to move, and he picked up the pace. The exertion warmed him, but it meant he was losing body heat in the cold conditions. It didn't matter. Either he was going to get them off this mountain, or they were both going to freeze.

After about an hour, Logan stopped to rest. Tepfer remained unconscious and looked worse than ever. Logan perched on a rock, breathing deeply, and stared back the way they'd come. It was only when he looked up the mountain that he realized how far they'd traveled and how much lower they were. The air was a little warmer now, and the breeze brushing against his skin held a touch of moisture. In the distance, a flock of the clumsy-looking, triangular birds fluttered through the sky like over-sized butterflies.

As he sat, Logan chewed on the other half of his ration bar. He tried to rouse Tepfer in case he wanted something to eat, but got no response. Leaving the soldier to sleep rather than force him awake, Logan picked up the poles and continued trudging downhill.

The snowfield thinned further as they descended, with tufts of green poking through in clumps. Through sparser areas of trees, the brown-green land was visible below as it flattened into the prairie. Logan tried and failed to spot the geological station, though he did see what had to be the Matchem River to his left. It ran more or less due east, joining up with several other tributaries before running through New Hope and into the sea at Saechao Bay.

The station was south of the river, so they wouldn't have to cross it. He aimed toward it—the building was less than a kilometer from where the river emerged from the mountains. After that, it was simply a question of grim-faced hard work. One foot in front of the other, each step bringing Logan closer to exhaustion. After another hour, the ground leveled off and, although still cold, the patches of snow were sparser, meaning he could walk more easily on the hard-packed clay soil.

He didn't dare move too far from the trees, though it would

have made the going faster. That would leave them exposed, and recon drones were so hard to detect that one could tag them without Logan spotting it. The trees offered some protection at least, even if the ground under them was knotted.

Finally, Logan saw a smudge of red and white, crying out when he realized it was the station. He stopped momentarily, the small building half hidden by the foliage, then redoubled his pace, pulling Tepfer along behind him.

"Tepfer? We made it, do you hear?"

Rushing forward, Logan's view of the station became clearer as he approached. It wasn't much to look at—a PlaSteel box with a red, angled roof crowded by antenna, along with a cupped anemometer. To one side was a tall pylon, topped with a large wind turbine that powered the station, its vertical cylinder spinning steadily in the gusts coming off the mountains. He was light-headed, not sure if it was from fatigue or excitement. Crashing to his knees, he fell facedown into the ground, the muddy soil smearing his face.

"Come on, Logan," he said, pushing himself back up. "Move your ass. You're not giving up now, are you?"

He scrambled back to his feet and seized the litter poles again. Clenching his teeth for one last push, he staggered toward the station. He could see the door now. *We've made it. We actually made it!* He wobbled again but recovered, stamping toward the building. The door was unlocked, and he pushed it open. Dropping the poles, he dragged the litter through the door, then closed it behind him.

The heat hit him like a sauna after being outside. It wasn't that warm in the building—it only felt that way in comparison. Someone had left a heavy, checked work jacket on a hook by the door, and Logan smiled. He threw it over him to add to his layers, though it was at least two sizes too big.

There was a modest heater by the wall, and Logan wasted no time in turning it on. It would drain the station's batteries quickly, but at that point, it didn't matter—they needed the heat. Once it was running, he uncovered Tepfer to check on his condition.

"We made it, Sergeant. We're going to be—"

Sergeant Tepfer grinned up at him. But there was no humor

in the soldier's dead eyes.

Logan hammered his fist against the wall and recoiled at the pain. It wasn't as though he'd liked Tepfer—his casual bigotry belonged to a time over a century ago—but Logan had been determined to get them to safety, if nothing else. And somehow his resentment of Tepfer's racism made him feel guiltier about the soldier's death. Would he have tried harder if Tepfer hadn't been so outspokenly prejudiced? Perhaps if Logan had been more in tune with the old ways, he'd have been able to pull it off. But would any of that traditional knowledge have helped on a completely different planet?

Logan rewrapped Tepfer in the parachute material. He should put the body outside where the cold air would preserve it, but he was reluctant. The idea of tanglefoxes and other native vermin chewing on Tepfer's body made him feel ill. The soldier deserved to be buried, but Logan wasn't sure he had anything to dig into the semi-frozen soil.

There was a roughly printed plastic stool in the corner by a bench full of monitoring equipment. Despite its appearance, it held his weight when he rested on it. His eyelids were like slabs of astrocrete. All he wanted to do was lie down. Instead, he ate another piece of emergency ration and followed it up with a Neetomint. They didn't help much and, although the calories brought a fresh boost of energy, it was a trickle rather than a flood.

The heat was building up. Logan realized he was dozing off and jerked awake. That wouldn't do. He needed to figure out what to do with the body, not to mention getting back to New Hope to find Aurore and Carl. Thinking about what might have happened to Aurore brought a renewed sense of determination, and he dragged himself up from the stool. There was a small closet in the opposite corner, away from the meteorology and ground sensing equipment, and he shuffled over to it.

Throwing open the door, Logan found a pair of heavy boots. They might have been useful, if they weren't several sizes too small. There was also a rubbery, yellow raincoat—also too small, a hard, white safety helmet, and a heavy-duty wrecking bar. He had no idea why the bar was there, but he could use it to dig into the ground, in a clumsy and inefficient way.

He grabbed the bar, then noticed a pair of tough-looking work gloves at the bottom of the closet. They were caked in dried mud but, for a wonder, were big enough to fit, though tight. He wrapped his hands with some of the parachute material as an extra layer, then forced the gloves on and went outside with the wrecking bar.

The bar broke up the ground easily enough, but he had to scoop the earth out by hand, and the gloves were soon soaked through. Luckily, the temperature was warmer than it had been on the mountain, and Logan ignored the discomfort. He was trying to decide what to do next. He needed sleep. He was already staggering as he moved, and his head was increasingly woolly. Against that was the adrenaline-filled yearning to find Aurore. If anyone had hurt her...

A flood of anger and hatred filled him, and Logan fought to suppress it. At this point, it would tear him apart for no good reason and wear him down further. Neither was a luxury he could afford, and he sucked in a long, deep breath of the cold air.

He wasn't sure who the enemy was. It didn't make sense for any of the Earth-based nation-states to attack—they all had a vested interest in developing the settlement through CESA, which left Luna Free State, the Atolls, and the Corporates. While Luna didn't have the resources to stage such an operation, the other two did.

The hole was about thirty centimeters deep now. Not deep enough, but he needed a break. His arms and legs were quivering with stress, and he'd nearly fallen into the hole twice already. The heat inside the station was like a warm blanket, but there was a trace of a growing stench that Logan didn't want to think about. After nibbling more of the ration pack, he went back to the closet and looked in. There was nothing that would help him dig any faster.

He pulled out the raincoat and held it against him. It was too small, but he might be able to fashion something from it to help, though the color made it a perfect antidote to camouflage. His hand caught something heavy in the left pocket—a small two-way radio.

It was a rechargeable unit, and Logan's first reaction was to switch it on to check if it was working. His thumb stopped barely a centimeter from the button. Would that put him in danger? It was a small unit, scarcely filling his palm, but any electromagnetic signal had the potential danger of being detected.

Deciding it was worth the risk, he pushed the button. The buzz of static bounced off the walls around him, and he turned the volume down, then checked the frequency setting. The unit was set to one of the settlement's general channels, so would normally pick up any routine signals, but there were none.

Logan switched the radio up and down the different channels looking for a broadcast, but found nothing. If their attackers were using regular radio signals, they were operating on a non-standard frequency. Though the chances were, their signals would be encrypted q-link transmissions that the small radio couldn't pick up. He was about to turn the unit off when the static vanished to be replaced by a three-toned pattern typically used to indicate an imminent broadcast. After several repetitions, a long beep sounded, followed by a deep voice.

"This is Colonel Rourke, commanding the Huanshi Colonization Force. We claim this world on behalf of the directors of the Xselsia-Surahman Combine and its shareholders. As you are by now undoubtedly aware, we have a sufficiently large cadre of people and equipment to make any resistance pointless.

"We have taken your capital and will track down anyone outside the town shortly. All survivors of your settlement will be shipped off-planet soon. I would prefer to avoid any further bloodshed. However, we are equipped to deal with any attempted resistance, and such acts will be dealt with severely.

"Turn yourself in peacefully and you will live. Attempt to fight and you will be eliminated. That choice is *yours*. But have no doubt, this world is *ours*."

Logan snapped the power off and sat until he warmed up inside the small shelter. His head was swimming with fatigue and the implications of what he'd heard. The Corporates had no right to this world. He'd discovered it, and Earth's nation-states had organized the first settlement. He slammed his fist into the bench, his anger rising once again. He would have been happy to leave the planet and let the politicians sort out this mess. But he wasn't going anywhere without Aurore.

Back outside, he continued digging. He'd reached a suitable depth for burying Tepfer when he heard a noise from the other side of the geological station. A metallic clanking from some sort of land transport bounced around the rocks to reach him, along with the hiss of what might have been other machines. Grabbing the short rifle, Logan ducked behind a stony outcrop.

The noises stopped, and voices drifted around the building. Logan couldn't make out the words, but it sounded as though there was some discussion as to who should check inside.

Logan edged around to his left to get a better view. It was slow work, but eventually he spotted a CEG AMTV—the militarized version of the Gators used by the settlement. Alongside it were several decidedly non-military air-scooters. A ragtag group of people clustered around the vehicles, and Logan saw several children among them. They weren't part of the invasion force, that much was certain.

Standing up, he clambered over the rocks in plain view, but it took several minutes for someone to spot him and raise the alarm. When they did, two people dressed in guard uniforms sprinted around the station, weapons at the ready. One of them was slim with a barely controlled crop of hair. The name tag on his uniform read "Berardo."

"Good to see you again, Giorg," Logan said.

Giorg's eyes widened. "Mr. Twofeathers?"

The other soldier stepped forward. Logan hadn't had much contact with her but recognized her face. Her uniform was the usual CEG one, but Logan spotted a United African Special Operations tattoo on the side of her neck.

"Sergeant Abena Diouf. I'm glad to see you alive, but we don't have time for long reunions." Her accent sounded French but with a harsher quality to it.

Logan pushed past the two soldiers, rushing around the

building to where the people were waiting. They were milling around, some of them looking directly at him, but most had vacant expressions, as if in shock. He jostled through them, his eyes taking in every face. He recognized them all, but the one face he was looking for wasn't there.

"Is everything alright?" Giorg was struggling to keep up with Logan's long stride. "We thought you were dead."

"Not yet," Logan said, grimly. "My wife, Aurore?"

Giorg shook his head. "We didn't have time to do a head count. We were lucky to get out of there as it was."

Logan gestured at the group. "They don't look in good condition. Where are you heading?"

Diouf spoke up. "Camp Botelho and the mine. There's a Nomad stationed there. We can use it to get to the *Hansen*."

"That sounds like a long shot."

Diouf's face screwed up. "You have a better suggestion?"

"I heard a broadcast. It said anyone who turned themselves in would be shipped off-world."

"And you believe that?" Diouf cleared her throat, her eyebrows lifting skyward.

"Corporate forces are professionals. They're not usually brutal for the sake of it. And it may well be these people's best chance."

"I have a duty to protect—" Diouf's skin darkened further.

Logan held up his hand. "That's my suggestion. You're in charge, not me."

Diouf lifted her chin a little and nodded at Giorg. She was heavier than he was. Part of it looked natural, but Logan suspected the usual Geneering accounted for much of it. "We're the only members of the Guard that got away, unless… Wasn't Sergeant Tepfer with you?"

Logan gestured at the parachute-wrapped pile by the mound of earth. "He was."

"*Salop! Cet enfoiré.*" Diouf squeezed her eyes shut. "I always thought he was too mean to die."

She strode over to the partly dug grave, her head hung low.

"She knew him?" Logan looked at Giorg.

"Could say that. They had a thing going on. Kept it quiet, I guess."

Logan thought it a strange pairing considering Tepfer's bigotry and Diouf's ancestry, but perhaps he'd misjudged the man. Diouf knelt next to the body and peeled back the layers of material to uncover Tepfer's face. He heard her say something, but the hiss of the wind obscured her words. After a few minutes, she re-covered Tepfer's body and rose to her feet, then walked back to Logan and Giorg.

"I'll finish digging," she said. "Thanks for trying to help him."

"We'll both finish it," Logan said.

Diouf grabbed a folding shovel from the AMTV, and with two of them sharing the work, it didn't take long. As they dug, Logan considered their situation. The Corporate forces would almost certainly know about the mining outpost and would have attacked it at the same time as the main settlement. Which meant there was likely nothing there to help the group, even if they made it.

"Botelho's a long trek from here by land. Especially if there's no one waiting. And how long do you think it will be before they hunt you down? You can't hide from them."

Diouf's smile was weak. "Might not be as easy as they think. We've got an EM nullifier on the AMTV. That's how we got away."

The nullifier would hide most of the EM signals from the vehicle, but it wasn't a perfect cover, and the sergeant had to know that. Plus, it took a lot of power to operate, which meant they'd be unable to move while it was on.

"I have to find my wife."

"She's not the only one." Diouf's words were clipped. "But we can't fight the Corporate forces. Our one chance is to reach the mine and hope there's a ship left. That way we can rendezvous with the *Hansen* and make the Jump back to Earth. They can send troops to tackle the Corporates, but we don't stand a chance on our own."

"What if they've destroyed the *Hansen?*" Logan said.

Doubt splashed over Diouf's face, and she took half a step back. "Why would they do that? The ship *has* to be there."

Logan sighed. "You have your plan, I have mine."

"I can't let you leave," Diouf said. "You could lead them straight to us. Besides, we need a pilot."

"How do you plan on stopping me?"

Diouf's hands tightened on her rifle, then she brought the muzzle up, pointing it directly at Logan's midriff. His stomach tightened and a chill came over him, much deeper than the one from the wind.

Chapter Six

*"When you are in doubt, be still, and wait.
When doubt no longer exists for you,
then go forward with courage."*
— White Eagle

Giorg's hand shot out, pushing the muzzle of Diouf's rifle down and away. "If we fight among ourselves, we've got no chance." He looked from Logan to Diouf. "Besides, our own people are back there. And to be honest, I'm not happy with the idea of leaving without knowing what happened to them."

Diouf lowered her gun but glared at Giorg, her face contorted into a grimace. "This is mutiny," she spat.

Logan spoke before Giorg, hoping to stop the soldier from digging himself a deeper hole. "If I can get close, I might be able to see the prisoners. At least then, we'd have a better idea of who's alive."

"You'll never make it on foot," said Diouf.

"I made it this far," Logan said quietly.

"And got a good man killed."

Logan felt a stab of guilt, though he knew it wasn't true. Tepfer had been wounded in the first few minutes of the attack, and Logan had done everything to keep him alive. "I'm not asking anyone else to go. You head for the mines."

"We still need a pilot," Diouf said pointedly.

"Then you'll have to wait until I get there, or someone else shows up."

Logan marched back inside the monitoring station. The wind was biting, but more than that, he didn't want to endure the anger and loss reflected in Diouf's brown eyes. Giorg came in and waited until Logan looked up.

Logan shrugged. "If you're here to convince me to go along with you, I can save you some time."

Giorg nodded. "I'm here to see how I can help. Our supplies are limited, but I'm sure we can do better than this." He gestured at Logan's makeshift clothing.

"You should save what you have. You're going to need it."

Giorg smiled unexpectedly. "Captain Manners was right—you are stubborn."

"She said that?"

"Several times." Giorg rolled open a bundle of clothing he was carrying. It was a large, gray-blue guard outfit. "This will probably fit."

Logan laughed. "They still making everything three times too big?"

"Sure thing. Need room for muscle growth."

Logan pulled off his clothes and tried on the uniform. It was labeled as "large," which wouldn't normally fit his sturdy frame, but in this instance was close enough.

"Tell me something." Logan sat back down and pulled on some thick socks. "If everyone in the military gets Geneered for added strength and stamina, where's the advantage?"

Giorg's boyish face turned pink. "Don't ask me."

"But you haven't done it. How come?"

"That's down to Poppa Berardo. He said a man should be able to make PFC on his own merit." Giorg tapped the Velcro patch on his uniform sleeve where insignia would eventually be placed. "I'm a woolly bear."

"Your father sounds like a smart man."

Giorg's thick eyebrows knotted. "Maybe. But right now I wish I'd signed up for the whole package."

"I don't suppose you have any size-thirteen boots hidden away?"

"Sorry, no." Giorg shook his head. "I'm coming with you."

"I can't let you do that." Logan stood and grabbed the carbine. "Besides, that would make you a deserter in Diouf's eyes, wouldn't it?"

"Unless I was ordered to."

Logan transferred his belt to the fatigues, then clipped the flashlight and Tepfer's pistol to it. "Don't look at me. I'm not connected with the military anymore and happy about that."

"I have orders from Captain Manners."

"She's alive?"

Giorg held up a small comm-link. Logan recognized it as a quantum-band transmitter used by the military to keep in touch during field maneuvers. "Let me speak to her."

"Short transmission. She's gone."

Logan frowned "What did she say?"

"To accompany you on a recon of New Hope."

While Logan appreciated the soldier's desire to help, it might not be a good idea to involve anyone else. "And Diouf heard this message too?"

Giorg's face was expressionless. "I don't believe she was hooked into the transmission."

"You'll have a hard time convincing her."

Despite Logan's assessment, Diouf put up little objection. Whether she believed Giorg's statement, or simply wanted to get as far away from the Corporates as possible, wasn't clear. Though she insisted on Logan agreeing to catch her up after he'd checked the situation in the city.

Giorg had persuaded one of the settlers to allow them to use their air-scooter, and they zipped over the brush at a steady thirty kilometers an hour, the maximum they could manage with the two of them weighing down the lightweight vehicle. The ducted fans on the scooter minimized noise, but even with its relative silence, they agreed to aim for the low hills to the north of the city to reduce the chance of detection. Logan calculated they'd reach the city around sunset, which would help conceal them.

They took turns grabbing some sleep while safely hidden, allowing time for the sun to set fully, then completed the last few kilometers on foot, not risking the low noise of the air-scooter. The

Corporate forces would be well equipped with audio monitors and surveillance drones, but they'd be inexperienced in this environment and still be finding their feet. Logan and Giorg crawled to the top of a hill, shuffling through the dense scrub until they were in a position to view the city below. Most of the lights were off, possibly because the invasion had caused power problems, or perhaps as a deliberate strategy.

Giorg pulled out a pair of enhancing field glasses and handed them to Logan. He scanned the area below, twisting the frequency dial so the glasses cycled through all wavelengths and highlighted different emissions. His jaw clenched when he saw the fractures and craters in the concrete of the main street. It was the only road in town that had so far received such luxury treatment.

"They've got laser, infra-red, and ultraviolet scanners, plus roving surveillance drones following what looks like programmed security patterns," Logan whispered. "There are several heavy fighters and HT-4 Futen troop transports in a compound to the southeast."

Giorg's reply was so quiet it was difficult to hear over the rustle of the wind through the bushes. "Any sign of our people?"

Logan did another scan of the town, then caught a flash as he slid the glasses sideways. Backtracking his movement, he ran up and down all frequencies. "Looks like a laser fence around the school."

He passed the field glasses back to Giorg.

"Automated sentry guns around the perimeter." Giorg made his professional assessment. "Looks like they're using the school yard as an exercise pen. If anyone reaches that fence, the turrets will slice them up. The school's separated from the closer buildings. Makes it harder to get close without being seen—or for anyone to get away."

"Good choice." Logan took the glasses again and zoomed in on the yard. His hands trembled with hope, making it hard to get a clear picture, despite the built-in image stabilization. Then, for a moment, the image cleared and he saw a familiar face. It was Carl.

He tried to find him again, but there were several dispirited-looking people shuffling around with hunched shoulders, their heads turned toward the ground. He didn't spot his nephew, but as he searched, the glasses detected a pattern in ionization frequencies—one that ran around the school yard inside the laser fence. "There's something else."

Giorg peered through the glasses. "That's a proximity field," he finally said. "I think they've tagged the prisoners. Anyone gets too close, their tag will be triggered. Might be hooked up to an electroshock unit—or a neural stimulator."

Logan grimaced in the dim light. It was bad enough to think of their friends and family being herded like animals, but using a stimulator on people was obscene and expressly forbidden by the Chengdu Articles on the treatment of non-combatants. Unfortunately, the Corporates had never recognized either the articles or the earlier Geneva Conventions.

Giorg tapped Logan's shoulder, and he looked around. The soldier had a finger pressed to his lips and tossed a small pouch to Logan, before tearing open a similar one himself. He peeled open a large sheet of almost invisible material and draped it over his legs, then pulled it up to cover him.

Logan had never seen one but he knew what it was—an EM Cloak that would dissipate and confuse any incoming scan signals, masking heat and visible light. He followed Giorg's example and snugged the sheet over him. As he did, a soft whirring came from above them, nearly lost in the wind.

Pulling the Cloak closer over his head, Logan peered through a slight gap between the folds of the blanket. The material felt peculiar against his skin, as though it were warm and alive. He froze as a small, blinking light came into view, the stubby, disk-like shape of a surveillance drone hanging in the air like a large coin, visible only when it blanked out the stars behind it.

The Cloak warmed against Logan's skin in response to a scan. The material was semi-passive but would react chemically to certain scan frequencies and sublimate various nanoparticles to further mask the user. The drone passed overhead, hovering over them, and he held his breath. A soft snap sounded on his right—a twig broken by some nocturnal creature, or perhaps a pebble caught by a gust. The drone spun on its axis, as if looking for the source of the noise, then Logan heard the wet snuffle of a rhison, one of the larger animals native to Kwelengsen. Finally, the drone moved again, heading in the same direction it had initially been following.

The grass prickled Logan through his clothes, and the soil's coldness seeped through him. A few minutes later, Giorg tapped his wrist.

"That was close," the soldier hissed. "We need to get our people out of there."

Logan wrapped up the Cloak and stuffed it in his pocket. "Are you sure about that?"

Giorg stiffened, swallowing several times. "You saw how they're treating them. We can't leave them like that."

Logan sighed. "I don't like it any more than you do, but they seem safe in there. They probably have somewhere warm to sleep and look as though they're being fed. Even if we could get them out, they'd be facing uncertainty, hunger, and the prospect of being hunted down. Is that what you think we should do?"

"We should—"

A shrill klaxon cut through the thick air, and they dropped to the ground. Giorg snatched the glasses up again. "There's someone by the proximity field," he whispered.

Logan reached for the glasses and studied the secured area. Sure enough, a man was on his back near the fence, convulsing so hard his body bounced up from the ground. He must have gotten close enough to the field to trigger it.

"That's Rod Albach," Logan said. "He's one of the field construction crew."

An armed soldier walked up and caught the squirming man by the ankle before dragging him a couple of meters away from the fence. The soldier lifted his arm close to his face, apparently talking into a wrist radio. Albach was quivering in the mud when Logan heard a piercing screech. He checked the area and saw a child struggling with a woman, recognizing them as Albach's wife, Jasmin, and their eldest boy, Benn. The boy was screaming, reaching out toward his father, as Jasmin did her best to hold him back while shielding the boy's sister.

The soldier was looking at the boy and didn't see Albach

clambering to his feet, somehow fighting the agony of the neural shock. When he noticed him, he barked an order. Albach ignored it and headed for the fence again.

This time Jasmin screamed too, but Albach didn't seem to hear. Whether he was deliberately ignoring it, or confused by the neural shock wasn't clear. As he approached the fence, he convulsed again, then fell to one knee before struggling back up. The soldier yelled another order, but Albach pushed on.

Logan wanted to look away but couldn't. Albach staggered to the fence, reached it, and stepped across. The lights from the laser detectors streaked across Albach's body, outlining him momentarily in a brilliant blue light. The glimmer caught the greasy strands of Albach's hair, illuminating it like a silvery-blue halo. Then he was through.

The closest turret burst into life, its own baleful, red-eyed sensors twisting to target Albach. There was a short burst of fire from the barrel, and moments later, the high-pitched tearing sound of a fully-automatic QuenchGun. Albach collapsed, looking like nothing more than a blood-soaked sponge seeping its vital stream of life into the ground.

The boy broke free of his mother and raced across the compound toward his father's corpse. As he got closer, the guard reached out and casually backhanded him with his armored fist, leaving the boy in the dirt like his father.

Logan handed the glasses back, not saying anything. A man had died because he'd wanted to be free. That was all—something that shouldn't have been a problem now the JumpShips had opened up space. But somehow humans always managed to be more inventive in finding ways of killing each other than living in peace.

"The bastards murdered him in front of his family," Giorg hissed. "And you *still* want to leave our people there to rot?"

The herd of rhison shuffled forward, their hefty bodies lumbering from side to side as they moved. Logan was in the middle, urging them in toward the city. The adult rhison were taller at the shoulder than he was and resembled one-eyed rhinos mixed with bison, which was how they'd got their name. Logan breathed through his mouth and kept a close eye on where he was walking. The pungent smell of the rhison wasn't helped by their thoroughly uncontrolled bowel movements. The mature ones tended to ignore him, while the younger ones seemed curious, circling repeatedly to bump their blunt heads into him.

They were the perfect cover. The creatures would confuse any scanning equipment, giving him a chance to get closer to the school. Seeing Albach cut down had changed his mind about the settlers being safe. Like the other native animals, rhison had learned to give the settlement a wide berth, but driven by his encouraging slaps, they were going to have a "night on the town."

They'd already crossed Third Street and were closing on the school before any of the enemy forces reacted. Logan heard some distant shouts and crouched lower as the zinging high-speed QuenchGun needles peppered the herd. The animals grew belligerent, stomping and snorting, but the needles were largely ineffective against their thick hides, and they continued to tramp mindlessly toward the buildings.

Logan poked his head up to check their position, then crouched again. It was hard keeping his big frame low, especially loaded down with the improvised pack he was carrying. Another few minutes would be perfect. The sky lit up with a yellow flash, and he was thrown face-first into the dirt. The bitter soil pushed inside his lips and he spat it out, struggling to regain his footing. He guessed someone had launched a grenade at the creatures to ward them off. Instead, it created panic, and they milled around, bleating in alarm.

His time was up. If he didn't act now, he'd lose the initiative. The enemy would recover from their surprise, and his chance would be gone. Logan pulled a micro-grenade from his pocket, flipped on the safety, and held the button down for five seconds before throwing it behind the leading rhisons. The device exploded, lighting up the area in a flash so bright it stabbed through his clenched eyelids, and the noise was loud enough to startle him, despite covering his ears.

He recovered almost immediately and yelled, stabbing the

nearest animals in the rump with the survival knife. The knife wouldn't cause any real damage, but it encouraged them to move, and combined with the flash-bang, it was enough to send them into a demented stampede toward the school.

Logan tried to keep up with the herd, but they were galloping too fast, and he slipped behind. He wrapped the Cloak around him as he ran, hoping it would obscure him from the enemy, though with the mud and dust the herd was kicking up, he was probably safe without it.

Sprinting to the closest of the sentry guns, Logan slapped another micro-grenade on its legs before rushing to the next. Before he got there, he heard a shout and looked around. An enemy soldier must have picked up his movements despite the Cloak, and was visually checking the area around Logan. There was no time to waste. He dashed for the next tower and planted another grenade.

A blast of needles tore up the dirt around him, and Logan dived to the ground. He wasn't sure if the soldier had seen him or whether the volley was a precautionary "spray and pray" reaction. The rhisons were charging in every direction, bellowing their fear and anguish. He crawled behind a boulder, hoping the rocky pile would shield him.

He was supposed to plant grenades on the other two sentry units, but he was out of time. He unfastened the cord holding the load on his back and pushed it forward. The device had all the signs of improvisation—he'd cobbled it together in about twenty minutes—and all he could do was hope it would work.

Tearing the tape off two torn wires, Logan jammed the ends together. A shower of sparks blinded him, his fingers burned, and all the hairs on his body stood on end. He held the wires together for several seconds, desperate to use all the power stored in the large capacitor he'd pulled from the hover-scooter.

The laser fence darkened, and the lights illuminating the compound went out.

"Come out from under the Cloak," a gruff voice barked.

Logan turned to see a guard staring at him, holding a short rifle. The light from both of Kwelengsen's small moons caught the edges of the soldier's body armor, outlining him in harsh angles. Logan pushed the Cloak back and stood.

"On your knees. Hands at the back of your head." The soldier rattled his rifle, pointing it at Logan's chest.

Logan did as directed. "I'm your prisoner."

"Sorry, man," the soldier grunted through his face mask. "Anyone found resisting is to be shot. Nothing personal. Orders."

He raised his rifle, aiming at Logan's head. There was too much distance between them—no way for him to do anything to stop the soldier.

"You don't have to do this." Logan kept his voice low.

"They own me. And my family."

The soldier's finger tightened on the trigger, and there was a metallic click. He turned the rifle on its side, threw out the magpack, and clicked in another.

Logan was already charging as the soldier brought the rifle up and pulled the trigger, but again there was the same useless click. Logan smashed into him, and both of them went down. Jumping on top of the soldier, Logan sliced the strap holding the other man's helmet in place and threw it into the darkness.

The soldier looked up, terror in his eyes. "Wait!"

Logan smashed his hand down without hesitating, hammering the knife-butt into the soldier's temple. The soldier jerked once, then his eyes closed.

"I'm sorry too, Sobol." Logan read the name tag on the man's armor.

Scrambling up, Logan sprinted past the now incapacitated laser fence. "Everyone, follow me," he yelled. "Quickly, while the fence is down."

Several people shuffled out of the darkness toward him, dazed expressions on their faces.

"The gun towers?" someone shouted.

Logan ran closer to the building, hoping to spot Carl, or better still, Aurore. He pressed the trigger on the detonator and the grenades he'd planted went off, sending the towers crashing down. He stopped and pointed north. "That way. Run. We don't have much time."

The EMP he'd triggered had worked perfectly and killed the

fence, but he had no idea what range of effect he'd get from the improvised device. Or how long it would last. The Corporates would undoubtedly have backups and countermeasures. So far nothing had recovered, surprising Logan at how well it had worked. People streamed past him and he pushed forward, then spotted Carl in the darkness. "Over here."

"What's going on?" said Carl.

"I took out the fence. Time to go." Logan grabbed the boy. "Aurore?"

Carl shook his head. "She's not here."

"Head toward Third." Logan slapped Carl on the shoulder.

He jogged away, and Logan turned to a group of people milling around hesitantly.

"This is your last chance. What are you waiting for?" he shouted, but no one else moved to leave.

A barrage of needles kicked up splashes of soil near him. Someone on the Corporate side was responding and had a functional weapon. Logan dropped, then twisted around and ran back to the fence. A woman was ahead of him, struggling with two children, one that she was half dragging. It was Jasmin Albach.

Logan caught up with her and swept the boy up. "Can you manage the girl?"

Jasmin nodded, her face a frozen mask. "They killed him…"

"I know."

Logan guided her across the fence. A number of people were up ahead, but he guessed fewer than fifty of them had risked making a break. He glanced back. Lights flickered on and off by the school. The systems were coming back online. It wouldn't be long before the enemy started chasing them down. Peering into the gloom forming a canopy overhead, he searched for a sign. Now it was up to Giorg.

Chapter Seven

*"You can't make an omelet
without breaking heads."*
— Grandfather Twofeathers

Logan carried the boy toward the largest group of people. Carl was there, and Logan gestured to him. "Keep everybody together."

"What now?" Carl's voice quavered. "We can't stay here. They'll come after us."

Logan examined Carl. The boy had turned eighteen a few months back and this was his first time off Earth. It was no wonder he was scared. Logan scanned the dark skies above them. "You have to trust."

The laser fence flickered, and the shimmering red lines stabilized as they were before. Logan spotted a number of shadows moving past it, followed by flashes of gunfire. One of the settlers screamed, then fell to his knees, and several others ran to help. There was a dark, angry wound in the man's arm where a needle had caught him. Logan pulled out Tepfer's pistol and raised it, lining up the sights with the first of the approaching shadows.

He squeezed the trigger, and the pistol recoiled. His target dropped, forming an unsightly mound on the floor. Whether dead or injured, Logan wasn't sure. He aimed and fired again. Unlike the QuenchGun of Sobol a few moments ago, his pistol was a cartridge gun and immune to the EMP. But the effects must be wearing off as the soldiers now shooting at them were using fully-functioning QuenchGuns.

"Everybody stay low," Logan called out.

An engine choked in the distance, then hummed into life. From the direction of the noise, it had to be a ground vehicle. Logan reached inside his pockets, pulled out the last two micro-grenades, and switched them to timer-mode. "Carl?"

The boy scuttled over.

"Do you know how to use these?"

Carl stared at the short, cylindrical grenades. "Not really."

"Pop open the safety like this." Logan demonstrated. "Hold the button down for five seconds. Then throw."

"Okay." Carl fumbled with the grenades. "Uh, but what…?"

"Use them on any vehicles or large groups of soldiers that approach. Okay?"

Carl looked doubtful but nodded.

Looking into the sky once again, Logan scanned for any signs of air-traffic but saw nothing. He spat out a curse and turned to check on the enemy's advance. Several were closer, shooting wildly at the escapees. A low-slung scout car moved up, its heavier weapons sounding like a roll of thunder above the smaller-caliber firearms.

"Carl?" Logan spotted him tucked behind a rock and sprinted over, keeping low. The boy's face was pale and he was trembling. "Grenade?"

Logan snatched the grenades from Carl. He triggered the first and lobbed it toward the car, following up with the second as soon as it was activated. He ducked back down, the explosions deafening even behind the rock. When he peered around the edge, the vehicle was out of action, surrounded by several bodies.

A high-pitched whine filled the air, and Logan glanced up. Three of the Futen transports he'd spotted earlier were dropping to the ground on the far side of the group. The lights on one of them blinked with one long flash and two short. "Come on," he yelled. "Everyone on board."

There was a pause, then the group scurried toward the transports. Logan spotted Giorg in the nearest one, and headed for the next closest. Carl followed him, keeping low and ducking every time a gun fired. Logan ran up the Futen's rear loading ramp, scrambling to the cockpit to drop into the pilot's seat. With a swipe, he disabled the remote pilot and took control of the bulky aircraft.

"Carl, see if anyone else is coming."

Carl headed back to the door to check. Most of the escaped settlers had boarded Giorg's aircraft, with only a scant few following them to this one. Logan wished more had escaped, but fear did strange things to people. It meant, though, that the remaining aircraft wasn't needed and would make a good decoy.

Logan took control of the third Futen, his fingers dancing over the console as he switched the spare aircraft out of "follow" mode and directed it to head due south. Returning control to his aircraft, he grabbed the flight stick as Carl skidded into the cockpit.

"I don't see anyone else."

"Strap in." Logan gestured at the co-pilot's chair and throttled up the engines. The spare transport was already airborne and receiving plenty of attention from the enemy weapons, as he'd hoped. But that didn't mean the Corporate forces had forgotten them. A regular trip-hammer of needles slammed into their aircraft, but nothing penetrated its armor.

Giorg's Futen lurched upward, and Logan pulled back on his controls, taking their aircraft up. The hail of shots increased as they lifted, dying away as the aircraft gained altitude. The comm system crackled into life.

"Where to, Logan?" It was Giorg.

Logan allowed himself the smallest of smiles. The EMP hadn't been powerful enough to reach the parked transports, which was what he'd hoped. "North, for now. Keep it low."

"I'll try," Giorg said. "I haven't done much of this."

The Futens were designed to be used by low-skilled operators, so he should manage. A high-pitched beep pulled Logan's attention to the instruments. The missile lock warning had activated. He stabbed the countermeasures control, and the cockpit lit up as a rain of flares shot out to decoy the missile. Then he twisted the Futen hard left, but the cumbersome transport was slow to respond.

"Giorg. Watch out. There's something else up here."

"It's an attack drone," Giorg shouted over the radio. "A Predator,

I think."

Logan had only a sketchy knowledge of those drones, but what he knew was bad. The Predator would be faster and more maneuverable than the transports, and would pick them out of the skies if it got a solid lock on them.

"Keep it at weed-cutting height. It's our only chance."

Logan drifted the transport lower, until it felt as though its underbelly was dragging through the prickly scrub covering the low hills. He glanced over. Giorg had dropped his aircraft too but didn't appear to have the confidence to fly as low.

The fat thruster housings on the short wings rotated down, making the aircraft more responsive to elevation changes but at the same time reducing speed. Logan glanced at the threat display. The Predator target track glowed red as it curved back for another pass.

"It's coming around. Watch your flank, and follow my lead." Logan twisted the controls and brought the transport on a head-on approach. That would present a smaller target to the enemy while maximizing the passing speed, making it harder to land a shot.

The Predator swung into view. Logan swallowed, his throat suddenly dry. The Futen was undoubtedly armed, but he wasn't familiar with the aircraft, and this wasn't the time to learn. Multiple flashes detached from the Predator, and the missile warning shrieked. Again, he launched a barrage of flares as he wiggled the Futen through dips in the hills. A hail of needles rattled across the fuselage. One caught the cockpit window, producing a crazed blossom of shattered glass.

"I've been hit." Giorg's panicked voice buzzed through the radio.

"How bad?"

Logan maneuvered his Futen behind the other. It was hard to see in the darkness, but a fountain of liquid was spraying from Giorg's rear starboard engine pod.

"Not sure." Giorg hesitated. "Warning from one of the tail engines. Temperatures are increasing."

"I see it. Tell the flight computer to reduce that engine's thrust limit by fifty percent. The others will compensate."

Giorg paused, then spoke again. "Done. I'm also seeing a drop in control actuator pressure."

With the damage to the wing, that was inevitable. But there was nothing Logan could do about it. "The ship will get slower to respond. Do your best and head north while keeping low. I'll see if I can distract the drone."

Logan checked the Predator's position. It was turning back again, and he brought the Futen around to face it.

"Carl, do you see the weapons controls?"

Carl scanned the panel in front of him. "There's a screen that says Fire Control. Is that it?"

"Anything else?"

"Locked."

The Predator was on another run. Logan saw its lights sweep closer. Flashes of fire flickered at the drone's side as it launched more missiles.

"See if you can unlock it." Logan jerked the controls to make the ponderous transport duck and dive.

I do not want to be shot down again. Logan forced the Futen lower, hitting the flare release once again. The cabin lit up momentarily, then darkness returned. He glanced down. The flare indicator was at zero.

"Hold on everyone!"

The Futen shuddered as a missile hit the rear. Logan checked the instruments. Both rear engines were damaged, and the stabilization system was struggling to compensate using the front ones, but it was a losing proposition. They'd never survive another hit, and the damage made them a sitting duck when the Predator came around to attack.

Logan swung the aircraft north, following the same advice he'd given Giorg earlier. Their best chance was to get far away from the town and the enemy forces. And hope.

Keeping one eye on the threat display, Logan pushed the Futen to its maximum speed. They were falling and rising in a series of sick lurches as the onboard systems struggled to keep them in the air. He followed the low dips and valleys to make it difficult for the Predator to track them, but the end was close.

"Giorg?" Logan had lost sight of the other transport. "I think I'm going down. Get as many people out of here as you—"

"Logan?" Carl interrupted. "There's something—"

Logan looked back at the threat display. The Predator was coming around, and they were in no condition to avoid it. He looked out, locating the enemy aircraft. It was already near and he could almost picture the gouts of flame as it fired another barrage of missiles.

Logan pulled the controls left, guiding the Futen into a ravine snaking northwest, but the response was more sluggish than earlier. He heard several people sobbing in the back, and a blanket of guilt wrapped around him. He'd given them hope, and now they were going to die.

A faint blue glow slashed overhead, and seconds later, they were buffeted by the turbulent air from a jet-trail. Logan guessed it was a second Corporate drone, coming to join in the fun.

The newcomer barely registered with the instruments, and Logan had a hard time tracking it. It was heading straight toward the enemy Predator, and he looked in that direction. The two points of light seemed to merge, then the landscape was lit by an immense orange flash of an explosion.

"What the hell?"

When darkness returned, Logan saw no sign of the Predator. He checked the instruments and found a faint trace of the newcomer, but nothing else.

"Mr. Twofeathers?" The comm system buzzed. "We've got your back. Take heading three-four-zero true."

Logan had wrestled with the Futen for two hours, and in the last thirty minutes, the aircraft had begun lurching more wildly. Both the rear thruster units were operating at under fifty percent, and the flight control system was increasingly fighting to compensate for the uneven thrust.

They'd been following a set of faceless instructions from the unidentified ship after it destroyed the Predator drone. Crossing over the lower slopes at the northern end of the Baraban range, then following the Tuck Mountains heading northwest. Logan initially thought they were headed toward Camp Botelho, but they'd changed direction multiple times and curved around to a southerly course. Giorg hadn't said a word, and Logan wondered if the soldier knew any more than he did. He would have asked, but they'd been directed to keep radio traffic to a minimum.

Their route skirted around the rugged edge of the Eastern Channel, an inhospitable coastal area that was so far unexplored, apart from routine satellite surveys and a few geological expeditions. The turbine temperatures on the damaged engines climbed again, forcing Logan to further restrict the power limits and slowing their airspeed.

The aircraft juddered, and Carl spoke for the first time since they'd escaped from the Predator. "Are we okay?"

"Engines three and four are taking a beating. One way or another, we're going down soon."

"Stay together, transport vehicles," the anonymous voice said.

Logan grunted. There wasn't much chance of that. He opened the comm channel. "We've got two badly damaged turbines. Any suggestions?"

"Stay together."

He closed the comm with a stab of his finger. "Come on, Logan. All you have to do is the impossible."

A flicker of movement caught his eye, and he glanced to the side. The other Futen had dropped back and was holding station ahead and left. Giorg had heard the broadcasts and apparently wasn't about to let Logan fall behind.

"Come around to one-seven-zero degrees," the voice ordered.

Under the silvery light from the moons, Logan spotted a break in the craggy shoreline and beyond it a wider expanse of water. They might be at Arakaki Bay, a wide estuary that cut inland about four hundred kilometers to join up with a large river emerging from the southern Magnier Mountains.

The water made it easier to control the transport as there were fewer disturbances in the airflow, and Logan relaxed his grip a little. He thought he knew where they were, but couldn't think of any obvious destination in this area of the archipelago.

The bay narrowed, and they followed the twisting river that fed it. Foliage hung over the water, forming a canopy over their heads, forcing the Futens to travel single file.

A high-pitched warble screamed inside the cockpit, and Carl looked at Logan in alarm. "What's that?"

"Thermal limit warning." Logan looked at the instruments. "The starboard rear turbine has shut down."

Carl's eyes were wide. "Can we make it?"

"If we lose the other rear turbine, we're done," Logan said grimly. "I wish I knew where we were heading."

Streaks of soft blue spread up from the horizon. Dawn was approaching, increasing visibility but also making it clear how narrow the gap in the trees had become. There was still no sign of the aircraft that had saved them. And the signals on the threat displays were so indistinct, he wouldn't have known it was with them but for the intermittent comm signals.

"Logan!" Giorg's voice sounded.

Logan looked ahead, his dark eyes taking in the scene. The river continued a few hundred meters then turned left, disappearing into the rock and leaving them facing a dead end.

The transport lurched and Logan slowed down, putting greater stress on the remaining rear engine. He couldn't hold the hover, and nudged the controls forward to ease the strain, but there was nowhere to go.

A diamond shape flickered into view ahead, and Logan recognized it as a Shuriken drone. A surprise, as he didn't think the Guard had anything so advanced on Kwelengsen. It was a reconnaissance and attack craft, armed with missiles and a Quench-Gun, and also equipped with the latest in optical and EM shielding, which explained why he'd had trouble picking it up on the instruments. The drones could be remotely piloted or fly autonomously as required. In this case, he imagined it had been under remote control, but who was behind it was anyone's guess.

"Move ahead," the voice ordered over the comm.

Logan was dumbfounded. The only thing *ahead* was the rock face, but the Futen's shudders told him he didn't have any choice.

An excited gasp came over the radio. "It's a holo-projection," Giorg said.

The other transport approached the rocks. At the point at which it should have smashed into the rough surface, Logan saw the nose disappear as the aircraft edged forward, its body cut off like a magic trick.

Another alarm warbled. The second of the rear engines was failing. Logan pushed on the flight stick and the Futen lurched toward the rocks. "Hang on tight, everyone."

Logan gritted his teeth as the Futen's nose reached what looked like a solid rock surface, then passed through. Even that close, the illusion was perfect and gave no clue there was anything unsubstantial about the cliffside. They crept in, and he held his breath as the rock appeared to slice through the cockpit and approach to within centimeters of his face.

An explosion pealed from the rear, and the tail bucked again. The Futen slid sideward as if falling off a precipice, and Logan yanked the controls to correct. The slide stopped, but then they lurched the other way, going into a spin as they careened through the fake rocks.

Logan blinked. The transition was extreme. One moment they were outside in sunlight filtering through the thick tree canopy. Then they were in a wide cavern, lit by stark, artificial lights. The river snaked left, while the other aircraft was sitting on a broad, flat outcrop to the right, leaving room for him to bring down his Futen.

A high-pitched grinding told Logan the engine was in critical condition, and he fought to level the aircraft enough to make a descent. The floor of the outcrop was flat and sandy, but there were enough rocks poking up to make precision necessary.

Despite his efforts, he couldn't stop the spin, and the aircraft swung around until they were facing the way they'd come in. From this side of the illusion, nothing looked abnormal—it appeared to be a regular opening to the outside world. But Logan had no time to wonder at the scenery.

Edging the Futen lower, he'd almost reached the point of first contact when a massive detonation shook the rear of the aircraft, the blast sending vibrations through to Logan's seat. The nose pitched up as the turbines overcompensated for the dead engines, and Logan killed the power on them.

They teetered momentarily in midair, then they were falling. Logan tried to shout a warning, but was too late, and the heavy aircraft crunched into the cavern floor. Despite the impact, it was tough and didn't crumple. Several onboard systems died in a shower of sparks, and the cockpit glass blew out as the impact buckled the airframe, but the ship held together. Despite that, there was a chorus of shouts and wails from the cargo area.

"Everybody out," he ordered, killing the engines—the last thing they needed was a fire or explosion.

Outside, several people ran forward with fire equipment. Logan unhooked his belt and looked over at Carl.

"You okay?"

Carl looked around feverishly, and he swallowed several times. "Are we safe?"

"I hope so. But we better find out who we're dealing with."

Logan clambered to his feet and shuffled toward the rear, with Carl following. Several soldiers in CEG uniforms were spraying liberal amounts of fire suppressant foam over the rear turbines. Logan cringed—the foam would make any attempt to rebuild the engines ten times harder.

The passengers they'd been carrying stood around huddled in small groups for the most part. Some were checking arms and legs that must have been on the receiving end of contusions or injuries sustained in the escape or subsequent flight. Logan counted—twenty-three settlers, well below the aircraft's maximum capacity. He hoped Giorg had done better.

Strident voices lifted over the constant rush of water and Logan looked up. More soldiers were arriving, but they carried guns instead of emergency equipment and pointed them at the settlers. One soldier wearing sergeant's stripes was arguing with an older man who was becoming increasingly agitated. Logan walked over, recognizing him as Bob McClour. McClour was another farmer, and one of the more outspoken citizens, but was usually levelheaded.

"What's the problem, Bob?"

"Oh, it's you, Logan," McClour said.

The sergeant seemed torn as to who to point his gun at. "I want everyone on their knees."

The sergeant's name badge said "Pendrey," but Logan didn't know him, and his uniform was decorated with the stylized eagle and lightning flash of USP Military Security rather than the circle and cross design of the CEG.

"I'm Logan Twofeathers, head of Kwelengsen engineering operations." Logan gestured at McClour and the others. "These are settlers, like me. I'm confused though. This planet isn't under MilSec jurisdiction."

"They want to take the kids away," McClour snarled. "What kind of people would separate children from their parents?"

"I told you, it's temporary." Pendrey glared at McClour. "Until we make sure we haven't got any Corporate infiltrators, security is our overwhelming concern."

"With all due respect, Sergeant, our people have been through a lot." Logan noticed Carl edging closer but waved him back. "I can vouch for all of them."

"Well, that's all nice and friendly-like." Pendrey pushed his chest out. "But who the hell is vouching for you?"

"I'm sure the CEG people wi—"

Pendrey cut Logan off, chopping through the air with his hand. "Enough already. Alright folks, on your knees, hands behind your heads. We'll process you as soon as we ca—"

"Wait a minute," Giorg pushed his way through to join them. "What's going on? Why are you pointing guns at these people?"

"Protocol dictates—"

"You're making a mistake, Sergeant. We wouldn't be here without Mr. Twofeathers, and these are people from the settlement. We rescued them from the Corporates."

"We have orders to make sure everyone checks out." Pendrey stared at Giorg like the private was an inferior species. "Now, I suggest you go find someone who can ID *you*, before I throw you in with these others."

Giorg's jaw set hard. "Yes, Sergeant. Is Captain Manners here?"

Pendrey's eyes widened. "The captain?"

"I was her assistant. She can personally identify me."

Pendrey waved to another of the MilSec people. "Watch them. If anyone tries anything—shoot."

The sergeant walked away, and Logan saw him talk into his comm-set. After a short discussion, he moved back.

"If Captain Manners is here, I'd like the chance to speak to her too," Logan said. "Like Giorg here, she can identify me."

Pendrey ignored him, waiting silently. After several minutes, Logan caught a movement in the cave behind the soldiers. Someone was approaching, but in the dim light within the cavern, he couldn't make out who.

"I'd know that walk anywhere," Giorg said. "That's the captain."

Three people marched up, and Logan spotted Manners at the front. She moved like a lioness—lean, hungry, and ready for anything. When she got closer, he spotted a mass of freshly wounded tissue on the left of her face, running from her jawline all the way to where it merged with her buzz-cut hair. She waved Pendrey to one side and strode forward.

"It's good to see you again, Logan." She looked across at Giorg. "Report for duty, Private." Giorg saluted and jogged toward the back of the cavern.

"Are you certain all these people are legitimate?" Manners asked.

Logan took his time looking at everyone. They weren't so large a community that he couldn't identify everyone by sight. There was no one there he hadn't seen before.

"All of them are Kwelengsen citizens."

"Make sure they're fed and looked after," Manners said to Pendrey. He saluted, and she turned her attention back to Logan. "That rescue was a brave attempt."

"I was hoping to find my wife. I don't suppose you know—"

"I'm sorry. I've no idea what happened to her." Manners frowned. "When we were attacked, everything was in chaos. She's not here though, or I'd know about it."

Logan let his head drop momentarily, knowing it was a slim chance. "Where *is* here?" He gestured at the MilSec soldiers. "You have some unexpected company."

Manners' golden eyes were impenetrable, and she pointed at the Futens. "Can you fix those?"

Logan stayed facing her. He didn't need to see them to know the answer. "Not the one I flew in—unless you have a source of high-thrust aviation turbines."

Manners gave a short shake of her head.

"The one Giorg flew might be reparable, if I cannibalize parts from the other."

"I'm glad to hear that. We're going to need it, if we're to have a chance of winning this war."

Logan's mind raced. "Winning? We don't stand a—"

Manners cut him off with a wave of her finger. "Come with me. This is no place for such discussions."

"My nephew..." Logan pointed to Carl. "I can't—"

"He's a fine-looking boy. Don't worry. He'll be taken care of too."

Logan locked eyes with Carl for a moment. The boy looked away. Even after everything they'd been through, it seemed his hatred of Logan hadn't softened.

Chapter Eight

*"What befalls the earth befalls
all the sons of the earth."*
— Chief Seattle

Manners guided Logan deeper into the cavern and, as they walked through the branching tunnels, he realized how vast the complex was. The entrance opened onto several passages, and at least some of them appeared to lead to other large caverns. He'd visited the Mammoth–Flint Ridge Caves with Carl's father when they were boys, and their sheer number and scale had impressed them both, but these appeared more extensive.

They followed a narrower passage to another cave, smaller than the first, but as large as a couple of basketball courts side by side. A ring of lights had been strung up around the craggy walls and in the middle were several pitched field tents, with a larger one set apart from the others.

Manners headed for the bigger tent and unzipped the front.

Logan peered in. There was a small, office-sized area, beyond which was a separate internal room. "Are there more of these?" he asked.

"Some. We might have enough to accommodate everyone, including your group." She sat in a creaky folding chair and gestured at its companion a couple of meters away. "I'm sure they'll appreciate a little privacy after what they've been through."

"Conditions in New Hope didn't look good. The Corporates

have everybody locked up at the school."

Leaning over, Manners scrabbled in a bag and pulled out a couple of bottles filled with a straw-colored liquid. "Green tea. Want some?"

Logan accepted, sipping at first, then gulping down the tea when he realized how long it had been since he'd drunk anything. The drink was sweet, with an unusual taste, and he checked the label. It was a fruit-flavored beverage that had been delivered all the way from Earth."

"You don't see much of this here," he said, holding up the bottle.

"It's a luxury, but the powers that be like to indulge me in small things, and send the odd case along with our regular supplies."

Logan took another sip, then closed the cap. "What do you want from me, Captain?"

Manners' impassive expression didn't change. "What makes you think I want anything?"

Logan was tired but stood anyway. He fingered the bottle of tea—Manners' friendliness made him nervous. "A private chat? Favoring me with your special supplies? We have a good enough working relationship, but not close enough to warrant this treatment."

"As you're the leader of the settlers, I want to make sure we stay on good terms."

Logan snorted. "I'm head of engineering. The council is in charge of the settlement."

"Do you have any of them with you?"

Logan hesitated. He hadn't seen any of the members. "I don't think so."

"I think most of the civilians would look to you for leadership, don't you? Especially after you pulled off such a dramatic rescue."

Logan's chest tightened. He wasn't comfortable with the idea, but she was probably right. "Even if that's true, it doesn't tell me what *you* want from me."

"We found these caves several months ago." Manners waved around them. "We don't know how far they run, but it's an extensive network. I decided it might be prudent to set up a bug out location in case some disaster struck, and this was the ideal spot."

"Nice of you to share that with everyone."

"A secret is only secret until one too many people know it. I diverted some supplies here to build up a decent cache. Then, a month ago, I received a request to allow a training team to do some work on Kwelengsen. It seemed an ideal opportunity to obtain some extra, much-needed supplies."

"And, as they were coming from MilSec, they didn't appear in any CEG inventory reports."

"You're a smart man, Logan." Manners tipped her bottle toward him. "An asset I can use. Everyone knows you, or at least knows of you. And I can't waste personnel babysitting civilians while we're at war."

Logan didn't know what secrets Manners had tucked away in the caves, but even with the supplies she'd obtained, he doubted it was enough to resist the forces he'd seen. "The Corporates outnumber you twenty-to-one, not to mention having orbital dominance. Do you really think you can take them on?"

"Perhaps not." Manners sipped her tea. "But even if I feel it's hopeless, I have a duty to fight back."

There was a hard edge to her voice that surprised Logan. Usually, Manners had a somewhat "by the book" attitude, but he'd never seen any traces of unreasonable belligerence. "Isn't your duty to protect the settlers? If you make trouble, civilians might die."

Manners closed her eyes as though meditating. When she spoke, her voice was calm. "My soldiers are primarily here to protect the settlement ."

"Exactly."

She smiled faintly. "You misunderstand. I mean the planet. You, of all people, must know how valuable it is."

"You're saying those people I brought in—and the ones being held prisoner—are *expendable*?"

"That depends."

"On what?"

"On whether they're willing to fight for this world."

"Fight? Does that include the children, and the sick or wounded, or are you limiting your press-ganging?"

"You said yourself—we're outgunned and outnumbered." Manners stood and kicked the chair to one side. "Don't they care about their world? Don't they want to fight for what they have? We need everybody we can get if we're to have the slightest chance."

Logan stared at her. "And that's all you'll have in the end, isn't it?"

Manners frowned. "What do you mean?"

"You said every *body*. You don't care if people end up as corpses, as long as you can play your games."

Manners turned away abruptly, her hands clasped behind her back. "Don't get the wrong idea, Logan. I can use you, but I don't *need* you. If you want to be difficult, that's up to you, but you're not going to interfere with my plans."

Logan had little chance of stopping her, whatever she chose to do. And he couldn't abandon the ones he'd saved. "What do you want me to do?"

Manners set her chair back on its feet. "Manage the civilians. Encourage them to help fight the Corporate invasion. And fix that troop transport."

"Encourage?"

"I'm not a monster, Logan." Manners smiled, but her eyes were cold. "I won't force anyone to fight. That's my promise."

"I'll do what I can then." Logan turned to leave.

"One more thing."

Logan stopped. "What's that?"

"Please inform everyone that although we have plenty of water, food—like everything else—is in short supply. In order to provide enough for my soldiers, rations for non-combatants will be limited to three kilojoules a day."

That was around a third of what was considered healthy, and Logan knew many of the settlers would struggle to survive on that. "Should I assume anyone willing to fight would not be restricted in such a fashion?"

"If they're part of my team, they get full rations, naturally." Manners didn't blink.

"I'll let them know."

Logan walked away, his hands clenching into fists. Manners

was supposed to be on their side. Every nation-state wanted to grab a bigger piece of Kwelengsen. That was why CESA had been formed, to stop one or the other from throwing in huge amounts of resources and effectively dominating the new world. What Manners was doing was wrong, but until someone official showed up to see what had happened, she was in absolute power. There was nothing he could do. It would have to be managed back on Earth. Right now, he had to deal with the current situation, and she was calling all the shots.

Not knowing the layout of the caves, Logan retraced his steps to where the Futens were parked. The settlers had dispersed, and other than a few guards, there was no one around. He should find out what had happened to them, but he was so disgusted with Manners' proposal, he didn't want to face them.

He walked around the back of the aircraft he'd piloted. Both the rear engines were caked in a greasy mix of blackened oil, suppressant foam, and soot. The starboard engine had several punctures on the casing, either from weapons fire or internal components exploding out. The control surfaces had been hit too, and now looked like the business end of a cheese grater instead of the smooth, aerodynamic surfaces they should have been.

The other Futen was in better shape. There were some scores and divots on the fuselage and signs of heat damage on the turbines too, but it might be possible to salvage it.

"Logan?" Giorg hurried toward him, wearing his seemingly ever-present smile. "Thanks. I owe you a lot."

Giorg held out his hand, and Logan noticed that the woolly bear patch on his sleeve was now hidden by a strip with a single yellow dot.

"You made PFC. Well done." Logan pointed to the new insignia.

Giorg's grin widened. "Yeah, the captain gave me the sunspot." He tapped the badge. "Said I'd earned it after what I'd done."

"I'm happy for you. Do you know where they've put the civilians?"

"I'll show you." Giorg led Logan back into the tunnels. "I wasn't sure if we were going to make it for a while."

"I know what you mean." Logan stopped, reaching out to Giorg. "Aurore's not here."

Giorg lowered his head. "I'm sorry, man. I know you were hoping."

"Did you tell the captain about Sergeant Diouf and the other group?"

"She wants the Futens working so we can bring them in." Giorg stopped. "She said it's one of her top priorities."

Logan's jaw tightened. To Manners, Diouf's group was nothing but potential recruitment material. "I'm sure that's right."

Giorg looked puzzled. "Did you fight with her?"

"No."

"Then what is it?"

Logan patted Giorg's elbow. "Come on. Show me where everyone is."

They walked to the right rear of the cavern then followed a narrower passage, twisting through the candy-striped umber rock. After about twenty meters, the tunnel opened into a rock hall larger than the one housing Manners' tent.

The area was littered with shelters. The dim light made it difficult to estimate numbers, but Logan guessed there were around forty such shacks, and the cavern had room for plenty more.

"How many are here?" Logan kept his voice low, seeing several people lying in the shelters. "Civilians, I mean."

"With the ones we brought, around two hundred."

"Did you know about this place?" Logan turned slowly, taking everything in.

"No. The captain kept it under wraps from all but senior staff and those assigned here."

"Isn't that strange? You're a small unit."

"You know the military." Giorg smiled nervously. "Need to know and all that. I just keep my head down."

"And the MilSec soldiers?"

"I'd seen the training request. But I didn't realize they'd arrived. Or that there were so many of them."

"How many?"

Before Giorg answered, a figure came through the passage behind them, the artificial lighting sending a shadow dancing through the cavern. It was Sergeant Pendrey.

"Berardo? Captain Manners is looking for you."

"Yes, Sergeant." Giorg saluted, then glanced back at Logan. "I better..."

Giorg hurried away. The setup had Logan on edge. He suspected Manners was cooking something up—something that would result in a lot of deaths, including some of the civilians.

It didn't take long for Logan to discover there was no real organization behind the accommodations. Some were military issue tents, but many were crude lean-tos fashioned from fabric, branches, and any other convenient materials. By the main entrance was a small stack of rations and a large, plastic water barrel, while down a short side passage, hidden by rough-cut pieces of tarpaulin, a couple of chemical toilets provided limited sanitary facilities.

He found Carl at the back of the cavern, throwing together a simple shelter. Logan eyed the rickety structure and shook his head. "You'd do better if you triangulated the supports. That would increase stability."

"Don't need your advice," Carl snapped, and continued tying branches together.

"We could make something large enough for both of us, if we do it right."

"There's more stuff in the corner." Carl pointed. "Make what you want. Just leave me the hell alone."

"If that's the way you want it." Logan suppressed his frustration. "Only trying to help. It's what uncles do."

"I don't want your help." Carl picked up a pebble and threw it pointlessly against the nearest wall. "And you aren't my uncle."

That was true, though Logan's closeness with Carl's father made him feel as though he was. "You can't do everything by yourself. Especially in circumstances like these. We *all* depend on each other."

Logan waited but Carl didn't reply. Finally, he headed for the pile of supplies.

"I'm not like you," Carl muttered.

Logan turned back. "No one expects you to be."

Carl was kneeling, digging at the sandy floor. "Don't know why you brought me to this damn place."

"I thought it would be a good change for you." Logan squatted next to Carl. "A new world, without the bad memories."

"What do you know about it?" Carl looked up, his dark brown eyes tight and accusing. "You've never done anything but run away."

Logan took a long breath. "What do you think I'm running away from?"

"Everything," Carl scoffed. "Your people. Your history. Your obligations. Everybody knows that's why you went into space."

"I went into space because I worked my ass off to qualify for a well-paid job." Logan's skin burned. "You might not have noticed this, but opportunities on Earth are getting fewer all the time. What do you think we should do—trap ourselves in the past, the way the Atolls trapped us on the planet?"

"We should have fought them." Carl threw down the sticks he'd been attempting to fasten together. "We outnumbered them."

"Some did. But the world was as badly fractured back then as it is now. And how do you fight someone who can destroy you by dropping rocks—or nuclear bombs—on your head?"

"And you don't want to fight now either, do you?"

Logan hesitated. The Corporate forces were vastly superior to theirs, and the addition of the MilSec contingent didn't change that. Without space support, the settlement was in the same strategic position as Earth had been under the Atolls, and the Corporates could take their time. Even if every surviving civilian joined in, it was hopeless. Then he remembered his discussion with Manners.

"We may not have any choice."

Logan moved away and circled the cavern, asking people to gather in one corner. At first, they were slow to move, but once a few got to their feet, it created a rush. After fifteen minutes, everyone from the shanty was waiting.

After pulling over an empty packing crate, Logan climbed on it, so everyone would be able to hear. He looked around at the expectant faces, recognizing most of those closest to him. He couldn't see everyone clearly in the dim light, but spotted Carl at the back of the group, arms folded. It didn't look like there were two hundred though—maybe half that.

"Thanks for joining me, neighbors. Before I say too much, let me cover a couple of things. First, if there are others not present at the moment, can you please tell them everything discussed here when they get back?"

"Who put you in charge, Twofeathers?" somebody called from the back.

"That's the second thing I want to discuss." Logan scanned the crowd. "I've only just arrived, so I have no idea who's here. Did any of the councilors make it? Or perhaps you've already set up an organization. If so, I'll be happy to hand things over. I'm an engineer, and make no other claims."

There were a few murmurs from one group on Logan's left, then someone lifted their hand. "Tejal's here."

"The administrator?" Logan looked around. "Where? Would you come forward, please?"

Several people moved to one side, leaving a narrow gap, wide enough for a single person. Tejal trudged toward Logan, in no hurry to bring himself to the front of the crowd. Logan stepped down and leaned in to talk privately to him.

"Administrator. You're the official CESA presence and *de facto* leader of Kwelengsen. I've spoken with Captain Manners and have information I need to share urgently."

Tejal's head was lowered, as though searching the floor for something. "Leave me alone."

"What?"

"I am no longer settlement leader." Tejal took several wet breaths. "There *is* no settlement. Don't you understand? The captain needs to—"

"You can't abandon everyone," Logan hissed. "Your duty—"

"My duty is to look after myself, and if you have any sense, you'll do the same."

Logan put his hand on Tejal's shoulder. "Don't lose it now. We need every—"

"We're finished, I tell you. The settlement is finished." Tejal was shaking. "My wife... I don't know what became—"

Tejal turned away and Logan grabbed his thin arm. "You're still the official administrator."

"I resign."

Logan's jaw tightened, and he pulled Tejal back. "If that's your final word, then so be it. But at least tell them." He nodded at the crowd. "They deserve to hear it from you."

Tejal stared at Logan briefly. "I doubt anyone cares."

Logan stood to one side and helped the administrator clamber onto the box. Tejal was silent, and people shuffled uncomfortably, the sand underfoot crunching and echoing around the rocky cavern.

Tejal swallowed. "Citizens of Kwelengsen, we face a bleak future. Our homes have been torn from us and our lives smashed. We have all lost… family… and friends. There is no hope left." His voice had dropped almost to a whisper, but then he dragged in a shuddering breath. "I've done what I can. Someone else must take over now. I resign." He went quiet, and the murmurs from the crowd grew louder. "Allah, have mercy on us all."

Logan felt the gasp from those nearest, and was sure it had been echoed by most of those present. Certainly, in the USP religion was frowned on, and public displays were seldom seen or heard. After the schism of the lower US States and the formation of the MusCat alliance, religion had become a dirty word. While that was different in the various nation-states, such expressions were largely kept private.

Tejal climbed from the box, and Logan took his place, holding his hands wide. "Easy, everyone. We've all been through a lot. I'm not saying I'm in charge—you need to decide that for yourselves—but I do have some information that you need to hear."

Logan spent the next few minutes explaining what Manners had told him, to the backdrop of increasingly loud grumbles and catcalls. "I understand you don't like what I've said. But losing your temper with me, or those around you, won't help. If you don't like it, take it up with the captain."

"They have guns," someone said from the back.

"Yes, they do." Logan sighed. "Captain Manners wants me to act as a liaison. Frankly, I don't want the job, so feel free to choose someone else."

Logan stepped off the box and made his way toward the exit. He wanted to put some distance between himself and the settlers. If he stayed, he'd be hit with a barrage of questions he had no answers for.

He ducked into a small, dark side cave that didn't appear to be in use for anything, and propped himself against the wall. He hadn't slept since before he and Giorg had tried to free the prisoners, and the lack was catching up with him.

After sleeping fitfully for a couple of hours, Logan wandered back toward the main cave entrance. Both the Futens had been dragged to one side of the rocky platform. As he approached, a MilSec guard wearing sergeant's stripes stepped forward.

"Halt. This area is out of bounds to civilians."

"Not if you want those ships to fly again." Logan carried on walking toward the nearer of the bulky aircraft. "You better get updated orders."

The sergeant was tanned and his skin looked slightly greasy as if he'd been working out. "You Twofeathers?"

Logan nodded.

"Then you're cleared. Sergeant Heskith, vehicle tech, level one. The captain thought you might need help."

Level one meant Heskith was qualified to do routine maintenance, and that was about all. Logan knew Manners had better people, but they were either on other duties or—more likely—hadn't made it. Still, Heskith's muscle might be useful.

"Nice meeting you, Sergeant."

"Call me Hesky. Everyone does." He looked Logan up and down. "Weren't you MilSec?"

"Not exactly." Logan frowned, not wanting to relive old memories. "Civilian contractor for SecOps. Consultant on a few jobs."

"Yeah. That's right." Heskith's face split with a wide grin, and he thrust out a meaty hand. "All part of the family though, right?"

Although he didn't necessarily agree, Logan decided it was easier to make friends rather than cause more friction. Things were going to be hairy if Manners went through with her plans. He gripped Heskith's hand. "It seems long ago."

Heskith pantomimed wringing his hand in pain. "Easy there, big guy. I ain't paid off all my Geneering yet."

"I better take a look at what we're dealing with."

The rear end of the Futen piloted by Giorg was scorched, with a coating of burnt lubricant that gave off a charred bitterness. The starboard engine was ruined. Several panels had blown off, and the inside was full of blackened parts. Other than that, the aircraft wasn't in too bad a shape. The titanium-carbon foam armor had absorbed most of the damage, though there were a few holes that had penetrated through to the inside.

He triggered the rear door and strode up the ramp when it hit the ground, making his way to the pilot's chair. After dropping into the seat, Logan flipped several switches to power up the systems and brought up the diagnostics. Without the adrenaline rush of the heat of battle, he found the controls well laid out and logical.

The Futen appeared to be fully armed. The decoy system was about half full, and there was a self-targeting QuenchGun turret at the nose. When he checked other supplies, he found the side storage bays were loaded with an array of missiles. While he didn't know the full specs of the weapons, he was sure they were effective. With more familiarity with the aircraft, they wouldn't have been such an easy target for the Predator.

"Damn it." He swore softly as he scoured through the different armament control options.

Heskith had dropped into the secondary piloting station and was watching Logan work through the controls. "What's wrong?"

"These things are equipped with EM cloaking. I wish I'd known that when we first took them."

"You didn't stop to RTFM, huh?"

Logan had triggered a full self-diagnostic when shouting from outside caught his attention. Giorg waved at them through the window. "Something's brewing," Logan said. "Back in a minute."

He scrambled out of the Futen. "What's happening?"

"I shouldn't be here." Giorg was hopping from one foot to

another. "There's another broadcast from Colonel Rourke. He mentions you and…"

"And what?"

"You better see for yourself. We've set up a screen in the settlers' cave."

An icy shaft stabbed upwards from Logan's stomach and wrapped itself around his throat. He broke into a run. When he arrived at the cave, a crowd was clustered around a small display screen set on top of a pile of empty boxes in one corner.

Logan pushed his way through, almost knocking over Carl who was at the front of the group.

Carl looked at Logan, his face pale. "It keeps repeating."

Rourke was visible on the screen, his long face and square jaw giving him a blocky appearance at odds with his athletic build. Behind him, fastened to the wall with MagCuffs, was a group of nine people.

"—four hours until we begin executions. Turn yourselves in, and cease these pointless hostilities. We will start with those behind me. And here's a special message for Logan Twofeathers.

"You were identified by our surveillance systems when you raided the refugee camp. We know all about you. You're a born troublemaker, who no doubt thinks he's some kind of hero. Well, I'm sure you'll be interested in my personal guest."

Rourke gestured off-camera, and a few seconds later a soldier pulled a screaming woman into view, dragging her by her hair.

Logan heard a loud hammering, then realized it was his own pulse, and the icy sensation in his stomach melted in a fiery wave as his fists clenched.

"I'm sure you remember your wife, Mr. Twofeathers." Rourke smiled mirthlessly, then struck Aurore across her face with a stinging blow. "Do you have a message for your beloved before you join the others?"

Aurore sobbed. Logan trembled as he saw the cuts and bruises on her face. Her upper lip had split and a knot of dried blood clung to her skin.

She looked directly into the camera pick-up. "Logan. Do as they ask, please. They'll kill us all if you don't." Her nose was dripping, and tears rolled down her cheeks. "I love you, baby, but do as they say. Stop this, please!"

Logan thought his head would burst, and the pleading in her voice tore at his core. He closed his eyes, then Aurore shrieked again, and he had to look. The soldier was dragging her to the wall, but she struggled against him, her hands beating at his face.

"No, don't. Please. Don't do it... Logan? Help me. Please!"

The soldier pulled his arm back and slammed his fist into Aurore's stomach. She bent over double, her words replaced by a wet gurgle.

"You have twenty-four hours," Rourke said. "After that, people will die. Starting with Aurore Vergari."

"Switch it off," someone mumbled. "Switch that shit off."

Carl reached out and killed the display. "Logan, what—"

Logan walked away.

Chapter Nine

"There is no honor in dying without purpose.
— Grandfather Twofeathers

Logan stalked into the main corridor outside the settlers' cavern. His instinct was to grab a gun, jump in the Futen, and head back to New Hope. But there was no way Manners would agree to that, and the damaged transport wouldn't make the journey in its current state. Hot and cold waves crashed through his body, and his gut screamed at him to do *something* to save Aurore. All the while though, his brain was busy working over his assessments of the damage to the Futen.

He tried to push the ideas away, but his mind habitually ticked through the work required. At least six hours to strip out the damaged turbine, assuming he had help. Then the same again to pull an undamaged one from the aircraft he'd flown. Re-installation would take a further eight, then an hour or two for the fine-tuning and balancing necessary to stop it from tearing itself apart as soon as it lifted off.

Twenty-two hours. And, if he was right about their position, they were at least three hours from the city, flying direct.

The main passage in the caves followed the path of the river but, over thousands of years, the course of the water had changed, branching and rejoining, leaving a maze of tunnels more complex than anything he knew of on Earth. He walked blindly, taking tunnels at random with no purpose except to be active, to keep his mind away from thinking about Aurore.

He might be able to shave a couple of hours off his estimate if there were no hitches, but long experience told him the reverse was usually true. And even if he was able to rebuild the transport in time, and persuade Manners to let him take it, what then? He wasn't Sergeant Tempest, super-soldier. He wasn't a one-man army. He wouldn't survive any longer than Aurore.

The tunnel curved sharply right and Logan followed it, noticing a smaller passage to the left. A cool draft carrying the crisp scent of fresh air and vegetation teased his nostrils. Was there another entrance? He followed the passage for a few meters before it opened into a wide chamber, rising into the air like a funnel several hundred meters tall. At the top, a roughly circular hole gave a view of the sky and let in a cone of nebulous light that washed the center of the chamber with a pale, milky luminescence, perfectly highlighting the angular bulk of a Nomad shuttle. But next to it was the much larger profile of something he hadn't seen in a while—an HPL-6C Planetary Lander, favored by MilSec.

Logan wandered around the large, green bulk, questioning what he was seeing. The landers had a high lift capacity and were used to deploy troops and military equipment. Each could carry up to three vehicles and as many as forty fully equipped soldiers. But without a mechanical payload, this one would be able to carry over eighty people into orbit. Using the Nomad as well, they'd be able to evacuate the entire group in two or three trips. *Why hadn't Manners mentioned them?*

A guard scurried around the Nomad, fastening his olive MilSec pants. He jumped when he realized someone was there, almost dropping his rifle. When he recovered, he brought it up and aimed it at Logan.

"What you doing here?" the soldier barked. "This area off-limits to civilians."

"Why?"

The soldier ignored him and activated his comm-set. "Gim, at the Cathedral. I have an intruder."

Logan didn't hear the reply.

"Stay," the soldier ordered. "You under arrest."

Logan's temper was already threatening to boil over, and he

wondered how difficult it would be to tear the soldier's QuenchGun out of his hands. But if he managed it, then what? He'd be trapped in the caves with no way out. Besides, that wouldn't help Aurore.

"Okay. Let's go," he said.

"No go. Stay. Guard come."

It wasn't long before Logan heard footsteps in the passage, then three soldiers emerged—two privates in MilSec uniforms and a lieutenant in a CEG uniform. The lieutenant was one of the CEG flight officers, and Logan recognized her without looking at her name badge.

"Hello, Idoya. I seem to have stumbled somewhere I shouldn't."

"You better call me Lieutenant Gallego under the circumstances. And yes, you certainly have."

Logan knew Gallego as a light-hearted, warm person who liked surfing and flying. While always conscientious about her duties, she was normally more relaxed than some of the others. Whether her change of attitude was because of the Corporate attack, or his current situation, wasn't clear.

"As you wish, Lieutenant. What now? Are you going to lock me up?"

Gallego gestured to the MilSec soldiers and they formed up on either side of Logan. Then she led Gim off to talk privately. Their voices became strident and, although they weren't loud enough for Logan to hear what was being said, the lieutenant appeared to be tearing several strips off the man.

When she rejoined them, Gallego nodded, and the soldiers guided Logan back along the narrow passage. Logan wasn't sure where he was. He'd not paid close attention to his route as he walked around the complex of caves. But from what he *did* remember, they were taking a different path.

After about fifteen minutes, they turned down a small passage on the right. There was an eFlimsy sheet taped to the wall with "Captain Manners" scribbled on it, and the opening showed unmistakable signs of being recently widened and straightened with rock cutters. Inside, Giorg sat at a folding table, and when he saw Logan, he glanced at the thin partition behind him.

"Please inform Captain Manners that Lieutenant Gallego is here with—"

"I monitored the transmissions, Lieutenant." Manners stepped out from behind the curtain, gestured them forward, then turned to Giorg. "No interruptions, Private."

Behind the partition, the area was well lit, and two more tables dominated by multiple data screens had been arranged in an L-shape. Unlike the cave where the civilians were housed, the walls had been squared off like the entrance, with five-centimeter channels scouring down the rock, as if some giant creature had been gnawing at it. The fresh surfaces had also been sealed with some type of shiny polymer, presumably to reduce dust.

Logan looked around. "New quarters, Captain?"

"We're making use of the facilities available. This *was* all rushed, as you know."

Logan spotted a large military comm-set on one side of the desks. "Won't the Corporates pick up any transmissions?"

Gallego stayed close to Logan's elbow as Manners sat.

"Is that your concern?" Manners said, leaning back in her chair.

"Anything that risks the safety of our people is my concern. Isn't that what you wanted from me?"

Manners' nod was hesitant, as though reluctant to agree. "There's a passive receiver planted high in the mountains above us. That's connected via an optical link to our internal data network, which is also an optical system running on micro-fiber. All of which is buried under several million tonnes of rock, so not much chance of the enemy picking it up. You see, we're not stupid, Logan. Despite what you think."

"Actually, I'm glad to know you're on top of things." Logan decided it was better to meet the issue head-on. "So, why am I here?"

"I understand you were found in a restricted area." Manners' thin-lipped smile made her look hawkish and predatory. "Or should I say, you were caught *spying*."

"I was wandering at random. I found the ships by accident."

"Shouldn't you be more concerned about your wife? Not to mention the others scheduled for execution in less than twenty-four hours."

The words hit Logan like blades slicing into his gut, and he fought to maintain his composure. "What I feel or think about that is my business."

"Seems to me, you're a time bomb." Manners rapped her knuckles on the plastic tabletop. "I will not tolerate a loose cannon. Perhaps I should lock you up, for yours and everyone's sakes."

"Who would repair the Futen then?"

Manners leaned back. "There's that. Though it might be better to plan things without it and have you placed under restraint anyway."

"People know I'm here," Logan said. "Wouldn't my disappearance need some explanation?"

"After Colonel Rourke's broadcast, I'm sure everyone would believe you'd left looking for vengeance."

Logan realized Manners was right. "Tell me one thing, Captain. Why are you hiding those ships? We can use them to take the civilians off the planet. Get away from this madness."

"I don't want to escape this *madness*." Manners' eyes were flinty. "Every time in these situations, the Corporates get to do whatever they want and never get punished for it. It's always too expensive or too risky—not politically expedient. But not this time. This time no one is around to interfere, and I'm going to take great delight in giving that traitor Rourke a bloody nose."

Something in Manners' tone suggested there was more to this than was obvious. "You know him?" said Logan.

Manners' lips pulled back from her teeth, but it wasn't a smile. "As you said a few moments ago—that's my business. Now, about those airc—"

"Out of my way." The voice came from outside the partition. "I insist. I must see Captain Manners, immediately."

The short figure of Wildan Tejal dodged around the edge of the partition. His brown skin flushed darker than usual, and his thick, black mustache twitched when he saw both Manners and Logan there.

"I should have known." Tejal sneered. "You're as guilty as she is. Both warmongers, manipulating the situation for your own squabbles."

"This is not the time, Tejal." The threat in Manners' voice was inescapable.

"This planet is far bigger than we can use for ourselves." Tejal rubbed his hand through his matted gray hair. "I've informed the

CESA authority of this several times."

Manners shook her head. "What are you blabbering about?" She raised her voice. "Giorg, call another security team."

"The Corporates have invaded, but it's our fault. They think we're shutting them out of this world. But it does not have to be that way." Tejal gripped the edge of the table, leaning over to stare at Manners. "We can give them room. Cede them their own territory. We don't have to continue the fighting and bloodshed. We can share Kwelengsen and live in peace."

"The Corporates aren't interested in peace," Manners said. "They came to conquer. Lieutenant Gallego, remove this man."

Gallego frowned at Manners. "But Captain..."

"Is everyone around here incompetent?" Manners yelled, and pulled out her pistol. "Get this fool out of here, then return."

"You cannot speak to me that way." Tejal drew himself up. "I am the chief administrator here. I am duly appointed by the CESA council and have the authority to direct affairs for the good of the community."

Logan thought about reminding Tejal that he'd publicly resigned a short while back, but didn't want to add to the chaos.

"I insist, Captain. We must do everything to make peace. I demand you listen to me."

Manners pointed her pistol at Tejal. "You have no authority over me or my personnel. Our duty—and our orders—are clear. We must resist this illegal Corporate attack as long as possible. This planet *must* remain in Earth hands."

"Even if we all die in the process?" Logan half-whispered.

Gallego grabbed Tejal and dragged him back from the table. The plump administrator struggled against her grip. "Take your hands off me. I'm the appointed representative."

Giorg appeared and took Tejal's other arm and, along with Gallego, wrestled Tejal around the partition.

"I will be filing a report on this, Captain." He gurgled as Giorg increased the pressure on him. "The CESA board will not ignore my mistreatment. You will get us all killed."

After the soldiers dragged Tejal away, Manners slammed her hand into the desk, sweeping several eFlimsies, a bottle of water, and various other items off in a spray of debris. Her lips were a pale, compressed line, and a bead of sweat trickled down her temple to trace a glistening line down the wound on her face. After several short breaths, she holstered her gun and turned her back on Logan.

"Tejal told the settlers earlier he was resigning as administrator," Logan said. "Why would he suddenly change his mind?"

Manners didn't reply right away, and when she did, the anger was gone. "You didn't catch the second of Rourke's broadcasts?"

"Second?" Logan realized he might have been walking longer than he'd thought. "What did he say?"

"Nothing much. He released the names of the casualties incurred in the aftermath of your and Private Berardo's little adventure at the camp. Several people were killed attempting to escape..."

Logan felt the coldness from earlier return like an icy punch.

"The list included Administrator Tejal's family."

Logan dropped his head, his shoulders as heavy and stiff as a steel I-beam. "I'm sorry. We did—"

Manners turned back to face him. "You did what you thought was right. I understand that all too well. To make an omelet, we have to break eggs."

Her words offered Logan no comfort. "How many dead?"

"Twenty-three." She paused. "Twelve men, seven women, and four children."

Logan closed his eyes as if that might take the pain away, but it didn't.

"Decisions have consequences, Logan. And they're not always good. Sometimes they may not even make sense. Tell me..." She paused. "What would you do with the ships?"

"Take the people away from here."

"And go where?"

He remembered his own discussion with Sergeant Diouf. The *Hansen* might not be in orbit any longer, and neither the Nomad nor the Planetary Lander had a Jump drive. "The *Sarabhai* may still be around."

"The Atoll ship disappeared before we were attacked, didn't it?" Manners said.

Logan nodded. "It appeared to, but the Corporates might have blocked our systems."

"True. But would you take that risk? And would the Atolls take in *scroffer* refugees?"

The Atolls' hatred of Earth people was well known. And since the attacks against them, that had increased. That one psychotic individual was responsible didn't matter—the Atolls blamed all of Earth for developing the Phage that was destroying their ships and space habitats.

"You're right, Captain. It would be a pointless risk."

"You can still call me Charlie." Manners sat again. "How long until you can get that Futen flying?"

"Not until too late for the hostages."

Manners' features hardened. "This will undoubtedly sound harsh, but they aren't my priority."

"They're mine." Logan tried to avoid thinking about the broadcast and the image of Aurore being beaten, but the memory was seared into his brain. There was Rourke, with the prisoners behind him pulling at the shackles, and Aurore being dragged in front of the camera pick-up and…

"Is there a recording of the broadcast?" Logan asked.

Manners frowned. "Recording the transmissions is routine. Why?"

"I need to check something. Can I have access to it and a portable viewer?"

Manners drummed her fingers on the tabletop. "I need that Futen…"

"Give me an hour. Then I'll get to work on it."

"What's going through your mind, Logan?" Manners screwed up her face.

He shook his head. "Nothing I can discuss now. Do I get the viewer?"

"Talk to Private Berardo on your way out." Manners pointed at the partition. "But whatever it is you're looking for, I'm the first to know."

Logan restarted the recording once again. The viewer was cradled in his arm as he sat on a rock ledge alone in one of the smaller caverns. He'd studied it in detail for the last forty minutes and lost count of how many times he'd endured it. The experience had left grim lines carved into his face the way the river had sliced passages through the rock around him.

A noise caught Logan's attention and he looked up to see Heskith's heavy figure by the entrance, the soldier's close-set eyes making him look as though he was squinting in the low light.

"Look, I saw what happened. Man, that's some kinda shitbake. Your wife and all... Manners told me to come and remind you though. We gotta get to work on that transport."

Logan checked the time. He stood and brushed the dust from his pants. "I need to see Manners first."

"Sure thing, big guy," Heskith said. "Let's go."

As they marched through the rocky tunnels, Heskith kept up a stream of chatter. "Looks like a bunch of your people decided there was something worth fighting for here. Heard a group of 'em have signed up. Though I ain't sure if a herd of recruits is gonna help us much. We need soldiers, not farmers and schoolteachers. No offense."

When they arrived at Manners' office, Giorg led Logan past the partition while Heskith waited outside. She was still at her desk, her eyes focused on the screen. After a few minutes, she closed what she was looking at and dismissed Giorg with a wave of her hand.

"So?" said Manners.

Logan pointed to a large display surface on the wall. "Can you bring up the recording?"

Manners' eyes widened a little, but she pressed several controls, and the screen lit up with Rourke's image frozen in the middle. "What now?"

"Advance the playback to two seventeen and hold it there."

Manners shifted the recording. Now the screen showed a closer image of the prisoners against the wall.

"That's the clearest frame I found," said Logan. "See anything?"

Manners scrutinized the screen. "Not really. A group of settlers lined up for execution, held there using standard-issue MagCuffs. They look scared." She shrugged.

"Do you recognize any of them?"

"I don't know everyone on Kwelengsen by sight."

"Can you zoom in on the faces? Take a good look."

Manners picked up a small control unit and focused the image on the people, moving from one prisoner to the next. "Some of them look familiar, but I'd be lying if I said I was able to identify them."

"Me too." Logan watched Manners' reaction closely. "And I've made a habit of acquainting myself with all the civilians."

"But you can't poss… there are too many of them."

"It's not as difficult as you'd think. But I'd lay money if you asked around, you wouldn't find anyone who can identify those people."

"I'm hardly going to do that." Manners kneaded her shoulders. "I doubt they want to be reminded that their nearest and dearest are being held for execution."

"That's not going to happen."

Manners stared at Logan and blinked slowly. "So who do you think they are?"

"Nobody. I don't think they exist."

"Apart from your wife, I take it? I couldn't fail to identify her, and neither can you."

"Maybe…" Logan glanced at the frozen screen. "Maybe not."

"What?"

"We've had the ability to create fake representations of people for over a century. I think they're playing dirty PSYOP games with us. Messing with our heads."

Manners tapped on the table. "Morale has been low since those broadcasts started, and it's getting lower. And it *is* the sort of nasty game Rourke would play."

"Let's see what the next broadcast brings." Logan hesitated. "In the meantime, there's a transport that needs some attention."

Manners nodded. "And if you're wrong?"

Logan hesitated. "Then I'll have to find a way to live with that."

He strode out to rejoin Heskith, and they made their way back to the Futens. Logan rechecked the diagnostics to confirm his earlier assessment, then moved to the control system and shut down the core, so he could work safely on the engine.

With Heskith's help, Logan soon had the engine cowling removed, and was disconnecting the intricate control interfaces from the damaged engine. Unfortunately, several had been burned and would need to be cannibalized from the other vehicle—making the job more difficult with the tools available and increasing the time required. He disconnected the main regulators and lifted out the housing, only to have it crumble in his hand—the composite material had the consistency of choux pastry.

"Another one lost to heat stress," he said to Heskith. "Replace RN-9017L—Inboard Low-Pressure Compressor."

The soldier made a note on a DataPad. "This thing took a beating."

"Yeah, I was there." Logan poked at the charred area underneath the regulator. "Adaptive Engine Controller is fried too."

Heskith's comm-set beeped. Logan couldn't hear the conversation, only an occasional inexpressive grunt.

"Yeah. Okay. Will do. Out." Heskith tapped the comm-set to end the call. "You're in demand again."

What this time? Logan wiped his hands clean of the black gunk from the burnt components. "I guess we need a break. Assuming I'm allowed lunch."

"I need to feed the inner man too." Heskith grinned. "And I ain't been told to stop you. But Manners wants you on the double."

"Anyone would think she liked me." Logan clambered off the tail housing onto the platform they'd set up. "Why don't you see what you can rustle up? I can find my own way to her office."

"Sure thing. Appreciate that."

Logan walked back through the passages to Manners' office. Giorg wasn't in sight, and he knocked on the frame holding up the curtain partition.

"Come in," Manners called.

She didn't appear to have moved from where he'd left her earlier. "I got a message you wanted to see me again, Captain."

Manners looked up, then leaned back and stretched her arms wide as she rolled her head and neck. "We can talk and walk at the same time," she said. "I need to move."

Logan fell in alongside Manners as she strode through the corridors. The cave complex was more of a labyrinth than Logan had first imagined, and there seemed to be multiple paths to almost everywhere.

"I asked you to watch over the civilians."

"You *also* ordered me to get the Futen working."

"I remember." Manners seemed more disappointed in herself than anything. "Tejal is gone."

Logan stopped. "Gone? Where?"

Manners reached into a pocket of her fatigues, pulling out a battered-looking eFlimsy. She thrust it into Logan's hand. "To save the world."

Logan read the note. It was scrawled, but he recognized Tejal's sharply-angled writing. It was difficult to make out in the dim tunnel, and he edged closer to the light to read it.

"Someone must stop this madness. We must seek peace, or we'll all die." Tejal's signature was scratched across the bottom.

"Did anyone see him leave?"

"No, but there are several unmonitored exits. Giorg has checked—no one has seen him for over three hours."

"He might be wandering inside the caves."

"Some food rations and a shoulder pack are missing," Manners said. "I've had search teams checking the caves and smaller exits. They found tracks leading into the bush outside one of them."

Logan frowned. "Then we need to get him back. The Corporates have enough hostages."

"I'm glad we agree." Manners started walking again. "I've ordered my people to use a Shuriken to locate him."

"How does that help?" The drone might locate Tejal but couldn't bring him back.

"It's the only thing we have that can fly undetected." Manners paused. "Unless the Futen is working again?"

"We're hours away from that." Logan understood Manners' dilemma. The Planetary Lander was too big and clumsy to use on a ground search. And while the Nomad could be deployed that way, both it and the Lander were capable of reaching orbit. With that much power, they'd light up the detectors on any orbiting surveillance systems. "I'll be in the search party."

"There won't be one." Manners' voice was flat. "The drone operators have orders to shoot on sight."

"*What?*"

"Tejal is a threat to everyone here—armed forces *and* civilians." Manners turned to look at him. "We can't risk him falling into enemy hands."

"That's crazy. Let me take a few people out there. He can't have got far. We can drag him back by force if you insist, but don't simply hand out a death sentence. He's not himself. Besides, we're many days' walk from New Hope, or any of the Corporate forces."

"They'll be scanning the surface. If they pick him up, we're all as good as dead. We haven't the equipment to defend against a full-on attack. And even if we could, I wouldn't risk it for one person."

"Then let me go. I can take my nephew." Logan gestured down the passage. It might help his relationship with Carl if he included him in something important like this and boost the boy's confidence. "He's done some hunting and tracking. We'll have Tejal back in a couple of hours."

"You have a job here. Without the Futen I can't retrieve Sergeant Diouf and her group. "Besides, your nephew isn't available."

Logan did a double-take. "What do you mean?"

They had taken a circular route and now stood at the desk outside Manners' office. Giorg jumped up at their approach.

"Simple. Carl Begay has signed up for the First Kwelengsen Volunteers—our new militia."

Chapter Ten

*"All birds, even those of the same species,
are not alike."*
— Shooter (Okute)

Logan's thoughts were a dust devil of crazy, unconnected ideas, and every time he tried to force different threads together they seemed to snap moments later. First, the discussion about Tejal, and now the bombshell about Carl. The boy wasn't a fighter. He'd said as much earlier. Logan's legs trembled, and his stomach gurgled. "Sorry."

"You haven't eaten?" Manners smiled faintly.

"Civilians are on short rations, remember?"

"That doesn't apply in your case. You're getting the Futen back in action. And if that weren't the case, I told you—families of those who sign up get full rations. So you qualify twice." Manners tapped her comm-set. "Send up two lunches. And some coffee."

Logan slumped in the chair opposite her, his mouth watering. He hadn't drunk coffee since before the Corporate invasion and felt the loss. "I can't get a handle on you."

Manners gave that smile again, as though she was pleased about something but didn't want to make it clear she was. "Why's that?"

"Can I be blunt?" He paused until she nodded. "Up to now, you've always struck me as being reasonable. You listened when there were differences over the best approach or utilization of resources. And came up with appropriate responses."

"And now?"

Logan wasn't sure how to answer that. The old Manners made some kind of sense, and he felt he'd come to understand her. But post-invasion Manners was a whole new ball game. Before, he'd have been comfortable telling her she'd crossed the boundary, but her new hard-line stance made him wonder if that would get him locked up. Or worse.

A corporal appeared from around the partition carrying supplies, giving Logan time to think as Manners unwrapped the food and poured coffee into beakers, as though they were sharing a picnic. Logan took a bite of his sandwich and found it soft and tasty, not typical of emergency rations. The coffee was good too and, as with the tea earlier, must have been imported.

A soft beep came from Manners' comm-set, and she put down her food. "One moment. Switching you to the speaker."

She tapped the comm-set three times and the desk speaker crackled into life.

"Please repeat," said Manners.

"Yes, Captain. I've located Administrator Tejal. He's two kilometers out. I have his location locked into the targeting system. Awaiting instructions."

Logan didn't recognize the voice, but he knew what those instructions were.

"You have your orders, Sergeant."

"But... Yes, sir." The voice went quiet for a moment. "Relaying optical feed."

The wall screen blinked into life and filled with a picture of the coarse vegetation outside. At first, Logan saw nothing, then spotted a flash of movement that resolved itself into the shape of Tejal clambering through the brush. His light-colored clothing offered little camouflage against the foliage.

"Target green," the anonymous voice said. "Deploying Quench-Gun."

Logan gripped the seat. "Captain—" The lights in the office flashed three times, and Logan heard several calls of surprise from outside. "What's happening?"

A voice echoed around the room and the corridor outside. "Enemy recon patrol detected."

Manners switched off the speaker and tapped her comm-set. "Shut everything down. Zero-EM protocol. And get that drone out of the sky, now!"

The lights faded, leaving a faint, ghoulish green from a bio-lume emergency lamp, and silence filled the darkness around them like a mudslide. Manners was a ghostly outline in front of Logan, but as his eyes adjusted, he saw more clearly.

"The Corporates are doing a high-altitude sweep," said Manners. "They've never been over here before. They must be spreading out."

"Aren't we safe in here?"

There was the briefest of hesitations before Manners replied. "We think so, but I'm not taking any chances."

Logan nodded, then remembered the administrator. "Tejal?"

"Yes, they could detect him." Manners' voice was tight.

Scanning systems were so refined that virtually nothing was undetectable if you were using the right frequencies. If the recon ships were at high altitude, the sensors might not have the resolution to pick out a single man from any other animal. But that was a fifty-fifty shot at best. "We can't leave him out there."

Manners shivered. "All we can do is hope they think he's part of the wildlife. If they capture him, we're finished. Even if he tells them nothing."

Logan understood. Tejal would bring the full attention of the enemy forces to the area, and the secrecy of the cave complex wouldn't survive such scrutiny.

"Let me get him."

"Out of the question. Then we'd have two potential security breaches wandering around out there, with twice the risk of being detected."

"He's only a couple of kilometers away. An EM Cloak will minimize my signals, and once I get to him, I can shield both of us."

Manners chewed her lip. "It's a hell of a risk."

"So is leaving Tejal out there." Logan paused. "He thinks we can negotiate with the Corporates. What if he spots their ship and signals them?"

Manners' eyebrows tightened into a barely visible harsh line, then she raised her voice. "Private Berardo. Fetch Sergeant Heskith, immediately." She looked back at Logan. "Do you need anyone else?"

Logan considered asking for Carl again but dismissed the idea. The boy hated him enough as it was. "Why increase the risk? Now I know where he is, I'll find him."

Manners gave a curt nod. A few minutes later, Heskith stuck his head around the doorway, his face tinged green by the eerie light of the bio-lume lamp he carried.

"Get Mr. Twofeathers a Cloak, and escort him to exit 11-South." Manners paused. "Do *not* leave the caves with him."

Heskith's left eyebrow twitched upward. "Yes, sir."

Logan stood. "Thank you, Captain."

Manners dismissed his words with a sharp shake of her head. "Don't."

Logan turned and followed Heskith out into the tunnels, the dim luminescence from the lamp making it difficult to pick his footing with any great confidence. As they walked through the passages, Logan spotted a few other areas with similar lighting. Clearly, not everything was shut down—only the large systems that had a chance of creating a detectable signature.

The unfamiliarity with the tunnels, along with the dim light, meant Logan was soon lost, despite his good sense of direction. After a five-minute walk, they entered a wider cavern piled to the ceiling with boxes and supply cases. Heskith checked the labels on several, then pulled down a large container. He opened it, grabbed two flat squares about ten by twenty centimeters, and handed them to Logan. "Better take a spare, in case."

"Thanks."

"Do you want a weapon?"

Logan thought about it. A weapon might be handy but would increase the chances of detection. "Sure, if you've got something invisible."

"Hang on."

After much delving around, Heskith pulled out a tubular object with a pistol grip at one end. "Speargun—all composite materials, almost undetectable," he said, handing it, along with a fabric pouch, to Logan. "Pull back the band, load up a bolt, aim, and fire."

"Sounds simple enough." Logan took the weapon and pulled

back the lever to draw the band back, finding it all too easy. "I don't think it's working."

Heskith laughed. "Nah, it's fine." He took the gun back, pulled a bolt from the pouch, and locked it into place. Pointing the gun at the ground, he pulled the trigger, and a loud crack filled the room as the bolt shot out and buried itself in the dusty floor. "The band uses non-linear metelastic materials. Super stretchy until you extend it to its fully-drawn position. Once that happens, the elastic properties return. Shoots at about two hundred meters per second. Enough to kill game, or an unarmored man."

Logan reached for the speargun and bolts. "I'll try not to use it."

"You do what you have to." Heskith slapped him on the back. "Come on."

They wound their way through several twisting passages, then Logan sensed a change in the air. It was damper, but also less stuffy. A short time later, the tunnel widened, and the distinct brightness of outdoor light overwhelmed the murkiness inside the caves.

They ended up at a narrow fissure that turned sharp right. Through the crevice, Logan saw signs of foliage backed by a pink-flecked blue sky. The caves had an air of timelessness, but here the real world followed its own unwavering dynamics and the sun was close to setting.

That complicated things, Logan realized. As the heat of the day faded, any nocturnal animals would be active, potentially providing a larger, more confusing, number of signals. But it also meant their infrared signatures would be easier to detect and limited the time he had to get to Tejal. Once darkness fell, it would be nearly impossible to locate the administrator. He opened one of the packets Heskith had given him and pulled out the Cloak, draping it over himself like a poncho.

"Good luck," Heskith said, then disappeared back into the darkness of the passage.

The sun sat low on the horizon, and Logan judged there was about an hour of light remaining. Despite that, the heat from the foliage around him made him sweat in minutes. They were closer to the equator here, which kept the average temperature higher than the site chosen for New Hope.

Although he'd been on Kwelengsen for close to two years, there was still so much about it that he and the other settlers didn't know. His ancestors had prided themselves on their knowledge of how to live in harmony with the world around them, but he'd never felt that connection. And, if he had, would it mean anything on a different world?

The man-made disasters on Earth were a clear lesson that a less exploitative approach was needed to ensure long-term sustainability. They'd been operating that way on Kwelengsen. But now that world was being engulfed and threatened by the Corporates. Logan's jaw tightened. The idea that history repeated itself appeared to be true. The invaders were different, but their motivations and attitudes were fueled by the same overwhelming greed, and the profiteering mantra—exploit, abuse, destroy.

Following a well-defined animal trail through the thick vegetation, Logan made his way northeast, in the direction he knew Tejal was heading. His long stride could have devoured the distance easily enough, but the need to be constantly on guard made progress slow.

The high-altitude recon ships weren't his immediate worry. He was more concerned the Corporates might have deployed a low-level sensor swarm of mini-drones to back up the search. But, if they had, he'd seen no sign of them so far. The sky had turned a deep vermilion, and the bush and rocks around him were splashed with heavy mulberry shadows. The sun was dipping below the horizon, leaving only the reflected pale glow from the darkening skies. Logan heard a crack ahead and stopped. It might have been Tejal or some indigenous creature.

Crouching, Logan waited for another sound to help pinpoint the location. For several minutes all he heard was the soft buzzing and chirping of the local insects. Then a distinct splintering as if someone had pushed through the foliage and stepped on a fallen branch.

Logan edged forward. He couldn't see anything, but judging

by the volume, it wasn't a small scavenger foraging through the undergrowth. Whatever it was, it didn't feel the need to mask its movements—which was what he'd expect from the unworldly administrator.

Creeping through the plants, Logan sensed movement ahead of him. The light levels had dropped to the point where he could make out little in the gloom. A noise to his right made him stop, and he twisted. A single green eye with a distinctive W-shaped pupil met his glance, and he smelled the creature's fetid breath from half a meter away. He jumped back and the animal did the same, braying loudly.

Several heads popped up from the dense brush. It was hard to make them out, but Logan was sure they were rhison or a close relative. The nearest one looked larger and meaner than any he'd seen, with a thick coat of matted bristles along its spine. Before he thought about bringing up the spear-gun, the animals ran, their high-pitched sonar-chips—used to supplement their single eyes—fading in the distance. Logan followed their movement by the scrape of scrub bush and the crash of breaking trees. He knelt, taking some deep breaths, then laughed softly. The creature had been as startled as he was.

His relief was cut short by a human scream up ahead. Logan hurried along the path of trodden-down foliage. After about forty meters, his attention was caught by a pitiful mewling, like an injured animal crying for help. Crouching low, he moved ahead, spotting a pile of pale rocks in the middle of the low bushes.

He heard the noise again and stopped to listen. It had to be close. Then he realized the "rocks" were the prone form of Administrator Tejal. Logan rushed and knelt alongside him. He was lying on his front, his tattered clothes scuffed and stained.

"Administrator?" Logan whispered.

Tejal moaned and tried to look around, but struggled to move. "It's Logan Twofeathers."

Logan examined Tejal, then eased the barely conscious man onto his back. "Can you hear me? I'm here to help."

"Monsters." Tejal's words gurgled wetly in his throat. "Monsters in the dark."

Tejal must have been caught by the stampeding herd. He didn't appear badly hurt, other than a few scrapes and bruises, but without a medical scanner, it was impossible to be certain. Logan took out the spare Cloak and wrapped it around Tejal, who kept up a steady stream of mumbling, but Logan caught only occasional disjointed words. Once they were both shielded, he stood.

"Let's get you to safety." Logan pulled the other man to his feet. "This way."

When Logan let go, Tejal slumped back down, whimpering in the dirt. Logan reached to help him but sensed movement behind him and froze. A moment later, the thin material of the Cloak grew warmer. They were being scanned.

Logan spotted the diamond outline of a surveillance drone, its dull surface catching the remnants of light in the gathering gloom. It was hovering about ten meters away, rotating back and forth on its axis, lights from its scanning beams gleaming like three red, demonic eyes.

Tejal was weeping plaintively. "Quiet," whispered Logan. "They'll hear you."

Tejal continued, seemingly oblivious to the danger. In desperation, Logan put his hand over the other man's mouth to muffle the noise.

The weight of the speargun pressed against Logan's back. There was little chance it would penetrate the drone's skin, but even if it did, it was unlikely to destroy it. Those things were built tough. More to the point, taking it out would alert its operators as much as if the drone detected them. Tejal wriggled, and Logan was forced to clamp his hand tighter. If they were detected, the whole base would be overrun.

A loud crash came from the direction the rhison had taken, and the drone spun around. After holding its position for a while, it flew off, following the trail the animals had made, passing over Logan and Tejal.

Logan waited until the drone had moved away before he checked on the administrator. When he slid the Cloak back, Tejal's head lolled in an alarming way. Logan's heart raced as he checked for a pulse. It was there, but faint, and Logan silently cursed.

He hauled Tejal's body onto his shoulders in a fireman's lift, then started back toward the caves. The sky was now a deep violet, with only a few stubborn streaks of red remaining, like bloodstains in the sky. The terrain wasn't too difficult, but the need to remain alert for other drones, combined with Tejal's weight, slowed Logan's progress and gave him far too much time to think about what had happened.

He'd *had* to keep Tejal quiet. If not, everything would have been over. But the thought that what he'd done might have led to Tejal's current condition dragged at Logan like a steel hawser. The entrance to the caves was difficult to find in the darkness, but eventually, Logan slipped through the rocky passage and, after a few turns, found himself back in the dim corridors. The smooth passages at least made it easier to move.

Heskith wasn't there—the sergeant must have returned to his duties, and Logan yelled at the first soldier he saw.

"Medical emergency. This man needs help." Logan sank to the floor, easing Tejal onto the rocky surface as gently as possible.

The soldier looked startled and disappeared, but returned shortly with several other people and a lightweight folding gurney. Logan was glad to hand over Tejal, but it did little to ease his guilt.

After carrying Tejal back, Logan was ready to spend several hours in a comfortable bed, but he doubted Manners would allow him that luxury. The scant amounts of rest he'd managed to grab over the last twenty-four hours were nowhere near enough. She'd want him back working on the Futen. He'd tried not to involve himself in the military operations, but both Manners and the invasion seemed intent on forcing that choice on him.

An idea occurred to Logan, and he headed for the Futens. The pilots' seats were heavily cushioned to protect the operators from g-forces in combat, which sounded like heaven at that moment. He scrambled into the main chair of the aircraft he'd flown in. No one had seen him, and he said a silent thank you as he sank into the padding. The seats had a recline feature, so he could lie almost flat. A wave of dizzy relief hit him and he was asleep.

Chapter Eleven

"An engine is like a person. You can work them non-stop, but eventually, both will explode."
— Grandfather Twofeathers

Logan was fighting for his life, but the enemy kept changing. Sometimes it was Tepfer beating on him with his powerful Geneered arms, then Tejal was smothering him in layers of blubber. Then it switched to an old foe, Gabriella, slicing his guts open with a large butcher's knife, which morphed into Manners doing the same. Finally, it was Carl, pinning him down and tearing his flesh like a half-human, half-arktomys were-creature.

His eyes snapped open and he jerked upright, not sure for a second if he was still dreaming. Carl was tugging on his shoulder.

"What is it?" Logan's brain struggled to catch up with reality.

Carl pulled away. "Captain Manners has been looking for you since you came back."

"Is something wrong?"

"Well..." Carl looked away. "There's been another broadcast from the Corporates."

"Rourke?" Logan swung out of the seat. "What's happened?"

"You better see Manners." Carl avoided eye contact.

A cold fear gripped Logan, and his stomach flip-flopped. Though he often found Carl taciturn and distant, this was something else—something personal. Clambering from the battered Futen, he left Carl inside and rushed to Manners' office.

Giorg looked up as Logan approached. "You'll have to wait. The captain is in conf—"

Logan brushed him aside and strode into Manners' office. She was drawing on the large display screen with two lieutenants watching. Logan recognized one as Zarah Morua, part of the CEG forces, while the other was MilSec with a name badge that read "Brierton."

"...the two lines of—" Manners broke off, her face an unreadable mask. She nodded at the others. "Come back in thirty minutes."

Logan waited until the lieutenants had gone. "Carl said there was another broadcast?"

Without a word, Manners changed the screen and brought up a recording.

Rourke was positioned on the left of the image like before. The prisoners they'd seen in the last transmission were again visible behind him, lined up against the wall. The location gave few clues as to where in the city it was. The wall could have been part of any of a dozen or so buildings. Logan examined the faces but still didn't recognize any of them.

"Today, I find myself faced with a difficult duty." Rourke spoke as if considering every word. "I offered everyone the option to lay down their weapons and return to Earth, but it appears my terms were too generous."

Rourke's long face tightened, his jaw becoming a hard edge. "Today's terrorist attack on our Corporate forces is unacceptable, and although designed to reduce our numerical superiority, it failed. The destruction of the temporary barracks is an inconvenience at best. Most of the soldiers inside escaped, despite being *asleep* at the time."

Logan stiffened. "You attacked them?"

Manners didn't answer, and the recording continued.

"Despite my natural tendency to be lenient, it seems you people haven't learned your lesson yet. So a graphic demonstration is clearly necessary." Rourke gestured off-screen, and several Corporate soldiers walked in front of the shackled civilians, accompanied by a sergeant.

Logan froze as the soldiers lifted their guns and aimed at the line of settlers.

"Understand, *you* have driven us to this." Rourke pointed at the prisoners. "I cannot allow the death of our troops to go unpunished, and the sentence for espionage is death. If the cowards who did this were here, I'd punish *them*, but perhaps all that is needed is to make a clear demonstration of our resolve."

Rourke raised his hand and gave the soldiers a sharp salute. Logan heard the sergeant call out, his voice quiet because he wasn't near the pick-up, but clear enough. "Squad. Charge weapons."

The soldiers pulled back the charging handles on their rifles.

"Squad, take aim... Fire."

Multiple high-pitched *thrums* filled Manners' office, followed by a series of terrible screeches from the prisoners. Their bodies jerked as a stream of high-velocity needles tore through them, daubing the wall behind with splashes of deep crimson like a Nitsch painting.

Logan closed his eyes but opened them at the sound of someone sobbing. One prisoner was alive, despite his chest and stomach being torn open by the salvo of needles. The man's entrails had slid out through ragged flaps of skin and pooled around his feet like a pile of slithering eels.

"God... help... me..." His voice was hoarse.

The sergeant walked over, pulled out a pistol, and fired a single shot through the man's forehead.

"I take no pleasure in this." Rourke frowned, the lines on his cheeks deepening into dark hollows. "But believe me when I say—if the attacks continue, so will the executions."

"I still don't believe—" Logan fell silent when Manners shook her head.

"I know you're behind these attacks, Mr. Twofeathers. Your efforts to encourage others to rebel are futile. We *are* in control. I'm sure you remember that I promised to begin the executions with your wife. Well, I decided that something else might prove more of a deterrent."

Rourke grinned, his narrow face turning hawkish. "And besides, troops in the field are so starved of... entertainment."

He gestured to one side, out of the range of the pick-up. Two other Corporate soldiers appeared, dragging someone between them. It was Aurore. The firing squad moved up, surrounding her until she was almost invisible behind them. There were a number of guttural laughs, and several soldiers reached out to touch her.

"Get back," Aurore shouted, "Stay away from me."

Every muscle and sinew in Logan's body tightened, his chest so compressed he could barely breathe.

One soldier snatched at Aurore's shirt, ripping the front open. She crossed her arms to cover herself, then another dragged the rest of the shirt off from behind. She fought, but she was impossibly outnumbered, and she fell to the ground screaming, "No. No. Stop!"

The pick-up changed angle to fill the screen with the image of the soldiers attacking her. Two others cut her pants with knives and tore them off. Another clamped a hand over her face, and her cries became muffled. The sergeant rolled on top of her.

Logan looked away. "Turn that filth off."

A few seconds later the sound stopped.

"I'm sorry, Logan," Manners half-whispered. "If there's anything—"

Logan's body was locked so tight he felt like he was made of glass and the slightest movement would shatter him to small pieces. His pulse hammered in his temples with a sickening wet throb. The look on Aurore's face as they dragged her down was etched into his thoughts like a laser engraving on titanium.

Hate and love were two sides of the same coin. And Logan was ready to destroy every Corporate soldier in existence. He'd willingly fly the transport directly to New Hope and plunge it into the heart of their forces. If that would guarantee Rourke's death, it would be worth it. That he'd be killed in the attempt was irrelevant.

"I told you, he's an animal." Manners slammed her fist into the table. "He'll stop at nothing to get what he wants. Do you believe me now?"

Logan fought down the anger, taking several breaths. That was the reaction they wanted. What Rourke expected the broadcast to achieve. And he couldn't let them drive him into a futile frenzy. He had to believe that Aurore was okay, wherever she was. If he stopped believing that, there was nothing left.

"That's not my wife." Logan sucked in air through his teeth. "It's fake."

"It looked convincing to me." Manners switched off the display and slipped into her chair. "How can you be so sure?"

"It may be simulated. They might have hacked our medical records and used other public information sources." Logan took another deep breath, forcing his pulse lower. "Generated using real-time simulation, or image swapping. It's not... the first time... someone's used those methods." The use of realistic 3V faking had been restricted since the European *Gefälschter Krieg* a hundred years ago. But the Corporates had ignored that treaty, along with many others.

Manners' eyes narrowed. "But why target you? What does that get them? Why not me?"

"Maybe it's a scatter-gun approach. Or because they know I was involved in freeing the prisoners. For good or bad, my name is inextricably linked with Kwelengsen. As for you, it could be that Rourke thinks you're already dead."

"He sees you as the potential catalyst for any resistance." Manners fiddled with the remote for the screen.

"If that's true, he's trying to manipulate me into doing something stupid. And the best thing I can do is not let him get to me."

"And what if you're wrong? What if it's real?" Manners slapped the control down with a loud crack. "Your wife *may* be alive, but those settlers are dead."

Logan's chest constricted, and his words came out in stabs. "Then Rourke has signed his own death warrant. But I won't be manipulated. By *anyone*."

Manners held his gaze briefly then looked away. "How are the repairs coming?"

The change of subject was jarring, but Logan was glad to be forced to shift focus to something else. "As well as can be expected. Heskith is a big help. Another seven hours should do it."

"Any way you can move that up? We've established contact with Sergeant Diouf, and I'd like to recover her group before sunrise tomorrow." She spread her hands. "If we can bring them in overnight, it'll reduce the chance of being detected."

"If we had a turbine balancer, I could do it sooner, but it'll take at least three hours to adjust the rotors manually."

Manners nodded, but a frown curled the corners of her mouth downward. "Do what you can." She hesitated, then patted his shoulder. "Again, I'm sorry about the transmission."

"*Did* you attack them?"

Manners stared at Logan, then looked back at the screen on her desk. "No. Either Rourke's lying to justify his actions, or there's another group operating somewhere."

"Others who escaped the attack?" A brief flash of hope welled up inside Logan.

"I don't know." She tapped something on her terminal. "But I intend to find out."

Logan sensed the hint of dismissal and stalked out. Despite what he'd said to Manners, he couldn't entirely suppress the images he'd seen on the broadcast and calm the volcano threatening to erupt inside his head.

As Logan marched toward the cave entrance, a figure rushed in his direction. Giorg skidded to a stop, and the clipboard he was carrying flapped against his chest. His gaze examined the rock passage, coming to rest on a spot past Logan's shoulder.

"Mr. Twofeathers... I was... That is, I'm on my way back to Captain Manners' office."

Logan stared at Giorg in the gloomy half-light. "Everything okay?"

"It's..." Giorg let out a short laugh. "Everybody's on edge, I guess. Including me."

"Because of Rourke's transmission? You think it's real?"

Giorg's eyes snapped to look directly at Logan but drifted away again immediately. "What do you mean?"

"What he said about an attack. Do you think there are others out there?"

"Oh that. Well, the captain seems... convinced."

"That will confuse things, I imagine," Logan said. "She wants the Futen ready tonight. Does Manners think Diouf's behind the attack? She was headed away from the city and didn't seem the type to turn back and pick a fight."

"I shouldn't talk about this." Giorg's glance slid away again. "And I need to get back."

Logan stepped aside as Giorg disappeared down the darkened corridor. Something had made him more reticent than usual. Manners was no doubt coming down harder on her people as the stakes increased, which would ramp up the tension for everyone.

Heskith was sitting by the Futen when Logan got back, puffing on a pungently spiced SootheStick that left a lingering acrid smell despite the ventilation from outside.

"Everything okay, big guy?"

"The usual seven-impossible-things-before-breakfast routine." Logan clambered up on the stubby tail wing. "They want this running by sunset."

Heskith nodded. "That's the army for you. Always a rush on for something."

Logan grabbed a wrench. "Let's do this."

He loosened the mounts on the damaged engine, but his thoughts were elsewhere. Whatever was troubling Giorg, it didn't seem to be affecting Heskith. Did that mean Giorg was overreacting, or was something going on in the upper echelons that Giorg knew about only because he was Manners' aide?

The one person Logan couldn't allow himself to think about was Aurore. Every time his thoughts edged that way, the memory of her being dragged down tore at him. It was almost more than he could stand, and he continually had to force his mind back to the work on the Futen.

Four hours later, they had the turbine unit swapped over. They'd tested it by bolting it to a makeshift stand, but had only got the high-thrust unit up to about a third of its operational speed. At that level, the balance seemed good, but there were no guarantees it wouldn't fly apart once they pushed it higher.

Logan connected the last control interface and torqued the fitting to the required specs. "It's make or break time." He gestured at the soldiers stood around the wide cavern. "We should clear those guys out. No point putting them in harm's way."

Heskith looked at him dubiously. "I'm not sure the captain would approve."

"So, let's not tell her." Logan wrestled the engine cover back in place. "I know. She doesn't exactly trust me, but if that turbine lets go, it'll be like the mother of all grenades going off. Anyone in here will be *sashimi*."

Heskith shrugged. "You sure you want to do the test? I could—"

Logan slid down and held up his hand. "I'm the best qualified to check it. Besides, I don't want *more* repairs on my hands."

Heskith snorted. "Okay, but I'm your co-pilot."

Logan was going to object but realized it was futile. No doubt Manners would insist, and her suspicions would increase if he tried to take the aircraft up alone. "Okay, let's get these guys clear."

While Heskith herded the soldiers to a safe place, Logan clambered into the pilot's seat. After wiping his hands, he powered up the instruments and ran through every diagnostic available. Everything showed green, and a few minutes later, Heskith slid into the seat next to him.

"Okay. They're standing clear." Heskith pulled the safety harness over his shoulders.

Logan flipped several switches, starting the front turbines. They zinged up to speed in moments, and a shiver of vibration trembled through the airframe. He checked the tell-tale displays were at safe levels and the engines were generating the specified thrust levels, then flipped the switches to initialize the rear turbines.

"Here we go," Logan said softly, not sure if Heskith heard him or not.

There was a rattle from the aft and Logan wondered if he'd missed something. But after a few hiccups, it smoothed out as the engines picked up speed. It might have been dirt. They weren't operating in clean room conditions. The rear engines wound up, approaching their idling speed of fifteen thousand RPM. So far, everything was good, but now came the real test. If the turbines were going to fail, it would be under load.

He pulled on a comm-set, so he could talk to Heskith over the whine. "Checking control surfaces and engine vectoring."

The controls responded and the aircraft juddered as the turbines rotated on their gimbaled mounts. Nothing showed red on the displays though.

"Okay, I'm taking her up."

Heskith circled his thumb and finger in an "okay" sign.

Logan pulled back the flight controls, easing the large transport into the air, scanning the instruments for signs of trouble. The scream of the turbines increased in pitch as their RPM climbed to produce the right amount of thrust. Takeoff was one of the most stressful points in a flight, and where the engines would most likely blow if they were going to.

Removing his hands from the controls, Logan checked to see if the Futen would maintain its altitude. It shook, and every surface rattled violently at the loading from the engines, but that was normal, and no warning lights triggered.

"Let's take her out," Logan said.

He turned the Futen, pushed the controls forward, and it edged toward the shimmering holo-projection. Their view flickered as they crossed the threshold, then they were outside in the tree-lined passage, the bright sky visible through the purple-looking fronds that closed over the river.

The instruments flashed red, forming a painful stroboscopic pattern of warnings. Logan heard a high-pitched screech, and the Nomad slid right, toward the real rock face. Heskith grunted, then Logan caught the slide and corrected. A moment later the engine cleared and the warning lights returned to green.

"What was that?" Heskith called out.

"Power fluctuation. Need to double-check the couplings. They might not be fully seated."

"We going back in?"

Logan shook his head. "Not if we want to make Manners happy."

The Futen's engines tilted to increase the horizontal thrust, and they darted along the river. Logan activated the EM Cloaking systems to make them less detectable. It would be dumb getting detected on a shakedown cruise. When the tree passage opened up, he pulled the flight stick back, increasing their altitude sharply before leveling off at three thousand meters.

"Seems okay now," Logan said. "The controls are a bit off. I'm having to compensate for some drift, but not enough to be an issue."

"It's kinda lonely up here." Heskith's voice crackled over the comm-set. "Feels like we're bare-ass naked."

Logan pitched the Futen back down toward the sea and relative safety. There was no point pushing their luck.

They dropped until the aircraft was skimming a few meters above the waves. Logan arced the Futen around, heading back toward Arakaki Bay. The glare from the sun would have made it difficult to see, but the image-enhancing cockpit filtered the light, overlaying a real-time display that made everything clear.

"Any idea what Manners is planning?" Logan said.

Heskith didn't answer right away, and when he did, his words were clipped. "You're asking the wrong guy. I'm not at that pay grade."

"The best thing would be to wait it out until we get some backup."

"You think any will come? Seems like a long shot. Besides"—Heskith stared through the window at the tree-lined coast—"the captain isn't the sit and wait type."

They were close to the river entrance now, and Logan guided the aircraft between the walls of trees. As the canopy closed above them, he lowered their speed to give them better maneuvering ability. "You're right, but I don't think it's the smartest thing to do."

They followed the winding river until they reached the cavern entrance. Logan's scalp itched as he brought them to a crawl, then edged back inside the caves. The rock illusion was far too realistic to make the passage entirely comfortable. He dropped the landing gear and lowered the Futen down to land. The hydraulics hissed as the gear took the aircraft's full weight. Once settled, Logan switched off the turbines and unstrapped.

"I'm going to double-check those power couplings. But you can tell Manners this thing is ready."

Heskith rubbed his hands together. "The captain will sure be happy to hear that." He unbuckled and clambered out of his chair, disappearing through the rear hatch.

The couplings all seemed firm, but Logan cleaned and reconnected them, trying to get the slightest speck of dirt off the surfaces. He was closing the cover when he heard footsteps approaching. He looked around and saw Gallego alongside the aircraft, frowning at the pockmarks in the damaged armor.

"This thing isn't pretty," she said.

"Best we've got given the time constraints." Logan tapped the hull. "It'll fly but I wouldn't push it too hard."

Gallego walked up and down the long fuselage inspecting it. She had a canteen with her and took a sip, then poked a finger inside one of the puncture holes. "*A beber y a tragar, que el mundo se va a acabar,*" she muttered, then looked at Logan. "Okay, wheels up. Let's get Diouf and the other strays."

Logan climbed through the side door and made his way to the cockpit. Dropping into the pilot's chair, he strapped in as Gallego did the same next to him. "Are you flying this, or am I?"

Gallego grimaced. "You've more experience with something like this. I'm used to fast-movers."

She used to fly interceptors, so Logan wasn't surprised at her willingness to let him take the controls. Flying something as cumbersome as the transport was a bird of a different feather—especially if the goal was to recover the AMTV. As Logan brought the turbines to full speed, Gallego leaned over, speaking louder to avoid using a comm-set.

"Just so you know—this isn't my idea."

Logan nodded. It was Manners dragging him into this ridiculous war. Kwelengsen was important, but a handful of poorly equipped soldiers and a bunch of civilians didn't stand a chance against the Corporates' elite forces.

The engines reached full power, showing none of the earlier glitches, and he smiled. But it was the briefest moment of self-congratulation. Despite the onboard cloaking systems and Gallego's presence, he had no doubts about how dangerous this mission was.

The die was about to be cast.

Chapter Twelve

"Have a vision not clouded by fear."
— Crazy Horse (Tȟašúŋke Witkó)

Gallego pulled a bulky remote-view helmet over her head, instead of the usual lightweight comm-set. It made her look like a cybernetic insect with the 3V projectors bulging out over her eyes.

"We're not going in alone." Her voice crackled over the comm-set. "I've got a fully-armed Shuriken online and ready for action."

Manners was taking the recovery of Diouf's party more seriously than Logan expected. "I'm surprised the captain would risk us *and* a drone unit."

There was an edge of sarcasm when Gallego answered. "Pah… It was my idea. I said we had no chance of pulling this off without fire support. *She* wouldn't risk another *crewed* aircraft."

"And she took your advice?"

Gallego's laugh was musical. "Sure. Once I told her I'd record an official objection in my notes if she didn't okay it."

That seemed more in keeping with Manners' recent attitude. He wanted to ask Gallego what she thought of the captain's behavior, but any cockpit transmissions could well be monitored.

Logan edged the Futen through the cave entrance and over the river. The night sky was purple-black, peppered with twinkling stars visible through the canopy. The length of time spent repairing the Futen meant they were late leaving, and Logan doubted they'd make it to Diouf's position and back before sunrise. Despite that, Manners had insisted they made the effort instead of waiting another day.

When they cleared the trees, he engaged the Cloak and lifted the Futen higher, while Gallego set up a series of waypoints heading northwest. "That's our route," she said. "It should keep us largely in regions shadowed from the Corporate sensor systems at New Hope. We need to stay below fifty meters though."

"And orbital recon?"

"Think small."

Logan grunted, transferring the waypoints into the live navigation. At that height, the autopilot wouldn't be able to safely follow the route and he'd have to baby the Futen. Which would make for a long, tiring journey.

"So much for technology," he muttered.

"I can only handle this thing on autopilot," Gallego said. "But once we're farther out we don't need to stay so low and we can take turns."

According to Gallego's information, Diouf had headed northwest, following the northern side of the Tuck mountains. That was on a direct route to Camp Botelho and away from the Corporates, but it wasn't the best choice. The only easy way to get to the mining station by land was via Daughety Bridge, a pontoon construction at the closest point between the Eagle archipelago and the mainland. If Diouf continued on the same course, her group would have to cross four hundred kilometers of sea, or follow the shoreline north for several days.

"Maybe Diouf was just putting distance between her and the enemy," Gallego said when Logan pointed out the problem.

"Possibly. The AMTV might be capable of crossing that much water, but the foot traffic with her wouldn't have a chance."

"Long shot, even for the AMTV." Gallego sounded unconvinced.

Their course took them up the west of the Baraban range, near the point where Logan and Giorg had crossed on their way to the base. Farther north, they'd hop between the Baraban and the Tuck ranges, before curving westward to pick up Diouf's trail. It was a long journey and, even at low speed, wouldn't have been possible without the power packs from the crippled Futen.

They'd been flying for over an hour when Gallego grabbed Logan's arm and stabbed her finger at the floor. "Put us down. Now!"

There wasn't much choice of landing spots, but Logan lowered the Futen into a large clearing. The wash from the turbines turned several large trees into matchwood as they dropped, and the Futen sank into the muddy ground. He looked across at Gallego. "What is it?"

"The drone picked up several scans—a combination of Reconsat pulses, and something closer."

"Looking for us?"

"Possibly. Might be part of a routine sweep though." Gallego gripped her armrests. "We'll know soon enough. The local signals will be on us any minute."

"What about the Shuriken?"

"Already on the deck. Kill the engines. Silent mode."

Logan switched everything off but the Cloak, leaving only a slight buzz from the cloaking field, plus an occasional creak and pop as the Futen dipped farther into the dirt.

Glancing out of the window on his right, Logan spotted something partly buried. "Is that what I think it is?"

"They're within five kilometers," Gallego said. "Following a northwest course."

Logan stared at the mound. When he'd first seen it, it had looked like a twisted mess of roots and rocks poking up from the ground. Then his brain resolved the shape. It was another Futen. He hadn't recognized it immediately in the faint moonlight because it was coated in mud, and all that was visible was the smashed-up cockpit. The large aircraft was wedged deep into the ground.

Logan guessed it had crashed either during the original invasion or not long after it. The bones of the cockpit frame and the front of the fuselage were nearly unrecognizable in the semi-darkness. Moss was already growing over the metal and composite surfaces. The cause of the crash was anyone's guess, but more critically, it showed that the clearing wasn't the haven it appeared from the air. Their Futen lurched, and a sharp pop bounced around the cockpit area.

"What the hell?" Gallego grabbed the frame next to her.

"We're sinking," Logan said. "We need to get out of here."

"If we move, we're done for," Gallego hissed. "That drone is right on top of us."

Gallego was wearing the helmet, so Logan wasn't sure what she was seeing. If she was hooked into the drone, she might not be aware of their circumstances.

"We must be on quicksand. And judging from that wreckage, it's deep enough to swallow us whole. If we don't move, we're going to be trapped. And it's a hell of a long walk back."

Gallego held up her hand. "They're overhead," she whispered.

Logan strained to hear but couldn't pick anything out clearly. He thought he detected a slight whistle over the general noise in the aircraft, but so indistinct it might have been his imagination.

"Lieutenant—" Logan stopped as they lurched once again, the whole cabin tilting left as though they'd slid off an island of stability.

Gallego didn't answer. Logan watched the display as the enemy drone slid over them, traveling eastward, a faint, nearly imperceptible star passing through the sky.

"You know what it's like when you get that sinking feeling..." Logan muttered. "Can we take it out?"

"Sure, but then they'd know something is here."

"If I don't restart the engines there may not *be* anything here."

The engines would have the lift to stabilize them and should pull them out, as long as they weren't already too deep. But every minute they waited would make it harder. The nose of the Futen tipped, pitching at least ten degrees down, and Logan grabbed the controls. "We *have* to move."

"One minute," Gallego said. "Then the drone will be over that ridge."

Logan flicked several switches, risking powering up the systems. A few seconds might make the difference between escaping or being completely stuck.

The drone's track vanished from the display, and Gallego slapped his shoulder. "Go!"

Logan jammed the throttle forward, bringing the turbines up to operating speed. When he tilted the thrusters down, the Futen twisted and rocked as if they were riding a horse that had been bitten by a snake. It lifted and leveled, then stopped. A painful vibration shuddered through the superstructure as the engines fought to drag them clear of the boggy ground. Every second of high thrust sapped precious power they could ill afford to lose. Even with the spare power packs, this mission was at the edge of the aircraft's flight range.

He found himself in a dilemma. A large amount of thrust in one boost might lift them clear at a high cost to their energy reserves. But if he tried to "tiptoe" free, it could end up draining the power packs more as it would take longer to pull them out.

He nudged the thrust control up.

"Logan... you have to—" Gallego sounded alarmed for the first time.

"I know."

The Futen lurched upward, almost coming away clean, but something snagged the front undercarriage, and they spun sideways, tilting dangerously and dipping one of the turbines close to the swamp. The thrust from the turbine sent a towering funnel of mud arcing several meters into the air, and a spray of liquid soil splattered across the cockpit.

Logan corrected the motion, and the nose came free, the aircraft bolting skyward like a champagne cork. Playing with the controls, he flattened their trajectory to keep them as low as possible and stabilized their course. He glanced at the threat display, but it was clear.

"The drone?"

Gallego grinned under her visor. "Heading due east. They didn't pick us up. That was some crazy flying."

"I learned from the best." Logan was thinking that his friend Joe would no doubt chuckle at such a wild maneuver.

"Well, I'm sure glad you're at the controls and not me." Gallego laughed. "The Shuriken is back in the air too. Let's get our people."

An hour later, the first pale splinters of light were breaking upward from the horizon, and they'd passed through the lower passage between the mountain ranges. The crossing was simple enough, and they were still shielded from direct detection from New Hope, but Logan felt increasingly exposed as the trees thinned and they passed over more and more rock.

"Won't be long now." Logan read the navigation display. "Should reach Diouf's group in about forty-five minutes."

It wasn't a moment too soon. Along with the imminent approach of daylight, their power reserves were edging toward the twenty-five percent line, and the flight back would be tougher as they'd be carrying the AMTV as well as the people. Manners had made it clear that rescuing the vehicle was her prime concern.

A transmission light flashed green, but Logan heard nothing on his comm-set. He glanced over at Gallego and noticed a hard edge to her jaw—the only part of her face visible. Presumably, she was getting a coded message on a military channel. "Rourke's made another broadcast." She took a deep breath and turned away.

Fear tore at Logan's insides like a rusty ripsaw dragging at a piece of lumber. "They relayed it to you?"

Gallego shook her head. "Only a summary. The bastards killed another bunch of hostages."

Logan waited for Gallego to say more. Finally, he had to ask, though part of him didn't want the answer. "Aurore?"

"I'm sorry, Logan..."

The words buzzed in his ears like a chainsaw on overdrive, and his knuckles whitened as he gripped the controls. Then he realized Gallego had continued talking.

"They didn't mention your wife," she said. "It must be awful for you after..."

Logan's breath released in an explosion. He hadn't realized he'd been holding it in. "Were any of the victims identified?"

Gallego hesitated. "Not that I know of." She flipped up the visor for the drone's alt-real display and looked Logan in the eyes for the first time since they'd set off. "You really think they're faking all this?"

"I'm certain of it."

"But why? Believe me, the Corporates have no reluctance to use violence and abuse. You must have heard about the Dresden Incident."

The incident was a mismanaged demonstration by a group of

young radicals over fifty years back. They'd been protesting large corporate funds and enterprises being shipped off-Earth to orbital residences and production facilities. Every company with the means was asset stripping its Earth-based operations, as numerous nation-states implemented responsibility laws designed to stop exploitation of people and Earth's resources.

The protesters had sneaked inside the International Congress Center in Dresden where the Commerce Executive, a group representing the combined interests of the larger Corporates, was negotiating with representatives from Old Europe. Despite a heavy security presence, the protesters managed to barricade the building, trapping the negotiators and demanding concessions and guarantees over future Earth-side employment ratios.

Twenty hours later, soldiers from BlackISE, the private security group preferred by the Corporates, made an assault to rescue their people. Although no one would normally have criticized that, the soldiers shot everyone on sight, unless they were wearing electronic Corporate ID tags. That included the local security guards and seven members of the European negotiating team. Only one person inside, other than the Corporate negotiators, came out alive. Something BlackISE described as an "oversight."

Despite the reminder, Logan didn't change his mind. "I can't explain it. But I know my wife is out there somewhere. And I know she's safe."

Gallego searched his face. "How can you be so sure after everything that's happened? And everything you've seen?"

"I guess you'd have to call it instinct." Logan smiled softly. All those years with Joe, he'd never been able to explain why he felt the way he did about certain things. Some might claim it was spiritual—his ancestors believed everything was connected—but that wasn't how Logan saw it. When he was younger, he'd questioned how he made those decisions when he had no rational explanation. Was it his subconscious mind aggregating details he wasn't aware of? Or an understanding that the Universe worked in specific ways? Whatever it was, it was rarely wrong, and he'd learned to trust it.

"The Corporates want us off Kwelengsen," Logan said. "They

want the planet for themselves."

"Of course." Gallego nodded. "It's the only viable piece of real estate we've found out here so far."

"Could they hold up against the combined Earth fleets?"

Gallego thought for a while. "Hard to say. We don't know what strength they have anymore. It's unlikely, but might be close."

"And what about their markets? Despite everything, they still sell over half of what they produce to Earth." Logan eased the controls to the left. "The Atolls buy some supplies from them, and that's increased since the Phage attacks, but not enough to make up for that kind of loss."

"You're right, but so what?"

"Kwelengsen's population is made up of members of every nation-state. Our leaders may not kick up much of a stink if the Corporates take over the planet and a *few* people die in the process. But it would be all-out war if it was carried out through brutal mass executions."

The alt-real visor clicked shut as Gallego pulled it back down over her eyes. "Nice theory. But I'm not sure the politicos care as much about their citizens as you think."

Logan checked their route. They were within thirty minutes of the meeting place. "I'm sure you're right. But politicians are sensitive to one thing—votes, or rather the lack of them. Can you imagine what would happen in the next elections if they let the Corporates willfully murder thousands of people's relatives and friends?"

Gallego's laugh came out as a bark. "Let's hope we don't find out."

They had a comm-link connection to Diouf, but up to now hadn't used it. Although there was no known way of decrypting a q-band link, the fact that it was operating could give away their location, so it wasn't worth the risk. But now they were close enough to need detailed information on how to find the group. Logan opened the channel, while Gallego monitored the area around them, using the drone's powerful sensors.

"Sergeant Diouf, this is Logan Twofeathers. We're approximately two hundred klicks from your position, following heading two-zero-eight degrees. Stand by for coded location packet."

He transmitted their current position, speed, and heading. That would allow Diouf to guide them to her position, and give them accurate estimates of when they'd reach her. A short time later, a routine acknowledgment signal came back, followed by the necessary course information. High-level cirrus clouds were showing pink on the horizon, and a thin band of blue was brightening by the minute, making Logan uneasy.

"I don't like this. Why no voice acknowledgment?"

"Minimizing transmission data?" Gallego said. "The LZ looks clear."

"Something isn't right." Logan glanced at the instruments.

"I'm not seeing anything," Gallego said. "This another of your hunches?"

According to the corrected navigation information, they were around eighty kilometers away. Not inside visual distance at their low altitude. But something still troubled Logan. He slowed the aircraft, dropping the Futen until they were half buried in the treetops.

"What are you doing?" Gallego hissed. "We don't have time to play games."

"I know." The power levels were below twenty percent. "Send the drone in ahead of us. If it shows clear, I'll follow it right in."

Gallego bit her lip, and he saw her Adam's apple moving. He guessed she was talking to someone back at the base, and it was likely a direct line to Manners.

"Okay." Gallego manipulated the controls. "Taking her in for an eyeball pass."

Logan put the Futen in hover mode. The main display flickered then stabilized, showing a viewpoint skimming over the trees. Gallego was relaying the optical display from the Shuriken. The drone was making good speed, but slowed as it approached the designated meeting place. There was nothing visible, then a highlight designator flashed on the right-hand screen. Diouf had transmitted updated location information.

"Probably wondering where the hell we are." Gallego altered the path of the Shuriken, sending it to the updated location.

"Slow down," Logan said. "Otherwise we'll see nothing."

"Don't tell me how to do my job. Jeez, this is stupid."

The drone slowed though, and it became easier to see the ground through the trees. Logan spotted the tracks first—a pair of churned, muddy trails, wide enough to be from a set of balloon tires. A moment later, the gray, bulky form of the AMTV came into view under the tree canopy.

Gallego swung the Shuriken around, losing track of the vehicle. Moments later, the drone passed over the AMTV again. There were several people stood around and, judging by their ragged, mismatched clothes, they were civilians.

"There!" Gallego called out. "So much for your instinct."

Logan had to admit it looked clear. The trouble was he couldn't rationalize why he felt uneasy, and Gallego would insist they moved in right away.

"Taking us in." Logan lifted them out of the treetops and nudged the throttles, moving the Futen at a speed not much more than a brisk walking pace.

"Why are you wasting time? We know they're there. Those are our people."

"Ancestral instinct."

"Logan, you're out of your goddamn mind. Manners knows what's happening. She's been tracking us all the way."

"That doesn't matter. I'm telling you—something is wrong."

Gallego paused before speaking again. "I have new orders. Turn the Futen over to me."

"Then who flies the drone?" Logan said with more calm than he felt. "I'm not experienced enough to handle that when things go wrong."

"I'll switch it to Autonomous Mode. I'm relieving you of any responsibility."

"I'll hand over control once we're grounded and have established contact with Sergeant Diouf. But not before."

A sharp click bounced around the cockpit, and Logan glanced at Gallego. She had her service pistol pointed at him.

"I'm sorry, Logan. That wasn't a request. I have direct orders from the captain."

Logan turned back to the instruments, keeping his hands on the controls. "If I'm wrong, we'll soon know. It can't be important enough for you to risk crashing."

Logan heard another, softer, click and wondered if she'd charged her weapon to fire.

"I've disconnected the transmission to the captain," Gallego said. "They can't hear us, but they can still track us. At this range, they won't have a good idea of what we're doing—or how fast we're traveling."

"Okay."

"What makes you so sure you're right?" Gallego hesitated. "Seriously. Explain it to me."

Logan thought about it. They were a few kilometers from where the AMTV was parked and would be there in minutes. Whatever had him on edge had to have a rational basis. There had to be something he could offer to justify his gut feeling.

Mentally, he reviewed what they'd seen as the Shuriken had crossed over their destination. The AMTV's gray, boxy shape was sheltered under the trees. People were casually standing around. They didn't react to the drone, but Logan doubted any of them were aware of it hidden behind its cloaking systems. Then it hit him.

"Did you see any children?" he said.

"What? No, why should—"

"There were at least eight or nine children with the group when I met them before. Where are they?"

"Sleeping?" Gallego sounded scornful. "It *is* dawn."

"Do you know any group of children of mixed ages where you wouldn't have at least a few of them milling around at all times? Especially when they're expecting to be rescued."

"Maybe nobody told them." Gallego's shoulders rounded. "Or they were all partying into the night. Who knows?"

"Even if the kids didn't know we were coming, would their parents leave them in bed?"

The AMTV was less than two hundred meters away. Logan had been slowing the closer they got. Now he wanted to run.

Gallego was intent on the data coming from the drone. "There's something... The Shuriken's picking up faint traces of... Incoming!"

The threat display flashed multiple times, and Logan spotted at least three missile tracks closing on them. The proximity warning was squawking continuously, the pitch rising as the missiles closed. He slammed the controls over, and the Futen snapped to the left, then back again as he threw the aircraft in the other direction. "Can they track us?"

"Ask me another," Gallego shouted, as the turbines whined with the violent maneuvers. The threat warning lit up again as another wave of missiles flashed toward them. "I'd say they're getting a partial lock."

"Who?" Logan pitched the nose down, weaving between several stands of trees, and bolting away from the AMTV.

"I have signatures for one—no, two—attack drones coming through. Here."

Gallego relayed the information from the advanced sensors on the Shuriken to the displays. The enemy drones winked into existence as red blobs, circling them like angry wasps. As soon as the information was available, similarly red warning triangles appeared on the cockpit windows, displaying the relative direction of the enemy aircraft.

"I'm tracking them. Got a lock. Preparing to fi—oh shit."

A new blob flickered on the display, larger than the other two. "What's that?" said Logan.

"Another Futen. They're locking missiles."

"Hang on." Logan dropped the aircraft into a gully, the right front engine clipping the edge and throwing a shale-encrusted mud shower into the air. The run was barely wide enough for them but offered temporary protection—at least until it ran out.

"Are you sure you—?" Gallego shouted, barely audible over the turbine noise. "Missile launched. Positive track."

Ours or theirs? The ravine they were following narrowed ahead, and Logan arced the aircraft upward, before killing the power to drop them back into the trees. How were the Corporates managing to field so much equipment? The ship he'd seen in orbit was big, but not large enough to carry what they were seeing on the ground, especially considering the enemy had lost several vehicles.

He focused on their attackers. The enemy aircraft was closing from the right, hopping over the treetops, while the two drones were circling around to cut them off in a pincer movement.

Logan activated the weapons controls, letting the missiles "see" the other Futen. A few seconds later, the lock whistled, and he pulled the trigger, launching several projectiles in its direction.

The missiles from the drones were still chasing them, and he turned hard left, scattering a stream of decoys behind the aircraft. The enemy was using the same gear and had a greater familiarity with it. Something flashed on the right, and a gout of orange flame rolled into the sky.

"One down," Gallego yelled. "Second drone is closing."

Logan threw the aircraft the other way, heading toward the mountain lowlands, hoping to find cover in the rocky passes and ravines. The enemy aircraft fell in behind them. It was a drag race into the rougher terrain. The other Futen made no headway, but the drone was faster. For the meantime, Gallego was keeping it occupied with the Shuriken, but it was a battle she'd eventually lose.

Another volley of missiles shot out at them, detonating against the rocks as Logan plunged their aircraft into another ravine. Ahead, he saw a rocky arch closing over the gully.

"Logan, I don't think we're gonna—"

The orange-brown rocks hurtled past, and Logan checked the rear display. The enemy Futen was chasing along the ravine too, only a hundred or so meters behind them. He saw flashes from the enemy's guns, and a split second later heard trip-hammer *thunks* as the needles slammed into the rear of the aircraft and engines.

The archway ahead formed a cave open at both ends, but it ran much deeper than Logan had estimated. Going through would be suicide under normal circumstances, but these were anything but. He brought up the weapons systems and targeted the rocks, waiting till the last minute to trigger the missiles.

The Futen plunged into the relative darkness, and for a moment Logan was blind. He spun the engines, using maximum braking. In the display, he saw the entrance fill with gouts of orange, billowing flames as the missiles detonated on the rocks, then the sky darkened as a cloud of deadly rocky fragments packed the entrance.

Logan could only imagine their pursuer's reaction, but nothing came through the cloud.

"You're certifiable," Gallego shouted.

"More than likely. But I'm also goddamn angry." Logan reversed the Futen from under the arch at a speed that had Gallego clinging to her seat.

The entrance was piled with fresh debris but was open, and they backed out into bright sunshine. The enemy had lifted to overshoot rather than risk flying through the maelstrom he'd left behind, and was now turning at the far end of the tunnel, waiting for them to emerge. Logan lifted their aircraft to target them. The lock shrilled. He squeezed the trigger, launching a full volley at the enemy.

The Corporate pilot had no time to respond. Logan doubted they had the chance to detect the launch. A second later, the enemy craft exploded, fiery trails arcing away as it plummeted to the rocks below. He didn't wait to gloat over the impact—there was the other drone. It could take them out as easily as the enemy Futen.

"Where's the other one?" he shouted, spinning their aircraft in search of it.

"It's okay. You can breathe. It's just sitting there."

Logan glanced at the threat display and realized Gallego was right. The drone floated over the rocks, not moving. "What happened?"

"Must have been on manual." Gallego operated the Shuriken controls, and a moment later, the enemy drone exploded. "Playing safe—didn't want someone to take it over by remote."

"Let's see what's down there."

Chapter Thirteen

"The skin of civilization is as thin as gossamer, and just as easily torn."
— Grandfather Twofeathers

Logan turned the Futen to take them back to the wooded area where they'd spotted the AMTV. Neither of them spoke, though Logan noticed Gallego silently reporting on the military channel. Ten minutes later, he set the Futen down in an open area near the armored vehicle. After unstrapping, Logan headed for the rear door, but Gallego stopped and pulled a short rifle and a pistol out of a locker.

"You should take this." She held out the pistol.

Logan looked at it for a moment. "I'm interested in rescuing people, not killing them."

Gallego jiggled the pistol, then tossed it on Logan's seat. "You can't be a bystander every time. Sometimes it's unavoidable."

Logan had been reminded of that all too recently, but despite that, he didn't feel that adopting a martial approach to everything was the answer.

The sun had crept over the horizon, and the sky was a rich, deep blue. But despite how pleasant it appeared, at this latitude, the winter chill turned their breath into foggy patches that drifted in the cool northerly breeze.

They edged their way forward. Gallego looked around at every step, scanning the ground as well as the bushes for anything that might indicate a trap. When they reached the closest figure, they saw it had been propped up using branches to set it into a roughly natural pose. Convincing enough to fool anyone checking the site from the air, but close up, the body was a brutal mockery of life.

Gallego lifted the man's head, and Logan winced. A single black hole had been drilled into his forehead by a needle round. "That's Jack Durden, one of the power generation guys."

"Friend?" Gallego said.

"Not especially." Logan looked away and shivered. "He was among the first to come here. An old-timer."

Gallego nodded. "I can do this myself, if you—"

Logan held up his hand. "I owe these people at least this much respect."

Gallego moved to the next one. "Keep an eye out for booby traps. God knows what those sick bastards have done here."

Logan didn't need the warning. Anyone who could arrange such a deception was capable of anything. He picked up a stick and examined another body, poking around it and moving the clothes to reveal anything out of the ordinary.

"That was Anna Binoche. She was a MedTech." Logan swallowed hard. He'd never had to face such wholesale barbarity before, not even when Gabriella, the mercenary, had tried to gut him at the top of the USP Space Elevator. "None of these people were soldiers. They were friends, neighbors, parents, husbands and wives."

Gallego grimaced. "Corporates don't give a damn about anyone unless they can make money from them."

They worked through the grotesque display, moving closer to the AMTV sheltered under the largest tree, the fan of its branches forming a protective umbrella.

Every person had a single needle shot to the head, execution-style. Waves of shock made Logan dizzy, and his feet dragged in the mud. These people weren't a threat to anyone—their deaths were completely unnecessary. One figure was left—tied more elaborately to an "X" formed by two heavy branches.

Logan knew who it was before they got close, the CEG uniform, ebony skin, and muscular build giving him all the clues he needed. Gallego checked for traps but found none and lifted the corpse's head. It was Diouf.

Unlike the others, Logan couldn't see any sign of a needle hole, though her midriff was thick with dark, oozing blood. She was hanging with her chin down and her body at an angle, so it was impossible to see clearly, but Logan got the impression she'd been gutted.

"What the hell?" Gallego's jaw clenched. "Why would they—"

Diouf's eyes opened, and her mouth sagged.

"Jesus!" Gallego tore at the zip-ties holding Diouf to the crossed branches. The sergeant's mouth opened and closed, and she gurgled as though she were choking.

"Children. In the—"

"Don't speak," Gallego urged. "Shit, the medikit's in the Futen."

Logan turned, but stopped as Diouf spoke again.

"Don't... children... AMTV..." The words were a sickening, wet rasp, and blood and bile oozed out of Diouf's mouth, dribbling down her chin.

Gallego removed another of the zip-ties, and Diouf fell. Gallego caught her, struggling with the sergeant's larger bulk. Logan jumped across to help, and together they lowered Diouf. Her mouth was working, thick rivulets of blood washing down her neck.

"Get the medikit!" Gallego barked. "Quick."

Logan stood, but Diouf grabbed Gallego's collar and fought to speak again.

"Children—" She let out a long wheeze, then collapsed back, her powerful hand losing its grip.

Gallego lowered her ear to listen, then looked up at Logan. "She's gone."

"She didn't deserve that."

"No one does." Gallego wiped the blood off her hands on the ground next to Diouf, then jumped to her feet. "The children are in the AMTV."

"Maybe, but—"

Gallego grabbed her rifle and marched toward the hulking transport. "You heard her."

Logan joined Gallego by the AMTV. There was a gentle popping as the tree above dropped its leaf polyps in preparation for winter, and they rattled against the vehicle's armor. In a week or so, every tree would be denuded and look like it was a long time dead, at least until spring arrived.

Then Logan heard something else. Like several small animals squeaking or squealing. A fear-filled ululation that rose and fell. But no animal on Kwelengsen made such sounds.

Gallego heard it too. "It's the children. They're inside, and they're alive."

"I understand. But we have no idea of what's really in there."

"It's the children, like Diouf said." Gallego was shaking, her eyes locked onto the back door. "Go upfront and take a look through the windows."

Logan nodded and made his way to the cab, dodging around the large tires and checking underneath. There were no signs of anything suspicious, and he soon reached the metal ladder bolted to the side. It led to the driver's door, and he scrambled up, keeping his head below the level of the window in case anyone was waiting inside. The armor here was thicker, and he couldn't hear the noises anymore. Edging along the vehicle, he crept higher to peek through a side window.

"The privacy screens have been activated," Logan called to Gallego, who was rocking from one foot to another. "I'll have to move around."

The windshield would be less dark, and Logan clambered along the fender to get a look inside. At first, he couldn't see anything. The glass wasn't as dark as the side window but was still enough to prevent a clear view. After a little while, his eyes adjusted and he detected movement inside. It wasn't clear, but it looked like the children were on the floor with their hands tied behind their backs. They might have been gagged too.

"They're in there. Alive from what I can see, but—"

"I'm getting them out," Gallego shouted.

"Wait. There might—"

Logan heard the clunk of the door being opened, and a fraction of a second later, the AMTV bucked underneath him. Instinctively, he threw himself backward as the armored panels split wide, and a deadly furor of whirling metal, glass, and streaks of white-hot flame surrounded him.

He spun through the air, and something hard hit him in the leg. His thigh felt as though it was being scoured of all flesh and muscle by molten steel, and he gasped as he flew back. He landed with a spine-numbing thud, coals of incandescent metal and plastic peppering the area around him, and he blacked out momentarily.

When he came to, the AMTV was engulfed in painfully white flames, the heat enough to burn his skin at a distance. Rivulets of molten slag ran down to congeal in hissing pools on the cold ground, sending up damp clouds from the sodden soil, but despite that, the fire raged.

Logan's skin burned and he was forced to crawl away from the flames. He had no choice—the enemy trap must have included some type of high-temperature thermal component. If he stayed close, he'd end up cooked.

Moments ago, the adults' deaths seemed like the ultimate depravity, but for someone to set such a trap using children as bait was monstrous. Some couldn't have been more than three or four years old.

He dragged himself to his knees, ignoring the pain from his leg. Lifting his hands into the air, Logan threw his head back and issued a primordial scream that echoed around the clearing, for a moment drowning out the crackling and hissing of the fire. He'd spent his life fighting to improve the world for people. That was why he'd gone into engineering in the first place. Drawn by the thought that, if he learned enough, and was smart enough, he'd be able to help people secure better lives, if only in small ways.

Now, it seemed everyone he had contact with, or tried to help, died. First Tepfer, then the settlers lost at the school. And now the children, Diouf, and Gallego. Manners and the rest would be better off if he never returned. For the first time, he gave weight to the idea that Aurore was dead. What would he do if she was? How would he manage? How could he ever forgive himself for getting her involved in this? It had been his idea for them to be part of the settlement efforts, after all.

He rolled onto his stomach, clawing at the ground, and choking, bitter soil muddied his lips as they brushed the frosty clay, like the antithesis of Aurore's warm kisses. The pain from his leg sharpened, and he turned back over to check it. A rough splinter of metal was buried in his thigh, dark blood oozing from the wound with every movement.

The sting of the cold air reminded him of their first winter on Kwelengsen. Aurore had insisted they went sledding and had arranged to print out a toboggan big enough for both of them. They'd joined dozens of others on the slopes outside town, spending hours sliding around like kids, before returning to their quarters and basking in the relative warmth, their bodies entwined.

Maybe he wouldn't survive. Perhaps he was as dead as the bodies around him. He focused on the sky, watching the clouds scurrying across, always moving. As if they had goals of such importance they had no time to stop, despite being nothing but water vapor that would sooner or later fall from the sky to mix with the earth and water below. That's what he wished would happen to him. That he'd dissolve into the ground, his atoms becoming part of Kwelengsen for all time.

Eventually, Logan dragged himself up from the ground using a tree stump. He stumbled almost blindly to the Futen and dug out the medikit, using a mixture of antiseptic wipes and local anesthetic to clean and treat the wound. Then he grabbed the metal shard and pulled on it.

The pain was so intense, he almost gave up. But he wouldn't be capable of flying the Futen with the debris stuck in his leg. It was embedded deep in the muscle, and he had to twist on it to loosen it, and finally, with a roar, he pulled it free. After cleaning the hole as best as he could with the wipes, he slapped on a dressing and sprayed the area with MediSkin to seal it. He pulled a folding shovel from its wall holder and limped back outside.

He moved the bodies to the center of the clearing, then examined the AMTV's remains. There was a dark mass a few meters away from where the rear door had been, and when he approached, he realized it was Gallego. Her face was burned and blackened to the point where she was nearly unrecognizable, and the rest of her body oozed blood from numerous holes, matting her charred uniform.

Logan lifted her in his arms, as though she were a child, and carried her over to the others. It didn't make sense to waste time over them. They were dead—beyond any help he could give. But he couldn't abandon them. Finally, he checked the AMTV itself. It wasn't something he relished, but he had to do it. The walls were gone, burned down to the vehicle bed. When he peered inside, there was nothing identifiable. All that remained of the children was dust that was already being picked up by the wind and blown away through the trees.

He hobbled back to the other bodies and began digging a hole next to them. It was difficult with the rocky soil, made harder by his wounded leg. After fifteen minutes, he was sweating, despite the low temperature, and stopped to remove his jacket.

"Logan Twofeathers."

The scratchy voice sounded from behind him and had a peculiar metallic edge to it. Logan turned and saw the black, diamond shape of the Shuriken drone hovering a couple of meters away.

"This is Lieutenant Brierton. Return to base immediately."

"I've got something to finish."

"Negative. Your continued presence on-site is a significant risk, both to our secrecy and your safety. The longer you remain there, the greater the chance that you'll be detected, captured, or killed."

"I'm busy." Logan lifted the shovel.

"This is an order from Captain Manners." Brierton's voice grew harsher. "Failure to comply is not—"

"Get lost."

Logan started shoveling again. He didn't hear it leave, but the next time he stopped, the Shuriken was gone. For a while, he wondered if Manners would order the drone to execute him, but realized that was unlikely while there was the slightest chance of getting her Futen back.

It took him over an hour to dig a hole big enough and deep enough. Then he placed the bodies in it, arranging them as though they were sleeping. Standing at the edge of the grave, he didn't know what, if anything, he could say, but they deserved something in recognition.

"I'm not much of a talker," he said, his words booming in the peace of the grove. "But these people didn't deserve what happened to them. May the Great Spirit watch over them, may the Circle turn their way again sometime."

He stayed silent for a minute, then covered the bodies and built a cairn with several rocks he'd dug up. He placed Gallego's piloting helmet on the top. Someday, people who knew the dead might be able to find them again. He hoped so.

Back at the Futen, Logan staggered to the pilot seat. The pistol Gallego had offered him was there, and he picked it up. He opened a storage hatch to put it away, then hesitated, staring at it. He pulled the gun from its belt clip, It was the same type of MalCheck pistol he'd used in the mountains. He pushed the gun back into the clip, fastened it to his belt, then climbed into the pilot's seat.

When Logan settled the Futen on the floor of the cave, a throng of CEG and MilSec soldiers rushed out of the passages around the area, Several of them were armed and most were scowling. After shutting off the turbines, he dragged himself from the seat and hobbled down the rear ramp. Some of the soldiers pointed their guns at him, but he ignored them, waiting for someone senior to arrive.

He hadn't communicated with the base on the flight back, partly because he didn't want to talk with anyone, but mostly because he'd been lost in his own thoughts. He'd hoped to escape the conflicts that surrounded Earth, but now that idea was nothing but a dream. Humans simply couldn't allow anyone to live that way. And if anyone tried, they were attacked—as his ancestors had found out to their bitter cost.

After a few minutes, Heskith muscled through the crowd, pushing down several of the raised gun barrels. "Awright, back to work, guys. You all know Logan. He ain't the enemy." Heskith moved up until he was standing in front of Logan and gestured at the aircraft. "The bird okay?"

Logan nodded. "Superficial damage. The energy cells will need a complete recharge, but other than that it's fine."

"I'm on it." Heskith jerked a thumb over his shoulder. "The captain wants a meet right away."

"I said the Futen's okay. I'm not." Logan pointed to his

blood-soaked leg.

"Ahhh shit... I'll roust up a MedTech and bring them over, but you better see Manners. Right now, she's angry enough to kill a rhison with her bare hands and eat it raw."

"Angry at me?"

The sergeant shrugged. "At everything. Something's going on, but don't ask me what."

Heskith led Logan through the throng. The crowd was dissipating, but he still had to bump people out of the way.

"I don't get it," Heskith said. "That was a big deal, you going after our people like that. Not to mention taking out those Corporate ships. But anyone would think we just lost the goddamn war or something."

"Where do I find a MedTech?"

Heskith stopped, turning to face Logan. "They usually hang out in the northern passage. There's a designated medical zone there. But please, Logan, see Manners first. Otherwise, she'll be chewing on my ass."

"Sorry, Hesky. This leg has been a partially open wound for six hours. I'm tired. I'm hurt. And I saw a lot of our people butchered for no good reason. So I'm putting myself first. If Manners wants to yell at me, she can do it while I'm getting treatment."

Heskith tugged at his ear. "Your call."

They backtracked and turned down a side passage on the right. This one was better lit than most, to make it easier for medical traffic. About fifty meters in, an area had been cut into the left of the passage to make a squared-off space about twenty by thirty meters. It showed evidence of the same polymer coating Logan had seen in Manners' office. Cots and beds were arranged throughout the space, some screened off, but most—thankfully—empty. Several figures in medical scrubs were milling between the closed-off beds.

"Doc, we got a casualty here," Heskith called out.

A woman looked around and gestured. "Bed seven."

Logan limped over and hauled himself onto it. He felt guilty, complaining of his wounds when so many others had died. But it wouldn't help anything if he ended up sick and sidelined. Heskith stood by the bed, fidgeting restlessly.

"I better get back to that Futen," he said.

Logan had the impression it was more that the soldier wanted to avoid the Manners explosion. "Sure, no point you standing about here. The doctors will fix me up in no time."

Heskith nodded, looking grateful at the chance to leave, and hurried away. After a short wait, the woman who'd responded earlier came up and jerked the curtains around the bed. Logan didn't recognize her and guessed she was MilSec. The badge on her tunic said "Havji."

She looked at Logan's leg and shook her head. "That's a mess. What happened?"

"Dog bite."

"Right..." She pushed the material of his pants away a little. "Can you take these off?"

Logan slid them off, grimacing as the fabric rubbed against the wound.

"Were you attended by a student carpenter?" She tutted. "That's the worst dressing I've ever seen."

"Thanks, I did it myself." Logan dropped his pants and lay back.

"Oh wait, you're the one from the—"

The curtains swished open. Manners was standing there, her normally pale skin suffused with pink. "One moment, Doctor. That man isn't to be treated. He's not part of the militia and doesn't qualify."

Havji continued examining Logan's wound. "Captain Manners... nice of you to stop by. Let me explain the function of a hospital. We treat wounded people. Regardless of their status."

"I'm giving you a direct order, Dr. Havji." Manners' voice was icy. If she hadn't already been angry, she was now. "This man's treatment is canceled until I say otherwise. His wounds aren't serious."

Havji straightened. "Thank you for your *medical* opinion, Captain. May I remind you that I'm the senior ranking physician, and treatment is at *my* discretion. I don't answer to you."

Manners hammered her fist into her hip. "Is his leg wound critical?"

"No." Havji bit her words out. "I could just let it drop off."

"There's no need for that attitude, Doctor. You may be MilSec, but it has been agreed I'm the leader of the joint resistance efforts."

"So go and do some resisting. And let me do my damn job."

It was obvious to Logan that neither woman would back down. "Doctor, is it okay if the captain talks to me while you check my leg?"

"If that's what you want." She gave Manners a sideways glance. "But don't think you can come in here and bully my patients."

Manners bristled then took a deep breath. "Thank you, Doctor. I appreciate that."

"I'm going to have to strip that MediSkin off so I can treat you. It's going to hurt."

Logan nodded. "I understand."

Havji started working on his leg, and Manners stepped closer. "Why didn't you call us?"

"I assumed it was better if I minimized comms traffic." Logan growled—Havji was pulling at the MediSkin patch. "Besides, I was busy flying."

"The autopilot wasn't working?"

"It works fine."

Manners brushed his answer off. "Have you heard what's happened?"

Logan snorted, then yelped as Havji probed the wounded area. "With all due respect, Captain, I flew back and came straight here. I haven't had time for chitchat."

"There's been another attack." Manners stared at him.

"By the Corporates? Who could they—"

"No, another attack on them. I thought..."

Realization dawned on Logan. "You thought I'd gone on a one-man vengeance mission? Perhaps I should have, after what I saw. But sorry, I was too busy trying not to pass out."

"*Your* mission was a tragedy," Manners said, her anger diminishing a little.

"Yes, there was no need for those lives to be lost."

"I meant the loss of the AMTV." Manners looked away. "It would have been a good addition to our forces."

Havji stopped. Her eyes caught with Logan's, and he shook his head in a tight movement.

"What about the attack?" Logan said.

"Rourke announced it in a broadcast." Manners clasped her hands behind her back. "They're going to double the number of executions unless the people responsible turn themselves in."

"And you believe it?" Logan winced as Havji cleaned his wound. "It's probably made up. Like all the rest."

Manners lifted a clenched fist. "We have proof."

"Oh?"

"We saw it. I had a second Shuriken in the air—watching New Hope in case they went after you and the others." Manners hesitated. "We thought it might be possible to warn you in time to..."

Logan wasn't sure he believed Manners. If she'd had the Corporates under observation, when had they set up the trap? They hadn't been waiting there by chance, and the bodies hadn't been sitting around in the wilderness for days either. Had someone tipped off the Corporate forces ahead of time? So they could arrange a trap with perfect timing? It didn't seem possible. As far as he was aware, few people knew of the plan, and none of those were likely to be in touch with the other side.

"The attack happened while you were on the way back." Manners' lips tightened. "You could have been part of it."

Logan sat up. "Who was it?"

Manners pretended to watch the medical monitor screen on the table next to the bed. "We don't know. But from what we could tell, they were using CEG equipment."

"You think some of your troops escaped the initial attack?" If that were true, there was a slight chance Aurore might be with them. That she might be okay.

"It seems the only reasonable explanation." Manners gestured at the pistol on the bedside table. "Does *that* mean you're ready to join the fight?"

"I'll fight. If I believe its the right thing."

"And if you don't?" Manners' tone was quiet, but threatening.

"Then I'll say I disagree." Logan gasped as Havji pressed a NanoBiotic dressing over his wound. "I'm not a soldier—I don't follow orders blindly."

"Well, I can't ask for more than that, can I?" Manners' smile made her face cadaverous. "We're trying to establish contact with this other group, but it's difficult. I'm sure you understand."

"This is your war, not mine. All I'm interested in is seeing as many people survive as possible."

"We have the same goals." Manners looked at Havji. "Doctor, how long will he need to stay here?"

"My patient is suffering from exhaustion and extreme blood loss. The NanoBiotics will fix him up, but it will take a minimum of three days." Havji held up her hand as both Manners and Logan opened their mouths to object. "I know. Let him at least sleep for eight hours. After that, most of the healing will have had a chance to take hold, and I'll release him for light work."

"Understood. Thank you, Doctor." Manners turned back to Logan. "See me as soon as you're up."

With that, she left, her boot heels leaving an echoing rattle behind her.

"She really is a hard-ass," Havji said. "If you need more time, I'll fight her over it."

"Thank you. You've done enough." Logan glanced down at his leg. "Is it going to be okay?"

"Your leg? Sure." Havji paused and whirled her finger in a circle. "All this? Who knows? But watch your back."

"Funny. I was going to tell you the same."

Chapter Fourteen

"Anything becomes edible with the right condiments—and hunger is the best seasoning."
— Grandfather Twofeathers

When he woke, Logan felt equal parts better and worse. His leg wasn't throbbing as much as it had been, and the pain seemed less angry. But at the same time, he was running a temperature, and his body ached all over. Havji walked across, a look of professional concern on her oval face.

"You look like hell," she said. "Take these."

Logan held out his hand and she dropped two off-the-shelf painkillers into his palm. "Do I call you in the morning?"

"No. Your body clock is fritzed, and so is mine." She smiled. "I've been on fifteen hours. Time to hit my bunk."

"Was there no one to relieve you?"

"Yes, but I stuck around in case our mutual friend came back."

Logan rolled his legs over the edge of the bed. "Thanks. You didn't have to do that."

"I know." Havji yawned. "I wanted you to get a solid ten hours."

"Ten?" Logan shook his head. "What happened to my pants?"

"I stole them so I could get a better look at those fine legs of yours." Havji grinned.

"I'm married."

"And I'm joking." She laughed, appearing a lot younger. "Sorry, I have a terrible sense of humor—not to mention bad timing.

Seriously, they were a complete mess. I tossed them and grabbed you some fatigues—in the drawer."

Logan got dressed while Havji waited.

"You'll pass," she said. "Watch that leg for the next few days. Put as little strain on it as you can. The NanoBiotics will make you feel crappy, so take painkillers if it gets too bad."

"Thanks, Doc."

"You can call me Neeta." She paused. "But don't call me after hours—my rates double."

"I'll remember that." Logan clipped the gun back on his belt and shifted his weight squarely onto both legs. "Not bad."

"Thanks." Havji covered up another yawn. "Sorry."

"Go on, scoot," Logan said. "I'll be fine."

"One thing, Logan."

"What's that?"

"I don't like repeat business, okay?"

Logan nodded, and Havji staggered off without looking back.

He should go to see Manners but was reluctant to face her so soon after waking. His stomach rumbled, and he limped to the settlers' cave to see if there were any rations available. He didn't care what it was, as long as it contained calories.

The cave was quiet, though there were a few early risers stumbling around. The table that had earlier contained only a few rations now housed a generous supply, which led Logan to guess that Manners' "recruiting methods" had been successful.

He grabbed a packet that claimed to be oatmeal cookies, along with some water, then checked the shelters he and Carl had set up. There was someone sleeping in his, and Logan didn't disturb them. There wasn't much point—he could sleep anywhere. When he checked Carl's though, there was no sign of occupation.

"They're not here," a woman called out, her voice rough, as if dazed from recent sleep. "All the militia people went into barracks."

Logan thanked her and hobbled to a small area where several folding chairs had been set out in groups. As he sat and opened his rations, a thin, rat-faced man walked by, then stopped abruptly. "Hey, Mr. Twofeathers. You shouldn't be in here with us. Soldiers eat in the official mess."

"I'm not a soldier," Logan said quietly.

"But Captain Manners said—well, it doesn't matter, no-one would stop you anyway." He pulled off a pair of wire-rimmed glasses and struggled to wipe them on his shirt. "But, you should go to the mess. Food's a lot better there."

"It's Jarret, isn't it?" Logan nibbled on a biscuit, then as quickly spat it out. Combat rations were never good, but this was stale beyond belief. "Are you eating there?"

"Me? Not a chance." Jarret shuffled over. "I don't have those privileges."

Jarret was in his mid-forties, with the type of thinning hair and squint that spoke of too much time working at a desk. If Logan remembered correctly, he'd worked in the administrator's office part-time, managing the tech systems as his community contribution. Though slightly built, there didn't seem to be any reason he shouldn't qualify for the militia—unless it was a matter of principle. The man looked in reasonable health.

"You don't want to fight?" Logan said.

"That isn't it. I have to think about the kids and all. They need better food than the crap they're giving us down here. But she called me useless because of this." Jarret held out his arm awkwardly.

"What happened?"

"Got caught in the attack. Explosion broke it and filled it full of shrapnel." Jarret's head dropped. "Lost Beth too. Now it's just me and the kids. I want to work, Mr. Twofeathers, I'm not one to sit around while there are jobs to be done. But—" He massaged his stiff elbow.

"What do the MedTechs say?"

Jarret looked away, his lips compressing into a bitter line. "They gave me a MediSkin patch and sent me on my way. They're not allowed to help civilians who don't sign up."

Logan suddenly didn't want to eat and dropped the stale rations onto a makeshift table next to him. "When did you and the others who can't fight last have a proper meal?"

"I don't know. Before the attack, I guess."

"Where's this official mess?"

"North Tunnel three. But"—Jarret looked worried—"Manners won't let us near it."

"She will today." Logan stood, a little unsteadily, due to the ache in his leg. "Gather up everyone in the same position as you, and we'll head over there."

Jarret's eyes widened. "Really? Manners will—I don't know what she'll do, to be honest. Shoot us?"

"She wants to talk to me anyway. Might as well do it over breakfast."

"Okay."

Jarret hurried away, and Logan headed to the entrance to wait. If they were short on supplies, that was one thing, but if the military personnel were living it up as part of their privileges, that was something else entirely. Ten minutes later, a bedraggled group had assembled, and Jarret came up carrying a girl who looked about two, while an older girl held onto his injured arm.

"That's everyone," Jarret said. "This is Missy and Flora. Say hello, girls."

The girl Jarret was holding waved, while the other mouthed an almost inaudible "hello."

"Need help with them?" Logan said.

"I'll manage. They're touchy with others... now."

Logan nodded, then faced everyone and raised his voice. "Okay, we're going to the soldiers' mess. Keep close, and be as orderly as possible. And whatever happens, don't worry."

Jarret led the group through the tunnels, and soon Logan realized they could have found their way to the mess purely by following the heady scent of freshly cooked food. By the time they finally turned into another large cave, he was drooling.

The mess cave was larger than the one used to house the settlers. It looked like the same tools that had carved out Manners' office had been used to open it up and give it a roomy ceiling. The flattened floor was packed with a number of tables and chairs that, while basic, were a significant step up from the broken-down amenities the civilians had to make do with. Along one side was a lengthy serving bar, stacked with a variety of large, steaming bowls, and even an array of what looked like fresh fruit. Several soldiers sat at the tables, and a man stood to attention by the bar, as if on guard.

Logan walked up and realized it was Carl. Without a word,

Logan took a tray from a pile and handed it to Jarret.

"What are you doing?" Carl hissed.

"These people need decent food. I'm making sure they get some."

"They're not authorized to eat in here." Carl glanced around. "I can't allow it."

Logan sympathized with Carl's plight, but it didn't change anything. "I'm sorry, nephew. They deserve decent food."

"I'm not your goddamn nephew." Carl placed his hand on a gun at his waist. "And those people aren't allowed to eat here. They have their own supplies."

Logan reached out and covered the hand Carl was resting on the pistol with his own. "Are you willing to shoot people for being hungry and sick?"

Carl's glance caught Logan's with a burning hatred. "Why are you destroying my life?"

"I'm sorry you feel like that," Logan said. "But it doesn't change anything."

Carl was silent for a minute, then twisted away from Logan's grip and stepped to one side. "Captain Manners will take care of you."

Logan turned to the settlers. Jarret and many of the others were looking around anxiously, as if expecting trouble any second. "Okay, everyone. Help yourselves." Logan gestured to Jarret. "Make sure everybody gets a good meal, but don't let them take too much. And make sure they clean up after themselves, okay?"

Jarret nodded and handed trays to people as they approached. Logan looked around to check the reactions from the other soldiers, but they were gone, no doubt to report to Manners. There was an old-fashioned rotary clock on the wall that showed it was five in the morning. The captain was going to have an unpleasant early call.

"After you finish here, go and find Doctor Havji in the medical center." Logan was talking to Jarret, who was busy feeding the two girls, though he hadn't yet eaten. "I'm sure she'll help."

"You think?"

"Tell her I thought she didn't have enough trouble and sent you."

A soft murmur of chatter had filled the cave, but now it stopped abruptly. Manners stood at the entrance, flanked by a lieutenant and two bulky sergeants: one CEG, one MilSec. She crooked her finger at Logan, gesturing for him to approach.

He patted Jarret's shoulder. "I better go. Good luck with the arm."

Manners' expression remained neutral as Logan approached. Carl took two steps closer, but she waved him back.

"I don't want a public confrontation, Logan." Her words were quiet, but her tone was as cold as a deep space comet. "You will follow me, however, and not make a fuss."

"Or?" Logan kept his voice at a similar level to hers.

"Or I might think to hell with it and have you executed in the middle of the mess hall."

Logan smiled. "You're far too smart for that."

"And you've acted like a stupid child. Are you coming?"

They left the mess, the hum of conversation already growing behind them.

"Are we going somewhere particular, or are you marching me to my execution?" Logan asked.

Manners kept her eyes straight ahead. "Be quiet."

After a short walk, they turned into Manners' office. Giorg sat at his desk but jumped to attention when they arrived. Logan noticed Giorg's uniform was disheveled, as though he'd been rushed in dressing. Manners, on the other hand, looked as though she'd spent an hour polishing her buttons.

"No calls, Private. No visitors of any kind. Not even if the Corporates come hammering on the front door…"

"Yes, sir."

Logan followed Manners behind the privacy screen. She walked around her desk, standing with her back to him, hands clasped behind her. She'd expect him to stand too, but his leg was bothering him, and he lowered himself into one of the chairs on his side of the desk.

After several minutes, Manners turned to face him, showing no sign of annoyance that he was sitting. "What do you want?" she said. "My job?"

"I'd like my old life back—wife, engineering, peaceful world." Logan sighed. "That's not going to happen any time soon though, is it?"

Manners glowered at him. "I get more trouble from you than every other person in this damn place."

"I'm sorry. But you're wrong to mistreat people. And when I see it, I have to do something."

"Something up to and including undermining my authority in a combat situation?"

"You gave those people food that was barely edible, while you and your soldiers ate a feast in comparison." Logan drew in several gasps of air. Manners' accusations needled him. "I thought they des—"

"I don't give a damn what you thought." Manners' nostrils flared, and she leaned over the desk. "Supplies are limited, especially food, so I allocated what I could to the non-productive members of the group. This ensures adequate rations for the people who are putting themselves on the line to preserve what little we have left."

"With you as the ultimate arbiter of who is worthless?"

"Yes." Manners stood back. "Yes, I am. I'm trying to hold everything together. We're buried in this cave. I have no idea when, or *if*, reinforcements will arrive. I've a limited number of experienced people mixed with the untrained and, in some cases, untrainable. And as if that wasn't enough, there's a rogue group out there stirring up the enemy, while a madman is executing and raping the people they've already captured."

Logan's stomach churned as if he'd been gut-punched. "I know the situation…"

"Well, why don't you act like you do?"

Logan leaned closer to the desk. "Didn't I show that I understood on the mission? If you'd seen those people, the children. All dead."

"Spare me the bleeding-heart liberalism," Manners snarled. "I know what you did. What you went through. You're not the first, and undoubtedly won't be the last. What makes you think that gives you any special privileges?"

"I don't think I have. But brutalizing our own isn't the answer.

Otherwise, we're no better than the enemy."

"And now you've created an expectation I can't satisfy. We don't have enough food to go around. Do you understand that?" Manners glared at him. "Who knows what you'll be up to next. I'm beginning to think my only option *is* to lock you up."

Logan stiffened. The expression on Manners' face told him she wasn't making an idle threat. "I guess you can do that. Though I don't imagine it will help your popularity."

"I'm not here to make friends."

"I understand that." Logan rubbed at his itchy leg. "So how about we work together?"

Manners lifted one eyebrow. "What did you have in mind?"

"Well, if what you say is right, it sounds to me like we need to do a supply run. I'll lead it."

"And I'm supposed to trust you?"

"No." Logan smiled grimly. "We'll have to trust each other."

Manners sat down, but she held herself tightly as if she'd explode if she relaxed. "Do you think we can, after what's happened?"

Logan thought for a moment. "How much logistical information have you got on the Corporate operations?"

"Nothing beyond what we've managed to gather from a few micro-probes. They knocked out our reconsats, and we've had no luck breaking into theirs." Manners looked apologetic. "My best tech specialist was lost in the invasion."

Logan frowned. If Aurore had been with them, she'd have had a good chance of accessing the Corporate systems. "How about maps of where they've set up?"

Manners activated the large screen. She brought up a plan of New Hope, then overlaid it with an intel data grid. Logan was familiar with the symbols from when he'd worked for SecOps and knew some of the enemy layout from the school break-out. "Most of the aircraft and related equipment are on the east side," he said. "The school is central. If your information is accurate, most of their people are housed in the buildings around that, and they're using our own warehousing in the south for supplies."

As they examined the military situation, Manners seemed to relax a little. "They've increased the guards around the aircraft and school since the attacks. But the warehousing is less well protected from what we know. But they'd be on us like a bad rash as soon as we went anywhere near it."

Logan peered at the screen. "When was this data collected?"

"That's from yesterday." Manners checked a display on her desk. "While you were away. Why?"

"That explains why one of their Futen transports is missing." Logan pointed to an empty area where the aircraft were sited. "Is there anything newer?"

"Lieutenant Brierton?" Manners said into the intercom. "Do we have any updates from the micro-probes?"

Brierton's deep voice sounded tinny over the speaker. "We have some updates that came in a while ago. But they aren't processed yet. Should be ready in a couple of hours."

Logan gestured to Manners. "Do they have any visuals on the aircraft yard?"

Manners waited while Brierton checked, and confirmed that they did.

"Create a new overlay of the visual data and send it through," she said, then turned back to Logan. "What have you spotted?"

"Just a gut feeling." A cold shiver tracked through Logan as he remembered his last conversation with Gallego.

A few minutes later, the screen beeped, and an indicator flashed showing new data was available. Manners tapped on it, and the images flickered.

"There. Do you see it?" Logan whispered.

"Nothing jumps out at me."

"Switch back to the previous data set." The image flickered again, and Logan indicated the aircraft area. "Expand that section and watch."

"I still don't see it."

"They have a full complement of Futen Transports," Logan said.

Manners leaned back in her chair and steepled her fingers. "You and Private Berardo stole two, and you destroyed another one in the fight over the AMTV, and yet they have six ready to deploy."

Logan nodded. "The same number they started with."

"They must have shipped extra vehicles. It's not unheard of in military operations."

"Okay, but would a military commander not use their full offensive complement in a battle?"

She reached behind her and pulled out a bottle of green tea—not offering Logan any. "There are tactical situations where that might be a valid option."

"Would you do that if you were invading a planet?"

"It's unlikely." Manners took a sip of her tea. "What's your explanation?"

"I think they're building them. That and any other equipment they need." Logan leaned forward. "Right here."

Manners snickered. "I'm sorry. How would they manage that? You're the engineer. Production of a single one of those aircraft would exceed all of Kwelengsen's current manufacturing capability."

"I know," Logan said. "They're manufacturing them in orbit."

"That's even crazier," Manners spluttered. "How the hell would that work?"

"I saw their ship before I was shot down. It's enormous—far bigger than any of ours."

"Big enough to hold spare aircraft?"

"Possibly. But think about it. They wouldn't necessarily know what strength of forces were stationed here, or whether the CEG would send reinforcements. The Corporates might have arrived here to find themselves overwhelmed."

"Or they load up on spare equipment and then deploy as necessary." Manners' jaw tightened. "They know we don't have ships large enough to carry the amount of hardware to challenge them."

"Have you heard of a UMAP?" Logan waited for a few moments. "A Universal Manufacturing and Assembly Plant. They've been used in industry for several decades."

"And you think they have one?"

"Not exactly." Logan tapped his chin. "They're usually limited in scale to a couple of meters in any given dimension. I think they have a super UMAP—something large enough to churn out a Planetary Lander, or pretty much anything else, overnight."

"Is that possible?"

"I'm not sure, I've never heard of one that big. But it's the only thing that makes sense. It would be huge, and they'd have to mine asteroids to feed it raw materials. But if I'm right, that would totally change the balance of power. No matter what we did, we'd never win. Whatever we destroyed, they could replicate in a few days."

Manners' face whitened, and for the first time since Logan had met her, she looked scared.

"You will not repeat this to anyone. Understood?" she whispered. "The effect on morale would be devastating."

Logan tended to agree. If the Corporates had such technology available, they'd be in a position to dominate every star system within Jump range. No Earth nation-state, not even a combine like the CEG, would be in a position to fight against such a tactical advantage.

"You think I'm right?" he said.

Manners shook her head slowly. "I don't know what to think. No JumpShip from Earth is as large as you've described. I didn't think it was possible to make them that size."

"Neither did I. But everything's theoretically impossible… until someone goes out and does it."

"How can I verify your idea?"

Logan thought about it. If they had a reconsat, or gained access to a Corporate one, they might detect supply traffic ferrying materials to the Corporate JumpShip. But both were remote possibilities. "We could send up a ship—the Nomad perhaps—and look for their supply ships. Or we could destroy a large amount of their equipment and see if they can rebuild it."

"Neither of those approaches is entirely practical," Manners muttered. "Is there any way to neutralize the advantage it gives them?"

"If we killed enough of their operators, we might reduce their capacity to fight, but autonomous technology is common enough. They could have several craft operated by one person."

"You make it sound impossible," Manners said.

"If my wife was here, she might come up with something."

Manners' eyes snapped from the screens to lock with Logan's. "That's not an option either."

"I'm well aware of that. So how do we get at their supplies?"

"*We?* We'd need a diversion to draw their forces away from the warehouses long enough for someone to get in and load up."

"The Futen has the capacity and stealth capabilities to do it without drawing too much attention. I'll pilot it."

Manners moved over to the large display. "Okay. We'd need to hit something big, that they'll try to defend. It would give us an opportunity to test your theory."

"Sounds interesting."

"We stage an attack on the aircraft, here." She drew a red circle around the location of the enemy Futens. "That would draw attention to that area and look genuine. Their aircraft are an obvious target."

"Could you sustain an attack for long enough?" Logan rubbed his jaw. "It would take at least thirty minutes to load the supplies."

"The answer to that is… maybe. But we have a different problem." Manners tapped the screen. "We'd have to deploy a significant force to look convincing, and the only vehicle capable of delivering our people is the Futen."

"So we'd need two operational?" Logan thought about it. "Can you spare Heskith and a few other people?"

"I could… if I thought there was a good enough reason."

"If we had a source of parts, it might be possible to repair the second one we stole."

"How are you going to do that? Walk into the Corporate supply depot and ask nicely?"

"Nope, but we may have an alternative."

Manners' eyebrows arched upwards. "If you're thinking about the one you shot down, you can forget it. There wouldn't be enough of it left to matter, and I can't authorize another journey all that distance."

"I'm thinking of something closer."

Logan outlined what had happened with the quicksand, and the crashed Futen they'd seen. "It's about two hours away. If we can pull it out, we can use it for spares."

Manners looked doubtful. "Would they be worth anything after being stuck in the mud?"

"Only one way to find out." Logan stood, regretting it as his leg nearly buckled under him. "It's the best chance we have to get the gear we need."

"I don't like it," Manners said. "But it seems to be the only option—better than dealing with food riots or starvation."

Logan ignored the barb, refusing to feel sorry for what he'd done. "If you have a better pilot, I'm happy to go along purely as a tech."

"I wish I had. Gallego was our sole remaining fully qualified pilot. No one else has anything but basic flight training."

This time Logan felt a sting of guilt, even though her death wasn't his fault. "So who's going to fly the other aircraft during the attack?"

"Private Berardo managed to get the Futen here."

"I'm not sure he's—"

Manners held up her hand. "The private will spend every waking moment between now and then in an Alt-Real sim improving his skills. I'll assign Heskith to work with you. He can choose who else he wants on it. But I'll be honest, I'm not expecting much."

"Understood." Logan moved to leave.

"Don't think this somehow makes us friends," Manners said. "I'm watching you. And if you step out of line again, I'll throw you in a cell. Regardless of the consequences."

Chapter Fifteen

*"I have seen that in any great undertaking it is
not enough for a man
to depend simply upon himself."*
– Shooter (Okute)

Logan headed to the entrance cave to check the Futen's condition. As far as he knew, other than a few improvised ventilation holes and the fact that the power-packs needed charging, it was in good shape after the last flight. As he was poking around, he heard some chatter behind him and turned to see Heskith accompanied by several other soldiers in a mixture of CEG and MilSec uniforms.

"Damn, Logan. You must have a Teflon ass," Heskith bellowed. "I was sure the captain would bang you up for that latest stunt."

"Feeding hungry people isn't a *stunt*."

Heskith shook Logan's hand, then pointed at the group behind him. "Well, we're here under your orders. The captain said it was some kinda shopping trip."

"Not exactly." Logan smacked the Futen's hull, the boom reverberating around the cave. "Is she recharged?"

"Should be. Been hooked up since you came back."

"Do we have any flotation bags in the supplies?" Logan said.

Heskith rubbed his jowls. "The MilSec guys might have some."

"Grab them. However many they have."

"What if someone objects?"

"Send them to Manners. And take the gear while they're gone."

Logan grinned. "We also need a couple of sets of diving gear and some heavy-duty line. Plus chains for hoisting, and a cutting torch."

"Sure thing. I'll drop down to the nearest Johnson's Hardware."

Logan slapped him on the shoulder. "Do your best."

Movement from behind the soldiers caught Logan's attention. Lieutenant Morua was approaching with four others in assorted uniforms.

"Hello, Zarah." Logan smiled. "What brings you this way?"

"Official duties," Morua said, as serious as usual. "We're your escort."

"I didn't ask for one."

"The captain thought you might need the extra protection." Morua leaned in and continued in a whisper, "I don't think you can refuse."

"I've no reason to."

"This is my team." Morua gestured at her troops.

Logan acknowledged them, then did a double-take as he spotted Carl at the back of the group, studiously avoiding eye-contact. Logan almost hadn't recognized him as he was sporting a newly shaved military-issue haircut.

"What's he doing here?" Logan said.

"Manners assigned him." Morua looked down, scraping her foot through the dusty ground.

Carl stood there chewing on a fingernail, pinpricks of sweat beading his forehead, despite the cool temperature in the cave. Logan was going to say Carl didn't have the experience for such a job. But he saw nothing but contempt in the boy's eyes and realized he didn't have the right to criticize Carl's decision.

Logan turned back to Morua. "We won't leave until Sergeant Heskith gets back. Until then, feel free to do whatever you like."

"If it's all the same, we'll wait here." Morua turned to the soldiers. "Smoke 'em if you got 'em."

"Suit yourself." Logan opened the Futen's rear ramp and climbed in, heading for the cockpit. The power packs were at ninety-five percent—already good enough, and they'd be full by the time Heskith returned. Logan ran through some checks to make sure he hadn't missed any problems earlier.

His review was interrupted by a cough. Carl stood behind the co-pilot's seat, twisting his CEG cap in his hands as though he wanted to say something, but wasn't sure what.

"If you're wondering if I'm going to ask the lieutenant to leave you behind," Logan said, "don't worry—I'm not."

Carl's face contorted as though he hadn't heard correctly. "You're not?"

Logan looked back at the diagnostics. "You're a grown man, you make your own decisions. I shouldn't interfere."

"But—"

"You made it clear." Logan sighed. "I was wrong. Wrong in bringing you to Kwelengsen and wrong in objecting to you joining the militia."

"Maybe I—"

"It's okay, Carl. You've decided to fight. I won't try to stop you. In fact, I'm joining you."

Carl looked puzzled. "You signed up with the militia?"

"No, but I'm working with Captain Manners. This mission was my idea." Logan swore the boy looked pale, though he had no idea why. "I thought you'd be pleased."

Carl looked away momentarily. "Guess so. I mean, sure."

"Go and be with your team. I need to finish here."

Carl nodded, his expression confused as he left. Logan turned to the instruments. It wasn't the reaction he'd expected. But how should Carl have responded? As if he suddenly decided Logan was the best person in his life? There was too much resentment and anger inside the boy.

Thirty minutes later, Heskith returned. He'd secured most of the supplies, and Logan helped the troops load them in the back of the Futen.

"Only found three flotation bags," Heskith said.

"That's three more than I hoped for."

"And we'll have to improvise the hoisting chains with an engine strap and some wire cable."

"It'll have to do." Logan waved to Morua outside. "Time to move."

"Okay people, you heard the man." Morua stood. "We don't need to be asked twice."

Two hours later, they were over the swamp where Logan had seen the remains of the other Futen. He brought their aircraft into a slow pass over the area, scanning the ground with the aircraft's sensors to gauge the extent of the marsh. In infrared, the wet areas showed clearly from the cooler soil around them.

"Do a couple of runs," Heskith said from the co-pilot's seat. "Should be able to combine the scans to highlight where it's shallower."

"Good idea." Logan turned the aircraft and swept the area again. After several extra passes, they had a clear map of the depth of the watery areas.

"Damn, we can't put her down close enough, and there's no good route in on foot," Heskith said. "Now what?"

"Let's drop everyone off out of the way." Logan drifted the Futen to one side and landed to let Morua and the others disembark.

Logan caught her as she was leaving. "Anyone in your team got any flight experience?"

Morua frowned. "Not that I know of. Why?"

"I need someone to fly this." Logan pointed to the Futen. "Carl, you ran construction drones didn't you?"

"Sure," Carl said. "They're easy though. But I couldn't handle that thing. It's way bigger."

"It's not much different when you're on automatic. You'll manage."

"Did you forget about me?" Heskith was by the rear ramp. "I can fly it."

"You'll be with me." Logan pointed out at the remnants of the Futen. "In the swamp."

"*In?*"

"Right." Logan turned back. "We're going mud diving."

"I don't like the sound of that." Heskith looked at the swamp and shivered. "I'm more your basic sun and sand type."

Logan climbed back on the Futen. "I'm open to other suggestions."

With Heskith and Carl on board, Logan lifted the transport back into the air and brought it over the shattered front of the wreck. Then he switched the pilot to hover and showed Carl how the controls worked.

"It's pretty simple. The control stick moves you left and right, forward and back. The throttle controls height, and the rudder pedals turn the craft. You try."

Carl moved the stick, and the Futen slid sideways then forward. "It's like the drones, but the controls are laggy."

"They operate in low sensitivity in this mode, but also this is a big machine to move around. Besides, we need control here, not speed." Logan smiled as Carl spun the aircraft around on its axis. "I'll back us up over the wreck. All you need to do is keep this one stable and follow instructions. Okay?"

Carl looked dubious. "I guess. We should head back. I mean, what if the Corporate forces show up?"

"Why would they?" Logan said. "They were here a few days ago and didn't find anything."

"But…" Carl turned away from Logan. "Nevermind."

"Don't worry." Logan patted Carl's shoulder. "You'll do fine. We'll use comm-sets to keep in touch."

Logan made his way to the rear of the transport where Heskith was waiting with the flotation bags and diving gear.

"What's the plan?" said Heskith.

"Suit up. We're going to get wet." Logan hit the door controls and the rear ramp whined into operation, lowering until it was fully open. The scream from the turbines was deafening as they fought to maintain altitude and position. The ramp was just beyond the nose of the downed aircraft. "Carl, nudge us forward about a meter," he yelled into his comm-set. The transport eased ahead. "That's perfect."

While Heskith was pulling on a diving suit, Logan wound out a cable and hook from a winch by the door. Lying on his stomach, he reached down and hooked it through a thick piece of superstructure on the smashed-up Futen.

Once it was secure, Logan grabbed the other suit. He wished he was as confident as the face he was showing the others. He'd done some recreational diving with Aurore off the coast at New Hope, but this was a different set of circumstances, and far more dangerous.

"We need to put those flotation bags inside the wreck. As far down as possible." Logan gestured to the aircraft below.

"Are you kidding me? In this swamp?" Heskith's eyes were the size of soccer balls.

"You don't like getting dirty?" Logan grinned.

"Even with the diving gear, that's suicidal." Heskith peered over the edge of the ramp. "Seriously, anyone trying that is likely to get sucked to the bottom."

"We'll use safety lines," Logan said. "Besides, I'm betting the mud hasn't got inside much."

"Maybe, but the water will be black as space. But less transparent. We won't see a meter in that crap."

"I never said it would be easy." Logan stared at the mangled cockpit and wondered if the crew had escaped. "If it makes you feel better, I'll do the diving. You hand me the bags."

Heskith looked relieved. "I guess. You sure you want to go down there?"

"Not really. But it's the only chance to get hold of more turbines. Keep a close eye on my safety line though."

Logan clambered over the edge and lowered himself onto the buried aircraft. Once he was sure of his footing, he gestured for Heskith to pass down the flotation bags. His idea had been to drag the wreck from the swamp so they could recover the engines, but now they were on-site, he wasn't sure it was possible.

"Think big," Logan muttered, then wormed through one of the missing windows, avoiding the jagged edges. The piloting seats were empty and half covered by the water. The stagnant liquid smelled like death itself, making Logan wonder again about the crew. And then there was the question of the swamp wildlife...

Most of the native life on Kwelengsen was relatively harmless to humans. From what they knew, life had developed on the planet relatively recently. The local fauna hadn't fought for survival over billions of years like Earth creatures and mostly avoided the humans. Any Earth species introduced to the planet, whether animals or plants, were so genetically strong by comparison they tended to replace the local "opposition." That said, the settlers had only explored a fraction of what was there in the short time they'd been on Kwelengsen.

Logan looked up as a shadow moved over him. Heskith was lowering himself through the cockpit framework, dragging a yellow flotation bag.

"Jeez, that stinks," he called out. "Rather you than me, buddy."

Logan tied a rope to the cockpit frame and the other end to the belt of his suit, then grabbed the bags. He stood on the pilot's chair, with his feet in the water. "Okay, here goes. Keep an eye on my line."

Heskith looked grim and nodded. "Don't mess around down there, big guy."

Logan glanced at the water, then before he thought too much about it, he lowered himself down.

Blackness surrounded him. At least it seemed he'd been right, and that so far, the Futen was mostly full of water. At first, he didn't think he could see anything, then after a while, his eyes adjusted. There was a lamp on his suit, and he switched it on—that helped but only enough to see perhaps a meter farther.

The inside of the craft was a mess, the bent, twisted framework looking like a set of kicked-in ribs. Logan dived deeper and located the cockpit access door. He yanked at it and found it stuck, trapped by the crumpled bulkheads. Bracing his feet on either side, he pulled but it didn't move. Looking around, he spotted a broken piece of airframe and used it to pry at the door surround.

After several attempts, the door popped open, allowing Logan access to the darker space of the main cargo hold. He aimed the light inside, but it didn't penetrate far enough to reveal anything. Grabbing the door frame, he pulled himself through and ran into what appeared to be a metal wall. Moving around, he realized it was the front of an armored scout car. So, it was possible the flight crew were the only ones on board.

Logan slipped past the vehicle's side, pulling himself deeper. The water was heavily silted now, with dark globs of unidentifiable matter floating around him like black stars. Beyond the scout car, the area opened up, but a shadow loomed in front of him. Then several faces appeared in the darkness, and he flinched. A lineup of armored Corporate soldiers was strapped to benches running the length of the walls. Like a silent, hellish jury watching his every move. Whether they'd died on impact, or drowned, wasn't clear. Logan clamped his teeth harder on the mouthpiece and pushed deeper.

Finally, he was near the Futen's rear ramp, where the flotation bags would have the greatest effect. He tied one to a stanchion and flicked the switch on the remote trigger. Then he moved to the other side and repeated the operation with a second.

The third bag needed to be secured higher to avoid interfering with the others, and Logan floated up toward the grim phalanx of dead soldiers. The one nearest didn't have a helmet, and his eye sockets were black, empty caves. Something had eaten the man's eyes. Logan recoiled, choking, his mouthpiece falling away, allowing the filthy swamp water inside his mouth. He turned away, scrabbling for the mouthpiece, then spotted something moving in the shadows.

It was long, thin, and almost black and zipped away from the light before Logan got a clear view. Another darted out from behind the bodies, followed by a third. He didn't know what they were, though they looked a little like eels. He shone the light in all directions, hoping to keep them away, then fastened the remaining bag to another part of the superstructure.

Something hit him from behind, and Logan twisted to see what it was, but it darted away. Another blow smashed into his shoulder. He whirled again, but the creatures moved too fast. Pushing off from the wall, Logan swam upward using his long arms in big strokes to lift him quickly. The things were snapping at his legs, and something nipped at his foot.

The scout car was ahead, and he had to move to the side to get around it, slowing his progress. One of the creatures bit into his suit, and Logan swiped at it. It scurried away, but he hadn't hurt it. He grabbed the vehicle tracks and used them to drag himself along faster, the impacts against his legs increasing as the creatures swarmed. Another bite, this time over the wound on his leg, and he jolted at the lightning bolts of pain.

A faint square of light loomed into view—it had to be the cabin door. Logan lunged for it and clambered through, turning to force it closed behind him. He heard several dull thuds, like the pounding of a hydraulic hammer on the bulkhead. The door held though, and he swam the short distance to the surface. Heskith was peering over the edge of the cockpit frame, his eyebrows drawn together. "You okay? Looked like you found a jacuzzi down there, and the line was dancing like crazy."

Heskith helped Logan clamber out of the water onto the other seat.

"Some beasties down there wanted to tango," Logan said.

He checked the leg of his diving suit. The bite had almost cut through the thick neoprene but had only pinched the wounded area. He couldn't tell if it had caused more damage until he took the suit off again.

"You get the bags secured?" Heskith asked, glancing at the brackish water.

"You can keep your socks dry." Logan detected a hint of pleading in Heskith's tone—the soldier looking even less eager to attempt a dive than earlier. "I got them all. Let's give it a shot."

They climbed back onto the ramp of their own aircraft, and Logan triggered his comm-set. "Carl, I'm activating the flotation bags. Be ready in case you need to manage the slack."

Carl acknowledged, and Logan focused on the sunken aircraft. "Here goes."

He thumbed the button on the remote activator, and nothing much happened. The bags must have deployed and filled with gas, but there was nothing to show it.

"It didn't work?" Heskith muttered.

"Maybe..."

Water suddenly churned and frothed like it was boiling in a giant pot, as the excess gas blew up through the fuselage like a giant belch. A shower of noxious water and rotting material filled the air, accompanied by the bitter stink of the inflation gases. A few minutes later, Logan saw what he'd been hoping for, as the buried aircraft lurched upwards, rising at least ten centimeters.

"Now we wait?" Heskith pointed at the crashed Futen. "It'll pop right out?"

Logan shook his head. "Not much chance of that. We'll need to give it some help."

The carcass of the wrecked craft shuddered again, and Logan let out some slack on the line he'd tied to the nose. "Let's secure that lifting strap."

The strap was bulky and awkward, but Logan hoped it would spread the load enough to allow them to lift the other aircraft, rather than tear through it. They looped it through the biggest intact stanchions and fastened it to some of the cable Heskith had scrounged. By the time they were done, the aircraft had risen higher, and Logan saw the faint outline of the cockpit door through the stagnant water.

"Let's give this thing a lift," he said.

After waiting until Heskith had climbed up, Logan followed. He made his way through the Futen and slid into the pilot's seat. Carl wrinkled his nose and turned away.

Logan put his hands on the controls. "I got it," he said, then triggered the comm-set to connect to Heskith. "I'm going to start lifting. You're going to have to be my eyes."

"Roger," the sergeant called back.

Logan teased the throttle, taking up the slack. The Futen's rearview camera had been damaged during their escape from New Hope. Their aircraft rose, then the nose lifted as the cable tightened. The autopilot corrected, but it was slow, and they see-sawed in the air until Logan dropped the throttle back a little. He made another attempt, with the same result. This time he was ready though and manually stabilized the aircraft faster.

"It moved around five centimeters," Heskith called over the radio. "Not nearly enough."

"Nothing's ever easy," Logan muttered.

Again, he operated the throttle, this time dipping the nose early to counter the pull and felt the cable catch on the crashed aircraft.

"You got it!" yelled Heskith. "Keep it coming. It's working. Dammit, move you son-of-a-bitch."

Logan pushed the throttle farther forward, to control the bucking transport. It reminded him of the time he'd tried bull riding. He'd done it once, showing off to Joe, and had been happy not to try it a second time.

"How's it looking, Hesky?" Logan fought the twitching controls. "Talk to me."

"I don't know. It ain't moving now, I think the—"

A snapping noise reverberated around them like a gunshot, loud enough to be heard over the protesting whine of the turbines. The Futen went wild, the tail spinning and flicking up as if released from the jaws of some huge beast. Logan snapped the controls over to avoid them flipping into the swamp, jamming the throttles back to their station-keeping position. The nose came within a meter of the swamp, then swung back up and steadied.

"You with us, Hesky?"

"Man, you drive worse than a virgin heading out on his first date." Heskith gasped for breath. "The cable snapped."

"Okay. Let's take a break."

Logan maneuvered the Futen over to the solid ground and dropped it down where the soldiers were waiting. He was glad to kill the engines, even if it was only a temporary break. He checked the power reserves and frowned. They were already down to less than fifty percent. Prolonged hovering was always wasteful, but pulling the weight of the downed aircraft had made their power consumption worse.

They clambered out, and Morua came up, her mouth turned down. "Not so easy, huh?"

"Well, it was for some people sat on their asses over here," Heskith muttered, then caught the look on Morua's face and saluted. "Sorry, Lieutenant."

She looked at Logan. "What now?"

He looked back at the swamp. "We take another shot at it. We have more cable. Right, Hesky?"

"Right. But it ain't going to hold, you saw that."

"We can double it up, or even triple. Give it a better chance."

"I'm against it," Morua said. Her face was neutral, but her jaw had a firm set to it. "I think we should cut our losses and head back. We're too exposed."

"I like that idea." Carl had followed Logan out and was standing to one side. "Let's go back before—"

Morua cut him off with a withering glance. "Thank you for your opinion, Private." She turned back to Logan.

"Manners won't like it," Logan said. "She wants two operational

Futens."

"We tried, we failed." Morua exhaled. "It happens."

"We're out of options, big guy." Heskith clapped his hand on Logan's shoulder. "No one can win 'em all."

Chapter Sixteen

*"Desperation and bravery are
two sides of the same coin."*
— Grandfather Twofeathers

Logan wandered over to a tree near the edge of the swamp and looked out across the treacherous surface to the buried aircraft. Freckles of bright blue flowers rimmed the shore, trailing into the swamp on the more solid areas. From that vantage point, it didn't look like they'd moved the trapped Futen in the slightest. He heard a rustle behind him and glanced around to see Carl holding a water canteen and some combat rations.

"Morua thought you might be hungry."

Logan took a bar and bit into it, chewing a heavy mouthful. While better than the stale supplies Manners had been feeding the settlers, it still tasted like sawdust and glue. "Thanks," he muttered around the crumbs.

"I shouldn't be here," Carl whispered, swatting ineffectually at the clouds of bugs around them.

"I know you didn't want to come to Kwelengsen. But what would you have done back on Earth? People are starving there, remember."

"That's not—" Carl looked away. "It's not safe here."

"Nowhere's safe these days." Logan finished his bar and washed it away with a couple of mouthfuls of water. "Would you prefer to die in a food riot?"

Carl's head snapped around to look at Logan again. "You're the one who—"

"You ready to go, Logan?" Heskith lumbered up. "Morua's getting antsy."

"Sure." Logan turned away from the marsh and followed Heskith, the buzz of insect life loud in the still afternoon. Then he stopped. "Hesky, there's an armored car in the back of that Futen."

"Yeah? No wonder we didn't stand a chance. Those things weigh eighteen, maybe twenty tonnes."

"That much?" Logan started walking again. "I don't suppose we could get it out?"

Heskith snorted. "You never give up, do you?"

"Something I learned from a good friend."

This time it was Heskith's turn to pause. "They're clamped for transport. That must be why that thing's sunk the way it has. All the weight's at the back."

"There'd be no power to unlock the clamps," Logan said.

"Manual override. Hydraulic."

Logan rubbed his jaw. "What about the cargo door?"

"That much weight would smash straight through it." Heskith slapped at a bite on his cheek. "You think it's possible?"

"Only one way we'll find out," Logan said, marching on a direct line toward Morua.

Morua took some convincing, but with both Logan and Heskith working on her, she eventually agreed. Logan gathered Carl up, and the three of them boarded the Futen once more. He brought the aircraft back over the wreck, then left the controls to Carl, who hadn't said a word since earlier except yes or no in answer to direct questions.

Logan was helping Heskith rig the pulling cable when the sergeant looked at him. "What's with that kid? I thought he was related to you, but he seems to hate your guts."

"We're not exactly related. But you're right that he hates me." Logan pulled the doubled-up cord over and wrapped it behind a large structural frame. "His father was Leonard Begay."

"The captain of that ship? The *Saca-wotsit*."

"*Sacagawea*." Logan looped the cables around a supporting strut that was part of the cockpit. "Leo was a close family friend. I thought bringing Carl here would help him move on. But all it seems to have done is make him blame me more."

"Blame you? For what?"

Logan shrugged. "For not finding his father alive, I guess."

"Kids... They don't make any sense."

Logan nodded his agreement. "I think we're ready to give it another try." He pointed at the filthy water. "After we release the armored car."

Grabbing his breathing tank and helmet, Logan pulled them on. He didn't relish another encounter with the eel-like creatures, but it was the only way to release the payload. "The manual release is at the front of the cargo space?"

Heskith's expression was grim. "Yeah, should be the same as on ours."

"Okay. No point waiting." Logan grabbed the safety line.

"I guess not..." Heskith hesitated. "Shit. Climb out of there, big guy. I can't let you do that twice."

"What?"

"It's time Hesky got his feet wet." Heskith clambered onto the second pilot seat and helped Logan take off the air tank. After strapping it to his back, he took the line and clipped it to his belt. "If you see this thing dancing, bring me up as fast as you can. Okay?"

"You don't have to do this," Logan whispered.

"Yeah, I do." Heskith spat into his face mask and smeared it around. "Can't let it be said that Hesky don't pull his freight."

"They won't while I'm around."

"The door sticks, you said?" Heskith dragged down a pack displaying a prominent explosive warning.

"It lifts up this way." Logan eyed the cylindrical objects Heskith pulled from the pack. "Grenades?"

Heskith grinned. "Figured they might stun the bastards, like with fish."

"Let's hope so."

"Remember. Watch that line," Heskith said, then dropped into the stagnant pool.

Initially, Logan followed his shape through the dark water, but after a while, there was nothing but a stream of bubbles to show

Heskith's progress. After a while, they vanished leaving only the safety line disappearing into the gloom. He thought he saw a dim light, then a moment later, the surface churned. There was another flash, followed by another belch of frothing water. Logan wondered how the blasts affected Heskith and hoped the sergeant didn't stun himself in the process. Then the surface calmed, the last few bubbles bursting to leave a perfectly black mirror.

Logan counted off the seconds. After two minutes, he was worrying. Surely the release shouldn't take this long to operate. There was a faint glimmer of another flash and he waited for another surge. Before that happened, the submerged aircraft lurched upwards, shooting at least a meter higher. A flood of turbulent water filled the flight cabin area, making it impossible to see anything.

"Carl, lift and take up the slack," he called into the comm-set.

Their aircraft lifted, staying clear of the rising nose. Heskith must have released the payload. Logan reached around, scrabbling for the line in the churning water. His hand snagged it and he heaved. For a moment, it felt like he was pulling on something heavy, then the line went limp in his hands. Furiously winding the line in, he dragged it upward, but when he lifted it clear, there was nothing but a badly frayed end.

"Heskith?" Logan shouted, knowing he wouldn't be able to hear while underwater. "Heskith!"

The crashed aircraft rose higher, and Logan realized that without the weight, now was the best time to lift it clear, before the swamp reasserted its grip. He waited another minute, his eyes scanning the water for any sign of the soldier, then reluctantly pulled himself onto their own aircraft.

Dashing through to the cockpit, Logan took the controls and pushed forward on the throttles to lift the aircraft. The Futen bucked under him, but not as wildly as earlier.

"Where's the sergeant?" Carl yelled over the deafening whine from the turbines.

Logan gave an abrupt shake of his head, a pit of anger burning inside him. Someone else who'd relied on him was dead. The Futen lurched upwards, and Logan glanced back through the cockpit. The other aircraft was almost clear. He moved the controls and dragged the wreck over the black morass, hauling the stricken aircraft over to rest on solid ground.

"Go release the cables," Logan said, able to talk at more usual levels now the turbines were no longer screaming like tormented banshees.

Carl hesitated, then jumped out of his seat and ran back. A few moments later, the tail lifted as the cable was released. Logan turned the Futen and positioned the ramp close to the wrecked aircraft, to make it easier to transfer any recovered parts. He landed, then closed his eyes, trying to shut everything out. Heskith had been a good man. And that was no way to go.

Morua clambered in. "You did it. Unbelievable." She stopped. "Heskith?"

Logan dropped his face into his hands.

"Damn." The word shot from Morua's lips like a bullet. "This was supposed to be a recovery operation. Not a body count."

"Do you think I don't know that?" Logan choked out the words in a half-whisper.

Carl staggered up. "That should have been you down there." He lunged for Logan. "You're the one who deserves to die."

"That's enough, Private." Morua pushed Carl back toward the door. "Outside. Now."

What sounded like a peal of thunder passed overhead and, moments later, Logan caught the angry buzz of QuenchGun fire.

"What the—" Morua looked through the door and yelled. "Incoming."

Logan looked up and caught the flash of an air vehicle overhead. It was smaller than the Futen but large enough to be an aero-scout. As it moved away, several figures jumped from wide doors on the sides, dropping like large rocks before landing without so much as a bounce.

"Drop-troops!" Morua yelled. "Get us up in the air. Now."

Drop-troops were the latest innovation in rapid troop deployment. Logan had seen some of the technology behind them. The soldiers wore reinforced exoskeletons with rocket assistance, allowing them to jump from a moving aircraft and land safely. This gave them the ability to be on-site faster than regular forces, and with heavier weapons.

Logan re-started the turbines, but it was too late—the enemy aircraft was already turning back to target them. Before the engines reached take-off speed, the sinister shape of the aero-scout dropped, hovering a dozen meters away with its weapons ready.

Several smaller attack drones swept up ahead of the charging drop-troops, their guns locking onto Morua's squad. Then an amplified, metallic voice sounded from the scout vehicle. "You have thirty seconds to lower your weapons, or we'll cut you down where you stand."

"How the hell..." Morua looked out. "We don't have a chance."

"Perhaps you should order your soldiers to stand down," Logan said. "This isn't worth more deaths."

Morua glanced at him, then nodded before jumping out.

"Squad, hold your fire, and lay down your weapons," she barked. "Repeat. Lay down your weapons."

Logan killed the turbines and wriggled out of the pilot's seat. The drop-troops were encircling Morua's squad, the attack drones swarming around on high alert.

As Logan jumped off the loading ramp, he heard murmurs and grumbles from the soldiers. Their position might have been hopeless, but the will to fight was there. Seeing the drop-troops closeup, Logan realized they had much heavier armor than the versions he was aware of. They looked like something out of a comic, but infinitely more menacing. They were also heavily armed, with rifles as big as a squad weapon, and each of them carried what appeared to be portable rocket-launchers on their backs.

A drop-trooper with sergeant's insignia stepped up. "Anyone carrying, lose the hardware. Then get on your knees."

Logan couldn't see the man's face because of a seamless visor that ran from the forehead all the way to the neck. And his voice had an electronic buzz. The soldiers weren't in exoskeletons, they were wearing full armor. That would be typical for space operations but it was usually considered too cumbersome for planetary actions. Logan unclipped his pistol and dropped it on the ground before sinking to his knees.

Morua's squad did the same and, finally, she lowered herself to her knees too.

"Okay, listen up." The Corporate sergeant turned to check there was no resistance. "If everybody's smart, no one needs to get hurt. Put your hands on top of your heads, and wait to get zipped."

Once their hands were zip-tied behind their backs, they'd be helpless, but Logan couldn't see another option.

"I'm in charge here," Morua said. "We have rights under the—"

"You have nothing," the sergeant snarled. "Except what I say you have."

There were only four Corporate troops, but even without the aero-scout and drones backing them up, Logan doubted Morua's people would have been able to fight back. Their light armor was no defense against the heavy rifles. Another Corporate soldier approached Corporal Marsalis, one of the MilSec team, and grabbed his wrists, forcing them behind his back.

Marsalis struggled and yelled, but even with his Geneering, he was no match for his opponent's mechanical enhancements.

A loud sloshing came from the swamp, and Logan looked across as a small tidal wave of muddy water rolled over the tail of the damaged Futen. The enemy soldiers were staring too, and several stepped back as a large shape lumbered out from the stygian quagmire, thick streams of sludge and rotting vegetation sliding off its back.

"What the..." The enemy sergeant lifted his gun at the strange object rising from the boggy waters.

Something at the front of the behemoth twisted around like a large antenna, then erupted with flame, Logan ducked as he heard the high-pitched thrum of supersonic needles fly overhead, followed a second later by a rippling crack tearing through the air.

The aero-scout lurched, its pilot fighting for control after being hit by a heavy volley of needles, the drones already vaporized. Then it spun away, smashing into the ground thirty meters from them before exploding in a fireball. It had happened so fast, no one had moved. But it galvanized everyone into action and Morua's team reached for their discarded weapons. Logan grabbed his pistol and aimed at the visor of the nearest drop-trooper. He pulled the trigger several times, then dived to one side as the large figure sprayed a burst of lethal needles in return.

Several others were firing, and someone let out a yell. Whether it was meant as a cry of rebellion, or from injury, wasn't clear. Heavy clanking sounded behind him and Logan turned. The thing had emerged from the swamp, and as the mud slid off it, he realized it was the car he'd seen inside the sunken Futen.

The "antenna" was a heavy QuenchGun that swung around, streaming a hail of needles into the drop-troops. Under the strength of its fire, they were falling back. While the needles weren't sufficient to take them out right away, they didn't appear willing to stand up to such fire for long.

An explosion swelled up in front of the drop-troops, followed by several others, forcing them to retreat. The armored car was firing, but now it was taking enemy shots too. The drop-troops' weapons looked as powerful as those on the ground vehicle. With their numbers, they'd eventually overwhelm it and get the upper hand if nothing changed.

Logan bolted for the Futen and clambered inside, triggering the turbine start sequence as soon as he was at the controls. Several loud pops sounded as shots hit the aircraft, but none were targeted well enough to do any critical damage. In a few seconds, the engines had enough thrust to lift, and he pulled back on the controls.

From the air, Logan had a clear view of the ground and the drop-troop positions. Their armor protected them, but also made them easy to pick out on the battlefield. Holding the Futen steady, Logan opened up the fire control systems and tagged each of the enemies for auto-targeting.

Immediately, the Futen shuddered as its weapons blasted several volleys at the enemy. Numerous threat warning lights came on, and Logan jerked the aircraft around to make it a harder target. Then he flew over the enemy troops in a short pass, the automatic weapons churning up the ground around them. They turned to engage him, but as they did, the armored car hit them from the other side, forcing them to defend themselves again.

As Logan spun the Futen to make another pass, he saw several more explosions detonate and one of the drop-troops went down.

He cleared it from the target list, focusing on the other three. The aircraft's weapons sent another glittering burst of shots into the enemy soldiers, and another one fell. Logan brought the Futen over their heads, jinking the aircraft erratically to avoid enemy fire.

He banked low, turning the Futen for another pass. As he lined up again, he saw the ground vehicle barreling toward one of the remaining drop-troops. Despite the roar of the turbines, Logan heard the collision and saw the enemy soldier punched back, slamming into a pile of rock before hitting the ground face-first. The remaining drop-trooper was swarmed by Morua's team, and Logan disarmed the auto-weapons, bringing the Futen back to land by the edge of the swamp.

After climbing out, Logan surveyed the area around him. Most of Morua's squad were clustered by the rocks where the drop-troops had made their stand. A few minutes later, the armored car rolled up, its tracks clanking and squealing in protest. After grinding to a halt, a hatch on top popped up, then squealed open, and a familiar round face with a beaming grin appeared.

"Hesky?" Logan laughed. "How in the hell did you manage that?"

Heskith slid down from the armored car and hobbled toward Logan. He had a nasty bite mark on the side of his head, a larger one on his shoulder, and yet another on his leg.

"No one makes fish food out of Hesky," he grumbled. "Those things tried to get me, so I hid in the car. I was trapped for ten damn minutes before I realized it had power."

"I'm glad to see you're alive." Logan reached out to shake Heskith's hand.

"Not as much as me." Heskith touched a finger lightly to the wound on his face and shuddered. "Never liked sushi, but now I'm gonna eat it every damn chance I get."

Logan chuckled. "Get them before they get you, huh?"

"You got it." Heskith looked over Logan's shoulder and his eyes widened. "What the hell?"

A grimace of fear mixed with anger distorted Heskith's brawny face. He slammed a meaty arm into Logan, knocking him aside, then snatched the pistol from his belt and raised it.

Logan tried to turn to see what what was happening, but

something slammed into his back like a plasma cutter drilling through him. He fell, then rolled over. Someone was walking toward him, but Logan's eyes wouldn't focus. A thick blur rushed forward and Heskith roared. The two blurs collided, and as they fell to the ground, Logan's vision dimmed.

Chapter Seventeen

"It does not require many words
to speak the truth."
— Chief Joseph

Logan opened his eyes and blinked several times. All he saw was polymer-coated rock above him, and when he tried to roll over, his shoulder burned with agony.

"Thought I told you—I don't like repeat traffic."

Neeta Havji's warm eyes swam into Logan's view. "I'm back at the base?"

"Been here three days," Havji said. "I kept you sedated until ten hours ago. Wanted to make sure your body had time to start repairing before you went off on another silly stunt."

"How bad is it?" Logan managed to twist his head and saw a drip on a stand next to him. Behind it, a life monitor's flickering readout tracked his heartbeat.

"On a scale of one to ten? About a two. Any lower and I'd recommend feeding you to the dogs."

"Dogs?"

Havji laughed. "Doctor humor, sorry. Your leg was infected, despite the earlier treatment. But the bigger worry was the shoulder wound. Somebody sure doesn't like you."

Logan tried to remember what had happened. "Who?"

"Ha. Like anyone tells me anything." Havji pushed a thermometer in his ear and held it there for several seconds. "Fever's down.

All I know is you were rushed in along with three others. Two of them didn't make it. The other guy—your friend Heskith—I treated for some of the nastiest bites I've ever seen—he's been in every day checking on you. What the hell did you get up to out there?"

Logan breathed deep, relieved to know that Heskith had made it, but wondering who hadn't.

"The ones who died? One of them wasn't a young settler?"

"No. Both were uniforms—had military IDs."

Again, relief washed through Logan, followed almost immediately by guilt. The men who died were no less deserving of life than anyone else.

"A needle round passed through your upper right thorax. You were lucky—a few centimeters to the left or lower and it would have been through your lung. Mostly soft tissue damage, but it nicked your scapula. That'll be sore until the bone heals."

"Thanks. I owe you—again."

"You'll get the bill in the mail." Havji hesitated as though she were going to say something else, but then her chin dropped and she sighed.

"You okay?" said Logan.

"You see a lot as a doctor." Havji turned to check the monitoring equipment. "People hurt, desperate, dying. It's all part of the job. But to see people killed, young people who've barely lived—that's simply too cruel, you know?"

Logan remembered the cries he'd heard from inside the AMTV, the children desperate for help, only to be burned to death moments later. Havji was talking about the soldiers, but the children's fate had been far worse.

"War is always ugly," he said.

"I know." Havji wept quietly. "I signed up for this. Seemed like a way to give something back. But I never expected I'd be in the thick of it. So many people do their term without seeing anything other than the odd broken bone, some cuts and bruises, and a few dozen cases of venereal disease."

"And now you think, *why me?*"

Havji nodded, and Logan reached out awkwardly to pat her hand. "My ancestors would say you're here because the Great Spirit wanted you to be. Here to make a difference."

Havji sniffed. "Do you believe that?"

"I think sometimes good people have to stand against the bad."

"Thanks, Logan." Havji squeezed his hand. "I thought I was the carer here?"

"I'm an engineer—I deal with machines. But people need maintenance too."

"Hey! He's awake." A bellow sounded from near the entrance and Heskith's bulky figure shuffled toward them.

"Hesky, you look like crap." There was a dressing covering the sergeant's face.

"Sure, but it's gonna leave a fantastic scar. The women will be all over me. Ain't that right, Doc?"

"It doesn't *have* to scar. Once the skin starts regrowing, we can apply ScarGone and it'll be almost unnoticeable."

"Now where's the fun in that?" Heskith pulled up a chair, sitting backward on it and leaning his thick arms over the backrest. "Eh, big guy?"

"I'll have to take your word on the fun part." The scar on Logan's chest was itching. "How are things?"

Heskith rubbed his jaw. "Well, you know—not so good."

Logan didn't know but sensed Heskith was hesitant to talk. "You flew the Futen back?"

"Yeah."

"I have other things to tend to," Havji said, then glanced at Heskith. "Don't tire him out."

As she walked away, Heskith admired her departing figure. "She is one cutey-patootie, don't you think?"

"She's a nice person."

"Come on. You're married, but you ain't dead. The doc's worth more than a look."

Logan kept his eyes on the end of the bed. "How about the turbines from the downed Futen?"

"Front two were trash. I guess the impact killed them, or they swallowed a ton of swamp at full speed and that was that." Heskith made an expansive gesture with his hands. "The two rear ones… well, they're in one piece but that's about all I can say for them."

"Bad?"

Heskith nodded. "Been in the water for days. Mechanically they look okay, but it's impossible to say if there's any hidden damage to the metal without a full-blown multi-frequency analyzer."

"I'm guessing we don't have anything that sophisticated." Logan was uncomfortable lying down, but every time he moved, his shoulder reminded him sharply not to. "We knew it was a risk."

"I've torn down both turbines and the gimbal mounts." Heskith brushed the wound on his cheek. "Damn thing itches like crazy. Cleaned everything up as best I can, and they're ready to put back together, but..."

"But you can't know for sure they're going to work."

"Exactly. And to be honest, I don't want to be anywhere near those things the first time they spin up."

"I'll check everything as soon as I'm out of here." Logan sighed. "How's Manners?"

"Frothing at the mouth." Heskith pulled out some gum and offered Logan a piece. "Not happy we lost more people. Fuming 'cause I won't put those turbines back together on my own. And ready to blow because we didn't bring that armored car back. And then, well, you know..."

"No. I don't know. The car was no good?"

"Power packs were shot, and the battle killed 'em. Everything was corroded to hell. I was lucky to get out of the swamp in that thing. Besides, we didn't have the room or the power reserves to lift it *and* the turbines."

"But that must have been Morua's decision."

"Sure, but it was on my advice." Heskith turned and showed his shoulder patch. The sergeant's stripes had been replaced by a corporal's. "Manners demoted me. Can you necking believe it?"

"That's crazy. Without you, we'd have all been corpses rotting into the ground." Logan rubbed his forehead. "When I'm up, I'll talk to her. See if I can clear this up."

"No offense, big guy, but you better leave it alone. She ain't real happy with you either. She'd be giving you hell in here if it weren't for the doc. From what I heard, Havji had to ban her from the hospital. I'm telling you, she's been like a cat with a mouthful of nettles since..."

Again Heskith fell silent. Logan knew there had to be more

but couldn't think what that might be, or why Manners would be angry at *him* again.

"Spit it out, Hesky. Something isn't right here."

Heskith chewed noisily on his gum, then leaned forward. "They picked up signals—before we left. A q-link stream from right here in the camp, and it wasn't under Guard or MilSec encryption."

"A traitor? Here?" It was possible. The Corporates had deep pockets, and people's scruples were often far more limited. But what did that have to do with him? "Wait. She thinks *I've* been contacting the enemy?"

"Not exactly..." Heskith shook his head, avoiding Logan's eyes. "That nephew of yours, Begay."

"Carl? That's ridiculous." The cave walls seemed to be imploding around Logan. "His father was killed by the Corporates. There's no way he'd ever—"

Heskith held up his hand. "They searched him when we got back and found a transmitter."

Was this some trick Manners was using to try and control him, Logan wondered. What possible reason would Carl have for throwing in with the Corporates? He couldn't believe it was about money.

"And he *did* shoot you..."

Logan's head buzzed as if someone was tunneling into his head with a rusty drill bit.

"Hey, you okay there?" Heskith leaned over Logan and shook him. "Should I get the doc?"

"Carl?"

Heskith's face clouded over. "Yeah. Sorry, I thought you'd seen."

Logan shook his head. "I saw *somebody*. It wasn't clear."

"Walked right up and shot you in the back. Seen guys like that in the service. Cold, dead eyes—usually snipers." Heskith looked around as if searching for the doctor. "I tried to get you out of the way, but wasn't quick enough."

"Thanks."

It seemed such a small word to express his gratitude, but Logan ached in a way he never had before and couldn't focus. Carl was family, or as good as. Hell, he'd cradled Carl in his arms when he was a baby. And Leonard had been a brother to him. Leo had been a year older than Logan, but they spent all their time together after the older boy had to repeat a year in school and ended up in the same classes as Logan. Logan never asked why Leo was held back—it had never mattered.

Logan had always been bookish, but with Leo around, things changed. Leo was so physical, and together they did things that, up to then, Logan had largely ignored. It was Leo who persuaded Logan to start working out and get in better shape physically. Leo who first encouraged Logan to date, taught him how to shoot, and how to drive.

And now, Logan was supposed to accept that Leo's son wanted to murder him? It was impossible. There must be some other explanation. But how could Heskith be wrong? He was a witness.

Logan realized he'd been lost in his thoughts and Havji was back alongside the bed. She was checking his pulse and waving a light in his eyes. "Logan? Talk to me."

"I'm alright." Logan pushed away the bedclothes. "Where is he?"

"You don't wanna know. Shit, I should never have told ya." Heskith gave Havji a pleading look. "He shouldn't be moving around. Right, Doc?"

Havji frowned. "Absolutely not."

"Where are my clothes?" Logan tore the various sensors from his wrists and leg, then eased himself upright. "Don't think of trying to stop me."

"Drawer on your left," Havji said. "You'll need to sign a release. I won't be held responsible when you fall over dead."

"Fine."

Havji left while Logan dressed. His shoulder was tight, as though the needle was still inside, and he winced at every movement. The pistol was fastened to his belt and Logan checked it, not thinking why.

Heskith moved around the bed. "You won't be needing that, buddy."

Logan stared at him. "You're right." He put the pistol back in the drawer as Havji returned. She held an eFlimsy with the words

"Patient Release" visible at the top. Logan didn't read it and jammed his thumb against the print-sensitive authorization area.

"You're making a big mistake," Havji said. "You need at least another thirty-six to forty-eight hours of recovery."

"Thank you, Doctor." Logan turned to Heskith. "Take me to him."

Heskith glanced at Havji, then back at Logan "Your funeral."

Logan trembled as he followed Heskith through the passages. Perhaps the chillier winter temperatures were having an effect, though the caves were closer to the equator than the city. Or maybe you shouldn't be moving in your condition, Logan thought guiltily.

They turned left into a tunnel that looked newer than the others, the rock rawer and less weathered. The passage ended at a makeshift gate, its metal mesh clearly fashioned from construction supplies.

"No guard?" Logan said.

Heskith shrugged. "Not needed. Someone comes in now and then to let him go potty."

Logan moved closer and peered through the rhombic holes, while Heskith stayed in the corridor. A cot filled most of the secured area, and a dark figure lay there facing the wall. In one corner, a small lamp gave out a pitiful dim glow that created more shadows than light.

"Carl?" Logan kept his voice low, knowing he wasn't supposed to be there.

"Leave me alone."

"It's Unc"—he stopped himself—"Logan."

"Come for revenge, is that it?" Carl rolled over and stared through the fence. He was back in civilian clothes and looked like he hadn't washed in days. "Want to butcher me while I'm trapped, helpless as a caged animal? That would be just your style."

"What is all this?" The conversation was getting away from Logan before it had even started. "They said you shot me."

"And? You don't believe it?"

"What on earth would make you do that?"

"We're not *on* Earth anymore. As you're so fond of pointing out."

"You're right, but that doesn't explain *this*." Logan pushed up against the cage. "You betrayed us to the Corporates. You tried to kill me. Why?"

Carl didn't say anything. Perhaps he didn't know the answer. After a while, Logan turned to leave.

"For him," Carl hissed. "For my father. He's dead because of you."

Logan whirled back. "That's nonsense. The *Corporates* killed Leonard. They blew up his damn ship with him and his entire crew on board. I know they did. I saw what was left of the *Sacagawea*."

"You killed him long before that."

Logan stepped back to the fencing. "That's crazy. We were friends. I'd give anything to have him back."

"You made him go away. You made him leave us."

"He joined MilSec. He wanted adventure." Logan's eyes welled up with bitter tears. "He wanted to prove to himself to everyone."

"He wanted to be an engineer. Like you."

"That's not—"

"He never told you, did he?" Carl sneered. "But he didn't because he couldn't get the grades. You beat him at everything, and when you won the scholarship to McMaster, it was the final humiliation."

"What do you mean?" Logan's head was spinning again, and he grabbed the mesh for support.

"You swore a blood oath, to always fight for each other. But you left. He knew he'd never be able to compete with you, so he joined the military."

"Did the Corporates fill your head with this crap?"

Carl leaped off the cot and hurled himself against the fence, the weight of his impact bending the metal mesh outward. "I found his journals—in his belongings. Shipped back to us, wrapped up in a goddamn USP flag."

The words slammed into Logan like the needle had done days earlier, and he turned away from Carl's burning eyes. "He was my best friend."

"And you were his worst," Carl continued. "It's all in there. How humiliated he was when you, the younger one, advanced so far ahead of him. How you left him behind. Even when he married mom and started a family, it couldn't ease his pain. That's when he decided to join up. And after that, we never saw him."

"He wanted—" Logan croaked.

"He needed to show you he was as good as you."

"No."

"I'm only sorry I failed him. And if I get the chance, I'll do it again." Carl's snarling face was next to the fence, almost touching Logan, the metal rattling as he shook it. "Who do you think betrayed the mission to pick up Diouf? Who made sure the Corporates knew you were going after that downed aircraft? They were supposed to do the job for me. But then I got caught up in it all and had to do it myself."

Logan forced himself to look at Carl, barely recognizing him. "You? You caused the deaths of all those people—those children. To get rid of me?"

Carl lifted his chin, and Logan raised his fist.

"Go ahead. Do it," Carl hissed.

The next thing Logan knew, Heskith had his arms around him, pulling him back from the fence. "That's enough, big guy. Only thing that's gonna do is make you feel worse."

Logan struggled for a moment, but Heskith was too powerful, and something tore in Logan's shoulder.

"You know what will happen to you?"

"I don't care," Carl whispered.

Heskith guided Logan back down the tunnel. "Christ, the doc ain't gonna be happy with me over this."

Logan glanced down to see fresh blood oozing through his shirt. "Don't worry. She knows it's my fault."

"Sure, but I was hoping to get closer to her, ya know? Why d'ya think I been visiting every day?"

A smile tugged at Logan's lips. "I'm not her patient anymore."

"Don't bet on it." Heskith turned into the larger corridor. "She was melting that eFlimsy as we left."

Logan leaned against the tunnel wall, hoping to draw strength from somewhere, but failed. The surface was like damp sandpaper, and he could taste the acidic rock. Tears mixed salt with the acrid limestone, and he wished he was that hard and unfeeling. "As long as she lets me use the bed."

Havji looked up as they shuffled in, Heskith half-carrying Logan. "That's about what I expected." She sighed. "Strip."

"You been holding the bed for me?" Logan winced as he took his shirt off, and Havji stepped over to help.

"I knew you wouldn't be out of it long." She helped him slip the gown on. "Who knows? Maybe I'll be lucky this time and you've done something I can't fix."

"Thanks."

"Shut up. And you..." Havji looked at Heskith. "Get back to work, and you can quit coming around here to ogle my ass under the pretense of checking on *him*."

"Sh..." Heskith's face whitened, then he saluted. "Yes, ma'am."

Havji waited until Heskith left, then peeled back the dressing on Logan's shoulder. "Hmmm..."

"Bad?" Logan murmured, his thoughts tied in knots.

"Yes, I'm afraid your head is about to fall off."

Logan stayed silent as Havji worked on the wound.

"He's a good guy," he finally said.

"Who? Hesky?"

Logan nodded.

"I know that. But right now there are much bigger things to think about."

Logan smiled. "I said the same thing for years. Until I met my wife."

"Did she change you much?" Havji prodded at Logan's wound, making him yelp. "Or have you always been a stubborn asshole?"

"Always. If you wouldn't mind leav—" Logan grunted again as she prodded the wound.

"I said *shut up*."

"You win."

"While you were gone, Manners called." Havji's cheeks dimpled. "She doesn't come down here anymore."

"What did she want?"

"You, of course."

"And?"

"I told her you were out cold."

"Thanks."

"Shut up." Havji resealed the dressing. "You're lucky. The damage was superficial. You tore the dressings open, though. And now you'll be here another seventy-two hours."

Logan opened his mouth to respond, but Havji waved her finger in warning. He shut up.

After Havji left, Logan lay back on the bed, thinking back to his days with Leonard when they were children. Yes, they'd sworn an oath. They'd put a nick in their thumbs, then clasped hands, swearing on the blood they'd shared to always back each other up. And they'd done that all through school when others turned against them. But later, it had been forgotten. One of those childish pledges made by lots of young boys, not something to be taken seriously as adults. Logan had excelled at math and had an aptitude for mechanics. He'd followed his interests, and Leo had done the same. Or so he'd thought.

After they'd found the *Sacagawea's* remnants, with everyone on board dead. Logan had ignored his anger and pain over the loss of his friend. Instead, all he'd thought about was leaving the violence behind. Was he running away when he'd chosen to cut his ties with MilSec? Was it idealism, or cowardice, that pushed him to look for a new life away from the fighting and hatred? Was the idea of building a world free from all that nothing but a gutless pipe dream?

He'd made the decision quickly, blaming it on his disgust at the USP's involvement in the development of the Contravalency Phage. But he'd never thought to take Aurore's feelings into account. Had she really wanted to give up her career to come to this backwater as a scientific dogsbody? Or had she gone along with it purely because he wanted it?

Was it possible to stay on the sidelines and never get involved?

Part of him wanted that more than anything. He wanted there to be somewhere in the universe where conflict and violence had no place. He wanted freedom from the messed-up crap that had come to dominate Earth and its politics. He'd tried to insulate Aurore from it, to build a perfect bubble around them. But it hadn't worked. Despite every effort, the violence had followed them and taken not only his best friend but Aurore too. He couldn't let things end that way. It was too late for Leo, but he wouldn't—couldn't— admit that was the case for Aurore.

Chapter Eighteen

*"Never let the silt of one day
carry over to the next."*
— Grandfather Twofeathers

The next couple of days were remarkably quiet, and Logan was glad of the chance to rest—though it gave him too much time to dwell on the recriminations that had welled up after talking with Carl. He was surprised that Manners hadn't shown up at the hospital, or sent a demand that he be carried to see her on a gurney. But according to Heskith, she was busy making preparations for the offensive against the Corporates.

Logan was increasingly restless. The forced idleness did nothing for his mood, and he obsessed over what had become of Aurore. He still believed she was out there somewhere, but where was anyone's guess. For some reason, he felt sure she wasn't, and never had been, in the hands of the Corporates.

"Hey there, big guy."

Heskith's booming voice pulled Logan out of his gloomy thoughts. The sergeant visited everyday, claiming he needed to keep Logan in the loop about the work on the recovered thrusters, though Logan was fairly sure *he* wasn't the attraction. Despite the slapped wrist from Havji, it seemed Hesky wasn't about to give up that easily.

"How are things?"

"Ahh, ya know. Same old shit. Manners is biting on my ass over the turbines. I'm sure gonna be glad when you're back on your feet." Heskith scraped a chair along the floor and sat beside Logan's bed. "I'm kinda hoping you can take some of the flak."

Logan stiffened. "With all this about Carl, will she let me near it?"

"I don't think she's got much choice." Heskith drummed his fingers on the back of his chair. "I'm struggling with this stuff, and she knows it."

"Still having problems?"

Heskith shifted his bulk. "I've cleaned up every part and done my best to bring 'em into working order, but those units are dead. Trouble is, Manners doesn't want that to be the case, so she won't accept it."

Logan snorted. "I imagine she's frustrated she can't change reality by force of will."

"Yeah, something like that."

"I'll be up and about tomorrow. And I'll dive straight into the turbines. Together we'll crack the problem."

"I hope you're right." Heskith shuffled on the seat. "Or both of our asses will take a chewin'."

Logan sipped some water. "When's the mission planned for?"

"You're not on the need-to-know list." Heskith grinned. "So, I'll tell you anyway. She's penciled it in a week from now. According to the weather data, a winter storm's gonna hit the capital, which would help keep our movements under wraps for as long as possible."

"Smart thinking. *If* we can get the birds in the air by then."

"She's counting on it. I'm not supposed to know this." Heskith glanced around, then leaned in. "Manners has blocked the Corporate broadcasts and only releases summaries, but they're still killing the settlers they captured. Rourke said he ain't gonna stop until the people who attacked them turn themselves in."

"How many?"

"Ten a day."

Logan rubbed his jaw. "Have any identities been verified?"

"Sorry, dunno."

If Rourke was still using that tactic, he was worried about

something. Perhaps Manners had more up her sleeve than Logan was aware of. Another thought occurred to him. "Is anyone guarding Carl?" Logan remembered there'd been no-one there during their fraught discussion.

"On and off. Can't afford someone to sit there and watch him sleep all day. He gets food and thirty minutes' supervised exercise, but that's about it. Why?"

Logan clapped his hand on Heskith's shoulder. "Nothing for you to worry about, my friend."

Heskith narrowed his eyes. "I'm starting to know that look, big guy. Tells me you're planning to do something you shouldn't."

"You may be right." Logan chuckled. "Don't worry. No one will get hurt."

"I hope so." Heskith leaned back. "Any ideas about the turbines?"

"Lots. But all of them could be wrong."

"You think I'm missing something?"

"I doubt it. But those are complex units. Until I examine them, there's no point speculating."

"I want to get them working, Logan. I mean it. It's more than pride. I want to give those Corporate bastards a bloody nose. Even if that's all we can do. You know?"

Logan closed his eyes for a minute. "I know. And I understand. I told Manners I was in for the fight and I meant it."

Heskith nodded his approval. "Good, but what I mean is, don't spare my feelings. If you see something I missed, shout out."

"Don't worry, I will," Logan said. "Though I might say it quietly."

Heskith looked down, not saying anything for a while. When he raised his eyes, they glistened in the hospital lights. "Thanks, buddy."

"Trying to make the best of things, like everyone else."

Heskith pushed the chair back. "I better be going. Don't want Manners to bump me any lower."

"See you tomorrow."

"You better."

After Heskith left, Logan felt uncomfortable. There was a lot riding on the mission, and though he didn't necessarily agree with all of Manners' motivations, he'd committed to helping. He wasn't going back on that—but it was far from being the best option available to them.

"What were you and that testosterone junkie conspiring about?"

Logan looked up to see Havji standing by his bed. "We were talking about establishing the Neeta Havji Hospital once we drive the Corporates from Kwelengsen."

"Right." Havji laughed. "We both know that's not going to happen."

"The hospital? Who knows? We'll need to do some rebuilding."

"That's not what I meant. We're not likely to be on the winning end of this, and you know it. A lot of people are going to die, and there doesn't seem to be any way of avoiding it."

Havji looked more serious than Logan had ever seen her. "Perhaps," he said.

"I feel like everyone I know is already a corpse." Havji shivered. "But they don't know it yet."

"That doesn't sound like the bedside manner you learned in med school," Logan said softly. "Maybe you need to take more time for yourself and spend less in here."

"And what? Sit in my cave mulling over the fact that we're all corpses-in-waiting?"

"There are worst things."

"Like?"

"Betraying your people, or your family."

"Sorry."

"You don't have to be." Logan hesitated. "But I do need two things from you."

"What are those?"

"A one-hour pass."

Havji stared at Logan for a long time but didn't say anything. When she did, her words were clipped and precise. "I don't know what you mean."

"I think you do." Logan swiveled to face her, his legs hanging over the edge of the bed. "And the only reason Manners agreed to stay away from me is because you said you'd watch me. If I leave here, I'm sure you have orders to tell her immediately."

Havji didn't reply.

"I have something I have to do. It won't take long, and no one is going to get hurt. "

"And the second?"

"I need an EM Cloak."

Havji's eyes opened as wide as craters. "I don't have anything like that."

"You have other patients. Check their gear. I'm sure someone will have one."

"You're asking me to steal from my patients?" Havji snapped. "What do you think I am?"

"A good person."

Havji stormed away, her footsteps echoing like gunshots in the confines of the cave walls. Logan cursed, then lay back, closing his eyes again. If nothing else, he could probably get a Cloak when he saw Heskith the following day, though that could be too late to help. Manners would expect him to work on the aircraft non-stop. If he waited until he was meant to be sleeping, he might—

"Here."

Logan heard a rustle and opened his eyes. Havji was standing there, holding a package he recognized as containing a Cloak. He nodded and reached out, feeling guilty because he'd persuaded her to do something she felt was wrong. "I'll return it as soon as I'm done," he said. "No one will know."

Havji reluctantly released the packet. "I will."

Logan pulled on his clothes and wrapped the Cloak about him.

"Those things are crazy." Havji was staring. "You look like a floating head. I can barely see the shimmer when you stand still."

"Good." Logan was going to take his pistol, but thought better of it, and instead handed it to Havji. "You better take care of this."

"Why?"

"Because it will make you feel better if I don't take it."

Havji gave a curt nod. "Good luck. And stay safe."

Logan pulled the Cloak over his head and headed for the exit.

As he walked along the passages, he kept glancing down to where his body should have been, but instead of seeing himself, there was nothing there. It was like having an out-of-body experience, his movements guided entirely by his body's internal sense of kinesthesia. He wondered if this was what his ancestors had felt like when they talked about dreamwalking. Could any of that be true, or was it the brain interpreting visions caused by meditation or narcotic experiences?

He stumbled, almost falling, but his body's natural sense of balance caught him and he lifted back up again. There were voices ahead, growing louder. Logan moved into a shallow dip in the passage, pressing flat against the wall, and held his breath.

Three young soldiers in a mix of uniforms ambled down the passage, chattering and joking. They passed within a couple of meters without apparently noticing anything. Then they were moving away and soon disappeared around the curve of the tunnel.

Taking a long breath, Logan continued his journey to Carl's cell. He'd only been there once but found the passage without too much hunting. As Heskith had indicated, there was no guard, and he hurried over to the metal mesh.

"Carl?"

There was the muffled sound of someone half-waking.

"It's Logan."

"What the... Go 'way."

"One question. Then I'll leave."

Carl sat up and looked around, rubbing his hand over his face. "I'm dreaming, aren't I?"

"No, I'm here. But hidden."

Carl stayed hunched on the bed, staring at the floor. "What do you want?"

"Did you tell the Corporates about this place?"

"What? Why does that matter?"

"Just answer me."

Carl shook his head. "No, I never did." They asked me, but I didn't."

"Why not?" Logan hissed.

"Because I didn't trust them." Carl hesitated. "And because I wanted them to kill just you. That's all. Are you happy now?"

'Yes. Thank you."

"Don't. I hate you."

"I know."

Logan backed away down the corridor. He inhaled deeply, realizing he'd scarcely breathed while talking to Carl. Once back at the main intersection, he turned left, determined to carry out the next part of his mission.

Logan avoided several more of Manners' team as he crept through the passages. The soldiers seemed relaxed. They must have felt relatively safe inside the caverns and weren't expecting someone to be slinking around hidden by an EM Cloak. Again, Logan had to check his bearings, but it didn't take too long to find his way to the large chamber holding the Planetary Lander and the Nomad. He waited by the edge of the tunnel to see if there was a guard, but it appeared there wasn't. With mission preparations underway, perhaps Manners couldn't spare anyone.

He entered, moving slowly to minimize any noise he might make, not entirely confident the cave was empty. The Nomad was the closer of the vehicles, its familiar bulk filling around a third of the chamber, while behind it sat the towering Lander, pointed upwards like a fat, oversized missile.

It reminded him of the classic *From the Earth to the Moon*, the Lander being the bullet and the lava tube above reminiscent of the inside of an enormous gun barrel. He wished life were as simple as in those old adventure books.

He climbed the ladder to the access door, and it slid open with a soft swish when he swiped the door patch. Normally access would be through the elevator door at the rear of the cargo compartment, but the noise would give him away to anyone within a few hundred meters.

Once inside the cavernous hold, he looked around. There was an internal elevator, but again, it would have been too loud. He'd have to get to the control room the old-fashioned way, and started climbing a ladder attached to the inner bulkhead. The cargo section had only appeared to be a few meters high, but the farther he went, the more he realized his estimate was an optical illusion. After several minutes, his injured leg was protesting, and trickles of sweat ran down his face and back.

He stopped, balancing with one foot on the ladder's rungs to give his injured one some temporary relief. "You're getting old."

Logan set off once again, struggling for grip as his hands grew slick with sweat.

Finally, he reached the access hatch and opened it manually, being as quiet as possible. After scrambling through, he lay against the bulkhead, catching his breath. When he looked up, he groaned. He was in a secondary cargo hold, identical to the first. Logan cursed—he'd have to repeat the climb. Yet another ladder stretched up to yet another bulkhead like an impossibly vertical railroad.

"One final push, old-timer." Logan imagined Aurore teasing him. She'd laugh seeing him struggling this way. "Maybe the soldiers have the right idea and when we get back, I should look at buying some extra muscle."

He knew he wouldn't do it. While Geneering could enhance you physically, the older you were, the less effective it was, and Logan was beyond the optimal age. He also wondered how appropriate it was—somehow it seemed like cheating. Besides, he couldn't afford it anyway.

The next climb was a pain-soaked blur. He was forced to stop twice to rest his leg, and when he reached the next hatch, he struggled to lift it.

"Which smart guy came up with this plan?" he murmured as he clambered to the next deck.

This section was set up with heavily padded, orange acceleration seats arranged in concentric circles, making the chamber look like a giant floral display. While passengers could travel in the cargo bays, they'd be more comfortable in this area. Again, he had to climb, but this chamber was shorter than the first two. Despite that, he swallowed a couple of painkillers he'd been saving for "just in case," his breathing getting easier as they took effect.

He dragged himself to the main control area. It had seating for a flight crew of five, with the usual dual pilot chair arrangement upfront and three additional positions arranged behind them. Logan used his last shreds of strength to scramble into the padded pilot's chair, fighting to keep his breathing from rasping.

"That's it," he muttered. "Next time, first-class all the way."

He took a few minutes to recover, then turned his attention to the instrument panel. He'd never flown a Lander of this design, but the controls followed the layout used by most modern spacecraft. The first thing he did was check on their loading, bringing up information screens on fuel capacity and load, maximum lift, and projected possibilities for launch.

He smiled. The ship was fully fueled and ready to leave at short notice. He did a quick estimate of the possible cargo and plugged that into the orbital computer. After a few seconds, it confirmed there was enough delta-v to achieve a stable orbit around Kwelengsen, with power to spare. That was what he'd been hoping for. He ran several further checks, but everything appeared to be in the green.

"Okay, Logan. Time to get your ass back down."

The return journey was easier, but still strained his leg. When he reached the bottom, he swung the hatch open, but heard voices and closed it again—leaving a small crack open. Had they heard him?

"—everyone's going nuts around here. Especially the captain," said a female voice.

"I know what you mean," said a deeper male voice. "All these goddamn alerts and exercises. Seriously, if I have to put on another alt-real visor, I think I'll puke."

"No kidding," said the woman.

The soldiers were moving, and Logan guessed they were a regular patrol circling the ships to check they were okay and that no one was stealing one from under their noses.

"I mean, jeez. When do these things ever play out like they do in the sims, anyway?" the man muttered. "You run all the variations the Battle Logistics Systems throw up, and I guarantee the other side will come up with something else."

"You know what BLS stands for, don't you?" The woman chuckled. "Bull Shit."

"And this no-frat rule sucks." The man's voice took on a different tone. "Don't you think, Francine?"

"I think you better keep your pecker in your pants and your mind on soldiering, *Corporal*." The woman laughed. "Otherwise, Manners will cut 'em off. Permanently."

"Sheesh, don't even joke about it." He hesitated. "It's enough to give any man the crumples thinking about it."

"I doubt you ever suffered that for long. Not from what I've heard."

"What does that mean? What did you hear, Fra…"

The voices trailed off as the pair moved away, and Logan took a breath. He sat down by the door, listening through the crack. It was no good moving right away. The soldiers might still be around, and the next job was simultaneously easier and riskier.

He leaned against the bulkhead, his muscles burning from the climb.

Logan woke with a start, not knowing where he was. When his thoughts cleared, he wondered how long he'd been asleep. He didn't have a watch but had the feeling that a significant amount of time had passed.

He pressed his ear to the door again and listened. The only sound was the ever-present hiss of air moving through the tunnels. After waiting a little longer, he eased open the door and climbed down the ladder. There was no sign of anyone, and he couldn't hear anything in the distance. Logan guessed it was deep into the night and hurried over to the Nomad.

Access to its control room was easier because the Nomad had an aircraft-like design and stood on its belly on heavy-duty landing gear. But it also meant Logan would be more exposed to a casual glance. He made his way through to the cramped cockpit and lowered himself into the pilot's seat. This was a ship he was familiar with, and it took him only a minute to retrieve the data he wanted. Like the Lander, it was flight-ready and fueled. Orbital status was well within its capabilities, even with a full payload, and it had plenty of delta-v for what he had in mind.

He deactivated the controls, hoping nobody had seen the glow from the instruments through the cockpit, and crept back to the side door. Again, he checked for sounds, but caught nothing and stepped out onto the rough cavern floor.

Making sure the Cloak was around him, Logan hastened down the corridors and headed to the hospital area. When he arrived, the lights were dimmed—confirming his earlier estimate that it was the middle of the night. He padded to his bed and stripped off the Cloak. As he did, he sensed movement behind him.

"Logan?" Havji hissed.

She had his pistol in her hands, holding it in the firm grip precisely described in the manual, though Logan thought he saw a slight tremble. "You're making me nervous, Doctor."

"*Me?*" Havji hesitated then lowered the gun, flicking the safety on with an audible click. "I thought you'd run out on us. It's been four hours."

"That long?" Logan looked down. He didn't want to admit what had happened but couldn't think up anything that would sound plausible.

"You said you'd be gone for an hour, max. I waited up, thinking something might have happened. Where have you been?"

Logan dropped onto the bed. "I fell asleep."

"You..." Havji's eyes were like twin searchlights, then she sputtered out a laugh. "Asleep?"

"Shhhh..." Logan looked around. "Don't wake everyone."

"Everyone else is out for the count." Havji clamped her hand to her mouth for a moment. "I... well, I dosed everyone with tranqs when you didn't come back."

"What?" Logan stared at her, then a small laugh sneaked past his lips.

"I know." Havji was still giggling. "I doped them up because of you."

"Will they be okay?" Logan asked, struggling to control his laughter.

"Oh sure. But a lot more rested and mellow come morning."

Logan smiled. "Remind me never to let you near any of my racehorses."

Havji giggled again, though this time it was softer. "Seriously, you own racehorses?"

"What? No, not really. We had a few horses on the compound where I grew up, but they weren't mine, and we never raced them. Too valuable."

"No kidding." Havji nodded. "I've never seen one outside a 3V."

"If we get out of this, I'll introduce you to them."

"I could get to ride one?"

Logan thought about how nervous Aurore had been when she tried it. He smiled again. "Well, maybe. Thanks again. Now get some sleep."

"You too."

Logan got undressed and slipped into bed, but he didn't sleep. He was thinking about Aurore and the time they'd spent together. Would that ever happen again, or was that all he'd ever have? Surely, if she was alive, there'd have been word by now?

When Manners had mentioned the other group, he'd hoped to find Aurore safe with them. But he'd heard nothing since. He wasn't even sure if Manners had established communications. That was one of the things he intended to find out the next day.

His mind filled again with the memory of Aurore on the horse. Despite her anxiety, she rode the animal like a princess. Though most people would find it difficult, her years of dance training gave her the posture and balance necessary to make it look easy. She looked like an amazon warrior as she trotted around the horse circle in the evening sun. The image burned inside Logan. He ached to be with her. He *had* to find her, no matter what it took.

Chapter Nineteen

"All dreams spin out from the same web."
— Crazy Horse (Tȟašúŋke Witkó)

When he woke, a large hand was shaking him, and Logan opened his eyes to see Heskith's jovial face. The soldier had a cup of what had to be coffee in his hand, while another was steaming on the bedside table.

"Come on sleepyhead," Heskith boomed. "Time to rejoin the working class."

Logan rubbed his face, clearing the mist from his eyes and his thoughts. He'd been dreaming about riding through sun-drenched fields of daisies with Aurore. It seemed so real, and now, the shock of reality hit him like a plunge into a cold ocean. He rolled off the bed, his legs unsteady from the previous night's climb. He swallowed half of the coffee, wincing at the bitterness.

"That's the same expression I used to see on my ex when she woke up next to me." Heskith laughed. "You snore as loud as she did too."

"I didn't know you'd been married." Logan pulled on his clothes.

"Long time ago and on a different world."

Logan nodded. He grabbed the pistol and clipped it to his belt. "Okay, let's go."

As they left, Havji emerged from behind the curtained area she used as an office and bunk space. She didn't speak but gave them a curt wave before going to check the other patients.

"I think she's glad to see the back of you." Heskith slapped Logan on the back.

"And I think you might be right."

The cave entrance had changed considerably since the last time Logan had seen it. Several benches were set up to one side, covered with a mountain of parts, while on the other sat a crudely assembled test rig holding one of the turbines, the gaping maw of the outlet pointing outside. In addition, a hoist and track had been bolted to the roof.

The other turbine rested on a pallet, looking less complete and in rougher shape from what Logan could see. "So, what's the story?"

They walked down to a freshly flattened area bearing similar marks to those in Manners' office and the hospital. Heskith pointed to the engine on the stand. "*Helga* is one hundred percent. Cleaned up pretty good, runs free, but I get nothing when I try wind her up on the test rig."

"Helga?" Logan raised his eyebrows.

"Long story. Remind me to tell it you someday." Heskith gestured at the unit on the pallet. "Now *Astrid* there—well, she's kinda rough, but as far as I can tell should work. I put her on there and fired her up, but she was so noisy I didn't dare push it anywhere near flight rpm."

Logan's mouth twitched. "I'm not sure I'm ready for the history behind those names."

Heskith stood next to Helga and gulped some of his coffee. "The way I see it—and I haven't told the captain this yet—but I think we *might* be able to get one of them running, but there ain't an ice cube in hell's chance of getting *both* functional."

"And you've been waiting for me to let her know?"

"Hey, would I do that?" Heskith winked. "I was busy conducting an in-depth analysis and assessment. Anyway, you know how important it is to get a second opinion on these things."

"Of course." Logan patted the side of Helga. "Let's check it out."

They started with basics and ran through the full checklist of standard diagnostic routines. Then, they carried out a number of additional ones they'd thought of. After four hours, they'd racked up a stack of negatives and not much else.

"We're getting nothing at the Main Control Interface," Logan said. "Which means one of two things. Either the individual control packs are no longer functional…"

"Or the MCI itself is blown. That's what I figured."

"I suppose it might be both," Logan mused. "Let's swap the MCI from Astrid and see if that changes anything."

The MCI was a large assembly with dozens of connections and took over an hour to strip off the other engine. As they worked, Heskith kept up a stream of chatter about his vintage Mach 4e Mustang. Logan wasn't especially interested, but at least it helped to pass the time.

"—could do with new battery packs, but finding good quality replacements is like excavating for unicorn poo. The ones I got in now have been rebuilt three times."

"Wouldn't it be cheaper to convert it to take modern carbon power cells?" Logan unfastened another of the myriad of connectors.

"Sure, but what's the fun in that? Nothing beats mid-twenty-first century LiAs. That baby puts out over twelve hundred Newtons. Zero to one hundred klicks in under two seconds."

"Reliable?" Logan asked.

Heskith guffawed. "Well, not so much. But you should see the styling, big guy. It's like they say—driving a 'stang makes you a man."

"Okay, that's the last." Logan pulled back from the turbine and eased the MCI off its mount to avoid damaging the connectors.

They transferred the unit to the good engine and connected it to the harness. With Heskith at the controls, Logan double-checked everything, then stepped back and gestured to the soldier to try the engine. The turbine hesitated, turned one complete revolution, then stuttered again, repeating the same sequence over and over.

"Same as before," Heskith called out. "What a pain."

"Hang on. I'll jiggle the control connectors." Logan moved back to the test rig.

"Watch yourself. There's a lot of juice running through that thing."

Logan was aware of that and approached the engine with a composite prybar. He planned to use it to prod at the connectors, hoping the material would isolate him from any shocks.

After tapping several of the subsystems, Logan noticed a change. "Hear that? It's spinning up twice now."

"Which circuit?"

Logan did a double-take. "Harmonic resonance controller."

Heskith let out a groan. "Typical—worst goddamn one to switch out."

It took another couple of hours to switch over the sub-controller and reassemble the turbine. Partway through, Heskith vanished and returned with a tray piled high with food.

"You eating for two?" Logan asked.

"You could say that."

Logan knew that the enhanced performance from Geneering came with a price, and this was a common issue. If you made the human body work at higher performance levels, you had to feed it more fuel—like any other engine.

After the brief stop to eat, they got back to it, but it was late afternoon before they were ready for another test. The long day had Logan frazzled around the edges so soon after being in the hospital, but he knuckled down and pushed through his discomfort.

This time when they tested the engine, it buzzed into life but then skipped and slowed momentarily. It repeated the same pattern, almost mirroring its earlier behavior. For the most part, it sounded healthy, but the hesitation was too strong to ignore. They stripped down the engine once again and swapped out the sub-controllers systematically. It was a long and painstaking job. By the time the engine finally turned over consistently, Logan was so tired he almost wished he was back under medical care.

With the turbine turning smoothly at its idle speed, Logan moved over to the controls and raised his voice to be heard. "Okay. Best we've got. Crank it up and let's see what happens."

Heskith rushed inside the damaged Futen, reappearing a moment later balancing what looked like a large glass tabletop over his head. He set it down in front of the test station, angling the top back. It was a safety screen, improvised from a dozen riot shields. While the shields were almost indestructible, Logan doubted that the ramshackle affair would provide much of a defense if the turbine let go at high speed.

Heskith muttered something into his comm-set and Logan guessed he was broadcasting a warning to stay clear. Heskith reached for the controller and eased the turbine speed up, creeping it higher and higher. After a few stumbles, the turbine hit its operational flight speed, the intense thrum from the impellers bouncing around the cave like a swarm of angry wasps played through a public address system.

Logan leaned over. "Are you going to go for broke?"

"Don't think the test-bed will hold it." Heskith goosed the control once more, and the scream of the turbine intensified.

Logan stuck his fingers in his ears, and both men staggered back a little. Heskith pushed the engine further, and Logan noticed the cradle creeping along the floor. He tapped Heskith's arm and pointed to the moving framework. The engine noise dropped as Heskith turned the controller back to idle and waited to let the turbine cool before cutting the power.

"Best test we're going to get," Heskith said, pressing a thick hand against one ear.

Logan nodded. Given their equipment and facilities, their only chance of running a complete trial would be by mounting it on the Futen itself.

"Good news, gentlemen?"

Manners marched toward them with her hands behind her back.

"We've had some success." Logan gestured at Helga. "On this unit at least."

"Excellent work. Now you just need to do the same with the other."

Logan tapped his hand against his leg. "That may not be possible."

"Oh?" Manners pinned Heskith with a withering glare. "A Futen Heavy Transport requires four engines, doesn't it, Corporal?"

Heskith studied the ground between him and the turbine. "Yes, sir."

"Then get on it, soldier."

Logan stepped forward. "We've been working for over sixteen hours. It's time for a break."

"*You* may rest any time you wish, Mr. Twofeathers."

"I don't think you understand. We had to—"

"I'd appreciate it if you'd address me correctly."

Logan stared at her. "Very well, *Captain*. As I was about to say, to get this unit working we were forced to cannibalize the other. It's not possi—"

"Thank you, Mr. Twofeathers. We value your input." Manners' eyes locked on Heskith once again. "What do you say, *Corporal*?"

Heskith was slow to answer and, when he did, he didn't meet Manners' glare. "I'll get right on it, Captain."

Manners spun on her heel and left. Logan waited until she was out of earshot, then turned to Heskith.

"What the hell? You know Astrid won't run. Not unless we pull the parts back out of Helga."

Heskith spat on the ground. "What a shitbake."

Logan nodded in sympathy. "Let's take a break, get some food at least."

"Sounds good, but I better stay here and look as though I'm working."

"Okay, I'll go get some. Anything specific you want?"

"Sure. Anything loaded with calories."

Logan left Heskith looking thoroughly dejected and headed for the passage leading deeper inside the caves. He was sorry about the corporal's predicament, but there wasn't much he could do about it. Manners was becoming increasingly irrational—first demoting Heskith, and now demanding the impossible.

At the mess, he loaded up as much food as he could carry. As he was walking back, he was thinking about the turbine. Even if they somehow found enough parts to fix the control system, the unit was in such poor shape it would probably detonate the first time they brought it up to operational speed. There had to be another way. What had Manners said? A Futen needed four engines. It was true. And there didn't seem any way around that.

Unless…

Logan hurried back into the entrance cave and found Heskith staring at Astrid as though his dog had run off with his lunch.

"Wrap your teeth around some of this, and stop feeling so glum." Logan tossed Heskith a ration pack.

Heskith frowned. "Fake turkey? Those are the worst. Couldn't you do any better?"

Logan chuckled. "You're welcome."

Heskith's lack of enthusiasm didn't stop him from tearing open the wrapping and taking a large bite.

"We need two aircraft for Manners' operation, right?"

"Sure." Heskith chewed noisily. "One to mount an assault on the Corporate vehicle yard, while the other goes after the supply warehouses."

"Okay. We have one working Futen but, as Manners pointed out, we don't have enough turbines for the other. But what if we didn't need four?"

"You lost me there, big guy." Heskith grabbed a second ration pack, tore it open and sniffed. "Fake beef and mustard. Better than turkey at least. You can't fly a quad-thrust with precision on three engines—the power levels would be so out of whack, you'd never control it, even with the compensators on full. Hell, you know that from when you flew that one in."

Logan glanced at the second Futen and nodded. "That's true. But how about reconfiguring it to use three turbines instead?"

"Now I know you're crazy. That's impossible."

"The Futen airframe is solid in the tail. We chop the two rear wing mounts off, then we splice the gimbal mounts and install the engine at ninety degrees."

Heskith stopped eating momentarily. "Like the old Skorpions? That'd be one hell of a conversion job. And those things weren't renowned for their stability."

Logan ran his fingers through his hair. The Skorpions were an older design of military transport that used three thruster units arranged in an equilateral triangle shape. They weren't pretty or effective, but he hoped modern flight systems were smarter than they'd been back then. "You're right, but what other options have we got?"

Heskith grabbed yet another ration pack. "None that I can see." He chewed for a couple of minutes. "How the hell would you control it? Flight system is set up for quad-thrust."

"My programming skills aren't exactly up-to-date." Logan considered the problem. "Did any of Manners' tech people make it?"

"Not that I know of." Heskith hesitated. "Oh, there's Brierton. He was some kinda technical officer, but not this stuff I don't think."

"We can check. Otherwise I guess it's down to me."

Heskith finished his ration block, screwed up the wrapping, and tossed it into Astrid's wide intake. "You think we can pull this off?"

"All we can do is give it our best shot. Get hold of Manners, tell her we need to talk." Logan cracked open a water bottle and sipped from it.

Heskith nodded and walked a few meters away. Logan saw him using his comm-set but couldn't hear what was being said. When the soldier turned back, his face was grim. "We're to see her immediately."

Five minutes later they were outside Manners' office. There was no sign of Giorg, and Logan wondered if something had happened to the young soldier. He hadn't seen anything of him for several days. Heskith was about to knock on the partition frame when Giorg showed up.

He glanced at Logan, then turned away. "She's not here."

"I just spoke to her," Heskith said.

"She's in the war room. Sent me to take you there."

"War room?" Logan couldn't believe Manners would think something like that was necessary. Their *forces* were barely enough to annoy the Corporates, let alone fight a war.

"This way."

Giorg led them through a few meandering tunnels and they finally ended up in a cavern that, based on the scrape marks on the walls and floor, had been recently excavated and given the same coating as the hospital. In the center, a number of tables were crammed with computers, and a large 3V display dominated the area. It looked like the one Logan had seen in Manners' office. Amongst the group of soldiers, Logan only recognized Brierton and Manners.

She was scrutinizing the tactical data on the 3V, with a sour look on her face that didn't bode well. "What is it now?" she said brusquely. "If you've got that engine working so soon, you must have lied to me earlier."

"It'll never work," Logan said. "But we have another option."

Logan outlined the discussion he'd had with Heskith, pointing out the benefits and weaknesses of the proposal. Manners waited until he'd finished, then scratched at her bristly, short hair.

"And you're sure this will work?"

"No, but it should. And, frankly, it's your best hope of having two operational aircraft." Logan shrugged. "I doubt that second turbine would run if we had a shop full of parts."

"And you agree, Corporal Heskith?"

"Yes, sir," Heskith barked.

Manners conferred quietly with her team. After a short discussion, she turned back to Logan and Heskith. "Get it done, and make it as fast as possible. The storm is moving in sooner than we thought. We need both those aircraft or we've no chance." Manners paused. "It's an imaginative solution, Mr. Twofeathers. You should be congratulated."

"It was Corporal Heskith's idea, actually. I only helped with some technical evaluation."

Manners opened her eyes wider. "Well, congratulations to you, Corporal. Dismissed."

Heskith turned to leave, but Logan remained where he was.

"Is there something else?" A muscle in Manners' jaw twitched.

"We'll have to reprogram the flight control systems," Logan said. "I've heard that Lieutenant Brierton has some technical skills. Perhaps he could assist us in getting the software into shape."

Manners hesitated, then looked at Brierton. "What about it, Terris? Is that within your field of expertise?"

Brierton was stony faced. "Not at all. My specialties are comms and signal processing. I'm afraid I'd be useless to you."

Logan detected a slight emphasis on Brierton's last word but didn't understand why. "In that case, would it be possible to co-opt Jarret Gillmore? He has some knowledge of data systems."

"Gillmore? Oh, the man from the mess." Manners laughed. "You're always looking to save people, aren't you?"

"Isn't that an obligation we all share, Captain?"

"Go ahead. We might as well get *some* use out of him, now we're having to feed him full rations."

Manners waved her hand in dismissal, but Logan stood his ground.

"There's more to discuss?" Manners said sharply. "Let me guess—your nephew? He's a traitor, Mr. Twofeathers. He betrayed all of us and got people killed. He's guilty of espionage, collaborating with the enemy, and sedition. If it wasn't for my regard for you, I'd have had him shot. Which is what he deserves."

Logan shook his head. "That's very magnanimous. He made his decision—he'll have to deal with the consequences. But that wasn't what was on my mind."

"Oh?"

"I have an idea, a plan you might call it, that might remove the threat of the Corporate forces entirely."

"Really?" Manners' voice dripped sarcasm. "And I'm sure it's something that would never occur to a bunch of stupid soldiers, like us."

"I'm not saying that. But I thought you might like to hear it."

Manners chewed her lip for a few moments. "We're in a strategic meeting, with a packed agenda. I'll probably regret this, but we can talk later, privately, if you wish."

"If that's your preference," Logan said.

"It is. But Logan"—Manners paused—"Don't expect me to be brimming with sympathy."

"All I ask is that you hear me out."

"Very well. See me in my office at twenty-one hundred."

Logan strode away, with Heskith falling in beside him. Neither of them spoke until they were well away from the war room.

"What the hell was that, big guy?"

"Which part?"

"About the tri-thrust being my idea. I ain't got the brains for that, and Manners knows it."

"Never undervalue yourself," Logan said. "I thought it might help you get back on her good side."

"She ain't got one."

They were almost back at the entrance, and Logan stopped at

the top of the ramped area. "I hope you're wrong."

"What's this other plan of yours?"

"I'll tell you after I've spoken to Manners. I want to get her reaction first. Besides, we've got some engineering to take care of."

"Okay. What do you want me to do? Despite what you told Manners, I ain't qualified for that kind of stuff."

"First thing is to fetch Jarret Gillmore, if he's awake. We need him on this as well. The sooner the better."

"Anything else?"

"Can you get me a large volume 3V visualizer, with engineering extensions?"

"Very funny." Heskith rubbed his wide jaw. "How about some large surface eFlimsies and a stylus?"

Logan laughed. "That'll do."

Heskith headed out, and Logan wandered over to the Futen. After grabbing a ladder, he climbed onto the back of the damaged aircraft. The width of the rear framework wasn't too far off the chord of the stubby rear wings supporting the turbines. That would make it easier to attach a reinforcing rig to hold the engine in place.

Moving back down he checked the area underneath the tail. It went up at a sharp angle, then continued as a relatively slim fuselage to the rear wings. This made room for the back ramp to come down, but Logan realized they'd likely have to sacrifice that to reinforce the new mount with sufficient cross bracing.

"Here he is," Heskith bellowed. "Had to arrange someone to look after the little tykes though."

Jarret trailed along behind Heskith, his face looking more haggard than when Logan had last seen him. Heskith had several large eFlimsies rolled up under his arm.

"Mr. Twofeathers? Is everything okay?" Jarret moved up next to Heskith, his almost skeletal frame contrasting so sharply with the soldier's Geneered bulk that they looked like a comedy act. "Are we in trouble over the rations?"

Logan held up his hand. "Nothing like that. In fact, you won't need to worry about that anymore. I need some help, and I'm hoping you might be the right person. Call me Logan, and this is Hesky."

"Welcome to the team, buddy." Heskith's large fist surrounded

Jarret's as they shook hands.

After Logan explained what they were going to attempt, Jarret shuffled on the dusty ground. "I don't have any engineering expertise."

Logan nodded. "I can handle that side of things. The biggest problem I see will be adapting the control software to work on three engines."

"Yes, the flight dynamics will be completely different," Jarret said. "Balancing the thrust vectors will be challenging, and the whole thing is going to feel like you're riding on a bubble. At least until you pick up speed…"

Jarret faltered, and his pale face reddened. "Sorry. It used to be a sort of hobby of mine."

"How so?" Logan looked up. He'd been sketching on the eFlimsies, trying not to waste too much time.

"Well, it all seems rather silly now." Jarret fiddled with the hem of his shirt. "I was hooked on Rocket Racing and was part of the university team running in the Junior Leagues. We got as high as the regional semis. I wanted to go pro at one time. It was software, but cool. If you know what I mean?"

Loan smiled. "Sure. What happened?"

"Well, the pro leagues are so competitive—a real dog-eat-dog affair. And then I met Beth and it would have meant a lot of time away from home so…" Jarret's voice faded, and a shadow seemed to cloud his face. "Anyway, I didn't want to do it anymore."

"I'm sorry," Logan said softly. "This is good news though. You worked on the control systems?"

"Control, flight stability, data acquisition, virtual interfaces. You name it." Jarret laughed. "There's no room for specialists in a junior team. I even wiped the bugs off the racer."

"Now I'm doubly glad we have you around. My skills are rusty, to say the least."

Jarret smiled shyly. "If you can get the thruster hooked up, Mr… I mean, *Logan*, I can make it fly."

"I'll hold you to that." Logan glanced at Heskith, who was doing his own inspection of the damaged aircraft tail. "How about that, Hesky?"

"Sounds perfect. We got a good team."

Logan saw the light on Heskith's comm-set flash. A minute later the soldier turned to face him. "Captain Manners is ready for you."

Logan dragged himself to his feet. "Wish me luck."

Chapter Twenty

*"The enemy of your enemy is
not always your friend."*
— Grandfather Twofeathers

Logan slowed as he got closer to Manners' office, unsure of what direction the conversation might go. While he'd faced her before many times, this was probably the most critical confrontation, and he was painfully aware of the need to convince her he was right. Giorg wasn't outside when he arrived, and he tapped on the frame of the partition.

"Enter."

Logan moved into the private area and stopped. Manners was lounging in her seat, dressed more casually than usual, with her tunic over the back of her chair. She leaned back, her lips curving into a smile. There was a small beaker on the table filled with a dark red liquid, and even from a distance, Logan caught the sweet scent of wine.

Manners noticed his glance. "Would you like one?"

"Thank you, but no. I'd like to keep my focus on the business at hand."

Manners picked up her drink and took a sip. "Very wise. Who knows what might happen if you… let down your guard."

"Are you feeling well, Captain?" Logan examined her face, sensing something wasn't right.

"Well enough." She smiled again. "And call me Charlie. We're old friends, aren't we?"

"I'm not sure how to describe our relationship, to be honest," Logan said. "I thought we were friendly, but we've disagreed a lot in the recent past."

"Sometimes friends *do* disagree." Manners sipped a little more wine. "You're a strong man, Logan. I like that, but I'm a strong woman. Sometimes two strong people can rub each other the wrong way. Doesn't mean they can't be friends, does it?"

"That's true…."

"Good." Manners moved around her desk and pushed Logan down in one of the chairs in a gentle but firm movement. Then she pulled hers closer so she was facing him, their knees almost touching.

"So what's your idea?" Manners said softly. "You've figured out a way to make a DNA-coded bomb to wipe out the Corporates?"

"That's impossible. There's no difference in our DNA and theirs." Logan shifted in his chair. "I think we should talk about this some other time. When you're more—"

"What? In the mood?" Manners chuckled.

"I was going to say more *focused*."

"Oh, but I am." Manners leaned forward, the neckline of her vest gaping. "Tell me something. Do you think I'm attractive?"

"Is that important?"

"It might be."

Logan decided he'd better outline his idea quickly. "I checked the Heavy Lifter and the Nomad. They both have the capability to achieve orbit with enough delta-v left for orbital maneuvers."

"Is that so?" Manners swallowed more wine. "You've been a bad boy—snooping around like that. I should punish you."

"I have an idea how to use them…" Logan hesitated, suddenly realizing why Manners looked different.

Her eyes were dilated and unfocused—as though she didn't see what was around her clearly, and her skin was slightly pink. It might have been the alcohol, but he didn't think she'd had enough for that. Neopenth would fit the bill, but she must be a relatively light user. It was highly addictive and destructive, and she wouldn't have lasted in her job if she used it regularly.

"I think you need a good night's rest," Logan said.

"I think I need a good, hard man." Manners laughed throatily. "And you fit the job description."

"That would be wrong in so many ways." Logan slid his chair back, but Manners grabbed his knee.

"Still worried about that wife of yours?" She leaned farther forward. "Don't worry, I won't tell."

"That's enough, Captain."

Logan stood, and Manners fell off her chair, landing on the ground on all fours.

"You want me on my knees, huh?" Manners giggled, shuffling closer.

"I better leave."

Manners' eyes opened wider. "You gonna walk out on me?"

"Goodnight, Captain."

"Jeez, if it makes you uncomfortable here, come back to my bunk. No one has to know. Hell, why are men so sheepish?"

Logan was worried. If anyone saw her in this state, she'd lose a lot of respect, and that would inevitably lead to discipline problems. Who would take a commander with a Neopenth habit seriously? But it would be almost impossible to get her to her bunk without being seen.

"It's hard, you know. All this..." Manners sprawled on the floor. "Keeping everyone in line. Managing discipline in the ranks. And facing up to what might happen with the Corporates. Those bastards. A group of bastards, led by the biggest bastard of all."

"Rourke?"

Manners grabbed her cup and swallowed most of the wine in a single gulp. "Colonel Tyson Bastard Rourke. The finest officer never to graduate from the academy."

Alcohol and Neopenth was a potent combination. Could he keep Manners talking until it put her out? It wasn't a great option but appeared to be the best one he had. Logan sat back down.

"How about that drink?"

Manners grinned. "Now we're talking." Staggering upright, she produced another beaker and filled it carelessly, then topped hers back up. "Cheers."

Logan took the smallest of sips. The wine was a dark, fruity

Merlot. In other circumstances he might have enjoyed it, but in the present situation, it was like drinking acid. "So how did that happen? With Rourke."

Manners gulped more wine, then banged her cup down, almost overturning it. She wobbled unsteadily. "Let's not talk about him. Let's talk about us. Do you know what really gets me going?"

Manners leaned down to whisper in Logan's ear, then overbalanced again and fell into his lap.

"Oopsie..." she said, snuggling against him. "This is nice. You have a nice chest. Anyone ever told you that? Strong, yet natural. Not all Geneered like those apes."

"So Rourke went to the MilSec academy?" Logan ignored the physical contact.

"We weren't lovers," Manners said abruptly. "We just used each other for sex."

"If that's all it was, why do you hate him so much?"

Logan didn't care what her relationship was with Rourke. But if he kept her focused on that, she might forget she was meant to be seducing him.

"Cadets aren't supposed to hook up with other cadets. It's 'gainst the rules. That gets broken more than any other, let me tell you. They say it leads to compli... complications and problems with judgment—but what the hell. It's no biggie."

"But you thought it was more serious?" Logan surreptitiously poured his wine on the floor, hoping it would trickle away and not be noticed. "Is that what happened?"

"Oh forget him. That's history—this is now." Manners pushed her lips forcefully against Logan's. "Let's have some fun."

Logan pulled away, wiping his mouth. "Sure. How about another drink?"

Manners laughed. "That's more like it. Hang on."

She drained most of her beaker, then refilled both from a large bottle stashed behind her desk. "Where were we?"

"Cheers." Logan picked up his wine before Manners decided to jump on him again.

"Down the hatch," she said, drinking another large draft.

"Rourke graduated at the same time as you?"

Manners wobbled again and plopped down in her chair. "No,

never did. Was supposed to. You going to fuck me or what?"

"So what happened with him?"

"Christ, you got a hard-on for that bastard or something?"

"I'm curious. They say it's better to know your enemy."

"Enemy? You don't know the half of it." Manners slurped her wine, then wiped her mouth with the back of her hand. "Week before the ceremony, he vanishes. AWOL. No one had a clue what happened. There's a big search—all the cadets pulled in for it. Combed all the training areas. Nothing."

"So what *had* happened?"

"Everyone thought he was dead somewhere. I thought he was… I don't know, dragged off by animals after an accident. Then, guess what?"

"I've no idea."

"Six months later, he's spotted in that firecracker at UW158."

Logan had never heard of the conflict but knew that Strategic AsteroTech had a lucrative extraction operation active on 2011 UW158. "The platinum mining operation?"

"That's the one. Strategic used BlackISE to take it, and Rourke was under contract to them. A goddamn first looey in six months."

The Corporates were known for rapidly promoting military people who showed promise. But Logan knew they were often bounced back, or even out, as fast. "And now he's a colonel?"

Manners snorted. "Colonel, my ass. All he did was job-hop from promotion to promotion. Talking of asses? Do you like mine?"

Logan had disposed of his wine and lifted his glass up. "Another round?"

"You trying to get me drunk or shumthing?" Manners laughed. "Don't need to, just take me to bed. Come on, we both need it."

Despite that, she refilled the tumblers and took another large gulp.

"Enough talk. Less get on with it." Manners giggled again. "Your place or mine?"

"I don't have a place," Logan said. He needed to change the subject again but was running out of ideas.

"Stop playing hard to get. You're not that innocent, buddy."

"How are the plans coming for the operation?"

"Who cares. Hey?" Manners staggered to her feet. "Do you dansh? Dance?"

"No." Not even with Aurore, Logan thought.

"Dansh with me."

Manners grabbed Logan's hand and pulled him to his feet. She fumbled with the controls by her desk and "She Thinks of Me," a slow jazz tune by the Silk Stephens Band, filled the small cave.

"They say dancing is musical foreplay." Manners pulled Logan to her and swayed, clumsily rubbing herself against him. "You think you…"

Logan waited for her to finish but she never did. She'd have dropped to the ground like a sack full of rocks if he hadn't held her up. He set her down in the chair and checked her vitals. She was breathing deeply and decidedly unconscious, but other than that, appeared to be fine.

"You'll have a hell of a headache when you wake up," Logan whispered.

With Manners safely diffused, he had time to think about what to do next. He checked the time, surprised at how late it was. Most people would be asleep, or at least in their bunks. He could have left her where she was and walked off, but people knew he'd been to see her. If he left her here, someone might put two and two together and get seven. But he'd never move her on his own in her current state.

Logan checked Manners' desk. Next to her comm-set was a dark blue-and-green blister pack of Neopenth. There were ten shots in the pack, but three had already been used. Manners couldn't have taken that much in one night. If she had, she'd have been out of it for a couple of days, not thinking about sex. He picked up the comm-set, fumbled to find the right connection for Heskith, then triggered a notification.

"Uhhh… yes, sir?" Heskith might not have been sleeping, but his voice was thick as though he had been.

"Hesky, it's Logan."

"Logan? What the hell? This is Captain Manners' code." There was the sound of people complaining in the background, and Heskith went silent for a few moments. When his voice returned, the noise was gone. "What's going on, big guy?"

"I need your help. I'm in Manners' office. Bring a blanket."

"Seriously? Jesus, what kinda mess are you in now, bud?"

"Not as much as I *will* be if you don't get over here quickly."

"Five minutes." Heskith cut the transmission.

Logan slumped on the chair and closed his eyes. He tried to imagine what might happen when Manners finally woke up. He couldn't help but think he might be back in her office early. After taking a minute to breathe, he cleaned things up a little, pouring his untouched drink back in the large bottle and awkwardly working Manners' arms into her combat tunic to cover her up.

There was a tap on the partition frame.

"Logan? It's me." Heskith stepped around the partition, his eyes snapping to Manners, her clothing still in disarray. "Neck. What the hell did you do, Logan? Is she…?"

"She's okay. Just drunk." Logan wasn't sure what to say. "We were talking, and she wanted to make it social, so we had a few drinks."

"A few?" Heskith hissed. "Looks like you got her shit-faced."

"It was her doing—not mine." Logan felt guilty over the lie. "I don't want to leave her here but can't get her to her bunk on my own."

"That's why you wanted the blanket—to cover her?"

"Better if no one knows about this."

Heskith pointed. "You grab her feet. I'll take her head."

He moved around the table and stopped abruptly. Logan followed the soldier's gaze to the Neopenth and cursed. He'd meant to put them out of sight before Heskith arrived.

"Is that…?"

Logan nodded. "I think she started with it."

"Shit. That ain't good."

"I know." Logan scooped up the drugs, then grabbed Manners' feet. "Not a word. Okay?"

"Makes me goddamn sick, I tell ya." Heskith's voice was low and angry as he wrapped the blanket around her. "Officers do that shit and get away with it. But let an enlisted guy get caught doing anything, even weed, they're up on a charge."

"Let's go."

They both lifted Manners and tried to move, but her dead weight made it awkward, and they were bound to draw attention if anyone caught a glimpse of them.

"Put your arm under her shoulder. We'll carry her between us."

That was easier, and they staggered off down the passage. The tunnels were empty, and after a few minutes, they made it to Manners' private bunk area. After dropping her on the cot, Logan pushed the Neopenth into her tunic pocket.

"Let's get out of here."

Logan headed for the door with Heskith close on his heels. After they moved away, the soldier grabbed his arm.

"What really happened?"

Logan sighed. "Another day perhaps."

Heskith locked eyes with Logan. "People like that have no goddamn right being officers if you ask me."

"She's under a lot of stress."

"You're a good guy, Logan. Sticking up for a piece of garbage like that. But she don't deserve it."

"Get some sleep. Tomorrow will be a long day."

Heskith nodded and turned toward the main military bunk area. Logan should have gone to the settlers' cave, but instead, he made his way to the hospital, hoping to find Havji.

It was quiet when Logan arrived. Only three of the beds were in use and their occupants were either asleep or knocked out. He moved to the partitioned area that Havji used for sleeping.

"Doctor Havji?" he whispered.

He heard stirrings from inside and a moment later Havji stuck her head around the screen, rubbing at her eyes. "Logan? Huhhh… what's wrong? Are you in pain?"

"I'm fine. Sorry for disturbing you, but I need to talk."

"Give me a minute."

She disappeared, and Logan heard the rustle of fabric. When she returned she was dressed in medical scrubs, and more alert.

"What is it?"

"Not here," Logan said. "Come on."

Logan led Havji to the entrance cave, guided her inside the rear cargo space on the damaged Futen, and closed the doors.

"What are we doing here?" Havji sat on the left side bench seat.

Logan sat opposite and leaned toward her. "I thought it might be the safest place."

"You think we're under surveillance in the caves?"

"I'm not sure. But I don't want to risk it." Logan hesitated. "Especially for you."

"Now I'm worried—what the hell's happened?"

Logan spotted a rivet on the floor and picked it up. He was struggling to put recent events into perspective. "Last night, I went to check out the ships in the big cave."

"That's where you were? Hell, if I'd known that, I'd never have helped. Manners is paranoid about those things."

"I know." Logan held up his hand. "I didn't do anything to them. I only wanted to check how flight-ready they were."

"I thought you were an engineer, not a pilot."

"I'm both. I specialized in space engineering. Learned to fly on the job, then qualified later."

Havji looked doubtful. "So what did you find?"

"Both of those craft are capable of making it to orbit, with a comfortable margin."

"That's good isn't it?"

"Sure. Except Manners doesn't seem interested in using them."

"I thought there was nowhere to go."

"We don't know for sure that the Corporates destroyed the *Hansen*. There was no one on it, so why would they? It posed no threat to them. But even if they did, we know there is *one* destination for sure."

Havji chewed at the inside of her cheek. "The Corporate JumpShip?"

"Exactly." Logan spread his hands. "If we take control of that, we'd severely reduce their ability to fight. And using both of our ships, we'd have the capacity to get all of the people here off-planet and back to Earth."

"Are you telling me you can pilot a JumpShip?"

Logan nodded.

"Then we have to go for it. It's too good a chance to miss." Havji paused. "Did you tell Manners this?"

"She knows from my records. Anyway, I told her about my idea a little while ago." The dim lights from outside the aircraft slanted in, creating a luminescent barrier between them. "When I first got here, I stumbled on the aircraft by accident. I suggested to Manners at the time that we should use them to make our escape."

"And?" Havji's eyes were wide.

Logan hesitated. It had been a private conversation between him and Manners, but now there was a different context to it. "She wasn't interested."

"Are you kidding…?"

"She told me she didn't want to leave, even if it was possible. That she *wanted* to fight the Corporates."

"That's crazy. Maybe you misunderstood her."

Logan shook his head. "Tonight I found out why. She was in a relationship with Rourke when they were cadets. She hates the fact that he joined the Corporates and advanced so quickly."

"That doesn't make sense. The captain is many things but she's not irrational." Havji frowned at Logan. "There's something else, isn't there? Something you're not telling me."

Logan sighed. "She's using Neopenth."

"What?" Havji stood, walked to the back door, then turned to face him. "Neopenth? That's one of the worst—are you sure?"

"I saw it. And I've seen the symptoms often enough to recognize the effects. I take it she's not getting it from you?"

Havji shook her head. "Of course not. There are almost no instances where Neopenth is a valid treatment. I don't even have any in stock."

"How would they affect her judgment?"

"Hard to say for sure." Havji thought for a moment. "Symptoms include anything from paranoia right up to full-blown hallucinations, irritability, irrationality, loss of inhibition. In advanced cases, it can bring about extreme dissociative states. The user has no connection with the real world—like someone hooked on Alt-real sims. You think Captain Manners is like that?"

"I don't think she's at that level yet. But she's definitely using the drug." Logan wasn't sure if he should say anything else but decided it was better to clear the decks. "She tried to seduce me. She'd taken Neopenth and was drinking heavily."

"Oh my." Havji gasped, then giggled. "She has good taste at least."

"This isn't a joke."

"I know. That's a potentially lethal combination. Did you...?" Her voice faltered and she looked away.

"I'm married. I don't *fool around*."

Havji looked back at him. "Good. This sounds messy enough." She sat down again opposite Logan. "What do you want to do about this?"

"I was hoping you might have an idea."

Havji didn't answer right away. "Technically, I have the authority to relieve her of her command on medical grounds."

"But?"

"I'd need far more evidence of irrational behavior and, ideally, support from the other officers." She twisted her lips. "Truth is, between you and me, the senior people are all thick with her."

"That's what I figured." Logan tossed the rivet down the cargo compartment, the pinging sound bouncing around inside the confines of the Futen. "I guess there's not much to be done. Sorry, I woke you for nothing. Thanks anyway."

"I'll keep an eye on her," Havji said. "If she displays clear signs of mental problems, I'll do something."

"Let's hope we're not all dead before that happens."

Chapter Twenty-One

"May hope forever wipe away your tears."
— Chief Dan George (Geswanouth Slahoot)

Despite the late night, Logan was up early the following day. He'd not slept well after his conversation with Havji, but regardless of that, he couldn't delay the work on the damaged Futen and dragged himself out of his sleeping area in the settlers' cave. After stopping by the mess to pick up a coffee, he headed for the main entrance, not in the least surprised to see Heskith and Jarret already waiting for him.

"Thought you'd decided to sleep in, boss." Heskith grinned.

"Rough night." Logan nodded at Jarret. "Kids okay?"

"Yes. Thanks to Hesky, I have a babysitter when I need it. And he got me this." He pointed to a portable terminal tucked under his arm. "What's the plan of action?"

"Simple. Hesky is going to detach the two rear tail wings and what's left of the turbines. You're going to study the flight control code, to see what we're dealing with. And I'm going to finish up the plans I started yesterday on how to rebuild the back end. How does that sound?"

"You want those wings off clean?" said Heskith

Logan looked at the back of the Futen. They'd need some of the components that were embedded in the wings. "As clean as possible. If the control interfaces get damaged, the game will be over."

"I'll need help getting the turbines down. Can't manage that alone, even with the hoist."

"You'll get it."

With their tasks assigned, they got to work. Heskith climbed onto the tail, to cut panels off and gain access to the wing attachment points, and Jarret vanished inside the aircraft to plug his terminal into the aircraft's diagnostic ports.

Logan was deep into the design work. He'd laid out the basic mounting idea and located the strongest mounting points for the reinforcing support frame. As he'd thought, the large rear door would be blocked, but he couldn't see any way around it given the resources they had available.

"Hey, boss?" Heskith shuffled up, his feet scratching on the gritty floor.

"What is it?"

Heskith pointed at his comm-set. "Manners wants to see you."

Logan put down the large eFlimsy he'd been sketching on—he'd been half-expecting this. "Okay. Hopefully, this won't take long."

Heskith nodded. "Watch your back."

A short while later, Logan was ushered into Manners' office. Her eyes were puffy and bloated. She gestured for Logan to sit, then glanced at Giorg.

"Private, fetch me some breakfast. I haven't had the chance to eat yet."

"Yes, sir."

"And take your time. I need to talk to Mr. Twofeathers privately."

Giorg's expression was carefully neutral, and he scurried away.

Manners waited a few minutes. "I'm not sure… things are a bit blurry…" She stopped as if collecting her thoughts. "Did anything *happen* last night, Logan?"

"Such as?"

"I'm not sure. I'm a little confused. Maybe I was dreaming."

"Too many short nights, I imagine." Logan wondered how much she remembered. Possibly very little. But if that were the case, he wasn't going to remind her. "We discussed an idea of mine on how we could use the Heavy Lifter and the Nomad."

"Oh yes..."

A momentary flicker of panic crossed Manners' face, and Logan knew she didn't remember. "I suggested using them to get people to safety off-planet and, at the same time, deal a strong blow to the Corporate forces."

"You did?" Manners shook her head slightly. "Yes, it's coming back to me. We talked about this before, I think. I told you, I'm not running away from this fight."

"You did. This isn't running away."

Manners scrunched up her eyes, and a muscle in her temple twitched. "Perhaps I misunderstood your idea. Would you mind explaining it again?"

"The Corporates have a large scale UMAP that can replace any of their equipment in short order. That, and the fact that they have orbital domination, gives them an insurmountable advantage."

"You mentioned this earlier. I wasn't convinced then, and I'm still not."

"But you can't deny their ship in orbit gives them complete superiority over us."

"Without similar ships of our own—yes."

"So, we can use the Nomad to launch an attack on their JumpShip. We fill up the Planetary Lifter with as many people as it will carry, we take over their ship, and then *we* are in control. They'd be cut off from their main supply source, and we'd be able to Jump back to Earth for reinforcements."

"And the Corporates are simply going to let you walk onto their ship?"

"I'm sure they have people on board, but it'll be a token force. They can't afford to waste soldiers babysitting their ship from an enemy they believe is trapped on the ground." Logan didn't bother mentioning his idea that the *Hansen* may be in orbit. With Manners' attitude, it was better to focus on military options.

"It *might* work..." Manners wiped her hand across her eyes. "When would be a good time?"

"If we did it while faking an attack against their forces down here, we'd have them off-balance at both ends. Might be good timing, no?"

Manners swallowed several times. "I don't remember any of

this…"

"I think you've been overworking." Logan smiled. "Could your other officers take on a bigger share of the workload?"

"No." Manners' tone was sharp. "You can't share command."

There was a tap at the partition, and Giorg stuck his head around the doorframe. "I have your breakfast, sir. Hope I'm not too soon."

"No. That's fine. Bring it in."

Giorg edged in with coffee and a plate loaded with various foods. Logan eyed it enviously—it looked like the private had grabbed one of everything, in the hope he'd find something Manners would enjoy.

"Will there be anything else, sir?"

"Not right now."

Giorg saluted and left.

"Did you ever make contact with that other group?" Logan tried to make the question sound as casual as possible. "The ones who attacked the Corporates?"

"What?" Manners was already chewing on a muffin. "Oh yes, we did."

"And?"

Manners' eyes widened. "And, they're a small group, fewer people than we have here. I hate that they managed to strike back before us. But they're closer to the city. We need to get both those aircraft functional. That's the number one priority."

"We're working on it. If you have any other vehicle technicians, they would help."

"Dammit, I want to give Rourke a bloody nose. Make the bastard pay for what he's done."

"Anything else about them?"

Manners seemed to refocus on him. "Oh, I see. You mean about your wife? Sorry, she's not with them."

"Who's leading them?"

Manners hesitated. "Staff Sergeant Carlson. Good man—a little unimaginative but competent."

"Don't recognize the name," Logan said. "I should get back to work, unless there's anything else?"

"He's new." Manners had a faraway look in her eyes. "No. No, I don't believe so. Let me know if you need anything else."

"Vehicle techs?"

"Oh yes. I'll see what I can do."

Logan walked out and came face-to-face with Giorg. The private locked eyes with him for a moment, then looked away.

"I'll be at the front cave if she needs me," Logan said.

He took his time walking back. He wasn't sure if Manners didn't see the potential of his plan, or whether her obsession with Rourke was making her oblivious. If they captured the Corporate ship, they'd cut the enemy's supply line, not to mention have a chance of getting the civilians safely out of the war zone. He'd be happier knowing he was fighting for the right thing.

When he got back, Logan was pleased to see Heskith had made good progress. Most of the panels around both rear wing roots had been peeled off, and the heavy-duty fastenings that held the wings to the superstructure were visible. Logan would have liked to cut one of those off and turn it through ninety degrees, but they didn't have the facilities to rework the TiCaLam composite of the superstructure. Instead, they'd have to use a much weaker and heavier steel space frame attached with bolts and adhesives.

Logan waved to Heskith as he approached, and the soldier dropped down from the wing, meeting Logan some way from the aircraft.

"Everything okay?" Heskith muttered.

"Yes. No problems. She doesn't remember what happened." Logan wiped his brow, unsurprised at the traces of sweat. "She's going to see if she can dig up some people to help."

"That would make things go faster."

"I asked about the other group out there. I was wondering if—"

"Your wife? What did Manners say?"

Something like a large stone seemed to settle in Logan's gut. "Aurore's isn't with them."

"Sorry, big guy." Heskith patted his arm. "I know how much not knowing is hurting you."

"She said it's a small group. Led by a Staff Sergeant called Carlson."

Heskith wrinkled his nose. "That don't make no sense."

"What doesn't? Do you know Carlson?"

"Nobody does." Heskith shrugged.

Logan froze, his muscles rigid. "What do you mean?"

"Carlson was assigned to us. But he was set to arrive on the *next* scheduled supply run."

"That can't be." Logan felt a new sensation in his gut, and it wasn't from fear of what had happened to Aurore. "Why would she lie about that?"

"Beats me. All I know is, the only way Carlson is on Kwelengsen is if he came as part of a black ops mission."

Logan stared at Heskith. Could there be a black ops team already working on the planet, fighting back against the Corporates? If that were the case, the ground war might quickly escalate into chaos, making it increasingly important to get the civilians off-world.

"Could she have made a mistake?" Logan said.

"Manners? Make that kinda mistake?" Heskith's face tightened. "I doubt it."

"But you saw her last—"

"Hey, Mr. Twofeathers. Glad you're back." Jarret wandered out from the Futen, blinking in the lights inside the cavern. "That control code is hellish."

"Call me Logan, please."

"Yes, sorry, Mr... I mean, Logan." Jarret smiled. "I'm not good at being informal, I'm afraid."

"The code is complex?"

"Extremely. The basic principles are all there, of course, but they're mired in so many security protocols and multiple redundancy packages that it's difficult to find a good starting point."

"Too difficult?" If they couldn't get the flight systems reconfigured it wouldn't matter how good the physical conversion was.

Jarret took off his old-fashioned spectacles and cleaned them on the bottom of his shirt. "I don't think so, but I'd like to get a second opinion on the areas I've mapped out—when you have time."

Some of Logan's tensions eased. At least it didn't sound like they were battling the impossible. "I'll make time this afternoon. How's that?"

"Perfect." Jarret glanced over to the passages leading into the caves. "Would it be okay if I checked on the girls? They're nervous with other people, and I worry about them."

"Sure, take as long as you need. If they're not comfortable, feel free to bring them here while you're working. If they're not in the way, there's no problem."

Jarret's face lit up, and he put his glasses back on. "Thank you. I appreciate that."

Logan watched as Jarret hobbled away, then turned to Heskith. "Did he see Dr. Havji yet?"

"Nahh. Said he had something scheduled for tonight, didn't want to risk leaving the kids until they had chance to settle with the sitter." Heskith looked worried. "Sure hope the doc can fix him up."

"She'll do what she can." Logan grabbed the eFlimsies he'd been working on earlier. "I better get back to it."

"Me too. I'm disconnecting all the control lines from inside the wings. They're a bitch to get at. After that, I'll need some help. It'll be time to unhook the wings and rotors."

Logan nodded. "Let's hope we have some extra bodies by then. If not, we'll have to look for *volunteers*."

Heskith snorted. "They're in short supply in this army."

"I'll settle for *voluntolds*."

It took another day and a half to complete the work and prepare the modified Futen for flight, with Manners calling for updates on an hourly basis. Logan and Heskith had been working around the clock, taking catnaps when they were too exhausted to carry on. Even Jarret had been putting in long hours, though he insisted on having meals with his children and sleeping next to them.

Logan checked through the modifications to the flight system. Jarret had done a good job on the changes and successfully modified the code to balance three turbines instead of the usual four.

"It's going to be like flying a unicycle," Jarret said, while he and Logan reviewed the code. "Even using the automatic systems, the pilot's going to have to watch the aircraft closely, or else it'll go haywire."

"That would be me then," Logan said.

"Seriously?" Jarret's eyes opened wide. "You're not going to let one of the military guys handle it?"

"I told Manners I'd fly one of them. And there's no one else better qualified. If there is, I'll happily stand aside."

Heskith had ambled inside the aircraft as they were talking. "You're nuts, big guy. I told you, no one volunteers." He spun a wrench around his finger. "I'm all done with the plumbing. Who knows if it'll work, though."

The three men left the Futen to look at the finished conversion. The turbine had been mounted to the back using a steel plate box affair, with a heavy-gauge tubular frame that attached the box to the airframe. It had eight triangulated supports running back to various points on the main chassis, designed to relieve the additional strain that the sideways mounted turbine would bring.

They couldn't weld it in place, so everything was bolted, glued, wrapped with wire, then more bolts and adhesive. It made the rear of the aircraft look as tidy as a porcupine that had argued with a bobcat and lost.

"Near as I can make out, either this thing's gonna fly"—Heskith gave a lopsided grin—"or drill a new tunnel all the way through the mountain."

"Thanks for the vote of confidence." Logan laughed and looked at Jarret. "What do you think?"

Jarret stared at the messy framework. "Sorry, I don't know anything about structural engineering. But it's ugly."

"The best things always are." Heskith's laugh boomed around the cave. "Look at me."

"Are we ready for a test?" said Logan.

"We better be," Heskith growled. "Manners ain't gonna take any more delays."

"Okay. What's left?" Logan asked.

"I need to verify the limiter code I added for the rear turbine," Jarret said. "It's glitching and there's a chance the unit could invert in some circumstances."

"I got to do another purge on the lines," Heskith said.

"Okay. Let's say thirty minutes." Logan looked at the time. "I'll check in with the captain."

"Check she's not messed up again, you mean?" Heskith's face darkened.

Logan shot Heskith a warning glance, but he stared back unperturbed. Since the night Heskith had helped Logan with Manners, he'd become increasingly and openly critical of her, leaving Logan worried that the soldier might end up in greater trouble if word got back to her.

Giorg was outside Manners' office, scribbling on several eFlimsies, but looked up as Logan approached. "She's not here."

Logan raised his eyebrows. The Captain was usually conscientious, and it was halfway through the morning.

Giorg looked away. "She's not feeling well."

"At the hospital?"

Giorg reddened and his voice grew quieter. "She's in her private quarters."

A surge of realization washed over Logan. Manners must have hit the Neopenth again. He couldn't help wonder if anyone else had been involved, but Giorg wouldn't say anything if he knew.

"We're about to test the repaired Futen. Would you inform her when she's available?"

"Certainly."

Logan waited for a few moments, but Giorg didn't say anything else.

"You've been avoiding me, Giorg. Why?"

Giorg blushed deeper. "Avoiding? I wouldn't say—that is, I'm not."

"I think I know you better than that."

"I've had a lot on my mind." Giorg's eyes darted around his desk. "Captain Manners keeps me busy. We *are* at war you know."

"Maybe, but there's something else. I can tell."

Giorg's jaw set, but he didn't answer.

"It's okay," Logan said. "You don't have to say anything. But remember, I'm here if you need a friend."

"Pasquale's dead."

Logan's ears buzzed as if they'd been flooded. "Debiasi? My electrical engineer? How do you know?"

"Linnie's with that group we made contact with. She passed on the message."

Logan had been so wrapped up in his own worries, he hadn't thought about Linnie or Pasquale since the invasion. They weren't soldiers, and he'd assumed they'd been captured with the other settlers.

"She must have taken it hard." Logan had assumed his two junior engineers were more than friends. They spent a lot of time together, even when they weren't working, though he hadn't realized Giorg knew either of them. "They were close."

"*They* weren't the only ones."

Giorg's words were nearly a whisper, and Logan realized there was more to the soldier's reaction. "You were involved with them?"

"Him." Giorg's voice cracked, and his head dropped. "He liked both. But all I wanted was him."

"I'm truly sorry, Giorg," Logan said.

"What difference does that make now?" Giorg stared at Logan as though he blamed him.

"I have to leave. We need to run a test." A thought occurred to Logan. "I don't suppose Linnie had any news about Aurore, did she?"

Giorg stiffened as if he'd been hit by several hundred volts. "Aurore?"

"My wife."

"No, she didn't mention her."

Logan nodded. "Okay. I keep hoping."

Giorg's mouth snapped shut, and after a short while, Logan left.

He headed back to the cave entrance, mulling over Giorg's reaction. He was upset about Pasquale, and trying to keep a lid on Manners' issues would undoubtedly put him under stress. But Logan was sure that wasn't the full story. Something else was affecting both Giorg and Manners, and possibly others besides, but he couldn't put his finger on the answer. Unless the knowledge of Manners' drug problem was now more widespread. Whatever it was, it had his stomach in knots.

Back at the aircraft, Logan found Heskith and Jarret drinking coffee and chatting like old friends. "I hope this tea party means you're all done."

"Couldn't be done-r," Heskith said. "How was Manners?"

Logan thought of ignoring the question, but it wasn't his job to protect her. Besides, he didn't want to lie to Heskith after all the man had done for him. "Unavailable."

Heskith snorted. "I guess preparing for the big offensive isn't important enough."

"She's ill." Logan kept his tone neutral.

"Right." Heskith's tone was so acerbic, even Jarret picked up on it.

"Is there something wrong with Captain Manners?"

Logan didn't reply and shook his head at Heskith, but the soldier ignored him.

"Nothing another *fix* won't cure." Heskith's face twisted up.

Jarret turned pale. "You mean *drugs*?"

"Got it in one. Our wonderful leader loves the old Neo-Nuggets."

Jarret looked from Heskith to Logan and back. "She's a Neopenth user?"

"Keep your voice down." Logan's whisper was sharp. "Captain Manners has some problems she needs to work through."

"Stop trying to sell him, big guy." Hesky downed the last of his coffee. "She's a full-on bean catcher."

Jarret turned to Logan. "She's in charge—of everything…"

Logan nodded. "I know. Sometimes it gets too much for her…"

"But Neopenth? Some of the other students in college destroyed themselves with that." Jarret's face grew longer. "And most of them didn't go down alone, you know?"

"You got it right, rocket-man." Heskith kicked at a rock and it skittered across the floor. "They usually go out in a blaze."

"Enough." Logan raised his voice. "This is a private matter. So let it drop."

"But—" Jarret stopped when he saw Logan's hard-faced expression.

Logan led Jarret away from Heskith. "Don't worry. She's not making the decisions on her own. She gets lots of feedback and advice from her staff."

"I'd feel a lot better if you were in charge, Mr—I mean, Logan."

"She's sick but getting the help she needs." Logan wished that were true.

"That may be so, but all our lives are in danger."

Logan couldn't think of a defense. Jarret was right, but they were stuck with her, at least for now. "I'd rather you didn't talk about this. Captain Manners needs our support."

"Does she deserve it?" Jarret watched Logan for a long minute.

"Many people would say no and maybe they'd be right. But what would happen to this group if it became widespread knowledge?"

Jarret didn't answer right away, and Logan guessed he was thinking about the panic such a revelation would bring.

"I won't say anything. You'll take care of it, won't you?"

Logan wanted to say he would, but he knew there was little he could do on his own. He also knew that without any clear signs of instability, the other soldiers would close ranks and protect her, no matter what. The only chance of stopping Manners was Dr. Havji, and she wasn't prepared to do anything without visible evidence.

Logan clapped his hand on Jarret's shoulder. "I'll take care of it."

Relief washed over Jarret's face, and Logan felt even guiltier. His reassurances were as hollow as the cave they were standing in. "Come on. We'd better get this thing tested."

They turned back to Heskith, who seemed deeply engaged in examining his own boot.

"You ready, Hesky?" Logan said.

"Sure. You taking her up?"

"Unless you know someone better qualified."

Heskith shook his head, and Logan moved toward the Futen's side door.

"I'm worried about the controller response curves," Jarret said. "They may need adjusting, but without seeing them in operation, it's impossible to know."

Logan stopped. "Can you monitor them remotely?"

"Yes. But I can't modify them. And you can't handle it while flying."

"Then I hope it's close enough."

Jarret scowled and his narrow jaw set tight. "I'm coming with you."

"I can't allow that," Logan said. "Think about your girls."

Stubborn determination filled Jarret's face.

"Okay. Let's go." Logan looked over at Heskith. "Do you want to make it a full family outing?"

Heskith wiped his hands with a rag. "I only fix 'em."

Logan nodded and made his way to the pilot seat. Jarret climbed into the spare, opened up his terminal, and plugged it into the diagnostic port.

The power packs were sufficient for any realistic test they might do, and Logan flicked the switches on the engine starters. The aircraft shook as the turbines came up to idling speed, and the framework making up the superstructure groaned and creaked.

Logan glanced at Jarret "There's still time to change your mind."

Jarret was tapping on the keys with one hand, while the other had a white-knuckle grip on the seat. "And lose my chance to be a hero?"

Logan made sure the turbines rotated fully, then pushed forward on the throttles, making them scream louder. The aircraft lurched but didn't take off. The airframe was juddering so much, it was hard to see the instruments. He found the bite point—where the thrust was balancing the Futen's weight—then eased the throttle higher and the aircraft lifted off. Almost immediately, it slid to the left, directly toward the other aircraft, and Logan fought to control the slide.

"I'm tweaking the control curves," Jarret yelled over the deafening roar of the engines.

Logan felt the slide weaken as Jarret manipulated the programming, and he relaxed the sidewards pressure on the controls. Finally, the Futen stabilized, and the turbines seemed to smooth out a little. He brought the aircraft's nose around, so they were pointed out of the cave mouth, then used the controls to edge them into the patchy sunlight under the canopy of trees. Once in the open, he increased the throttle, dropping the nose and letting the engines increase their airspeed.

"That's close," Jarret said, staring at the rush of water.

Logan balanced the engines, and they leveled off. "Should have brought fishing gear."

They were a couple of meters from the river below, and the tunnel-like foliage flashed by on three sides. The top speed was lower with the transport being short a turbine, but also because the modified rear unit only pointed left or right. But despite that, the ride seemed more than fast enough in the confined area. Logan saw a clear patch of sky ahead where the trees opened up and pushed the throttle to full power.

Jarret let out a gurgle as they shot out from the trees and soared into the air. As exhilarating as it was, Logan felt the lack of performance and the logy response of the controls.

Logan remembered an old phrase—the amazing thing about a dancing bear is not how well it dances, but that it dances at all. He put the aircraft through a series of twisting maneuvers, to explore the limits of performance. Although he couldn't hear anything over the roar of the turbines, he could imagine the airframe creaking in protest.

Looking over at Jarret, Logan gave a thumbs-up. They now had two aircraft capable of operating—barely in time for the planned mission, now only a day away. He turned the Futen back toward the base and dropped back down to skim over the water surface. No more excuses. No more preparation. It was time to fight.

Chapter Twenty-Two

*"My ancestors fought for their lands.
Who am I to break with tradition?"*
— Grandfather Twofeathers

"The attack will be a three-part operation." Manners stood at the head of the war room, with the full assembly of soldiers standing to attention in ranks in front of her. On her right, a large 3V screen displayed a solid map of New Hope and the surrounding area.

"Meteorology says a storm will hit at zero three thirty Juliett. Team One—led by me—will drop into the enemy shipyard at zero four hundred. Our goal is to damage or destroy as much of the enemy's air capability as possible, by any means."

The 3V animation showed a rendering of the Futen landing near the Corporate aircraft, followed by several explosions. The ripple of applause from the soldiers was interspersed with muted cheers, and when they died down, Manners continued.

"Team Two will be led by Lieutenant Brierton. Their job will be to hit the industrial area in the south of the city." This time the 3V displayed the Futen touching down by the warehouses. "At zero four fifteen they will land and recover as many supplies as possible, and destroy the rest."

Fear bit at Logan. "Captain Manners?"

Manners took her time acknowledging him. "I'm sure everyone recognizes Mr. Twofeathers. He'll be flying the transport for Team Two."

"I thought the second team was supposed to recover supplies as stealthily as possible."

"The plans have changed." Manners' voice was coldly threatening. "The more damage we can inflict, the more it disadvantages the enemy and increases our chances of success."

"We aren't going to win this," Logan said. The soldiers closest to him muttered and edged away. "The enemy has far greater resources available."

"The plans are final, Mr. Twofeathers. They've been agreed through consultation with the senior *military* personnel."

"What about my suggestion for leaving Kwelengsen?"

"It was considered. And discarded as impractical," Manners snapped. "Now, please. This is a mission briefing, not a debate. If you continue this interruption, I'll be forced to have you removed."

Logan knew she meant it, no matter how much she'd needed him to repair the damaged Futen. She'd certainly find someone to replace him if he made too much of a stink—regardless of how bad a pilot his substitute was. "Very well, Captain."

Manners gave a slight nod. "At zero three forty, before Teams One and Two deploy, Team Three, the group we recently established contact with, will launch a ground attack in the west. Their objective is to draw as much attention to that area as possible, giving the other teams the best chance of success."

The 3V showed several ground vehicles and people on foot making their way to the city, then firing weapons.

"At all times, you are to be on the lookout for targets of opportunity," Manners continued. "Any chance to reduce enemy numbers or damage their operation must be taken, and could turn the tide in our favor.

"Squad leaders will fill in the details." Manners pointed to a group of soldiers sitting off to one side. "Any questions, ask them. Dismissed."

Logan pushed his way through the ranks as they broke into groups, and walked up to Manners, interrupting her talk with Brierton.

"This is not the time for discussion," she said. "If you disagree with the mission, you can withdraw."

Logan choked back his anger. "I agreed to do this. I'm not going back on that unless you force me."

"Then I suggest you tend to your responsibilities."

"Perhaps we should discuss what happened the other night," Logan said. "The one you don't remember very clearly."

Manners stared at him as if he were a slug that had crawled out from under a rock. "I don't know what that might be, but this operation will dust off in two hours. We're going to give that bastard Rourke something to make him regret invading this planet. Isn't that right, Lieutenant?"

It was obvious Manners wasn't going to let anything stop her plans. Even if Logan told everyone about her drug problem, he doubted anything would change. The mood in the room matched hers—they all wanted a fight.

Brierton nodded, his dark brown features impassive, but his eyes gleamed. "It's a solid plan and has a good chance of working."

"One question," Logan said.

"Yes?" Manners sighed.

"Did you decide to change the plan before, or after, I fixed the Futen?"

Manners frowned. "Does that matter?"

"I just want to know how badly I was played." Logan spun on his heel and headed toward the exit.

Once outside, he stopped for a minute, gasping to release his anger. If they had to fight, then he was ready. But to do it in such a careless and pointless way was crazy.

"Logan? You okay?" It was Dr. Havji. She was staring at him with concern on her face.

"What did you think of the show?"

Havji stiffened. "What I think doesn't matter, does it?"

"So you agree with Manners' plans?"

"I think her plans are going to cause a lot of deaths."

"And you can't stop her based on that?"

Havji gave a sad smile. "We're the military. That's what we do."

Logan noticed the doctor had a pistol strapped to her waist. "You're going too?"

"If someone's going to get hurt, it's my job to be there to help."

"I'm sorry."

Logan left Havji and headed for the cave entrance. He wanted to be alone for a while to gather his thoughts. Inevitably, he thought about Aurore, and where she might be. Was she alive? Given the fact that no one had seen her at the prison camp in the city, or with any of the three groups that escaped, it seemed impossible she was. He slammed his fist into the passage wall as he walked. Maybe Manners was right, after all. Maybe all that was left was to take revenge on the people who'd invaded their world—retribution against those who'd destroyed paradise. Memories returned—Diouf and the children, his struggles with Tepfer in the mountains, and his failure with Carl, all tearing at his core of belief.

"Hey there, big guy." Heskith came up behind Logan, holding out his hand. "Time to say goodbye, bud. They're breaking up the team."

"You're part of Team One?" Logan rubbed his hand over his face. "Who's flying?"

"Who'd ya think?" Heskith grinned.

"Wasn't Giorg going to—"

"He sucked in the Alt-Real training." Heskith shrugged. "Besides, if you have to fight, I always say you might as well be at the front. Who wants to live forever, right?"

Logan felt numb but gripped Heskith's hand firmly. "See you when we get back."

A stream of soldiers emerged from the tunnels at the rear of the cave, heavily loaded with weapons, and marched toward the two Futens. Brierton was among them and headed straight for Logan.

"You ready, Mr. Twofeathers?"

"Call me Logan. Everyone else does."

"Very well." Brierton turned to face the bustle of soldiers and raised his voice. "Team Two—assemble on me. Team One—follow Corporal Heskith."

When everyone was in position, Logan was dismayed to see almost two dozen people lining up for their flight. It was a battle unit, not a provision-gathering team. He glanced toward Heskith—Team One was larger.

"How are we going to fit in the supplies if we're carrying all of these people?" Logan said to Brierton.

"We don't expect them all to come back." Brierton's voice was grim.

Logan wondered how many of the soldiers were aware of that. "What do the combat sims estimate our losses will be?"

"Sims?"

"I presume you've run some?"

"Captain Manners doesn't place a great deal of faith in simulations." Brierton smiled. "Neither do I."

Logan didn't say anything, but his fears ratcheted up another notch. Brierton was cut from the same cloth as Manners. At that moment, she marched down the ramp and approached the other aircraft. Every inch of her body appeared to have a weapon strapped to it, and she was carrying a heavy QuenchGun.

"Time to board, I believe." Brierton handed a comm-set to Logan. "This is set for the Team Two frequency."

Logan climbed through the narrow side door, moving through to the cockpit. Brierton followed and slid into the co-pilot's seat next to him.

"What's the state of our weaponry?" Brierton locked the harness straps around him.

"Two automatic QuenchGuns that can run either autonomously or under control," said Logan. "They're about two-thirds full. We also have a grenade launcher. There's only one ammunition pack for that—thirty-six rounds."

Brierton nodded. "Anything else?"

"Sixteen missiles, configurable air-to-air, or air-to-ground. And an active cloaking system."

"I guess that'll have to do." Brierton clicked the last of his straps into place. "We'll do two passes to the west of the city as we come in, to reinforce Team Three's diversion on the ground and make it appear we're mounting a strong offensive there."

Logan snugged his harness tight. "That wasn't mentioned earlier."

"Direct orders from Captain Manners." Brierton checked his rifle. "You missed the meetings."

"I was busy. Perhaps you noticed."

"This should help." Brierton pulled the weapons control interface close to his lap. After checking out the onboard ordnance, he established a connection to a Shuriken Attack Drone. "Take her up."

Logan checked the power packs. They were charged, and he ran through the full range of pre-flight checks. He started the turbines and waited until they came up to speed.

"Two, this is One Actual. Follow us out." Manners' voice buzzed in the comm-set.

The turbines on Heskith's Futen started spinning. The vibration from the engines shook the aircraft, and the scream of the engines filled the cave, even temporarily drowning out those on Logan's aircraft. The other Futen trundled a couple of meters, then lifted into the air and vanished through the cave entrance.

"Hang on," Logan called out, then increased the throttle.

The modified Futen lifted, and Logan guided it through the cave's maw. It was dark outside and he switched on the cockpit nighttime mode to enable him to see. The enhanced image filled the windows around them, showing their surroundings clearly, and illuminating the cockpit with a ghostly light.

Heskith's Futen was moving ahead through the tree-lined passage, and Logan pushed the throttle forward to follow them. They were supposed to stay together until they reached New Hope, and Logan hoped Heskith remembered to allow for the lower performance of their patched-up aircraft.

"Activating EM-Cloak." Heskith's voice sounded somehow smaller than usual.

"Acknowledge." Logan did the same.

The Cloak was slow in deploying, and Logan worried that it wouldn't engage. The tail conversion had been so rushed there hadn't been time to inspect all the other systems. But finally, the indicator lit up, telling him it was operating, and he breathed a sigh of relief.

Heskith spoke again. "Engaging autopilot."

Logan acknowledged but didn't switch on their autopilot. Although Jarret had managed to get the flight stability systems under control, the autopilot still thought they had four turbines, and kept trying to tip the rear engine into a horizontal flight configuration.

"Why aren't you using the autopilot?" Brierton yelled.

"I'm it," Logan said. "This will be a strictly hands-on experience."

Brierton shook his head. "You better not fall asleep then."

Logan turned the aircraft, following Heskith's. They were heading straight for the Magnier mountains, planning to cross and drop down the other side, then make their way northeast until they hit the city. It was risky, but cut down the flight time, and meant they'd be trailing behind the predicted storm front, which should provide cover.

As they flew east, the sky clouded up. Soon they were in the foothills and started gaining altitude to slip over the peaks. Some of the mountains were higher than even a healthy Futen's maximum ceiling, and the route avoided those, but Logan wasn't sure his modified aircraft would make it even over the lower path.

He kept a close watch on the instruments. As the air thinned, it reduced the turbine's performance, making the aircraft reluctant to climb. Heskith wasn't having the same issue and was leaving them behind. The ridgeline was still several hundred meters above them when the Futen shuddered, and the nose dipped despite Logan's attempts to correct.

"We can't make it," he called to Brierton.

"We have to."

"We'll need to find another way."

Brierton hesitated only a moment. "Stay on course, Logan. That's an order."

"You can order *me* all you like, but you can't order the laws of physics." Logan struggled to level the aircraft. "If I follow that course, we'll fly right into the mountain."

Brierton tapped his comm-set, and Logan knew he was talking to Manners on a private frequency. He banked the Futen northward. The peaks were more rugged there but offered a chance to slip through a lower pass.

"Logan?" Manners sounded in his comm-set on a direct channel. "Is this some sort of game?"

"We'll never get over that ridge. If you want us on this operation, we need a different route."

There was a long pause. "Very well. Reconnect with us as soon as you can. I'll confirm with Lieutenant Brierton."

Logan opened the navigation maps and zoomed in on their current area. A narrow ravine cut through the mountains about fifty kilometers to the north. It looked like it led to a series of canyons that might provide a way through. If they could get past the first ridge.

Silently, Logan adjusted their course, heading for the gap.

As they traveled north, the temperature dropped, and the sky grew cloudier. Neither of Kwelengsen's moons had risen at that point, which Logan knew had been another reason for selecting this date. The lower temperature helped the turbines because the air was thicker and more effective at providing lift, but it also taxed the power cells. By the time they reached the crevice Logan had spotted, their power reserves had dropped thirty percent.

When he brought the Futen around to the east, Logan realized the maps had been deceptive. The ravine was narrower at the bottom than it had appeared. Despite this, he maintained course. While the night enhancement mode was good, it provided a slightly distorted view of the world around them. When the base of the crack was directly in front of them, Logan brought the aircraft to a hover. The sensors showed the passage was barely fifteen meters wide.

Brierton noticed for the first time what they were facing. "Are you suggesting we go through there?"

"It's that or we find somewhere else to cross. And we're already using too much of our power reserves."

"That's suicide."

"Isn't that the point of this mission?" Logan brought up an aspect projection onto the window display and targeted the crevice. The projector overlaid a one-to-one outline of their craft sized to the distance of the gap. "We've got about a meter clearance."

"Is that enough?" A bead of sweat ran down Brierton's temple.

"We're about to find out."

Logan nudged the throttles forward, steering the aircraft into the gap. It was a risky maneuver. The wash from the turbines hitting the rock would make them more unstable, and they were already "riding the bubble" as Jarret had described it.

"I need to power down the Cloak, shut down the enhancement, and switch on the exterior lights," Logan said.

"I should have known." Brierton's tone was scathing. "This is all a plan to give away our position."

"The Cloak uses power and we need everything we have. And the night vision system provides us with a slightly distorted view." It wasn't the time or place for arguments, and Logan held his voice level. "Your choice. Do you want me to be able to see those rocks clearly, or not?"

Brierton paused before giving his clipped response. "Do it."

The glass went dark momentarily and then lit up again as Logan switched on powerful searchlights. He was taking a risk, but they were so deep into the mountains, it seemed reasonable. A tightly focused recon-sat would have to be positioned directly above to pick them up.

They crept closer to the ravine, the sharp, rocky walls more menacing in the natural light. Logan coaxed the Futen a few meters higher, giving them about an extra half meter on each side. As they slipped through the ravine, it felt like they were close enough to reach out and touch the craggy escarpment.

The Futen lurched, and Logan wrestled with the controls as they sideslipped toward the deadly, jagged surface. It might have been a gust of wind or the control system glitching, he didn't know. The front-right turbine housing thumped the rock, but it wasn't hard enough to make them fall. From the yells in the cargo section, though, he was sure several soldiers would be looking for laundry services when, and if, they returned.

"That's plenty close enough," he muttered, nudging the aircraft away from the rock once more.

The narrow passage was nothing like straight, and the rocky walls weaved, forcing Logan to constantly shift direction. It taxed his control over the aircraft, but after ten minutes of crawling, the crevice opened into a much wider valley.

Logan brought their speed back up to its maximum. His pulse was hammering and his hands were clammy. The return trip back through the crevice would be harder, and he wasn't hopeful they'd make it. Once clear of the rock, he switched back to the enhanced night mode and reactivated the EM Cloak.

"That was some kind of flying," Brierton said. "Sorry I got antsy earlier."

"You weren't the only one." Logan wiped his palms on his pants.

Their route had put them a long way behind Team One, and Logan pushed the Futen hard to catch up. If they were late, everything would fall apart, but there was little he could do to move the repaired Futen any faster. He lifted the aircraft high over each of the mountain rises, making use of any updrafts, before letting it plummet into the lower areas, using gravity as an assist to give them greater speed. While it helped, it also took its toll on the power packs.

Brierton watched him closely, confused by what Logan was doing but, after a little while, he relaxed as though he'd worked it out.

"Is there anything the team can do to help?" he said.

"Beyond jumping out?" Logan grinned at the lieutenant's expression. "It's simple. So much power can move so much weight at a certain speed. I don't see any way of changing that."

"In *Space Force: Marines*, Tech Sergeant Howie always has some trick up his sleeve."

Brierton sounded serious, but when Logan glanced over, the lieutenant had a smile on his face.

"I'd be glad to pick him up if you tell me where. Besides," Logan said, "I thought you were a technical officer."

"Sure. But not with this type of tech. I was in comms and visual systems."

"Interesting," Logan said. "No offense, but I'm surprised with that background the captain put you in charge of this team. Wasn't there anyone with more experience?"

"I'll try not to be offended." Brierton kept his eyes on the weapons controls. "I'm still military. And outside my specialty, I graduated top of my class at the academy in leadership and field tactics."

"Good to know." Logan executed another plunge. "The only

way to lighten the aircraft would be to dump the ordnance we're carrying."

"That's not an option."

"I didn't think so," Logan said dryly. "In that case, ask your team to blow backward."

"I didn't realize you were such a wit, Logan." Brierton chuckled. "Does it get you into trouble much?"

"Not as much as some."

The light on Brierton's comm-set flickered. But Logan didn't hear anything. After a short delay, the lieutenant nodded, and the light went out. "That was Manners. She's made contact with Team Three. They've made their way from their hideout to the outskirts of the city. They can lay low for an extra thirty minutes, to give us some catch-up time. Team One has also slowed."

"They don't want to start the party without me. I'm honored."

"Team Three can't hold position beyond that without being detected. So we need to get there quick."

Logan checked the reserves. Sixty-three percent left. Which looked good, but they'd be carrying a heavier payload on the way back and—he glanced back at the soldiers lining the cargo section—possibly a lot less.

They caught up with Heskith's Futen about two hundred kilometers from the capital, but there was no time for pleasantries. Team One would skirt the city, giving it a wide berth, then approach from the sea on the eastern side, giving them a greater distance to travel. Logan was taking Team Two straight in from the west.

The storm front was hanging over New Hope, hiding the details of what was happening, though Logan picked up traces of explosions on the threat display.

"I'm turning over control of Shuriken One to Team Three," Manners hissed over the comm-link. "They're taking a pounding down there. Logan get your ass up there and help out."

The instruments told Logan they were fifteen minutes away. "I'll be there."

"I think it's time to use *our* ace in the hole too," Brierton said.

Logan saw the soldier tapping in commands on the Shuriken interface, sending it ahead. The drone was much faster than the

Futen and would add to the confusion.

"Second Shuriken deployed in support," Brierton broadcast over the comm-set.

The cloaked Shuriken showed no signals on the Futen's instruments, but Logan spotted a much larger number of explosions ahead, where Team Three had engaged the enemy. How many civilian casualties would there be? The original plan would have minimized those risks.

The weather closed in around them, and waves of rain-heavy wind slammed into the Futen, buffeting them like a dinghy in a mid-ocean storm. Several gouts of orange flame reached skyward ahead of them, and Logan dropped the aircraft lower to make a pass over the area Team Three was attacking.

Brierton identified several targets on his screens, but the Futen's auto-targeting systems picked up more, and the aircraft lurched as their weapons fired. There were shouts from the cargo space, but Logan had no time to check if everyone was okay. Battle had been joined.

Chapter Twenty-Three

*"Force, no matter how concealed,
begets resistance."*
— Crazy Horse (Tȟašúŋke Witkó)

Logan banked the aircraft around after they'd made the first run and brought the Futen back over the target area for a second pass. Their weapons had caused considerable damage, and flames leapt from several buildings, illuminating the rain-soaked skies with a hellish red glow.

While helping to conceal them at a distance, the rain also gave away their position as it clung to the hull forming a visible haze. This was confirmed as a trip-hammer of pops and bangs impacted against the aircraft's fuselage. Logan heard screams from the rear compartment and gritted his teeth as he threw the aircraft left and right in a series of evasive maneuvers. It worked, but the Futen's sluggish reactions were worrying.

"We can't risk a head-to-head fight," Logan yelled. "We don't have the mobility."

"Targeting hardened enemy ground forces," Brierton said. "Bring us around for another pass."

Logan hoped the lieutenant had taken note of what he'd said, and turned the cumbersome aircraft around. Several targets had been designated by the ground forces, and Logan fed the information through to the swivel-mounted QuenchGuns.

When they came into weapons' range, the Futen juddered as

the recoil from the QuenchGuns shook the aircraft. A missile warning flashed, and Logan tried to turn them onto a different course, but it was like trying to throw a punch underwater. The airframe shuddered as the defensive systems deployed a wave of decoys and flares to lure the missiles away.

"Do you see it?" Logan shouted.

Brierton stabbed at the systems in front of him. "No. Something in the air. That's all I know. Re-assigning Shuriken to defense mode."

Logan dropped the Futen until they were almost clipping the tops of the larger buildings, and the wet roofs glistened as they flashed below. This had been the main housing section of the city, but now there was no sign of life—everything in darkness apart from the flames.

Brierton put his hand on Logan's shoulder. "We've done what we can. Head for the warehouses."

Logan turned the Futen as directed, wondering how much extra damage Team Three would suffer having no air support. While they'd agreed to the operation, had Manners been any more honest with them than she'd been with him?

The southern part of the city was quiet. The diversion was working so far as Logan could tell. The slab-like warehouses were all dark, with no signs of fire. A large yard adjacent to the buildings provided a convenient landing site. According to their surveillance data, the Corporates would usually have guards posted, but anyone assigned there must have been called to respond to the attack in the west, leaving it empty.

"Bring us in low over the main warehouse roof," Brierton said.

Logan hovered the aircraft a meter above the flat roof.

"Washington, Pidhajeck. You're up," Brierton called into his comm-set. "Keep us covered."

There were a couple of quiet confirmations, then the side door indicator lit up. A few seconds later, it closed and Logan lifted the aircraft clear of the building, drifting the Futen toward the yard at the front.

"Hold here," Brierton ordered. "Give the guys time to look around."

After a few minutes of hovering, Brierton gave the go-ahead and Logan lowered the aircraft, the thrust from the turbines so intense it whipped up a storm of small stones despite the floor being hard packed. Brierton was out of his seat before the engines shut down, and by the time Logan made his way back, the cargo bay was empty.

"One Actual." Manners' voice sounded in his comm-set. "We're coming down by the shipyard."

Outside, Logan found several of their team positioned around the aircraft in defensive positions, while the others were hurrying after Brierton toward the warehouses. The unaccustomed cold bit deep as the wind buffeted Logan, carrying with it a faint smell of burning. The warehouses were dark gray blocks against the faint orange halo as the rain bounced off them. Without thinking, Logan ran after the soldiers. They had no time to waste. Every minute's delay meant fewer supplies for everyone.

The warehouses weren't large by Earth-based standards. As yet, Kwelengsen didn't have much need for mass storage—other than the centralized emergency food storage areas. Before the invasion, domestic farming had reached a point where the settlement was largely self-sustaining, though with the help of the various CESA-contributing nation-states, stockpiles had been laid in to buffer against the worst of circumstances.

Inside the warehouse, Logan found Brierton dispatching the soldiers. The corridor split in two directions. The passage to the right led to the food storage, but Brierton was sending his soldiers in the other direction—to the industrial areas.

"Wait a minute." Logan grabbed Brierton's arm. "The food is this way."

Brierton shrugged Logan off. "Do you think we'd risk all this for better quality rations?"

"Let me guess. You found out the Corporates are using this area to store weapons and decided you needed an advantage."

"We're leveling the playing field," Brierton snarled. "We can't win a war without ordnance."

"We can't eat guns."

"If you want to risk your neck collecting cookies for lazy settlers, go ahead. But the equipment is first priority."

"We'll see about that." Logan yelled into the comm-set, "Manners—Lieutenant Brierton is recovering enemy equipment instead of food. Order him to carry out his mission."

Some of the soldiers stopped to listen, but Brierton waved them on. "Move it. We need every weapon we can get our hands on, the heavier, the better." He turned back. "You're wasting your time, Logan."

"One Actual. This is Logan. Please order Lieutenant Brierton to pick up food supplies as planned."

Logan waited, then the comm-set buzzed.

"This is One Actual." Manners' voice was cold. "Charges planted. The rocket goes up in two minutes."

"She doesn't care, Logan," Brierton said. "She was happy to go for this option. Especially after I introduced her to the powers of Neopenth."

Logan spun around. "You?"

"Why not? Oh, I didn't force her, she wanted it. All I did was *encourage* her to relax a little."

"But why?"

"Isn't it obvious?" Brierton spat. "No, I suppose it wouldn't be to you. You chose to come here—I didn't. Back on Earth, I had it pretty good. The salary for less senior officers isn't great, but with my Neopenth contacts, I was clearing three hundred thousand a year. Soldiers will take anything, as long as the price is right and the hit is good.

"Then my CO got wind of it. And I found myself assigned to this shitball of a planet."

Logan reached for his pistol.

"Now, now," Brierton snapped up the barrel of his short rifle. "Be a good civilian and don't do anything stupid. This war is the best damn thing that could have happened. It's time for the grown-ups to play."

Logan edged his hand away from his pistol.

"That's better. If you're a good boy, I'll let you fly us back." Brierton's voice turned to a growl. "If not, we'll leave you here for the Corporates to take care of."

A stream of soldiers returned along the corridor, struggling with large crates of Corporate weapons.

"That's what we need." Brierton grinned. "Why don't you run along and pick up some candy canes? We'll see if we can find room for them."

There wasn't much Logan could do, and he headed for the food supplies. There was no one in sight, only lines of supplies stacked high in long rows. He cursed. In ten minutes, the team could have loaded enough to provide for their people for months. Now there was only him.

Hastening down the closest aisle, Logan found a pile of emergency rations stacked in cubic-meter bundles. Despite their unpopularity, they were the best combination of nutrition and calorie density. The pile was far too high for him to reach the top without a hoist, so he grabbed the lower bundle and heaved.

The pile wobbled but stayed upright. He tried once more, his muscles burning as though they were tearing under the strain. The stack wobbled again, then toppled over. Logan jumped to the side, narrowly avoiding being crushed under the heavy packs. Grabbing a bundle, he rolled it onto his back, bending under the weight, and staggered toward the doorway. Outside, the soldiers were loading military crates onto the Futen, and Logan dropped the rations by the door.

"What about this?" he said.

The soldier glanced at the pack. "Talk to the lieutenant."

Logan didn't look for Brierton and instead headed back for another of the ration packs, deciding that the more food he got out of the warehouse, the better chance he had of getting it on board. As he lifted another pack, the *zing* of a QuenchGun followed by the buzz of fully-automatic fire reached him. He dragged the ration pack over to the corridor and peered through a window. The soldiers by the Futen had crouched down and were firing across the street, but Logan couldn't see their target. It could have been an enemy drone, a ground patrol, or something else.

Logan lifted his pistol and edged his way to the warehouse entrance, clumsily dragging the rations behind him with his free hand. The high-pitched scream of an air vehicle sounded overhead, and he jumped to the nearest window, spotting a Predator drone flash by.

Then a regular thumping sound reached him, mixed with the grinding of gears and the oily whine of large hydraulic systems in action. He caught a movement and spotted the source of the noise. Logan had never seen one before, but had read enough about them in the military press while he was in SecOps. A Mule Attack Transport lumbered toward them like a giant, four-legged metallic insect, its weapons turrets firing a nearly continuous stream of needles at the soldiers and the Futen.

There were screams up ahead as Logan reached the entrance. A few of the soldiers were trying to crawl away from the opening, but most were down and not moving. Brierton was crouching behind a crate of weapons and Logan jumped over to him.

"Where's the Shuriken?" Logan said. "Target the Mule."

"It's gone." Brierton blinked slowly, and he didn't seem to recognize Logan. "Their Predator took it out on the first pass."

"Well, do something." Logan shook Brierton. "Don't just hide."

"I'll be killed."

Logan looked at Brierton in disgust. "Isn't this what you wanted?"

Brierton didn't reply, and Logan pushed him away. Staying low, he examined the soldiers on the ground—all dead. One had dropped a rifle with a grenade launcher, and Logan snatched it up, checking to make sure it was functional. It wouldn't dent the Mule's armor but might slow it down.

A ladder down the corridor led to an elevated walkway. Logan slung the rifle over his shoulder and clambered to the top, moving to a window overlooking the yard. He used the rifle to punch the clear plastic out of its frame and looked out. He had a perfect view of the Mule as well as several enemy foot soldiers sheltering next to the nearer buildings.

Logan didn't hesitate and pointed the rifle through the opening. The gun recoiled heavily as he launched a grenade. His aim was off, but he was closer the next time, and the third hit the Mule on the front of its body. Keeping the weapon at that angle, he launched round after round at the giant vehicle. He wasn't hoping for much, but maybe it would damage the weaponry or the vulnerable leg joints.

When the launcher clicked empty, Logan ran back to the ladder and slid to ground level. The Mule reeled as the grenades hit, lurching from side to side like a moose under siege by flies. Logan broke from the doorway and sprinted toward the Futen, several shots ricocheting off the gravel around him.

"Stand clear," Logan called to the soldiers hiding behind the aircraft.

"Wait, don't..."

Logan plunged inside the aircraft, and seconds later, he was in the pilot's seat. The Futen was their only hope against something as tough as the Mule. The turbines buzzed into life and were up to operating speed in moments. Logan yanked back on the control stick, and the aircraft jumped into the air.

The storm of metallic hail faded as the Futen lifted. Logan had his hands full controlling the aircraft but managed to bring the weapons console online and set the front turrets to auto-target and fire. The weapons AI didn't target the Mule, recognizing it as too big for the turrets. He was pleased it was intelligent enough to suggest using the grenade launcher and stabbed the button to okay it.

While the Mule was a good weapon against ground targets, it wasn't anywhere near as effective against an aircraft. Logan spun the Futen away, moving over the nearest buildings and dropping below the Mule's line of sight. Then he circled around, randomly popping up from different points long enough to allow the auto system to launch grenades before dropping back down.

A missile warning lit up, and Logan banked the Futen hard, triggering decoys. Nothing appeared on the threat display except the approaching missile, but the Predator was out there somewhere. He lowered the Futen until its undercarriage was almost scraping along the street. Slipping the aircraft crab-wise, he used the improvised rear turbine to spin the aircraft on its axis.

He was looking for the smallest of traces. Drones by necessity didn't have the power reserves of a full-scale aircraft, so they only ran their Cloaks for limited periods of time. He spotted a flash as the Predator appeared out of nowhere and then saw the brighter flare of rockets launching. Logan stabbed the targeting display, directing the turrets manually, and twin streams of needles spat out at the drone.

The Predator jinked several times to avoid the volley, and while it didn't go down, its left wing dropped and its Cloak didn't reactivate. Logan reconfigured his next missile for air-to-air operation and punched the fire button. The missile shot out, a wriggling trail of smoke belching in its wake. Again, the Drone tried to avoid it, but this time it was less successful and exploded in a gout of flame that sent orange flickers dancing across the nearby walls.

The rear of the Futen twisted as though a giant had slapped its tail, and Logan wrestled the controls. The Mule had tracked him and moved into the streets leading from the warehouse to get a clear shot at him. Its thick, metal foreleg swung wide, smashing through a prefab building and sending up a cloud of splintering debris. The Mule's right leg wasn't moving the way it should, and Logan guessed some of the grenades had found their mark.

He switched the missiles back to ground attack mode, targeting the damaged leg. If he could cripple the Mule, they might have a chance. Four missiles shot out, streaking toward the legged vehicle. One missed, but the other three scored direct hits on its already damaged leg.

The Mule's guns flashed in response, and Logan twisted the Futen to the right. It was too slow, and he heard sickening metallic thumps as the needles slammed into the aircraft. The warning sounded again, as the Mule launched its own missiles. He ducked the Futen behind another building, the corner vaporizing as a missile slammed into it.

Again, Logan let the aircraft slip sideways, hoping to confuse the Mule's operators. He brought up a list of the Mule's weapon points, selecting the front QuenchGun turrets as targets, and also designated the right "knee" as a priority aiming point. Then he lifted the aircraft once more to give the weapons systems a clear view.

Before he could have possibly reacted, the AI triggered a full barrage of attacks on the points he'd selected. The enemy targeting responded as fast, and another hail of needles rattled against the aircraft. Two more enemy missiles launched, but Logan was already dropping, and the missiles smashed into nearby buildings as they turned to track him.

Logan moved the aircraft a good fifteen hundred meters from where he'd last emerged, hoping to make it harder for the Mule's weapons to target him. When he popped up, the Mule was on a three-quarter angle with its damaged leg closest to him. The volley of weapons automatically fired. He punched the override and manually triggered a second volley. The Mule hadn't returned fire, even as he sank out of sight.

After moving again, Logan waited, randomizing the timing as much as possible.

"One Actual." Manners' voice buzzed over the comm-set. "Objective achieved... heavy fire... heading out. All forces, pull—"

The signal cut off. Logan tried to get it back but he wasn't sure if the comm-link was working anymore. Manners' transmission had been almost too garbled to hear. His jaw tightened. *Or maybe they didn't make it.*

Logan switched off the AI weapon system, wanting to assess the situation. When he spotted the Mule, it was bent over at the front, dragging itself around. The right leg was broken, giving it the appearance of a metal animal lamed after being caught in a trap.

He didn't feel any sense of victory. If Team One was gone, they'd lost a lot of people, and he had no idea how many of his own team were alive. And if Team Three had been up against Mules, they'd have been through hell too. The cost seemed too high, no matter what they'd supposedly achieved. He turned the Futen into the rain and headed back to the warehouses.

There were no signs of life as Logan landed, and he wondered if Brierton or any of his team had survived. He left the turbines running at their idle setting and clambered out through the side door, drawing his pistol. The supplies he'd saved were nothing but a wet pile of smoldering ashes, muddying the gravel with gray streaks. He edged close to the entrance, flattening himself against the wall. "Brierton? Anyone? It's Logan Twofeathers."

There was no reply, and he slipped inside, checking the area where he'd last seen Brierton. The weapons crate and bodies were there, but the lieutenant had vanished.

"Brierton!"

His yell faded away to silence. Logan was torn between going deeper into the equipment warehouse to search, or loading as many rations as possible and getting the hell out. If Manners was gone, the situation would rapidly turn to chaos back at the caves.

"Freeze, traitor."

The cold muzzle of a gun pressed against the back of Logan's neck. He made no attempt to turn around. "Glad you made it, Brierton. Did any of the rest of the team survive?"

"Drop the pistol."

Logan's gun clattered onto the floor. "Why are you calling me a traitor?"

"You ran when we were attacked. Left us to die." Brierton slammed Logan against the wall.

Logan gasped, feeling a sharp stab in his ribs. "No one will believe that."

Brierton used his Geneered strength to whip Logan around, bouncing him off the other wall. "They will if I'm the only one to report back."

Logan threw his arm up to block a punch, but the soldier was too powerful, and Logan stumbled back, skidding along the floor.

"Sure, then you can tell them anything. And there won't be anyone left to report your drug dealing and cowardice."

"Exactly." Brierton swung his boot at Logan who managed to roll away. Then a hammer blow hit Logan in the neck as he tried to rise, and he collapsed again in the dust.

"You better make sure you kill me," Logan gasped.

"Why's that?"

"Because if you don't, I'll hunt you down no matter where you go."

Brierton swung again at Logan's head. This time, Logan managed to partly block the blow, sending the soldier spinning. Summoning all the strength he had, Logan jumped up and smashed his fists into Brierton's spine. Lashing out, Brierton caught Logan on the nose. Logan's sight dimmed momentarily, then refocused on the image of the grinning soldier, a pistol in his hand.

"I doubt that. But there's no point risking it, is there?" Brierton raised the gun.

The warehouse wall imploded, and a flash of fire engulfed the corridor, sending Brierton crashing into the opposite wall surrounded by a storm cloud of shattered composite sheeting. When it cleared, Brierton's gun was nowhere in sight. Logan grabbed the splintered framing of the wall nearest him and pulled himself upright.

"Want to try that again?"

An aircraft's thunderous whine passed overhead and Brierton whirled around, his eyes darting in all directions.

"That's right, Brierton. They're coming for you." Logan laughed, tasting blood running into his mouth. "I'm a civilian and unarmed. All they'll do to me is lock me up, but you'll be fair game for the Corporate soldiers."

"No." Brierton scrabbled around in the wreckage searching for his gun. Then he looked up again as the noise of the aircraft increased again. "No!"

"They're going to come in here and slice your cowardly ass into small pieces." Logan pushed himself more upright. "They'll bleed you to death slowly, until they extract every drop of information out of you. And once they're done with your body, they'll pull your mind apart like cotton candy."

"They won't catch me," Brierton screamed. "I'll take the Futen and return to base."

"Who's going to fly it?"

"Those things practically fly themselves, and you know it." Brierton ran for the door, and in seconds he'd vanished into the deluge outside.

Logan struggled to his feet and limped to the entrance. He heard the turbines winding up ready for takeoff. Leaning on the charred door frame, he watched as the modified Futen wobbled, then lifted off the ground, heading up into the sheets of rain and buffeting winds.

About a hundred meters up, the Futen lurched. Logan saw the turbines spinning wildly on their gimbals as the autopilot fought to balance the thrust. The engines screamed as the control system tried to correct, each attempt more extreme. The aircraft shuddered, then went into a spin that pulled it away from the warehouses and behind nearby buildings.

A yellow-white ball of flame lifted into the night sky, followed a fraction of a second later by a painful blast that might have been thunder if Logan hadn't known better. He cradled his arm around his ribs to ease the pain and stumbled out into the sleet-filled night, welcoming the wintry chill as it numbed his body.

Reaching up, he tapped on his comm-set. "This is Logan Twofeathers, Team Two. Can anyone hear me?"

He waited, but the only noise was the wet splatter of the sleet hitting the ground and the hiss of the wind.

"Logan Twofeathers. I'm at the warehouse complex. Is anyone out there?"

Logan sank to his knees, no longer caring about the cold or damp. He was tired, more tired than he could have imagined possible. With both Futens destroyed and the soldiers dead, he'd be a prisoner as soon as the Corporate forces arrived. They'd lost their best chance of getting off Kwelengsen alive.

And, he realized, he'd lost Aurore—he finally accepted she was gone. Whatever happened, whether he lived or died, didn't matter. Tears fell from his cheeks in a steady stream, mixing into the sludgy snow and washing away. He wished he could do the same. There was nothing left—he was already dead.

The roar of an aircraft grew louder and, a few seconds later, brilliant lights lit up the area around him. Logan barely glanced up—there was no point. If the Corporates shot him on sight, he'd be grateful. The engines screamed as the aircraft settled, kicking up a blast of gravel and snow. He heard the faint sound of a door opening, then a shadowy figure holding a short military rifle moved toward him, silhouetted against the powerful lights.

"Just do it," Logan growled.

Chapter Twenty-Four

"Death and failure are opposite, but unequal."
— Grandfather Twofeathers

The figure took several steps forward, waving a hand in the air as if trying to get a clearer view. "That you, big guy?"

A second later, Logan was staring into Heskith's face as the soldier lifted him from his knees. "Hesky?"

"Heard your call," Heskith said. "Couldn't leave you here."

Logan struggled to believe Manners had allowed him to take such a risk. "The captain?"

"She caught a couple in the chest." Heskith looked away. "She ain't dead—the Doc is working on her. I took it on myself to pick you up."

They hobbled back to the Futen, with Heskith half carrying Logan. Logan felt as though he were the shell of a tree rotted on the inside—appearing strong but, in fact, long dead.

"The supplies?"

"No time." Heskith pushed Logan inside the aircraft. "The Corporates will be on top of us in minutes."

Logan clambered into the Futen's cargo bay. There were only about half a dozen people in there, most with their heads down, and several bloodstained. Near the front, Havji was attending to someone slumped on a cot, blood dripping onto the floor. As he walked past, Logan recognized Manners.

"Can you fly?" Heskith came up behind Logan.

Logan dropped into the pilot's chair without answering and checked the controls.

"I was hoping you'd say that," Heskith yelled over the turbine noise. "I figure I'm better on defense."

Logan nodded and lifted the Futen into the air. Once clear of the buildings, he activated the Cloak and headed north, so they wouldn't lead the Corporate forces straight to the caves. When they were away from the city and Logan was sure they weren't being tracked, he'd cut back to a southwest direction.

"What happened?" Heskith said.

"Brierton wasn't there for food supplies. Manners ordered him to pick up as much weaponry as possible."

"Can't say I'm surprised." Heskith was checking the threat displays. "The captain always saw the civilians as a nuisance."

"How bad is she?"

"She got drilled by a couple of needles when the Corporates counterattacked. I ain't an expert, but I doubt she's gonna make it. Something like that's gotta mess up your insides." Heskith grimaced. "It wasn't clean."

"Havji will do her best." Logan pushed the aircraft to cruising velocity. "And the shipyard?"

"We took out all but one of their aircraft. And that one was damaged."

Logan relaxed. Hopefully, that meant there was little chance of them being followed or attacked. "A successful mission, then."

Heskith grunted. "As long as you don't count the cost."

Logan was flying by instinct, not focusing on the task at hand. The aircraft seemed to stutter several times, lurching through the sky. He looked down and realized it was him. His hands were twitching, pushing the controls around in jerky motions. After switching on the autopilot, the Futen stabilized.

"That's a bad gash." Havji stuck her head between them. "Any other damage?"

"Ribs," Logan said.

"Broken?"

"Maybe."

Havji pursed her lips. "Nothing I can do about that until we set down. Can you manage?"

Logan considered asking for painkillers, but given all the people who had died and his feelings of emptiness, it would seem like a betrayal to take anything to ease his own discomfort. "I'll be fine."

After forty-five minutes, Logan changed their heading to take them on the most direct route to the base.

"Power is at forty percent," he said to Heskith.

"That enough?"

"Ask me after we land."

Heskith frowned. "You okay?"

A ghost who'd been wandering the land for centuries, in search of something but never finding it, couldn't have felt emptier or lonelier than Logan did at that moment. After all they'd gone through, they were no better off. And, in fact, probably in worse shape than before they'd carried out the mission. If he was right, the Corporates would re-equip in days, making their losses pointless. And without Aurora, none of it mattered anyway.

"Yes," Logan finally said.

"You sure?" Heskith shifted in his seat. "It's like something's got a hold of you and won't let you go."

Logan wanted to say something to reassure Heskith but nothing convincing came to him. Outside, dawn was breaking. Patches of gray, windswept clouds smeared across the sky like stirrings in mud. *Perfect for a funeral.*

By the time they crossed back over the Baraban Range and entered the cave complex, Logan was sweating from the ongoing pain. As he landed the Futen, his aches seemed to multiply. After turning off the engines, he looked up to see an anxious crowd of soldiers and civilians lining the cave. Most were quiet and looked pale. He spotted Jarret holding his two daughters—a picture repeated throughout the cave. "Do they know what happened?"

"I sent a signal ahead," said Heskith. "Didn't go into detail."

Logan watched as Heskith climbed out of his seat and moved to the side door, surprised his friend didn't check on Manners. He took several heavy breaths, then dragged himself from his chair to follow.

Havji handed him a blanket as he passed. "Report to the

medical center. I'll take a look at those ribs."

He nodded but didn't answer. Wrapping his right arm around his chest to ease the pain, Logan climbed through the door. Instead of going to the hospital area, he stumbled to the back cave opening he'd used in his search for Tejal. It seemed like months ago, and yet he realized it was only a couple of weeks.

He had no plans. All he wanted was to get away from everyone, and this seemed the best place to do that for the moment. Logan found a crevice where he'd be hidden, and leaned back to watch the sky. The winter storms had been left behind on the journey, but even this close to the equator, clouds skittered through the sky.

Wrapping himself up in the blanket, Logan made himself as comfortable as he could. The pain from his ribs nagged constantly, no matter what he did. It was over—they'd fought and lost. Aurore was dead. The settlement was dead. All that was left was for him to lose himself and everything would be perfect. He dropped into a painful, hazy sleep, dreaming he was an eagle soaring high over Kwelengsen. The rush of air rustled through his feathers as he danced and soared in thermal currents, staring down and taking everything in with eyes far too powerful to be human.

He flew high over the city. Only now it was much bigger than he knew it to be. An elevated mag-rail system ran around the center, with branches running off into the distance like giant spokes of a wheel, and many of the buildings were skyscrapers. He banked and wheeled, diving for a closer look. Animals were grazing below the concrete tracks, but they were all wrong. The animals weren't native Kwelengsen creatures. Instead, they were from Earth—cattle and sheep among them.

It made a curious sense. Kwelengsen lifeforms were so underdeveloped that Earth species tended to muscle them out of the way, and the settlers had been pushing to build up livestock levels. But they hadn't reached anywhere near the population density that Logan was seeing. A sharp stab lanced through his wing, and he twisted to escape it, but it cut at him again.

"Wake up, Mr. Twofeathers."

Logan stirred, reluctant to leave his dream world. When he did, he was staring at Jarret Gilmore's long face.

"What's wrong?"

"Everyone's looking for you." Jarret looked at him curiously. "You vanished. No one knew where you were."

"How long?"

Jarret spread his hands. "It's been six or seven hours since you returned."

Logan looked up through the cave exit. Judging from the position of the sun, at least that much time had passed. He pushed himself up, but the pain in his chest was like a knife twisting in his side. Jarret reached down and helped him to his feet.

"Manners organized a search for me?"

Jarret shook his head. "The captain is under sedation."

"Who's running things?"

"Lieutenant Morua and Dr. Havji are handling everything for now."

Logan raised his eyebrows. "Interesting development."

"They're the ranking officers while Manners is out of it." Jarret pointed at the darkened passage. "We should get you back."

They passed several civilians and soldiers as they made their way through the caves. Each time, the people stopped whatever they were doing to look at them.

"I didn't realize I was so fascinating," Logan growled.

"Havji and Morua made finding you the priority. Even the children have been involved."

"Why do they want me?"

Jarret shrugged and turned down a side passage. When they emerged they were in the war room. Unlike earlier, it was occupied by Morua and one other soldier sitting at the screens in the center. Both looked around as Logan and Jarret entered.

"You found him?" Morua's face lit up in relief. "Thank goodness."

Logan clutched at his side, his breath coming in rasps. "Do you mind if I sit?"

"I should have thought." Morua turned to the other soldier. "Sam, let Mr. Twofeathers have your chair please, then inform Dr. Havji he's here."

Jarret left at the same time as the soldier, and Logan prepared himself for an interrogation. "Whatever you think I've done, I'll save you a lot of trouble and admit to it now."

Morua tilted her head. "Without knowing what it might be, or what the punishment is?"

"You can't punish me anymore."

"I'll wait for Dr. Havji, if you don't mind."

It didn't take long for the doctor to show up. She was carrying a portable medical scanner, dark rings under her eyes.

"Before we discuss anything"—Havji moved next to Logan—" I want to check him out. Okay?"

"Of course," Morua said.

"Logan, is that okay with you?"

He shrugged. "You're the doctor."

Havji switched on the scanner and Logan's ribs warmed under its beam. When she finally finished, they were throbbing and he wished he hadn't been so quick to agree.

"You've got three cracked ribs—one possibly broken, I can't tell for sure with this. Also, multiple contusions and abrasions. That wound under your eye needs fixing too, but it's been without attention so long it'll likely scar."

"I've got others."

"Other than that, you need food, rest, and medication to manage pain." Havji looked at Morua. "At least three days—with NanoBi-otics."

Morua nodded but didn't say anything.

"Is that when you're going to execute me?" Logan said. "It's pointless nursing a man back to health to kill him."

Morua looked from Logan to Havji and back. "What makes you think that's going to happen?"

"I failed. We didn't get any weapons or food supplies." Logan winced as Havji pressed a Biojet injector against his ribs and triggered it.

"NanoBiotic." Havji gave a bleak smile. "Might as well start."

"There are others in greater need than me."

"That may be true." Morua tapped her fingers on her knee. "But none of them are more needed by us."

"I don't understand." Logan felt a burning sensation as the shot worked on his damaged tissues.

"Dr. Havji told me you have a plan to get us off-planet. Is that true?"

"The Planetary Lander and the Nomad can both reach orbit and get to the Corporate JumpShip. We might have to fight our way in, but if we did that, we could make it back to Earth. Why?"

"Then that's our strategy," Morua said.

"Just like that?" Logan frowned. "What about Captain Manners?"

Morua leaned back in her chair and gestured to Havji.

"The captain's in a coma," Havji said quietly. "Lieutenant Morua and I have assumed joint command. It's our feeling that the best thing would be to leave as fast as possible and attempt to return to Earth."

Logan thought for a moment. "How many people are left?"

"Sixty-seven in total," Morua said.

It was too many for the Nomad, they'd have to take the Planetary Lander. That didn't present Logan with any piloting problems, but the larger ship would make it difficult to board the enemy vessel with any degree of surprise. "Can anyone else pilot an orbital ship?"

"I don't think so," said Morua.

"Does that change things?" Havji voice carried an edge of anxiety.

"My idea was to use the lander to take the civilians into orbit, while the Nomad would carry a military team to commandeer the JumpShip. But without another pilot, we'll have to do something else."

Morua stared at Logan. "Are you in?"

He didn't answer immediately. While it was his idea originally, he no longer wanted to leave the planet. He'd rather stay and die here with Aurore. Nothing they said would change that. But he'd found Kwelengsen. He was responsible for people being here, and ultimately, Logan felt an obligation to keep them safe. He couldn't abandon them when they needed him the most.

"I'm in."

"Let's get you treated," Havji said. "I don't want you losing a lung on takeoff."

Two days later, Logan felt stronger—at least physically. Inside, his thoughts were just as dark. He split his time between brooding and going through the possibilities with Heskith.

"I could program the Lander to take off automatically," Logan said.

"We've been over that already. Launch-to-orbit has too many variables—it ain't going to work without someone at the controls."

"I know. Which is why you'll be there. You can take over if anything goes haywire."

"Look, big guy. I can just about get by flying something like the Futen *if* I got the benefit of automatic flight. I ain't no rocket jockey and we both know it."

"I can give you a crash course."

"Poor choice of words." One of Heskith's thick eyebrows lifted. "And that's how it would end." He pantomimed a ship crashing into Logan's bed with his hand.

"How many p-suits do we have?"

"Two emergency suits in the HPL." Heskith frowned. "Zip in the Nomad."

"If we can't take control of their ship, we risk everybody."

"I know. But I don't see how we can avoid it. We're stuck with one ship."

Logan felt the same way, and it dragged him down further. Whatever they discussed, it always came down to one ship, and one pilot—him. Dr. Havji walked up. Since their return, she'd been distant, and her earlier playful tolerance of Heskith's lechery had vanished.

"Visiting hours are over. He needs rest."

"Is it that late?" Heskith tried to make his comment sound light, but there was something else in his voice too. "Sure thing, Doc. He's all yours."

After he'd left, Havji turned to Logan.

"Do you feel strong enough to take a little walk?"

"If I have to." Logan swung his legs off the bed. "Are we going somewhere special?"

Havji pressed her finger to her lips. "You'll see."

Logan was still unsteady, though the NanoBiotics had accelerated his healing. He struggled to keep up with Havji as she led him across the cave to where Manners' bed was hidden behind a partition screen. She held back the screen and waved him in. "Go ahead."

"You sure?"

Havji nodded and Logan slid past the partition. Manners lay there, her breathing so shallow she could have been dead. There was a large dressing around her upper chest and shoulder, and several intravenous drips feeding into her arm. To the left of the bed, a monitor ticked softly, measuring each pulse. Its screen should also have shown the dancing trace of her brain's activity. But it was flat.

Logan spun around to face Havji. "She's brain-dead?"

Havji shook her head once. "Heavy doses of certain anesthetics stop the readouts from picking up brain activity."

Logan was puzzled. "Is she that badly injured?"

"Not really. I decided to keep her under. Initially, out of medical concerns, but also because I found significant traces of Neopenth in her blood samples. Keeping her under stopped her from having to deal with withdrawal. She doesn't need to be that deeply sedated now..."

"Then why?"

Havji reached into her pocket and pulled out a bottle containing two silvery needles. Both were gnarled and twisted, indicating they'd been fired and hit something. "These are the remnants of the needle rounds I removed from the captain. They're too damaged to identify by eye, but under a microscope, you can see they're not of Corporate origin..."

Logan leaned over, gripping the rail at the end of Manners' bed. "One of her own team?"

"I'd say that was likely."

Logan felt light-headed. "Does Morua know about this?"

"Yes. It was a joint decision to keep the captain under." Havji hesitated. "We decided it was best for her safety. If she recovered, someone might try again. At least with her here, I can monitor traffic. But also..."

"What?"

"We'd already decided the best strategy for us was to leave." Havji faltered momentarily. "It's not a very courageous thing, is it? Or ethical. And if anyone finds out, we'll no doubt be court-martialed."

Logan reached out and squeezed her hand. "If it's any consolation, I think you're doing the right thing."

A single tear trickled down Havji's cheek. "Thanks, it is. Maybe they'll let you speak in our defense at the trial."

Logan looked down. Although Manners wasn't the easiest person to get along with, he couldn't see why anyone would want her dead. "Will she be okay? We'll be hitting five gees on launch."

Havji's brow creased. "It's a risk, but one worth taking under the circumstances. I've got the same concerns over you."

"I'm doing okay. The nanos have fixed me up."

Havji hesitated. "They've started repairing the tissue, but such stress might put you right back. Besides, that's not what I mean. You've changed, Logan. I don't need to be a fully trained psych specialist to see that."

Logan frowned. "Everything's changed. *You've* changed."

Havji guided Logan out from behind the partition. "When we first met, you had *something*—hope, perhaps. But there was something inside, driving you forward."

He stayed silent, and finally Havji continued.

"Now it's gone. Whatever was keeping you going, it's not there anymore."

"I'll get everyone to the ship and back to Earth."

"Everyone, but you?" Havji took Logan's hand. "You've lost so much, I know—so many have. Don't let them take away everything that's left."

Logan gently pulled away. "They already have."

He limped back to his bed and slumped down on the mattress. Havji had his best interests at heart, but Logan didn't want her sympathy. All he wanted was to be free from his responsibility so he could—

Could what? What *was* he going to do if they got back to Earth?

Chapter Twenty-Five

"May the stars carry your sadness away."
— Chief Dan George (Geswanouth Slahoot)

Havji had insisted on one more day of rest for him, and this time Logan wasn't inclined to argue. While his ribs were healing, they remained sore. Five gees always felt like getting mugged by a gang of elephants—not pleasant even if you were in good shape.

A sense of defeat hung in the air like a poisonous cloud drifting through the caverns. Everyone was walking around with blank expressions, as though they couldn't believe they'd be leaving soon, or maybe because they were losing everything they'd worked for. When the time came to board the ship, there wasn't a great rush, and barely a sound as the remaining soldiers and civilians gathered in the corridors leading to the Planetary Lander.

Logan bypassed the lines and made his way to the ship. Heskith was already there, suited up. Collectively it had been agreed that Morua and Heskith would board the Corporate ship. Logan had argued that he had the most ZeeGee experience, but that was dismissed as he was needed to fly the Lander.

"You ready?" Logan said.

Heskith grinned. "Always. But make sure we ain't on our own too long. I don't like our chances if there are more on board than we think."

"I'll have this thing hooked up within five minutes of your signal."

Heskith frowned. "I'm counting on it, big guy."

Morua shuffled over. She was wearing a matching p-suit, but where Heskith's bulk filled his, Morua looked like the Michelin man from vintage advertisements, despite her own Geneering.

"Time to get everyone on the ship?" she said.

"Try to keep the weight distribution as balanced as possible. It'll help minimize our fuel use." Logan looked at Heskith. "I better get upstairs."

Unlike his previous visit to the Lander, this time Logan didn't have to climb the ladder, something his sore muscles were grateful for. The built-in elevator platform hoisted him to the cockpit area, and soon Logan was checking orbital parameters in preparation for takeoff. The base's proximity to the equator made the launch easier, as it would require less of a trajectory shift as they climbed, but he was leaving nothing to chance.

The steady rattle of people boarding the decks below filtered up to Logan. Most people had been through this before when they'd left Earth, and it wasn't an experience they'd anticipated repeating anytime soon. But for some of the younger children, it was their first time, and now the moment was here, their excitement was growing, if only because it meant an end to the nightmare they'd all been suffering.

Logan activated the instrument panel and checked all the main diagnostics. Everything showed green, and the controls returned the correct responses when he tested them. They were as ready as they'd ever be. All he needed was the go-ahead when everyone was on board.

"Logan, we're bringing in Captain Manners and the prisoner now." It was Havji's voice on the comm-set.

"Okay. Make sure they're secured before Heskith comes up." Logan was sorry for Carl, and couldn't help wondering what punishment he would face on their return to Earth.

Havji acknowledged, then the transmission cut. Logan wondered what people thought of leaving, after working so hard to make the planet a new home. Perhaps some would have stayed if they'd been given the choice. But that wasn't going to happen. If nothing else, at least they had the option of escaping the fighting—for far too many, that chance was gone.

Logan glanced over his shoulder as the elevator whined, and saw Heskith rising through the bulkhead separating the cockpit from the cargo area.

"They're buttoning everything up downstairs." Heskith hoisted himself into the copilot's chair. "Should be ready in a couple of minutes."

"You don't have to sit up here." Logan glanced over at Heskith. "I can handle the launch on my own."

"I know that, big guy." Heskith buckled up his harness. "But it makes me look good to be part of the flight deck crew."

Logan shook his head. "Always trying to impress the ladies, huh?"

"You know it."

Logan saw the hatch lights for the lower doors turn green, then Morua's voice came over the comm-set.

"Everyone's settled. We're ready for launch."

Logan acknowledged, then started the ignition sequence and switched on the internal addressing system. "All passengers prepare for high-gee boost."

He waited until the timer ticked down. "Primary engines start." He checked the indicators held green. "Secondary engines start." He pushed the throttles forward, and the ship shuddered. "Sixty percent throttle. Hang on everyone."

Logan was driven hard into the seat padding as the Lander hurtled up through the rocky passage toward the hole at the top of the mountain. The confined space made the sensation of speed immense, though they weren't traveling that fast yet, and the bright patch above plummeted as if the sky were falling.

The roar from the engines was deafening as the sound reflected from the tunnel, and the flight stabilization system fought to keep the ship from hitting the rocky walls. Then they shot out like a bullet, the horizon opening up as the ship arced up into the blue.

"Roll seventeen," Logan announced, as they rotated to make orbital insertion easier. "Altitude ten kilometers and rising." He glanced at the controls. "Passing Max-Q, preparing for throttle up."

Up to now, the acceleration had been at three gees, but it jumped to five as the full thrust of the engines kicked in. Logan fought to control his breathing, his damaged ribs screaming for relief. The boost continued as the sky outside changed from azure to dark blue, and finally to inky black as they approached the atmosphere's edge. The autopilot throttled back as they no longer needed the massive thrust necessary to escape the planet's gravity well.

"Prepare for primary and secondary engine cutoff. ZeeGee in five. Four. Three. Two. One."

The engines died, and the control room took on an eerie silence before cheering erupted below. Logan had placed the ship in a slow-decaying orbit. Without correction, they would drop back to Kwelengsen in a few hours, but now they were clear of the atmosphere, he could use the scanners to locate the Corporate vessel. He found the signal easily enough and fed the information into the navigation systems.

"Anyone who feels comfortable moving around can do so. But remember the rule—you bring it up, you clean it up," Logan broadcast through the ship. "Flight time will be two hours. Course correction in fifty-three minutes."

"Jeez, that's a goddamn whale." Heskith had been checking the displays and brought up an image of the enemy ship. "Transponder says it's a DX-600 class—the CSS *Morrigu*."

"Never heard of it." Logan checked the data. Heskith was right—the ship was over three hundred meters long. "That's the one I saw on the day of the attack. See if you can pick out the docking ports on the scans."

Heskith nodded and worked the controls. Once they moved closer, they'd be able to select the best airlock. Kwelengsen lay beneath them, a green-and-blue ball with white clouds scudding over it like the wisps of an old woman's hair. It looked as friendly and hospitable as the first time Logan had seen it, but now it was full of violence and fear. The Corporate invasion was entirely illegal, but since they didn't recognize Earth's jurisdictions, that was irrelevant—at least to them.

It would be the same old story—complaints would be raised and ignored, threats issued, and deadlines would pass unheeded. After trying to avoid the issue didn't work, Earth's governments would impose sanctions of varying severity on the Corporates. And when all the shouting and protests were done, the Corporate soldiers would remain on the planet. Their paymasters would soon fill it with their own people to plunder the planet's assets—and then claim it was *naturally* theirs.

"Where did you get the name from, anyway?" Heskith had noticed Logan staring at the planet.

"It's from my people's language. The main island reminded me of an eagle when we first saw it."

"Yeah? That's pretty cool. I hope they keep it."

Just under two hours later, the Lander was on approach to the Corporate JumpShip. So far, they hadn't been challenged, which confirmed the idea that there was only a skeleton crew on board.

Heskith and Morua had selected a docking port they believed gave them the best tactical point of entry. It was closest to the engines, giving them an opportunity to plant charges and destroy the *Morrigu*, if necessary. Though that was the last resort—and would leave everyone stranded. The ports conformed to international Earth standards, so they'd have no problems connecting to the docking tube.

Logan nudged the Lander closer, like a minnow edging up to a battleship, and shuffled in his seat.

"You okay?" Heskith said.

"Sure. It bothers me though." Logan's gut instinct was playing up again, but as usual, he didn't know why. "I was half expecting some kind of challenge."

"Don't try to make things worse for us." Heskith laughed. "If they were on the ball, that thing would blow us out of the sky."

Logan brought the ship within a few meters of the *Morrigu*, the last adjustments tickling the Lander into position. The auto-docking system picked up the port and interfaced with it, bringing up a display that showed how close they were to lining up with the airlock. A few tiny thrusts stabilized their position, and the display turned green.

He tapped the controls to engage automatic station-keeping. "That's all I can do from here."

"Time to earn my pay." Heskith clambered out of his seat,

floated closer to Logan and held out his hand. "Thanks, buddy."

"Don't thank me." Logan locked the controls. "You're the one spearheading an assault on an enemy JumpShip."

Heskith snorted. "That's why they pay us the big bucks."

With that, he was gone, and Logan stretched. He could get the ship close, but the final docking sequence, where a flexible transfer tube would come out from the *Morrigu*, had to be triggered from inside the Corporate ship. After a brief delay, he saw their inner airlock light come on, then it died again to be replaced by the airlock cycling light. The vibration of the air being pumped from the airlock buzzed through the walls, then the outer door indicator flashed as the two soldiers moved outside.

Logan opened up several exterior views and found a decent outside shot of the hull. Heskith and Morua were gripping handholds on the outside of the Lander, and as he watched, one of them pushed off for the *Morrigu*. A minute later, the second followed. He tracked them as they crossed—two bloated human shapes, floating across to a metallic cliff that contained an airlock virtually identical to theirs.

"We're on board." Morua's voice crackled over the comm system. "Ready to override airlock security."

There was a short pause. "It ain't secured," Heskith said.

"That's surprising," Morua said. "I guess they weren't expecting us to get up here. Okay, inside in… Three. Two. One."

The airlock slid open and the space-suited soldiers entered. Logan saw the door close behind them.

"We're inside and I don't think we've triggered any alarms," Morua said. "Going to cycle the 'lock."

Everything was quiet, then Heskith's voice came over the comms. "Stand by for transfer-tube."

A ring of blinking lights appeared around the *Morrigu*'s airlock, then the tube reached out like a blindworm searching for food. Logan switched their own system to accept the connection, then lifted from his seat. He wanted to join the boarding party when they crossed. By the time he reached the airlock, the tube had already sealed against it, and a number of soldiers were in position by the door.

"Keep your hands on the guideline at all times," Logan said. "Whatever you do, don't free float as we cross—even if you've had ZeeGee training."

The pressures equalized and the lights flickered as the static charge on both ships balanced. Logan hit the 'lock controls and the door slid open, revealing the thin tube across to the enemy ship. "Follow me."

He grabbed the guideline near the top of the tube and pulled himself out. Bands of lights were embedded in the support rings every few meters, and Logan detected the burned plastic odor that he always thought of as the smell of vacuum. It didn't take long to cross, and he opened the outer airlock door, squeezing inside with the other soldiers. The airlock vibrated as it cycled, then the door opened and he walked into the enemy ship.

A line of Corporate soldiers faced them, weapons at the ready. One of them held the struggling Lieutenant Morua. Logan automatically reached for his gun, but a large fist clamped around his wrist.

"I wouldn't do that, big guy. It'd be a shame if you got hurt now."

Logan glanced behind him only to see Heskith's grim smile.

"Sorry, buddy. Game's up." Heskith tilted his head to one side. "But look at it this way, you still won."

"How do you figure that?" Logan growled.

"Because soon you'll be reunited with all the other settlers on the *Hansen* and can go home. Ain't that what you wanted?"

Logan and the others from the Lander were in a large area that he imagined was a wardroom. It was filled with an array of tables, and several large 3V screens were set on the walls, all showing the blue-green vista of Kwelengsen from orbit. Corporate guards armed with neural whips and short-barreled QuenchGuns were positioned around them ready to stop any trouble, but no one was in the mood to fight.

The large double door swished open and Heskith strolled in. He wasn't armed, and that, plus the fact he was accompanied by two armed enemy soldiers, indicated to Logan that Heskith wasn't fully trusted—despite his defection.

"Looky here, people." Heskith raised his voice so everyone heard him. "Colonel Rourke will be here in a moment to talk, and he don't want no trouble.

"He sent me here upfront so you'd know everything was okay. And so some of the more hot-headed ones among us"—Heskith looked at Logan—"won't be tempted to do anything ill-considered."

Heskith moved over to Logan, flanked by the Corporate guards, and leaned over to speak to him privately. "Don't screw it up for everyone, okay?"

"Why don't you come a little closer and tell me that?"

Heskith chuckled. "Sorry, buddy. This is all for the best. You'll see."

The door opened again and several more Corporate soldiers entered, followed by a sable-haired man with a prominent facial scar. Logan was surprised to see he looked relatively trim, without the excessive muscle favored by most Geneered soldiers. The man stepped onto a small platform that had been placed at the front of the room and clasped his hands behind his back. He looked around the browbeaten settlers as though he were Caesar surveying his domain.

"I'm Colonel Rourke. You may recognize me from the transmissions I've made."

"Murdering bastard," someone muttered from the back, followed by a ripple of jeers.

Rourke continued as if he hadn't heard anything. "This planet is now under direct control by the Xselsia-Surahman Combine. All existing residents and armed forces are to be relocated to Earth immediately.

"The JumpShip *Hansen* is currently being loaded with those captured in the initial attack on your illegal settlement, and in"—Rourke checked an old-fashioned wristwatch—"approximately four hours, this ship will complete a transfer orbit to rendezvous with it so you can join them.

"I know some, perhaps many, of you, see this planet as your home, and that can still be the case. I've arranged for a number of our immigration staff to be available for anyone wishing to apply for Corporate citizenship. We can also offer welcome bonuses for those deemed to have useful local knowledge."

Logan was struggling to absorb what he was hearing. "And the executions?" he said. "Are we supposed to simply forget them?"

"There were no executions," Rourke said. "The only people killed were those who resisted the initial reclamation operation, and, of course, any subsequent military actions."

"Reclamation?" another voice said.

"Yes, we claimed this star-system long before you people knew of it. We're taking back our property, that's all."

"That's a lie. I found this system," Logan said.

"You're Twofeathers?" Rourke inspected Logan for a few moments. "I'm glad you made it. Unfortunately, when you first visited, we already had a station on the outskirts of the system establishing habitation rights. You need to make your surveys more thorough, I'm afraid."

"What about the children you killed when you attacked the group north of the Tuck mountains?" Logan's anger boiled over at Rourke's hypocrisy. "Were they a valid *military* target?"

Rourke glanced around, and another officer hurried up to whisper something to him.

"Oh yes." A shadow seemed to fall over Rourke's long face. "That was a most unfortunate set of actions resulting from the misdirected enthusiasm of one of my officers and triggered by incomplete information from a contact within your group. I believe you know him."

Logan's head dropped. He hadn't seen Carl since everyone had been brought on board the *Morrigu*. Perhaps, like Heskith, he was getting special treatment. "*Unfortunate?*"

"We were led to believe that only military personnel were among the target group. Rest assured though, the officer in question has been fined and demoted."

"I'm sure the relatives of the dead children will be comforted to hear that," Logan spat.

"If there are no questions, I have nothing more to say." Rourke looked around. "I'm sorry things turned out this way, but you can't steal and occupy other people's territory. I know you thought you were building something special here, but desiring something doesn't make it yours. Heaven favors those who fight for what they want."

Rourke stepped off the podium and marched through the door.

No one said anything, and Logan understood why. Rourke had stripped them of everything they thought they had, but Logan knew the man was lying. There'd been no Corporate habitat in the system when they'd found it, though he had no doubt the Corporates would fake "evidence" to justify their claim.

Heskith approached again. "Come with me."

Logan followed the corporal as the Corporate soldiers flanked them both. They went through the large doors, turned left, and a little farther down the corridor entered another, much smaller, room. It was empty apart from four white chairs clustered around a plastic table.

"Sit down, buddy."

"Stop calling me that," Logan said.

Heskith waved the soldiers back, his face grim.

"You know, don't you?" Heskith half-whispered. "You figured out who killed cock robin…"

"I don't know what you mean." Logan didn't look at him.

"Sure, you do. You know Manners wasn't shot by the Corporates. And you know who did it."

"I've had my suspicions."

"But you didn't say nothing. How come?"

Logan leaned away from Heskith. "I was hoping you'd come to me on your own. If I'd known what you were planning to do, I wouldn't have been so patient."

"You really do believe all that crap about people being basically good and living all happy ever after, don't ya?"

The weight of Logan's anger pressed down on him as though they were still boosting at five gees. "I think people always have reasons for doing the things they do, even if they don't make sense to anyone else."

"That bitch would have gotten everyone killed. You know that." Heskith turned toward Logan, his heavy jaw locked tight. "She wasn't interested in getting stuff to help people. She only wanted to make the fight as big as possible. Regardless of who got hurt in the process."

"And you wanted to stop that." Logan shook his head. "By any means necessary. Even if it meant betraying your own people?"

"If they knew"—Heskith jerked his thumb over his shoulder—"They'd be calling me a hero and giving me a medal. I saved all their asses—and yours."

"You don't need to remind me, but that doesn't give you the right to be judge, jury, and executioner."

"She's a goddamn drug addict. Who knows, maybe she was a dealer too and developed too much of a taste for her own shit." Heskith's words came out like bullets. "You have any idea how many soldiers get hooked on Neo?"

"A lot." Logan took a deep breath. "She wasn't the dealer though, it was Brierton. He used her addiction to control her. He was the one who pushed her to escalate things."

"Yeah?" Heskith grunted. "Well, good riddance to him too. Officers… all goddamn parasites."

"What do you want from me now?" Logan said.

"Nothing. Nothing at all." Heskith shrugged. "I knew if I did this, I'd never be able to go back, but I was willing to risk that to save people."

"And the Corporates undoubtedly pay better…"

Heskith gave a rueful grin. "Well, it don't hurt." He stood. "Your kid will be here in a couple of minutes. He was asking what happened to you. Take it easy on him, would ya? He was scared, like a lot of people."

"I won't see him. Take me back to the others."

"Okay. Play it tough if you like."

Heskith tapped a button on his wrist-comm and the soldiers reappeared. Logan followed them to the wardroom. When he sat, he was trembling and his hands were clenched tight. They'd lost everything, and there wasn't the slightest thing they could do about it. And he'd lost even more, including his reason for living. The journey to Earth was going to be a slow one, no matter how quickly the Jump took them there.

Chapter Twenty-Six

"Loss makes grievers of us all."
— Grandfather Twofeathers

The room on the Bengkulu Elevator station was small, even by space-station standards—a four-meter cube with a fold-down bed and a single seat where the occupant could watch 3V. The washroom facilities were communal and down the hall. Usually, such rooms were used by travelers on temporary stopover and weren't intended for stays longer than a day or two, but with the unexpected influx of Kwelengsen refugees, the station's facilities were strained. It was clean enough, finished in an antiseptic white, with nothing to disturb its pristine appearance other than the large beaker of coffee attached to a sticky pad on the table.

Logan cared nothing about the spartan room decor. It was designed for transients and that was what he felt like. The journey back to Earth had been incident-free, and despite now being surrounded by the security of the station and under the protection of the various Earth nation-states, he knew he didn't belong.

He was still overwhelmed by the sense of loss. He had no doubt his friend Joe would be more than happy to have him on the Taikong Gaogu program. But Logan couldn't see himself there. Aurore had been a vocal supporter of the habitat concept as humanity's future home, and the idea of living there without her made him sick in his stomach.

When he and Aurore had connected, he'd felt as though his life finally found its focus, like she was the missing puzzle piece he'd been lacking all those years. Now, without her, nothing made sense. With his guilt over Carl, he couldn't go back to the family compound, and the apartment he'd shared with Aurore had long since been leased. Even if it hadn't been, it would have been too full of ghosts. Nothing was less useful, or insignificant, than a man without a home. For the first time, he wished he had Joe's tolerance for alcohol. The oblivion it promised would be welcome, if temporary.

Logan switched on the 3V and selected the Space-24 news channel. They were talking about Kwelengsen, as they had been doing since the day the settlers returned.

"General Eluise Mkandla announced today that the USP has directed that significant forces be made available for any future operation on Kwelengsen. This follows similar statements from the Pan Asian Confederation and the United African Democracies, who have both offered to reinforce CESA's position and military strength."

Mkandla appeared on screen, a somber expression on her face. She was wearing a black t-shirt bearing a cartoon image of bombs dropping, along with the slogan "War is diplomacy through physical means."

"Will there *be* a war, General?" an off-camera reporter asked.

"Of course there will." Mkandla looked around. "War is inevitable, as long as people are willing to fight for what is theirs."

"But will there be a war with the Corporates over Kwelengsen?"

"I'm a soldier. I don't make that call."

A different journalist managed to raise his voice over the barrage of questions. "What about the reports of the Corporate Destroyers? Do they give the Corporates an overwhelming advantage and mean that war is no longer an option?"

"The information we have on the large Corporate ships doesn't suggest they are invincible. I don't consider they offer more than a temporary strategic advantage. And I look forward to proving that in the near future."

"Is there any truth in the story that Corporate forces have barricaded the Kwelengsen system?"

"Utter nonsense." Mkandla pushed her way through the throng. "You can't cut off an entire star system. Now, good day."

Mkandla climbed the broad stone steps leading to the USP Ministry of Strategic Defense and vanished inside.

"There you have it, ladies and gentlemen." A female reporter stepped in front of the camera to fill the screen. "With General Mkandla's presence here at the Ministry, it seems certain we can expect some military response in—"

The door announcer chimed, and Logan switched off the 3V. He couldn't imagine who'd be looking for him. He'd already been through days of debriefing by what seemed to be every security agency on Earth. He activated the security camera and saw Giorg Berardo's narrow face looking back at him. He hadn't seen Giorg since they'd returned to Earth and didn't welcome the intrusion now. Whatever the soldier had to tell him, Logan was sure he wouldn't like it. Despite that, he opened the door.

After an awkward silence, Giorg said. "Can I come in?"

"We don't have anything to talk about, do we?"

Giorg shifted from one foot to the other, glancing over his shoulder. "I need to speak to you, but not out here."

Logan stepped to one side. "If you're looking for privacy, you're in the wrong place. All of these compartments are monitored, I believe."

Giorg jerked his chin up and down. "I know, but at least it's not public."

Logan sat in the solitary chair, deliberately leaving Giorg standing. "So?"

Giorg took off his cap and screwed it up in his hands. "I thought you might like to know—there will be no action taken against Carl Begay."

"Why's that?"

"They decided punitive measures would stir up bad publicity and not serve the public interest."

"Lying through omission sounds like a bad strategy." Logan stared at Giorg. "And I've never seen the military worry about bad press when they have a nice, juicy war on their hands."

Giorg's smile faltered as soon as it began. "You're right. But

Captain Manners also recommended that no further action be taken."

"Manners? That's hard to believe."

"I believe she feels Begay has been judged too harshly. And, as Carl has now signed up as a full member of the Guard, she believes he should be given a chance to redeem himself."

That didn't sound like the Manners Logan knew. While he was happy that Carl was no longer in serious trouble, he couldn't help but wonder if it wasn't a case of jump-or-be-pushed.

"You didn't need to come out here to tell me that. An e-message would have done the job."

Giorg looked away. "That's not everything…"

"What else?"

Giorg glanced at Logan but couldn't hold eye contact. "Those messages showing Rourke executing the prisoners, and then… Aurore… they were faked."

"I figured that out for myself back on Kwelengsen. Part of Rourke's dirty tricks campaign."

"No." Giorg's voice choked into a whisper. "Manners ordered it."

"What?" Logan was on his feet, the memories tearing at him like a freshly opened wound. "What does that mean?"

Giorg's head was bent low, and Logan realized the soldier was sobbing.

"Brierton had the skills. She ordered him to do it."

"For god's sakes why?"

"The captain knew you were key to getting the civilians involved in her plans. That was her idea of getting you onboard. She thought—"

"And no one stopped her? No one objected?"

Giorg shuddered. "No. None of *us*."

"You knew?" He squeezed his eyes shut. "Get out. While you can."

Another tear dripped down Giorg's face, but Logan didn't care how wretched the soldier felt.

Giorg sniffed. "There's something else…"

Logan clenched his fist. "Whatever it is, it doesn't matter.

Nothing could be as bad as what you've just told me."

"It's worse." Giorg took a deep, half-gurgled breath. "This I didn't know about. I guess the captain didn't trust me *that* much."

Logan waited.

"The leader of Team Three... that made the diversionary ground attack..." Giorg choked out the words. "It was Aurore Vergari."

Logan's knees buckled and he sank to the floor. When he finally spoke, his voice was blurred and thick. "Where is she now?"

"As far as we know, still on the planet. If she survived." Giorg waited as though expecting a reply, but after several minutes, slipped away.

Logan curled up on the floor, his head throbbing like a fusion power-pack on overload. He had a purpose once more.

He was heading back to Kwelengsen—to find his wife.

End

Acknowledgements

Thank you for reading!

Please consider leaving a review or rating at your favorite book retailer. Even if it's only a line or two, I would very much appreciate it. Or, if you prefer, send me your feedback via the contact page on my website. Your opinion is very important to me.

This book would not have been possible without the help and support of my family, friends, and other members of the writing community. I'd like to thank them all and especially my wife, Hilary, for her constant love, support, and patience.

A special mention must go to my editor, Michelle Dunbar (http://michelledunbar.co.uk) who helped polish the raw manuscript into the masterpiece that lies before you. ;-)

For a complete list of my books, please visit my website (http://davidmkelly.net/my-books/) and consider signing up for my email updates at http://davidmkelly.net/subscribe/. I won't share your information with anyone for any reason and won't bombard your mailbox either. You'll be the first to hear about new releases, as well as receiving occasional free stories.

Thanks again.

David M. Kelly

Also from David M. Kelly

The Joe Ballen series is a near future, sci-fi noir thriller series, featuring a smart-mouthed space engineer, engaging characters, cynical humor, and plausible science.

Mathematics Of Eternity (Book one)
You can ask Joe Ballen anything, except to give up.

Joe Ballen, a half-crippled space engineer, dreams of returning to his old life in space while scraping a living illegally flying cabs in flooded-out Baltimore. But when one of his passengers suffers a grisly death, Joe is dragged into a dangerous conspiracy centered around a prototype Jumpship.

As the bodies pile up, Joe becomes suspect number one, and his enemies will stop at nothing to hide the truth. With the help of a disturbed scientist, a senile survivalist, and his glamorous boss, can Joe untangle the puzzle and uncover the truth before he becomes another dead statistic?

The future's about to get a lot more action-packed!

https://books2read.com/MOE-JB1

Perimeter (Book two)
In space, treachery runs deep.

Joe Ballen's working on a new ore-processing platform in the harsh environment around Mercury. When a savage Atoll attack decimates his crew, Joe is injured and returns to Earth to recover. But vital starship engineering files are missing, and Joe is bulldozed into the not-so-choice assignment.

But he's not the only one in the hunt and Joe is dragged into a high-stakes game of cat and mouse. It's a journey that will take him to the perilous depths of space, where no one is quite what they seem. Can old enemies ever make good allies? And can Joe trust even the people closest to him?

Ballen's back in another action-packed, sci-fi noir thriller, guaranteed to keep you turning the pages.

https://books2read.com/per-JB2/

Transformation Protocol (Book three)
Change can be deadly!

With his life crumbling around him, Joe Ballen is close to going out in a blaze, fuelled by cheap alcohol and self-hatred. But when something "out there" starts destroying spaceships and stations, the only JumpShip available to investigate is the *Shokasta*—locked away by Joe in an attempt to get justice for his family.

But when an old friend offers him the chance to return to space to search for a missing JumpShip, it proves more complicated than either of them imagined. Joe realizes some people will go to any lengths to get what they want, and when his past catches up with him in a way he couldn't have seen coming, he must battle enemies new and old as well as his own inner demons.

https://books2read.com/TP-JB3

For a complete list of my books visit http://davidmkelly.net/my-books/

About The Author

David M. Kelly writes fast-paced, near future sci-fi thrillers with engaging characters, cynical humor, and plausible science. He is the author of the Joe Ballen series (*Mathematics of Eternity, Perimeter, and Transformation Protocol*) as well as the short story collection *Dead Reckoning And Other Stories*.

Originally from the wild and woolly region of Yorkshire, England, David now lives in wild and rocky Northern Ontario, Canada, with his patient and long-suffering wife, Hilary. He's passionate about science, especially astronomy and physics, and is a rabid science news follower. When not writing, you can find him driving his own personal starship, a 1991 Corvette ZR-1, or exploring the local hiking trails.

Find out more at www.davidmkelly.net

To sign up for the mailing list, go to www.davidmkelly.net/contact

You can also follow David through the following channels:

Facebook: facebook.com/David.Kelly.SF

Twitter: twitter.com/David_Kelly_SF

Goodreads: goodreads.com/DavidMKelly

Manufactured by Amazon.ca
Bolton, ON